SILVERY WORLD

AND OTHER STORIES

SILVERY WORLD

AND OTHER STORIES

Edited, Annotated, and
with Introductions by

MICHAEL J. PETTID

ANTHOLOGY OF KOREAN LITERATURE VOLUME 1

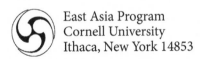

East Asia Program
Cornell University
Ithaca, New York 14853

The Cornell East Asia Series is published by the Cornell University East Asia Program (distinct from Cornell University Press). We publish books on a variety of scholarly topics relating to East Asia as a service to the academic community and the general public. Address submission inquiries to CEAS Editorial Board, East Asia Program, Cornell University, 140 Uris Hall, Ithaca, New York 14853-7601.

This publication is published in part with generous support from the Literature Translation Institute of Korea.

Number 192 in the Cornell East Asia Series
Copyright ©2018 Cornell East Asia Program
All rights reserved.
ISSN: 1050-2955
ISBN: 978-1-939161-02-4 hardcover
ISBN: 978-1-939161-92-5 paperback
ISBN: 978-1-942242-92-5 e-book
Library of Congress Control Number: 2018961659

Cover image: Makdill. Antique Korean Style Traditional Wooden Main Door with Steel Plate Engraving, Seoul, Korea. Shutterstock ID: 670822081.
Cover design: Mai

∼ CONTENTS

∼ INTRODUCTION

MICHAEL J. PETTID

The fall of the Chosŏn dynasty (朝鮮 1392–1910) resulted in changes that would absolutely shake its peoples and customs to the core. However, that is not to state that Chosŏn was not a dynamic country over its 518-year existence. Quite to the contrary, there was much change and innovation throughout the dynasty. Examining the culture and society of early Chosŏn, one would find nineteenth-century Chosŏn to be quite different if not almost unrecognizable in some respects. Particularly, the late Chosŏn brought a great shift in how Confucianism, the hegemonic ideology of the ruling classes, functioned within society. While Confucian mores remained quite important at various times and places, in other spaces it yielded to an ever-growing desire to examine the world from a more pragmatic lens. This "substantive learning" (實學 sirhak) allowed the opening of new areas of studies and new actors in creating these studies.

There was further increasing interaction with countries and peoples beyond the more-or-less traditional East Asian sphere that had dominated Chosŏn since its inception. New thought systems such as Catholicism became known to Koreans and attracted numerous converts. Of course this was far from acceptable to the ruling powers and the execution of foreign priests led to the first military actions by Western countries against Chosŏn.[1] The weakened Chosŏn had little choice to accept the treaties with the Western powers and this, too, brought about even more change. The colo-

---

1. See Ki-baik Lee, *A New History of Korea,* trans.Edward W. Wagner with Edward J. Shultz (Cambridge, MA: Harvard University Press, 1984), 264–266.

nization of Chosŏn was still some thirty years in the future, but the end of the dynasty was clearly underway by the 1870s.

This brief introduction is aimed at helping readers understand the historic backdrop of the writings that follow. Literary creation most certainly does not occur in a vacuum and the writers of the following stories were living in highly turbulent times. Their writings reflect what they saw and what they understood to be happening to their country. The voices of these men are far from uniform, as they all had their own ways of explaining the colonization of their country and how the situation should be remedied.

CHOSŎN AND THE EAST ASIAN WORLD ORDER

Chosŏn had long existed within the sphere of Chinese influence and actually relished this big brother–little brother relationship with the Ming dynasty (明 1368–1644). Politically this was necessary given the great size of China vis-à-vis Chosŏn, but it also benefitted in terms of intellectual transfer between the two states. Far from a one-sided relationship, the exchange was dynamic and brought reward to both. After the fall of Ming and the rise of the Qing dynasty (清 1644–1911), the ruling powers were less enamored with their Chinese neighbor whom they saw as being a barbarian power that had usurped the Ming. Nonetheless, after the initial fifty years or so, the relationship fairly much continued as it had in the past.

Japan, on the other hand, was more of a rival state that the Chosŏn powers viewed with a general distrust. This was the result of the Japanese invasions of the late sixteenth century that had devastating consequences for not only Chosŏn, but also the Ming dynasty that came to its aid. So while it is safe to state that Chosŏn continued to look at its eastern neighbor with a degree of distrust, there was also a continuation of intercourse between the two states. Japan remained very interested in the cultural offerings that Chosŏn could offer in the form of Confucian and Buddhist texts as well as ceramics that were highly valued in Japan. This relationship would transform greatly in the late nineteenth century as Japan desired to make Chosŏn the first conquest in its imperial empire.

In terms of social structure, Chosŏn was a highly hierarchal society, led by the royal family. Below were scholar-officials known as *yangban* (兩班) who occupied the highest civil and military positions.[2] The next tier below were the freeborn commoners on down to the lowborn that included slaves, female entertainers, shamans, Buddhist monks, itinerant entertainers, and butchers among others. While *yangban* status was something that could be lost—in fact the late Chosŏn period saw an increasing number of "fallen" *yangban*—powerful families managed to enjoy their high status for generations. On the other hand, the lowborn status was not something that could be overcome and that status was passed from generation to generation. While these status distinctions were formally eliminated with the Kabo Reforms of 1894 (甲午更張), in practice the limitations of status based on these groups remained strong in early twentieth-century Korea.

Of central importance to the writings in this volume are the events that unfolded in the late nineteenth and early twentieth centuries that witnessed the subjugation and colonization of Chosŏn by Japan. For each of the stories and writers in this volume, these events weigh heavy and greatly influence their literary creations beyond all else. Thus, a closer examination of those times will allow better appreciation of the stories that follow.

CHOSŎN IN THE NINETEENTH CENTURY

While the start of Chosŏn's decline is certainly seen in the weakening of the monarchy at the hands of the powerful descent

---

2. The *yangban* were the two orders of officialdom: the civil and the military.

were also marshalled forward, such as establishing modern schools throughout the country, founding paper mills and textile plants, and developing a system for the defense of the country.[9] Yet, the Club pushed its political agenda centering on reform too far and this invited a backlash from conservative elements that had surrounded King Kojong. Consequently, the King ordered the Club to be disbanded and prohibited its further activities in December 1898. This effectively ended any attempts for the reform of the government that was now under the control of a weak monarch who had surrounded himself with a band of toadies.

Despite the shutdown of the Independence Club, the individuals who had helped in its activities continued to push toward modernization in their own ways. Newspapers were established and become very important instruments for spreading ideas and knowledge.[10] Kojong had renamed Chosŏn as the Great Han Empire (大韓帝國) in 1897 and he and his government set out to build railroads, telegraphs, streetcar lines, and the like in the hope that Korea could remain independent of the foreign powers that were now at every turn. However, this would prove to be a case of too little and too late for Korea.

RUSSIA, JAPAN, AND KOREA

Russia and Japan had emerged as the chief contenders for the Korean peninsula by the turn of the twentieth century. Both desired control of Chosŏn. For Russia it was the prospect of an ice-free port on its Eastern border, and for Japan as the colonial stepping stone to the continent. The two sides poked and prodded one another with troop movements, attempting to establish military bases and the like before finally entering into negotiations over Korea and Manchuria. But no compromise could be arrived at,

---

9. Eckert et al., *Korea Old and New*, 233–235.
10. Hwang, *A History of Korea*, 148.

and thus Japan took matters into its own hands and launched a surprise attack on Russian bases at Port Arthur.

Despite the fact that Korea declared neutrality at the onset of the hostilities, the Japanese troops present in Korea intimidated the weakened government; Japan forced Korea to sign a protocol agreement that allowed Japan to use military force on the Korean peninsula whenever and wherever it saw the need. Japan also took control of waterways, insisted that all Korean treaties with Russia were void, and required that the Korean government use Japanese advisers in ministries such as that of finance and foreign affairs. The advisers had the effect of passing the administrative authority of Korea to Japan, and was vividly clear in that Korean diplomats stationed around the globe were recalled in the aftermath of this agreement.[11]

The war itself was brief and one-sided with Japan easily defeating the Russian forces in battle after battle. Russia sued for peace and the American president Theodore Roosevelt brokered an agreement that allowed Japan dominance of Korea.[12] Resultant from this granting of Japanese hegemony over Korea was the Protectorate Treaty of November 1905 (乙巳保護條約), which Korean ministers were forced to sign under coercion. While the formal annexation of Korea by Japan would not happen until 1910, the measures put in place in 1905 ensured that it was just a matter of time for the complete colonization to occur. Now Japan controlled the foreign and financial affairs of Korea. In 1907 the Korean government attempted to appeal to the international community by sending a secret mission to The Hague, but this was discovered and Kojong was forced to abdicate the throne to his son Sunjong (純宗 r. 1907–1910). At this time Japan was allowed to

---

11. Lee, *A New History of Korea*, 307–309.

12. Ibid., 309. It should also be noted that the United States acknowledged Japan's dominance over Korea for Japanese recognition of American hegemony over the Philippines. Britain also signed a similar agreement with Japan that recognized Japan's "right to take appropriate measures" for the control of Korea.

decide on appointments to government posts and also disbanded and replaced the Korean army with its own police force.[13]

In May 1910 Japan appointed General Terauchi Masatake (寺內 正毅 1852–1919) as the new Resident-General of Korea with the expectation that he would annex Korea. He immediately shut down the newspapers and along with Prime Minister Yi Wanyong (李完 用 1858–1926) drew up the terms of the annexation which was formally announced on August 29, 1910.[14] Kyung Moon Hwang points out that Yi, now regarded as one of the great traitors of modern Korea, was actually a brother-in-law to Kojong but was the one who signed over Korea to Japan. Hwang goes on to write of how there were direct benefits for some to collaborate with Japan— high office and financial reward, while for others it was the promise of material improvements and new culture that caused them to support, or at least not directly fight against, the change. Finally, there was a large group of Koreans who had little to gain at all by fighting Japan as their lives would change little in rural Korea.[15] What is inescapable is that the collapse of Chosŏn seemed certain from the very beginning of the nineteenth century, a time that saw widespread corruption and powerful families more interested in their own welfare and gain than for that of the country.

COLONIAL KOREA

The thirty-five year period under Japanese colonization brought about change on a scale that had never occurred before in Korea. This period is one that Koreans still recollect vividly and the brutality of the Japanese rule still plagues both intra-Korean relations and that of the Korean states with Japan. The "cooptive political control policies exacerbated internal cleavages" within

---

13. Hwang, *A History of Korea*, 154.
14. Lee, *A New History of Korea*, 313.
15. Hwang, *A History of Korea*, 158–160.

the anti-Japanese movement in Korea and have remained problems until the present day.[16] The very fact that there remain serious unresolved issues between the Korean states and Japan over seventy years after Korea's liberation helps us understand how consequential these three and a half decades were in Korean history.

The colonial machine of Japan was powerful and far-reaching, reaching every aspect of life by 1945. This certainly did not happen overnight with the annexation treaty in 1910, but rather through a string of policy enactments that allowed Japan to rather easily take over its target. And this was done with the cooperation of some Korean elites. After annexation the "royal family and prominent elites were eased into submission through lavish monetary sums, nobility titles, and sinecures."[17] While there was certainly armed resistance to the Japanese colonial government, by 1910 the superiorly equipped and trained Japanese police had wiped out most of these efforts on the Korean peninsula.[18]

The workings of the Government-General of Chosŏn (朝鮮總督府 J. Chōsen Sōtokufu) have been well detailed elsewhere, but for the purpose of this volume an examination of how this period influenced literary production is of the utmost importance. Even before the formal 1910 annexation of Chosŏn, the Japanese had been enacting laws that allowed increasingly greater control of the press. By 1907 a law was passed that allowed the government to regulate newspapers, and this had a detrimental effect on Korean newspapers and their ability to publish freely.[19] After annexation most major newspapers ceased publication, leaving just the pro-Japanese *Maeil sinbo* (每日申報 Daily news) delivering the news for the first years of Japan's rule over Korea.

Such censorship also had a significant influence on what sort of literary production was possible by Korean writers. History-

---

16. Eckert et al., *Korea Old and New*, 255.
17. Hwang, *A History of Korea*, 158.
18. Eckert et al., *Korea Old and New*, 255–256.
19. Lee, *A New History of Korea*, 330–331.

based, heroic biographies of famous personages of the past were a popular form of fiction in the early twentieth century and undoubtedly were aimed at bringing forth emotions concerning Korea's past and present situation among readers. These were quite naturally banned once Japan took control of Korea and writers had to move on to other topics such as self-improvement and enlightenment that is strongly featured in the "new novels" (*sin sosŏl*) of the first decade of the twentieth century.

The first decade of the colonial period was one of heavy oppression of the Korean people in practically every aspect of life. Censorship of the press, closing of private schools, exploitation of the resources of Korea, and the incarceration of anyone suspected of conducting anti-Japan activities were hallmarks of this time.

The stifling military rule of this period was aimed at suppressing any sort of expression for independence by Koreans. However, this very strict rule fostered anti-Japanese sentiment among the people and led to the outbreak of the March 1 Independence Movement of 1919. The former king, Kojong, died in February 1919 amid rumors of having been poisoned by the Japanese. The leaders of the independence movement both in Korea and abroad had planned to use the funeral as a time to declare Korea's independence from Japan and appeal to the world powers for intervention.

The declaration was sent to the Governor-General, the police, and read to crowds at Pagoda Park in Seoul. The demonstrations that erupted were eagerly joined by the people of Korea and spread in the ensuing months throughout the country with over one million Koreans taking part. The Japanese, who had been taken completely by surprise at the demonstrations, responded with brutality, arresting or even killing hundreds if not thousands of Koreans.[20] However, for all the success of the demonstrations, this had no consequence on purging the Japanese rule or in gain-

---

20. Eckert et al., *Korea Old and New*, 278–279.

ing significant attention of the international community. Yet the demonstrations did bring about some change in the Japanese rule over Korea as Japan wanted to change the image of their colonial rule in the eyes of their Korean subjects. The result was the so-called Cultural Rule.

The outward loosening of policies in Korea was aimed at bringing more Koreans into the colonial system by giving them a stake in the growth of the colony. Resultant were a relaxing of publication restrictions, allowing more native enterprise and also more freedom for Koreans to form social groups that were able to focus on a wide range of interests such as education, religion, youth, self-improvement, and so on.[21] This had the effect of greatly increasing the intellectual vigor of Korea in this period.

Notwithstanding the reforms in the Cultural Rule period, the Japanese colonial government also worked at the same time to increase the effectiveness of its rule over Korea. The administrative system was tightened, economic exploitation was fine-tuned, and the police control was made more efficient. While publication restrictions were eased, censorship and the threat of arrest still hung over publishers and writers alike. In the schools, Japanese language and history were still taught as primary subjects, as was the Japanese version of Korea's own history. And as can be expected, the easiest way for Koreans to socially advance was to hop onto the Japanese colonial bandwagon, for the best paying jobs, educational opportunities and the like were all linked to cooperation with the colonial government and at the very least outward acceptance of Japanese culture.

The works translated in this volume were all written within the first thirty years of the twentieth century, save for *Im Kkŏkchŏng,* which was serialized over an eleven-year period beginning in 1928. Thus the backdrop for the works is this very turbulent pe-

---

21. By September 1922 some 5,728 societies and organizations had registered with the colonial police. See Eckert et al., *Korea Old and New,* 286–287.

riod that saw Korea lose its independence to Japan, endure a very harsh period of iron-fisted rule, and then transition to a somewhat more relaxed rule that granted greater freedoms. Literary journals flourished in this period of the Cultural Rule and this in turn helped spur publication of works focusing on the plight of the people, the failure of the capitalist economic system, and the need for equality among the people in areas such as gender and education.

LITERATURE IN CHOSŎN

In the eyes of the Confucian ministers of the early Chosŏn dynasty, literature was inseparable to human society and culture.[22] The very advent of human civilization was bonded with literacy and the creation of literature. Of course this largely meant literature written in Literary Chinese (漢文) as Chosŏn, along with contemporary states in Japan and Vietnam, was a part of this great sphere of Chinese influence even though it had developed its own vernacular script by the mid fifteenth century (today's *han'gŭl*). And literature was to be primarily didactic and means to further the needs of the state or reinforce Confucian morality. At least that was the early goal in Chosŏn.

In the Chosŏn dynasty intellectuals understood there to be a clear and rigid hierarchy between writings in Literary Chinese and those in the Korean script. Even the creation of the Korean script was highly opposed by some, such as Ch'oe Malli (崔萬理 d. 1445) who cited the break from China and its script as being a detriment in Chosŏn-Ming relations, a break from the ancient traditions of China, and a setback to the advancement of Chosŏn's culture.[23] Indeed, the new script was referred to as the vulgar script (諺文

---

22. See Michael J. Pettid, Gregory N. Evon, and Chan E. Park, *Premodern Korean Literary Prose: An Anthology* (New York: Columbia University Press, 2018), 1–3.

23. See "Ch'oe Malli: Opposition to the Korean Alphabet," in *Sources of Korean Tradition: Volume One: From Early Times through the Sixteenth Century,* ed.

ŏnmun), whereas Literary Chinese bore the appellation of true writing (眞書 *chinsŏ*). Of course much of this disdain for the new script, termed "the correct sounds to teach the people" (訓民正音 *hunmin chŏngŭm*) had to do with power relations and the desire to keep the ability to read and write within a very small group of mostly men. Veiled under the mask of trying to emulate China was an underlying desire to keep the common folk away from literary production and consumption. However, this failed when King Sejong (世宗 r. 1418–1450) rejected the vociferous arguments of some of his minsters and promulgated the new script in 1446. His reasoning was that the common people were unable to express their minds in Literary Chinese, and thus the creation of this new script would allow them to easily learn and use the writing system in their daily lives. There was also a practical and perhaps more important aspect of the new script and that centered on being able to spread Confucian didactic works to those unable to read in Literary Chinese.

Despite the creation of this new writing system, Literary Chinese remained the official written language of Chosŏn until its end. Unless a work was intended for the common folk, all governmental publications were in Literary Chinese. The Korean script is seen in educational works and guidebooks, but these were aimed at commoners and womenfolk, not the male elites that shaped policy. While the Korean language soon found its way into literary creation, this was hardly the goal of the elites when the script was conceived, but rather an unfortunate consequence of letting the genie of writing and reading out of the bottle.

For the Chosŏn elite, the zenith of all literary activity was poetry. Poetry, in various Chinese forms, was seen as a Confucian exercise in morality, a means to self-reflect and improve one's self. Such poems, written in either Chinese verse forms or the Korean

Peter H. Lee and Wm. Theodore de Bary (New York: Columbia University Press, 1997), 296.

short form of the *sijo* (時調), were a means to demonstrate one's mastery of the vast East Asian literary tradition and to measure oneself with the writers of past ages. The ability to compose poems on a whim was a skill that was highly prized by the intellectuals of Chosŏn. Focusing on the perfection of nature was a common theme, if only as a way to demonstrate the imperfections of the human world.

Yet all poems were not this abstract or aimed at a higher purpose. *Sijo* and *kasa* (歌詞) poems were meant to be sung, and as such the entertainment value of these poem-songs cannot be dismissed. Indeed many of the *sijo* that can be classified as love songs were performed by female entertainers (妓生 *kisaeng*) for male audiences. The open-ended *kasa* covered a wide range of topics such as travel, lamentations, everyday life, and seasonal customs that were not so much didactic as entertaining or placating. And as the dynasty moved into its second half, the composer group of these Korean script poem-songs greatly expanded to include commoners and women. This reflects a larger trend within Chosŏn society of a broadening of social participation beyond simply a very narrow, all-male ruling class, and one could posit that this was, in part, made possible by the Korean script.

Notwithstanding the prestige of verse, fictional literature grew from early on and prototypes of the novel are seen in the writings of some Koryŏ dynasty (高麗 918–1392) men.[24] While fictional works such as the novel were officially scorned by the ruling elites, in practice these same men were oftentimes either the producers and or consumers of the works themselves. Hypocrisy aside, entertainment and escapism have always been hallmarks of fictional writing on some level, and the readers of Chosŏn were little different than the readers of today in that regard. The fiction of Chosŏn did follow quite similar patterns in some aspects such as the reward

---

24. See Pettid, "Koryŏ Period Prose Works" in *Premodern Korean Literary Prose*, 18–20.

of good and punishment of vice (勸善懲惡 *kwŏn sŏn ching ak*) and also the presence of stereotypical characters like the evil stepmother or bumbling patriarch of the household, but these reflected didactic elements that ran deeply in the worldview of the times.

The word novel (小說 *sosŏl*) is somewhat misleading in the premodern usage. As Ji-Eun Lee aptly demonstrates, this term covered a wide range of writings in premodern Korea and moved easily between fiction and nonfiction.[25] We also should be cognizant that the premodern novel readily used various forms of verse within the flow of the story. The use of verse was oftentimes a means to reveal important information to the storyline, to reveal a character's innermost thoughts, or to foreground an event that would come to be. Poetry was the highest level of literary expression and thus it was very much used as a window into a character's mind and heart.[26] Thus we can state that the premodern novel resided in an area that is quite different from that where the modern novel is found.

By the mid 1890s with the Tonghak Rebellion and Kabo Reforms taking place, the need to create writings in Korean script were seen as being very important. There was clearly a link between raising a consciousness of the people about events concerning the country and the need to communicate this in the Korean language. It is also a part of the desire to bond the language of everyday life with literature (言文一致), and thereby use Korean script for Korean writings. This is seen in the creation of the *Tongnip sinmun* by the Independence Club, as it was a newspaper for the people of Chosŏn in their own language.[27] Perhaps a backlash

---

25. Ji-Eun Lee, *Women Pre-Scripted: Forging Modern Roles through Korean Print* (Honolulu: University of Hawaii Press, 2015), 21.

26. Michael J. Pettid, *Unyŏng-jŏn: A Love Affair at the Royal Palace of Chosŏn Korea*, translation by Kil Cha and Michael J. Pettid (Berkeley: Institute of East Asian Studies, 2009), 42–43.

27. Cho Tongil, *Han'guk munhak t'ongsa* (A complete history of Korean literature) (Seoul: Chisik sanŏpsa, 1992), 4: 229–230.

against the imperialist environment of those times, the use of Literary Chinese was viewed by some as being a detriment to Chosŏn realizing its full independence and place among the modern nations of the world. But this was also a part of modernization in general and the wish to see Korea stand fully on its own, even in regards to written texts that would allow all Koreans access to literacy for the first time in its history.

Such a movement toward enlightenment is also seen in the types of novels that were published in the period from the 1890s until annexation in 1910. Historical novels featuring long-dead heroes and the glory of past days stood in stark contrast to the decaying and tumultuous times of the present period. Kwŏn Yŏngmin also cites the advent of fables and satires that centered on "human activity or moral positions that created social problems."[28] This brought to the fore the very situation that Chosŏn was now confronted with.

Another important factor is the advent of modern educational institutions, which also contributed to the shift away from using Literary Chinese. In 1883 the first modern school, the Wŏnsan Academy (元山學舍), was founded in the port city of Wŏnsan. This school was founded due to the initiative of the residents of the town. Other schools followed quickly, including Ewha Girls School (梨花學堂), the first modern educational institution for women in Korea, founded by U.S. missionaries in 1886.[29] By the time of annexation, there were some three thousand private schools in Korea

---

28. Kwŏn Yŏngmin, "Early twentieth-century fiction by men," in *A History of Korean Literature,* ed. Peter H. Lee (Cambridge: Cambridge University Press, 2003), 391.

29. I hesitate to state that Ewha was the first educational institution for women in Korea's long history as there are records that demonstrate the existence of such institutions in the Three Kingdoms period (三國時代 ca. 300–668 CE). One such example concerns the *wŏnhwa* (源花 original flowers) of the Silla kingdom (新羅 trad. 57 BCE–935 CE), a group formed for the education of young women. See Iryŏn, *Samguk yusa* (三國遺事 Memorabilia of the Three Kingdoms) (Seoul: Ŭryu munhwasa, 1994), 308–309. So, while Ewha is certainly the

and these were certainly a source for the nationalist movement.[30] Once Korea was annexed by Japan, the colonial government implemented reforms that required both government permission for the operation of schools and the use of approved textbooks. This resulted in the closure of many schools.

Koreans of the late nineteenth and early twentieth centuries also went abroad for study in good numbers. The Chosŏn government had established scholarships to support students in an effort to bring greater technical and linguistic abilities to the country. Thus students went abroad to study languages such as English, French, German, and Japanese, among others. In particular, many students travelled to Japan. The hope was that these students would learn from the leading countries of the world and bring back to Korea the knowledge needed for the country to advance among the modern nations of the world.[31]

The overall result of this new emphasis on education and understanding the larger world beyond East Asia was a flourishing of literature and a cavalcade of new ideas. Students were exposed to new intellectual trends and a vast new world of writings that would reshape their worldviews. Returning to Korea, this new knowledge was spread among the larger population in various means including literary production.

LITERATURE IN EARLY TWENTIETH-CENTURY KOREA

The early years of the twentieth century were fraught with hardship for the Korean nation and people. Japan's encroachments on the sovereignty of Chosŏn were plainly evident and oftentimes

---

first *modern* educational institution for women, it was not necessarily the first in Korea's history.

30. Lee, *A New History of Korea*, 332.

31. Yi Wŏnho, *Chosŏn sidae kyoyuk ŭi yŏn'gu* (A study on education in the Chosŏn period) (Seoul: Munŭmsa, 2002), 459.

this period. Well-known poems and novels were translated and revealed new ideas and attitudes toward the world that no doubt inspired Koreans to think differently. The importance of the French Decadent movement, particularly as developed by Paul Verlaine (1844–1896), is noteworthy in the development of Korean poetry[33] and we can note a strong influx of Western novels and biographies during this same period. Of course the *Bible* was one of the first works translated into Korean, but so too were works such as *Aesop's Fables*, *Pilgrim's Progress*, *Uncle Tom's Cabin*, and *Gulliver's Travels*, among many others. These works were widely read by Korean audiences along with those translated from Chinese and Japanese, providing interesting and thought-provoking new material for Korean readers.[34] In short, this period was one of great change in the literature of Korea and a first introduction for many Koreans to the world beyond the Korean peninsula.

Another consideration when examining literature in this period is linked to increased educational opportunities for Koreans in general. A result of this broader educational opportunity would seem to be increased literacy among the general population in the early twentieth century when compared to the late Chosŏn dynasty. However, this is difficult to ascertain and most accounts seem to indicate that literacy was not particularly widespread among the lower social status groups even by the time of liberation in 1945. There was, however, a growing group of educated readers—both male and female—and these individuals were consumers of this new literature.

A final point to examine is the purpose behind writings of this time. While it is too simplistic to state that Chosŏn authors were all Confucianists who sought to enlighten others with their writings, I believe we can assert that the writing of Chosŏn was not

33. Kim Yunsik et al., *Uri munhak 100 nyŏn* (One hundred years of our literature) (Seoul: Hyŏnamsa, 2001), 41–42.

34. Cho Tongil, *Han'guk munhak t'ongsa*, 4: 366–368.

1

THE SILVERY WORLD

Introduction

The so-called new-novel (*sin sosŏl*) was brought about as writers attempted to move beyond traditional forms and also as a result of readers seeking new types of reading experiences as traditional society continued its precipitous decline as the nineteenth century waned. These Korean language works were generally serialized in newspapers—in dire need of content—and were able to capture audiences by broaching new subjects and themes that hinted at great changes to come. Beyond that, the novels were used as means to introduce new, at least for early twentieth-century Korea, ideas and ways of life.

Yi Injik (李人稙 1862–1916) is given much credit, fairly or unfairly, as being at the van of this literary movement. Yi was born in Ichŏn of Kyŏnggi Province and came to age during this period of great decline of the Chosŏn dynasty. His family, once of elite *yangban* status, had fallen upon hard times. Nonetheless, as a member of upper status rank he was able to study abroad in Japan via a Chosŏn government-granted scholarship in 1900. While in Japan, he also received training as reporter at the *Miyako shinbun* newspaper (都 新聞社). During the Russo-Japanese war of 1904–1905 he served as a translator of Korean for the Japanese Navy. And after the conclusion of the War—a resounding Japanese victory—he was able to secure employment as a translator for the Japanese government. It is this such background that has resulted in Yi being viewed quite negatively in contemporary Korea as a Japanese collaborator, a view that seems completely verified by some of his writings as well.

Upon returning to Korea Yi served as the editor-in-chief for two newspapers before being appointed as the president of the pro-Japan *Taehan sinmun* newspaper (大韓新聞) in 1907. His literary activities began in earnest with the publication of the first new-novel *Hyŏl ŭi nu* (혈의 누 Tears of blood) in 1906 followed by *Ch'iaksan* (치악산 Mount Pheasant) in 1908 and *Ŭnsegye* (은세계 Silvery World] also in 1908. His life during this period and until his death in 1916 was closely linked to the Japanese colonialists and he is, for that reason, widely regarded with disdain as a traitor in contemporary Korea.[1]

Silvery World is set against the backdrop of the tumultuous years of the late nineteenth and early twentieth centuries. Particularly, readers learn of the failed Kabo Reforms of 1894. The Reforms were a series of initiatives issued at the behest of the Japanese during the Sino-Japanese War of 1894–1895. Japan used troops present in Chosŏn to carry out a coup of sorts and removed King Kojong and replaced him with his father as the figurehead of the Chosŏn government with a pro-Japanese cabinet. The reforms were sweeping and had a great importance on the modernization of Chosŏn, but that aspect is tainted by inroads Japan made in further integrating itself into Chosŏn's economy and government. Conflict arose between the Japanese and Russian factions within the Chosŏn government, and one consequence of this was the Japanese assassination of the pro-Russia Queen Min (posthumously, Empress Myŏngsŏng). The other main consequence was the aforementioned Russo-Japanese War.

Also central to the novel is the 1905 Protectorate Treaty between Chosŏn and Japan.[2] As an outcome of Japan's victory in the Russo-Japanese War, The Treaty of Portsmouth that was concluded

---

1. He is prominently listed on the rolls of Japanese collaborators that have been published in the past fifteen years.

2. For more on this period, see Ki-baik Lee, *A New History of Korea*, trans. Edward W. Wagner with Edward J. Shultz (Cambridge, MA: Harvard University Press, 1984), 306–315.

in September 1905 gave, among other stipulations, international recognition of Japan's paramountcy over Chosŏn. With no international support, Chosŏn had no hopes of avoiding this illegal treaty that was drawn up by Japanese and presented to the Chosŏn court by a Japanese minster accompanied by an escort of Japanese troops. When the Chosŏn government's attempt to appeal the illegality of this treaty to the international community was discovered by Japan, Kojong was forced to abdicate the throne to his son Sunjong. Sunjong in turn was made to accept a new agreement that established a Japanese Resident-General who now had formal authority to intercede on all matters related to governance. This was, for all practical purposes, the end of the Chosŏn dynasty.

Silvery World is largely divided in two halves: the first half taking place in Chosŏn Korea and the second unfolding in the United States before the conclusion where the protagonists, garbed in Western dress, return to a downtrodden and shoddy Korea. Within the work, we clearly see more-or-less traditional motifs such as the reward of good and punishment of vice, supernatural intervention, rather one-dimensional characters, and strong themes of Confucian morality in this work. Yet, these are tinged with the enlightenment ideals that are common to many of the new novels such as the need for modernization, education for all people, human rights and the need to discard the old, stagnant social systems in favor of new, Western ones.

Also prominent in the novel are the oratorical segments in which various characters launch into very sophisticated dialogues where they espouse their views of the world, politics, and the need for change. Characteristic of the new novel, these rather lengthy interventions in the text are rather uniform in voice and demeanor, notwithstanding the differing backgrounds, ages, and genders of the speakers. However, similar to such episodes in traditional novels, these moments give space to the authors to espouse their own worldviews to their readers. Thus even with the change in epoch, there remained a strong didactic function with the new novel, much the same as we note in many premodern novels.

Finally, we see the way in which the work was written was heavily dependent on Literary Chinese terminology and literary allusions to various personages and events in East Asian history. While the work is composed in the Korean script, the text is also full of terminology taken straight from Literary Chinese. Thus we can see that the writer's ability to compose in pure Korean was quite limited; further, that understanding the work would also require a readership who was aware of both Literary Chinese and the larger traditions surrounding premodern literature.

Written in the Korean script, *Silvery World* was published by Tongmunsa (同文社) in 1908. In examining this novel, we can state with authority that it clearly demonstrates the pro-Japan bias of Yi; this is not necessarily true of his other works. The first part of the novel is argued to have been "borrowed" from a *ch'angguk* (唱劇 song-drama) performance entitled "Ch'oe Pyŏngdo t'ar-yang" (최병도타령 Ballad of Ch'oe Pyŏngdo) performed at the Wŏn'gaksa (圓覺社) Theatre of which Yi was in charge.[3] To this popular performance Yi added a second half featuring the children of the deceased protagonist going to America where they complete their studies and gain a wider appreciation of what needs to be done to help Korea join the great, modernized nations of the world. Thus their motive changes from revenge on those who killed their father to supporting Japan in its efforts to bring modernization to Korea and its people.

The writer's disdain with the corruption of the late Chosŏn is clearly seen in the opening paragraphs of the novel. This, perhaps, owes its roots to the above mentioned "Ballad of Ch'oe Pyŏngdo," a song that no doubt grew from any number of oral narratives con-

---

3. Ch'oe Pyŏngdo is the protagonist in the novel as well. See Cho Tongil, *Han'guk munhak t'onsa* (The complete history of Korean literature) (Seoul: Chijik sanŏpsa, 1992), 4–354.

strike out at anyone and everyone they saw. They burst in and thrashed and kicked the servant, declaring that a crime had been committed. The servant fell onto the snow and shouted for help.

The servant's wife, who had no idea what was happening, jumped with fright, opened the back door of their quarters, and ran in her stocking feet, stumbling and falling over herself, into the courtyard that was filled with snow up to her shins, where she promptly got stuck in the middle gate. She tumbled into the backyard of the inner quarters and rapped on the mistress's door.

"Ma'am! Ma'am! Hoodlums have broken in! They're beating Ch'ŏnsoe to death!"

At the servant's cries, Madam Ch'oe, who had been weaving cloth on a loom, threw down the shuttle and bolted upright, but the thread from the loom caught on her waist and did not give. In terror, she called out to her sleeping daughter: "Oksun! Oksun! Get up! Hoodlums have broken in!"

Madam Ch'oe unraveled the thread from her waist, opened the door, and stepped out. Oksun, woken from sleep, cried out to her mother, but her mother did not respond and instead ran outside in her stocking feet, rapped on the door to her husband's study, and called out to him. But it was the same timid voice she had always been accustomed to using, ever since she was growing up in her parents' home.

"Oksun's Father! Oksun's Father! Hoodlums have broken in! Whatever shall we do?" She did not dare raise her trembling voice any louder. There was a door between the master's and mistress's quarters, but it was so thickly papered on both sides that any small sound outside the door could not be heard clearly from inside. Her husband did not answer, so she repeated her words over and over. In the meantime, Ch'oe had closed the shutters tight, spread out his mat, turned the oil lamp up high until it gave off black soot, and was sitting inside arranging counting sticks, each of which was the length of the space between his extended thumb and forefinger, adding up *one chim two mut* of land, *two chim five mut* of land, and so on, calculating the tax he owed. He lifted his head at the sound of rapping at his door, the distraction causing him to set a counting stick down in the wrong place. Finally, his wife's voice reached his ears.

Ch'oe asked, "What do you mean, hoodlums? Where are these hoodlums?" He sprang up and shoved open the door. But his wife had been standing on the other side with her face pressed against it. It smacked her in the face, and she fell over with a gasp. Ch'oe clung to the doorframe and peered outside, muttering in confusion. Meanwhile, the men who had been beating the servant in front of the gate had come running to the other side of the master's quarters and were stepping into the wood-floored hall outside Ch'oe's study. When they heard the back door open, they thought Ch'oe was trying to make his escape.

"Hold it right there!" they yelled.

They stomped across the hall and shoved open the door to Ch'oe's room. Swift as sparrows, the men rushed in like lightning. But Ch'oe had no intention of running away. His first intent when he heard that hoodlums had broken in was to go reassure the others in his household without giving them a shock. Then when he saw his wife get hit in the face and fall over, he meant to step outside to help her up. But when he realized what was happening inside, he turned to go back in.

"Who are you, and what do you want?" he asked.

Without a word of response, the men grabbed Ch'oe, who had no idea what was going on, and tied him up. Upon hearing the commotion, Madam Ch'oe, a pretty young thing of just twenty-seven or twenty-eight years, peeked inside the study, all atremble, without a single thought to the pain in her face or to her modesty around these men.

The men who burst into Ch'oe's house had been sent from the provincial government office of Kangwŏn Province on a secret mission to arrest a man living in Kyŏnggŭm Village who went by the name of Ch'oe Pyŏngdo. Ch'oe, whose courtesy name was

Chusam, hailed from an upper-class family that had lived in Kang-nŭng for several generations. According to the customs of the countryside, members of the gentry who did not hold government posts were referred to by the name of their wife's village. Ponp'yŏng was the name of the village where Ch'oe's wife was from. The family name of the governor of Kangwŏn was Chŏng. Ever since he was sent down from the capital, he had been running wild, stealing the wealth of the people of Kangwŏn. He had his errand runners lined up in every corner of all twenty-six counties, racing around at his beck and call to seize commoners from each village who were well off. Whenever an order like that came down, the governor's men were the first to benefit.

The men seized Ch'oe and immediately demanded that he pay them off in exchange for his release. Eyes blazing like emissaries from the underworld, they glared at Ch'oe like his life was hardly worth that of a dog's. They roughed him up, shackled his wrists, and demanded money. Ch'oe had no intent of not paying them off, but the amount he offered did not satisfy the governor's errand runners, who were intent on fulfilling their greed.

The greed of such men who go about arresting people is far worse than that of thieves who dig up graves and demand ransoms in exchange for the skulls. Grave robbers are all cowards, but the governor's errand runners were thugs with no sense of fear. The errand runners for the provincial government office of Kangwŏn were especially overjoyed at having gained a monstrous scoundrel of a governor, and all of the petty government officials and messengers were delighted at the windfall. With every word, they flaunted the governor's authority; with every word, they wielded the power of one who has come to arrest a criminal, while demanding their "errand fees." They called it "errand fees," but it was really just greed for other people's money. If you offered them ten coins, they snorted in disgust. If you offered them a hundred coins, they still snorted in disgust. They even snorted at two or three hundred coins. At the time, brass coins were being used for curing him what was happening. Ch'ŏnsoe, who was well known for being dramatic, made a loud fuss, as if the errand runners were killing the young Master Kim. He urged them to return to Ch'oe's house, to the farmers' great alarm.

The farmers shouted, "Let's go!" They stepped into the courtyard of Ch'oe's house, each of them swept up in the confusion.

In a flash, Kyŏnggŭm Village was turned inside out. Rumors spread about the commotion taking place in Ch'oe's house, and gentry and commoner, old and young alike came running, trying to crowd into Ch'oe's house. The courtyard was so small that latecomers were unable to get inside and stood outside the front gate, curious and asking each other what was happening.

The main courtyard of Ch'oe's house was in quite an uproar. At young Master Kim's command, the errand runners from Wŏnju were dragged out and sat down in the courtyard. Kim's voice was as cold as frost.

"You call yourselves government officials? Men like you who abuse your authority and do terrible things deserve to die. Do you not know that when the peasants rise up, the rulers die at the peasants' hands, and when the army rises up, men of power die at the army's hands? You have embarrassed me. Normally, if I had something to say to you, I would address you in my own house. But since you were intent on arresting Ch'oe and taking him to the government office right away, my request to speak with you was urgent, so I stood here and asked you to step out of the room, whereupon I was humiliated. Aye, there are no two ways about it. Men like you should be beaten to death for the trouble you cause. Other officials will have to take care when they visit the countryside. We cannot let you live after this."

Then he turned to look at the people of the village again.

"Listen up, everyone. Today, I am leading a revolt and killing these men from the Wŏnju government office. Are you with me?"

The villagers became excited, and the courtyard rang with their shouts.

days, there was a thing called Metal Eater. It ran around wild, stealing and eating metal. The children's song must have been created after the governor came down from the capital to Kangwŏn Province and began taking everyone's money. Now, far from being just a children's song, anonymous petitions were posted several times a month outside Chinnam Gate in front of the government office. But the governor feigned ignorance and went about his work.

What work was that? Shakedowns and buyoffs. Who was he shaking down, and who was he buying off? He took wealth from the people of Kangwŏn Province and gave it to his masters in Seoul. Of course, when I use the word masters, I do not mean the governor was a slave with the documents to prove it. I mean that he feared them, trusted them, and served them no differently than if they had been his masters, because turning your back on them meant certain death.

Serving such masters was both easy and difficult. What was difficult about it, you ask? If you were a clean public servant who worked hard for the people and did not offer bribes to your masters, then you were bound to have your official seal taken from you. Deadlocked, you would never get another government position again. That's why I say it is difficult to serve your masters.

And the easy part? As simple as placing the first stone on the *umulgonu* game board, you win by bleeding the people dry and offering it up. The governor of Kangwŏn at the time was especially good at that. He must have had many trustworthy masters. You would need a written list to remember all their names. The prime minister who pulled all the strings was one of his masters. Even the king's personal retainer was one of his masters. Those crafty eunuchs were also his masters. There were many other masters, as well, including one that was especially trustworthy.

As the parent of a master, she should have been addressed as "Mother," but as that would have been embarrassing at that age, she was instead addressed as "Older Sister." It was with her pull that the governor's seat was won and her pull that he relied upon as he plundered the people's wealth. Lurking behind his thievery were his many henchmen, like a row of tortoises basking in the sun.

The petty officials of Kangwŏn Province were famous for their ability to nickname people well. Every member of the governor's household had a nickname, and they were indeed apt.

The governor was Metal Eater.

The chief officer of taxes was Serpent.

The chief officer of rites was The Governor's Right Arm. The chief officer of the military was Meathead.

The chief officer of public works was Busybody. The governor's advisor was Gap-tooth.

The governor's concubine was Troublemaker. The *kisaeng* who served him in bed was Vixen.

Their nicknames differed, but deep down they were all the same. If you wonder what I mean by that, I mean that the governor and his underlings were all wicked at heart. Like rice cake and the crumbs that fall off the rice cake, like noodles and the curved ends of the noodle dough that are cut off, like thread and the fibers that come off of the thread, whenever the governor haggled over some request in order to get money out of the person, the lion's share would go to the governor while the middleman earned only a government post without having to take the government service examination, yet there were still plenty of people below who profited from the transaction. The governor and his lackeys ran amok, eyes red with excitement, while the people of Kangwŏn Province were uprooted from their homes. In the courtyard of the main building at the provincial office of Kangwŏn Province, the sound of executions never stopped, while from inside the building, the sound of music never ceased. In a voice like a nightingale, a flowery *kisaeng* sang of the famous rocks of Yaksandong-dae[3] and offered up a cup

---

3. One of the eight wonders if Kangwŏn Province, this scenic spot is located in contemporary North Korea.

of wine with jadelike hands. An old man with a white beard ogled the face of the *kisaeng*, drooling with lust for the girl, while the governor, too, seemed to enjoy the view as he received the cup from her.

The black zither plunked. The dulcimer plonked. The flute whistled. The hourglass drum thumped. Fluttering like a butterfly in a field of flowers, Kyehwa danced to and fro, here and there. The other *kisaeng* kept time with their shouts, turning the place into a frenzy of nightingales.

The governor was so carried away with the fun, distracted by the *kisaeng* and tipsy from drink, that even if war had broken out in Shandong, he would not have been moved. Of course, Shandong is in another country, but it would have been the same even if chaos had come as close as Yŏngdong, so engrossed was he in play. At times like that, no matter what came up, the petty officials would not address the governor but would wait until the fun had ended or report it to him the next day after investigating the matter. Of course, when it was an extremely pressing matter, they reported it to him immediately.

A herald with a good voice stood atop a stone step and called out majestically, "The errand runners have returned from Kangnŭng!"

The governor's ears perked up at the announcement. The music stopped abruptly, and the herald's voice continued.

"Call forth the chief officer of corrections. Have Ch'oe Pyŏngdo of Kyŏnggŭm Village in Kangnŭng put in jail. Proceed quickly."

As soon as he gave the order, officers shouted in response and poured out like wind and rain. Ch'oe was dragged away in the melee, and the government office was turned inside out. Innocent or guilty, Ch'oe felt his liver shrink in fear, while the governor's liver must have spread until it filled his torso. If a liver shrinks when you're afraid, what must you be feeling to make it spread to such a size? His lips writhed with excitement.

Like a tiger that has caught a deer, the governor's heart leaped at the thought of the meal before him. Like a snail that has met a stork or a heron, Ch'oe's heart trembled at the thought that he was about to be trounced upon by the governor.

An officer with a loud voice took the governor's order and charged Ch'oe with his offence.

"Listen up, Ch'oe, and do as we say. You, a so-called well-educated man of high standing in the countryside, have been un-dutiful to your parents and have feuded with your brothers. Your crimes are unforgivable. I will inform you of the laws pertaining to cultural edification."

The officers lined up on both sides of Ch'oe for the hearing of his sentence shouted so loud their voices could be heard from out-side, and you would have had to have been especially brave not to lose your senses. When Ch'oe heard the charges, he was aston-ished and beat his hands against the ground. A man of letters, he expounded on each of his words as he spoke.

"It is an old saying, but we owe our fathers everything for be-getting us and our mothers for raising us. A person who fails to do right by their parents is unforgivable. But if that is the case, how could I have committed the sin of not repaying my parents' kind-ness to me? My mother died before I was twenty-one days old due to complications from childbirth. My father carried me around to the neighbors to try to feed me, but he died before I was a year old and did not get to see me grow up. I was raised by my mother's sister. I never had the chance to serve my parents so much as a single bite of rice from my own hands. What worse sin could there be? Among the five penal laws, there is none worse than being undutiful to your parents, but how could I have avoided it? Also, it is said that brothers must be at peace in order to get along amica-bly. But I am a third-generation only son. Without even a sister, I have lived on my own with no one to turn to. Of course I would fail in my brotherly piety if I lived my whole life without knowing any. I never had the chance to practice filial piety or brotherly piety. Though I do not resent being charged with a lack of piety, I did not

from one mouth to two, from two to three, and so on across the entire village. The story was gradually added on to, until what went around was completely false. The false rumor swung about like a whirlwind, until it had reached the same pair of ears three or four times in a row. Every single person believed the rumor to be true. One elderly woman living nearby, who had lost her only son a couple of months earlier, had plenty of sorrow of her own. She went to Ch'oe's house, flung open the door to the inner quarters, and burst in.

"How could it have happened? They are saying Master Ch'oe has passed away." The old woman let loose with her pity and wept with abandon. Madam Ch'oe, who had been crying as well, was startled at the sound and lifted her head.

"What did you say? Who told you that? Woman, stop crying and tell me what you heard!"

Though Madam Ch'oe was the one who should have been crying, she pulled herself together to speak as the old woman kept bawling, unable to answer. So the younger farmers' wives answered for her.

"I heard it, too." "So did I." "Me, too." "Me, too." As they all chimed in, Madam Ch'oe could not bring herself to say anything further and broke down into tears. Every single person in that village felt bad that Ch'oe, an innocent man, had been arrested. It was not because they felt that warm-hearted toward Ch'oe, but because they were all living under the tyranny of the governor of Kangwŏn. Birds of a feather, they resented both the governor and Ch'oe's predicament. So when they heard of Ch'oe's passing, it was a matter that concerned all of them. So everyone, old and young alike, from the village gathered at Ch'oe's house, built a bonfire, and spent the night there, busily discussing the matter.

Ch'oe's family was left without a man of the house. So the people of the village felt it was their duty to help take care of things as if it were their own family. It was decided who would go to retrieve Ch'oe's body, and while discussing the funeral arrangements, an elderly man called Pak was put in charge of the ancestral rites.

Pak had led the ancestral rites ten years earlier, and he knew how they were supposed to be done. He asked if they had received official notice of Ch'oe's death, and he pressed to find out the source. In the end, he realized it was only a rumor and sent a girl to explain in detail to Madam Ch'oe that the story was false. He also sent another person to go to Wŏnju to find out what was happening. They were all so happy to hear it was only a rumor that tears fell from their eyes and smiles brightened their faces.

As it was the middle of the night, it was too dangerous to send just one or two people over the steep peak of Taegwallyŏng, no matter how much of a rush they were in, so they selected four or five strong young men to go. But Madam Ch'oe asked them to take her with them on a palanquin, saying that she had to see her husband's face at least once more in her life. The farmers were eager to volunteer their labor and stepped forward to offer themselves as palanquin bearers. But they were awkward at the task, so eight strong young men wound up taking turns carrying the palanquin and holding it so the others could rest. There were two people who lamented the fact that they could not ride the palanquin like a swift horse or sprout wings and fly. That was Madam Ch'oe and her daughter seated inside the palanquin.

When they saw a row of houses giving off smoke through the clusters of trees at the base of a distant mountain facing them at the tavern by the fortress gate, they knew it was the provincial governor's office of Wŏnju. The palanquin bearers set the palanquin down to rest, pointed toward the governor's office, and said loudly enough for Madam Ch'oe to hear that there were about ten *li* left, that they were nearly there, and they would sit and cool their sweat for a bit before going the rest of the way. As they dawdled, Madam Ch'oe peeked through a crack in the palanquin and gazed toward the governor's office. As she did so, she became worried anew about her husband. Her heart raced and her body trembled, while her tears fell. Oksun saw her mother weeping, and she began to cry, too.

Just then, the sound of boys singing and tapping the legs of their A-frame carriers in time as they headed toward the slope of Chiak Mountain in search of firewood reached Madam Ch'oe's worried ears.

The governor of Kangwŏn is like a cliff. Once you pass through those round pillars and step through the black gate, you fall. Oh, save us!

Though he steals, he struts around as if he is above the law. Though he does terrible things, he shakes his finger at other people. Oh, save us!

Though he feeds on the fattened commoners of the remote villages of Kangwŏn Province, he does not shit blood or suffer any stomachache. Oh, save us!

A hungry ghost has come. A hungry ghost has come. A hungry ghost has come to Kangwŏn and haunts our land. Oh, save us!

If we set out rice cakes for the spirits, we can free ourselves of this ghost. But he has taken all our food and is starving us to death. Oh, save us!

The hungry ghost is reborn as a donkey. The governor of Kangwŏn meets his downfall, and the governor's office is turned into the floor of a stable. Oh, save us!

It bites the mud pail and kicks its hooves until it is fed. Then it huffs and puffs. Oh, save us!

All that biting and kicking has hurt many, but how cruel to kill the only son for three generations in someone else's family. Oh, save us!

Next spring, do not go to Ch'iak Mountain to cut wood. The man from Kangnŭng will not return. He will become a cuckoo instead and cry all day and night. Cuckoo, cuckoo, cuckoo! Who wants to hear your mournful song? Oh, save us!

Madam Ch'oe heard the song and, as if her organs had gently melted away, she stopped longing to see her husband. She melted like snow in her seat, fading away, thinking only that she wished she knew nothing of the ways of the world.

The palanquin bearers were so busy talking amongst themselves that they did not hear the boys singing as they gathered wood. They tapped their pipes, reshouldered the palanquin, and hastened toward the governor's office. In about the time it took for wet tobacco to light, they reached the office.

Ch'oe Pyŏngdo was famous all over Kangnŭng for his clever ways. In 1884, the year of the Kapsin Coup, Ch'oe was twenty-two years old. That spring, he went to Seoul in search of Kim Okkyun, the famous leader of the Enlightenment Party.[4] Kim was generous in both appearance and attitude, and always treated others as if he were Lord Xinling, from the long-ago Warring States Period in China,[5] greeting a guest. Ch'oe became Kim's right-hand man and seemed to love him very much. And Kim loved Ch'oe in turn, holding him dear, and spoke with him about what was happening in the world. He told him much about the good and bad in our country's politics, but he did not tell him of his ambition to reform the country. When the Kapsin Coup took place in the Tenth Lunar Month of that year, Kim escaped to Japan. Afterward, Ch'oe went down to the countryside and began amassing his wealth. His plan was to save up money and take his wife and daughter to a civilized country to study. His goal was to return to Korea, after acquiring enough knowledge, and save the people. Ch'oe heard his fellow villagers refer to him as a man who was tightfisted with his money, but his desire was not to save just one or two people. He aimed to save the people of all eight provinces of Korea from misery.

---

4. Kim Okkyun (金玉均 1851–1894) was a reform-minded politician in the late Chosŏn who advocated using foreign resources to advance the country and keep it independent. He was assassinated in Shanghai.

5. Lord Xinling (信陵君 d. 243 BCE) was a prominent aristocrat of the Warring States period (戰國時代). He was famed for providing for talented men.

But Ch'oe had one major problem, and it was a problem that could never be fixed. He was a great man who certainly did not flinch when faced with an easy adversary, and so he was not the type to lose when faced with a high-ranking person intent on abusing their power, or someone using their power to keep others down, even if it meant suffering a death by a thousand cuts.

For some reason or other, he did bribe the errand runners when he was taken to the governor's office. But after arriving, he spoke his mind even while being beaten so badly, and he refused to give a single cent to the governor, even though he spent over half a year locked up. When people from his village went to visit him in jail and saw the state he was in, they pitied him and said, "Don't hold onto your money. Do whatever it takes to convince the governor to let you go." But Ch'oe refused to listen.

Governor Chŏng and Ch'oe were like the crane and the mud snail: the crane tries to eat the mud snail, but the mud snail tries not to be eaten. The governor, who would have gladly set Ch'oe free after taking his money, went wild when he realized Ch'oe would not give him any money. For Ch'oe, it was not that he was too tightfisted to spare even a spoonful of leftover rice, but rather that he detested the governor's ways. In other words, it was not about money, but about the fact that the governor, who was treating the people so badly, was a traitor to the nation and an enemy of the people. Ch'oe wanted to see the head of this wicked man lopped off with a sword. He did not want him to get even a single coin. The stronger Ch'oe felt about it, the stronger the words were that came out of his mouth. Perhaps the governor had heard what Ch'oe was saying about him. Between his anger at being badmouthed and his anger at not getting any money, the governor's tightly laced headband snapped and he gave immediate orders. The government office was in an uproar.

"Prepare the executioner's slab. Bring out Ch'oe of Kangnŭng. Ready his execution."

The governor was using his power to call for Ch'oe's immedi-

ate execution. Ch'oe stared him down and shouted: "For what reason have you arrested this innocent person? What did I do to be
beaten and locked away for half a year? Why do you keep dragging
me back out to flog me again once my wounds have healed? For
what crime am I now to be executed? Punishing an innocent man
and killing him is something that even an emperor would not do,
and moreover something he cannot do. The people of Kangwŏn
are not your people, they are the people of the nation. If I were to
be executed for committing a crime against the country, I would
die according to the law of the country. I would not be dying at
your hands. Right now, you are killing me for personal vengeance,
not for legal reasons. If you kill this innocent man, you will be
committing a crime against the country. Do not do it. Please, do
not do it. The death of this humble body does not concern me, but
there are greater things at stake. If you fail to govern the people
with kindness and treat criminals properly in accordance with the
law, then how will the people of Kangwŏn ever trust you? If the
people are oppressed, this country will not last. So think broadly,
think deeply, on behalf of the people. This is an old saying, but,
"The people are the roots of the nation. The roots must be strong
for the country to be at peace." Think about those words and do
not hold the people in contempt. Do not regard them as something to be sacrificed or treat them as enemies. If you think of
them as a part of yourself, regard them as younger siblings, and
love them like your own young children, the people will enjoy
eternal happiness, and this country will know a peace that is as
lofty as a mountain and as firm as bedrock. But should the people
suffer because you failed to do that, then this country will be stolen
out from under us in the name of saving the race by those from
more civilized countries that know how to govern. Right now,
there is not a single country still standing that treats its people
poorly. Egypt fell, and Poland fell. India, too, fell. If our country, as
well, rules its people with tyranny, then even if you do not see this
country fall, your children will."

Ch'oe's words poured out without pause, like a cataract. The governor had been waiting for Ch'oe to say something, anything, that he could fault him for, so engrossed was he in his desire to execute Ch'oe. When he heard him say that the country would fall, he leapt up, excited, like a fish on a hook, and gave the order for Ch'oe to be prevented from saying even one more word.

"What? How dare you say the country will fall! Smash his mouth in and execute him at once!"

The moment the order came down, officers swarmed in from both sides like bees and began beating Ch'oe's mouth with the red club used for breaking a man's shins. How could so much blood come from such thin, shrunken cheeks? Fresh blood gushed out of his mouth as his teeth were shattered, his gums split, and his jaw dislocated. Ch'oe could not say another word and merely bobbed his head with each fall of the club.

Meanwhile, Madam Ch'oe was making her way to the governor's office. The palanquin bearers were dripping with sweat under the scorching sun, and the *makkŏlli* they had drunk at the tavern by the fortress gate had turned them red-faced and tipsy by the time they reached the governor's office. As they carried the heavy palanquin, they danced about lightly as if excited over something. The palanquin bearer in the front led the way, bobbing his head gently beneath his pleated soldier's hat, his words coming out tenderly like a poem.

"We've come to a stream, and the stones are slippery. Mind your step as you cross the log bridge. Match your pace and mind the palanquin."

They made their way from the tavern by the fortress gate into town without stopping to rest, chatting all the while. Swift as an arrow, they made their way, completely oblivious to what was taking place at the governor's office, thinking only about making their lodgings at a tavern outside Chillam Gate. When they reached Chillam Gate, they found there were so many people gathered there that they were unable to push their way through. They stood there holding the palanquin, asking to be let through. Not only did none of the people gathered there make way for them, but they were so crowded together that the people in back shoved the people in front, while the people in front clamored for those in back to stop shoving as there was no room for them to move forward. So curious were they to find out what was happening, the people in back did not move even though they could not have seen anything even if they'd had eyes that could pierce through the crowd like an awl. What they were missing was the sight of a criminal being beaten to death in front of Chillam Gate. It was market day in the town of Wŏnju, yet no one was buying anything. So the market had been moved to right outside the gate, as if people had come just to see a body. The palanquin bearers set the palanquin down by the side of the road and asked the onlookers what all the fuss was about. Shocked, they rushed to the front of the palanquin.

"Madam Ch'oe! They say Master is being beaten to death in front of the gate!"

Madam Ch'oe was aghast and began weeping loudly inside the palanquin. She cried as if in her own home, without regard for the fact that she was on the side of a large street within a sea of people. Such was her sorrow and grief and bitterness, that she felt no fear of the governor; even if he had dropped out of the sky just then, she would have only continued crying and cursing him.

Those closest to the gate witnessed Ch'oe being beaten, and those closest to Madam Ch'oe's palanquin heard her crying. Those witnessing Ch'oe's beating felt their skin crawl with horror, and those listening to Madam Ch'oe's tears felt their noses sting and their eyes well with tears. Of course there are those who cry easily at others' misfortune, but even if those listening to Madam Ch'oe's tears had been born with hearts made of stone, they still would have found their hearts crumbling at the sound of it.

Madam Ch'oe's voice was as faint as a mosquito's, but the sound of her sad tale was so clear and pure that it seemed to rise into the air and pierce the clouds.

"Don't do it. Please don't do it. Governor, you are a person, too, so how can you arrest an innocent man and punish him so, just to take his money? How can you kill someone just because he will not give you his money? They say you are having him beaten to death in front of Chillam Gate. Is he a villain who killed your father? A foe who killed your mother? For what crime is he being put to death? Oh, you rotten thief! You can have all my money, just spare my husband! You take other people's wealth and act rashly, as if you will live for a thousand or ten thousand years. But your life, too, is as fleeting as the dew on the grass. After your dreamlike life has passed and you die, you will become a rotten ghost and go to hell, where you will be punished for all your crimes. And even after a million years have passed, you will still have not paid for all your crimes. There will be no end to your suffering. My husband and I will become bitter spirits, and we will be your jailers, ruling over hell.

"Oh, to whom can I tell my sad story? Even if I submitted a written petition to the ministry of justice, there would be no point. Even if I were to protest to the king himself, it would be no use. How is this evil to be repaid? Oksun, Oksun! Let's die together and petition the Creator himself! What is the point of you living in a world that kills people so unfairly? Let's go, let's go! Let's petition the Creator! The world seems bent on killing the people of this country. So let's make haste and rush to make our voices heard. Oh, such sorrow! They say that even if you live a full life and die of old age, your wife and children still grieve for you, so how much more painful is it when a man loses his life at the hands of another? Lord, lord, look down upon us and see what is happening."

The elderly women of the town stood along the palanquin from front to back, crying as if everything she said had happened to them and calling the governor a rotten scoundrel. Suddenly, the crowd began to disperse, as soldiers began pouring out in search of the palanquin bearers from Kyŏnggŭm Village. They ordered them to take up the palanquin and leave Wŏnju at once, beating the men to hurry them on. Frightened, the palanquin bearers picked up the palanquin and ran away toward the tavern by the fortress gate. In the open field outside the northern gate, the sound of Ch'oe's wife and daughter wailing carried toward the tavern.

Perhaps because the greedy governor kept so many procurers and spies whispering in his ears, even people with minor requests tried to puff themselves up and look important, which meant that bad rumors found their way to the governor's ears all too easily, and many of his guests were ready to squeal on others at the drop of a hat. He had been told that Madam Ch'oe was out there, weeping and wailing and cursing his name. Had she been a man, there might have been severe repercussions, but because she was the wife and daughter of a high-ranking family from the countryside, there was little else to do but banish her from the area under the charge of disturbing the peace. Thus, Madam Ch'oe's palanquin was driven out.

By then, the day was nearly half over, and Ch'oe's life seemed on the verge of ending. The chief officer of taxes approached the governor and, in some fit of kindness, spoke on Ch'oe's behalf.

"If you are going to kill Ch'oe, it would be better to hand him over to the soldiers. He should not be killed at the government office. If anyone should hear afterward that he died, they will say he died without having committed any crime. It would be better for you to be patient and withdraw the order for his execution."

"So you are saying I should let him live?"

"Even if we release him now, there is no way he will survive. If you send him away quickly, before he breathes his last, no one will hear that the governor killed an innocent man, instead they will think you released him for good reasons. But he will not last long. Ch'oe's wife was chased out of town after causing a scene in public with her daughter. So if Ch'oe is executed today here, the rumors will be very bad. It would be a good idea to lift the execution order."

After hearing what he had to say, the governor gazed silently at the chief officer, seemingly deep in thought. The governor did not say why he stared at him so or what it was he was thinking, but he suspected the sly officer of having been bribed by Ch'oe. His conclusion, though, was that regardless of whether the officer had taken any money or not, there was clearly nothing to be gained from killing Ch'oe, who was not long for this world. So the officer seemed to make a good point. The officer began to say something else, but the governor cleared his throat and gave the command for Ch'oe's execution to be stopped and for him to be released. A crow, crying at the rays of the sun setting behind the towering peak of Ch'iak Mountain, circled and alighted on a crooked willow branch in front of the tavern by the gate, pointed its tail toward the evening sun hanging in the western sky, and shook its beak toward the east as it cried out.

"*Kkamak kkamak kkak-kkak, kka-ok kka-ok kkak-kkak.*"

As the crow warbled, the willow cast its shadow over the western window of one of the guest rooms in the tavern. The birdsong was heard clearly by Madam Ch'oe, who was staying overnight in the room. Her ears rang, her bones ached, and her insides seemed on the verge of melting as her tears poured down like rain. But she could not bring herself to wail openly in the tavern. So instead she sobbed and voiced her grief to young Oksun.

"Oksun, Oksun! It's true what they used to say about crows being wise. Your father has come to the governor's office in Wŏnju, where he does not know a single soul and even the mountains and rivers are strangers to him, and is dying bitterly. Though there is no one here who can tell us when he has passed on, that wise crow is cawing so to inform us of his fate. We have been kicked out by the governor's men and driven back here, so there was no time to think. But now let us send someone to find out what has happened."

In the midst of her turmoil, Madam Ch'oe pulled herself together and called for Ch'ŏnsoe, the servant who had accompanied them, in order to send him back to the governor's office.

Ch'ŏnsoe was not especially devoted to his master, whom he had freeloaded off of for two or three years as a farmhand, but he seemed to feel bad for the situation his master was in. Though he was sluggish from the long journey and the ten-mile walk back to the tavern, he brushed off his fatigue and hurried back to the government office, singing as he went. From the mouth of that unlettered peasant came an erudite song.

"Sunlight sinking behind the summit of Mount Ch'iak, I know you are busy on your way, but please think of Madam Ch'oe and stay atop that mountain. Do not go just yet. Kim Ch'ŏnsoe is on an urgent errand to gather any news of Master Ch'oe. If I cannot make it back tonight, Madam Ch'oe will not sleep. She will spend the night crying with Oksun. Even Lord Jing of Qi stopped to shed a tear at the sunset over Wushan before continuing his three-day march."[6]

He sang as he ran, kicking up wind. In the grassy field, the sunset was faint and far off, and his song was bright and clear. Just then, he saw a palanquin heading east, descending upon him like a rainstorm. The palanquin was a large affair that could be rented for just a few coins. A dozen palanquin bearers in pleated soldier's hats were switching off every few paces. When Ch'ŏnsoe saw the palanquin bearing down on him like a galloping horse, he stepped out of the road to let them go ahead. As it passed, he stole a peak inside the palanquin and let out a sudden shriek, calling out his master's name.

The palanquin was carrying Ch'oe Pyŏngdo. Ch'oe had been released that day and sent to the tavern. Covered in blood from head to toe, anyone looking would have agreed that he would not survive. Ch'oe, as well, knew he was not long for that world, but his mind was still sound. If he could just hold on for a few more

---

6. Lord Jing (齊景公 d. 490 BCE) was the ruler of Qi from 547–490 BCE and was a major power during the Spring and Autumn period (春秋时代).

mountains where not a soul could be found were Ch'oe's wife and daughter, who were filled with only thoughts of shock and sorrow from the cruel and heartless way their husband and father had been taken from them. As deep as the mountains were, even deeper was what lay beneath the soil. Ch'oe's body went into the earth, and the sound of the wooden tampers rang out.

Ŏyŏra, tamp the earth!

Once you leave your family behind and take that path alone, you cannot come back. The road is without measure.
Ŏyŏra, tamp the earth!

They say the other world is a far-off place, yet here it is, close at hand. A distant place, yet it lies just beneath the grass of your grave.
Ŏyŏra, tamp the earth!

Do not ask about the ways of man. Not even the plants and trees know. The green shoots of spring return year after year, but not even the king's descendants can look back once they start along the road to the underworld.
Ŏyŏra, tamp the earth!

Such is the way of life. Your punishment was cruel and your death tragic. Such a pity.
Ŏyŏra, tamp the earth!
When innocent men are not killed and innocent men are not punished, don't the people live in joy and peace?
Ŏyŏra, tamp the earth!

Though we continue to live like victims, we grieve
for your unfair suffering and death.
Ŏyŏra, tamp the earth!

Place a board over the coffin, lay the last board
down. We will not see your handsome face again.
Ŏyŏra, tamp the earth!

We will miss you, we will miss you. We will miss seeing your face. Looking at the light of the lonely moon
over the empty mountain, can it compare to the face of
the one who has passed?
Ŏyŏra, tamp the earth!

If, in your untimely death, there were words left un-
said, tell them to us in our dreams, sing it to us like the
Song of Bamboo Branches.
Ŏyŏra, tamp the earth!

When the sound of the men tamping the soil down had
ended, a round burial mound had appeared. The grave perched
on top of the mountain like a bird on a wire. In accordance with
Ch'oe's final wishes, the head of his coffin pointed toward Hanyang, while his feet pointed toward his hometown. Hanyang was
the national capital, so it expressed his concern for the country
and his desire to keep watch over the capital. And his hometown
was where his ancestors were buried, where his poor wife and
daughter lived, and where he had friends who likewise worried
about the nation. His concern for his wife and daughter were
great, but his desire to protect the nation was also shared by his
friend, Kim Chŏngsu. Ch'oe's deceased spirit shuffled its feet in
anticipation, waiting for Kim to do his part to help their country.
But once a person was dead, that was it. Ch'oe was to bid farewell

to human life and walk that endless road, while his wife would spend her life weeping at the world.

The day her husband died, Madam Ch'oe wanted to die, too. And the day he was buried, she wanted to follow him into the earth. But there were two things that held her back and kept her from dying with him.

One was that she could not die and leave behind her eight-year-old daughter, and the other was that she was nine months pregnant.[9] She stayed alive in the hopes that the child would be born a boy, and Ch'oe's family line would not end with his death.

But Madam Ch'oe was filled with sorrow day and night. She wept at the sight of a mountain. She wept even at the sight of water. When she ate, she had to wipe away her tears before eating. And when she slept, her tears flowed in her sleep. She felt as if her liver was melting, her heart was stopping, her intestines were breaking, and her chest was being stabbed with a knife. She told herself not to fuss and not to despair, but her heart did as it pleased. There was one more thing for her to worry about. What worry was that? That was the worry that the baby she carried would fade away with the rest of her rotting insides. But the baby knew nothing of those worries and continued to grow inside of her.

After ten months, the baby came into the world, crying, "Wah, wah!"

Though the labor was long and left Madam Ch'oe fatigued and distracted after giving birth, she wanted to know immediately whether it was a boy or a girl. She asked the midwife, "You there, do I have a son or a daughter?"

The midwife replied indifferently, saying, "What does it matter? Just be happy it was a safe delivery."

Madam Ch'oe heard what she said and felt shocked and disappointed. Either it is a girl or it's a cripple, she suspected, then felt

---

9. It seems the author has lost track of time here—if Ch'oe had been imprisoned for over a year, this is not possible.

afraid. Her hopes fled, replaced by sad thoughts, and her pillow grew wet with tears. Already weak in constitution, Madam Ch'oe had been barely alive, just a skeleton that could be called a person because it spoke and a person because it ate, from the day her husband was arrested to the day he died, and from the day he died until the day she gave birth, so frail she looked as if the wind would blow her away, like a flame that would go out if pinched. She was so shocked by the midwife's words that she weakened even more after giving birth. A bubbling pot of rice and soup was placed before her.

"Mistress, please eat some soup."

Ch'ŏnsoe's wife urged her to eat. Madam Ch'oe opened her eyes and looked at the bowl for a moment. As tears welled up, she said, "I don't feel like eating. I'll eat in a little while."

Then she closed her eyes again and lay back down. Her face was pale and cold. Strange things began to appear before her eyes, and strange words came out of her mouth. Once known for her impeccable manners, Madam Ch'oe went insane and became like a wayward girl.

As it turned out, she had had a son, a precious bundle of joy. So why did the woman who helped deliver him give Madam Ch'oe such a shock? The midwife did not intend to startle her. She had picked up this way of speaking from somewhere. If you say the baby is a girl instead of a boy, then the boy will have a long life, or so they say. So that was why she did not say it was a boy. Her good intentions made Madam Ch'oe sick instead. Though she took ill easily, getting better was more difficult. She was given herbal medicine to restore her and nourish her blood, including *tanggui, chŏn'gung, sukchihwang, paekchakyak, wŏnji, paekpoksin,* and *sŏkch'angbo,*[10] but her heart meridian grew hotter and hotter, and the sickness crept into her bones.

Her precious son, born after his father's death, could not nurse at his mother's breast, so he was given to the nursemaid to look

_____

10. These are all traditional medicines made largely of herbs.

after. Born in chaos, the little baby knew nothing and only ate, slept, woke, ate, and grew. The pitiful one was Oksun, who was older and clever. Each time her mother had one of her fits, Oksun would cry, "Mother, mother! What's wrong? Look at me, Mother. I'm Oksun!"

Fearful thoughts would come to her young mind, and she would often call for Pong'nye. Madam Ch'oe would sometimes mistake Oksun for Governor Chŏng and chase her around with a kitchen knife, demanding vengeance, so helpers had to stay in the inner quarters at all times, day or night, and not leave her side for even a moment.

Someone had given the baby boy a name, and it was Ongnam, which meant "a boy as precious as jade."

Though his father had died unfairly, and his mother was terribly ill, the boy continued to grow. Seven years passed, during which he grew up without knowing his mother's face. Was that because she had died? No, she was alive, eyes open wide, but he could not meet her.

Had he grown up without a mother, he could have put her out of his mind entirely. But he heard with his own ears that she was alive yet he could not see her. What kind of twist was that? When Madam Ch'oe went mad, the one who had kept an eye on everything that took place in their home was Kim Chŏngsu. Also, Ongnam's nursemaid was a commoner from the village. When Madam Ch'oe's illness did not improve right away, Kim declared that it would be better for Ongnam to grow up without knowing he had a mother, and he gave Ongnam's nursemaid plenty with which to feed and raise him then sent them far away.

When Ch'oe was arrested by the governor, Kim was the one who had stood up against the officials without regard for his own life. He had then gone into hiding for a while, after which he heard about Ch'oe's death. Determined to be arrested, too, he had returned to Kyŏnggŭm Village and watched until Ch'oe was buried. But he was originally a penniless libertine. Even if he had been arrested, the officials would have traveled over three hundred *ri* and gotten nothing for it. And even if he had had money, he was not the type to give it away. Furthermore, Kim's scolding of the officials had already blown over without incident. So no one had come from the governor's office to arrest him, and he had stayed at home.

It sounds like a lie to say that he loved and cherished someone else's child more than his own, but Kim did in fact love and cherish Ongnam more than his own son. Long ago, Cheng Yin had abandoned his own son to save Duke Mu of Qin,[11] and Kim would have done no less to save Ongnam. Ongnam grew up thirty *ri* from Kyŏnggŭm Village. Kim traveled that distance frequently to see Ongnam. Whenever he arrived, Ongnam would run to him happily, as if greeting his own father, calling out, "Uncle! Uncle!"

Kim found this adorable, how Ongnam clung to him even though they were not the same blood. He adored Ongnam so, not simply because of his affection for Ch'oe, but because the more he saw how clever Ongnam was, the deeper his love for the child grew.

Yulgok Yi I was known from a young age for his wisdom, gained through logic, and Maewŏldang Kim Sisŭp was known from a young age for his writing.[12] Though Ongnam could not be compared to those sages, people who saw him all praised him, saying they had never seen such an intelligent seven-year-old.

"Uncle! I've come to see you, Uncle," said Ongnam, as he ran into the courtyard of Kim's house.

"Ah, who is this? How did you get here?" said Kim, as he opened the door and looked out.

---

11. Cheng Yin (程嬰). Duke Mu (趙武 d. 621 BCE) of Qin (秦) greatly expanded the territory of Qin and is considered one of the Five Hegemons.

12. Yi I (李珥 1536–1584), courtesy name Yulgok (栗谷), was one of the two most prominent Confucian scholars in the Chosŏn dynasty and further an accomplished poet. Kim Sisŭp (金時習 1435–1493), penname Maewŏldang (梅月堂), was a brilliant literary man and best known for writing the novel *Kŭmo sinhwa* (金鰲新話 New tales of Mt. Golden Turtle).

Ongnam led the way with his nursemaid following behind. Kim frowned, as if he were not happy to see them, and looked deep in thought.

"He kept badgering me," the nursemaid said, "saying he wants to see his mother, so I couldn't take it anymore and brought him here."

Kim gazed at Ongnam without responding then bowed his head. "Uncle, I walked thirty *ri* all by myself. Aren't I strong?"

"You mean this child walked all that way?" Kim said. "If you had told me, I would have sent a palanquin."

"I was so excited to see my mother," Ongnam said, "that my legs aren't tired at all."

Kim raised his head as if to say something but instead licked his lips without a sound.

"Uncle!" Ongnam said. "Please grant me this wish. I know my mother is alive, but I have never seen her face. I am dying to see her. I heard that she went mad after giving birth to me. If only I had never been born, maybe she would not have gone crazy ..."

As he began to weep, the nursemaid looked at him and began to cry along.

Kim's wife stroked Ongnam on the head and said, "Poor Madam Ch'oe. To experience such misfortune and then become so terribly ill ..."

The words stuck in her throat and she was unable to finish speaking as the tears began to fall. Kim's head sank lower. His head was bowed deeply, like the head of a monk who was falling asleep while chanting Buddhist prayers.

Kim's wife looked at him and said, "Husband, it would have been better if Ongnam never knew about his mother. But we cannot stop him from seeing her now, can we? I will take him there so he can meet her. Come, Ongnam. We will see your mother briefly, then you must return home with your nursemaid right away. But if you are thinking about staying there and insisting that it's hard to leave her side once you've seen her, then I won't take you."

Kim lifted his head and said, "Yes, my wife will take you."

At that single statement, Ongnam, his nursemaid, and Kim's wife all smiled, their eyes filled with tears.

At Ch'oe's house, the windowed double doors of the inner quarters were shut tight front and back, crisscrossed with long boards, and sealed with large nails, making them look more like the sides of a cliff than doors. Only the lattice door between one of the rooms and the central hall was left open. The room was bare of any furniture or dishes; the only thing in there was a ghostlike person.

Her hair was a rat's nest, and her face looked like it had not been washed in years. The pile of bones that looked barely capable of life, so pale was she, sitting alone and mumbling, was Madam Ch'oe.

Why were the doors all sealed with only the lattice door left open? When Madam Ch'oe's fits of madness were especially bad, she sometimes tore off her clothes and tried to run outside, and she also sometimes did not recognize Oksun and chased after her with a club, trying to beat her. Therefore she was kept locked up in her quarters, like a prisoner in jail, and several elderly women kept watch over her like jailers and kept anyone else from going into her room. The innocent person locked up in that dark, lonely room was Madam Ch'oe. And the one who opened the door to that room and stepped in, while calling out, "Mother!" was Ongnam.

Following on his heels were Kim's wife and Ongnam's nursemaid. From the opposite room, Oksun saw them and came running into her mother's room. Just then, Madam Ch'oe was sitting alone on the warm part of the floor, thrusting a kitchen knife into a pillow, and muttering about taking her vengeance on the one who took her husband's life. When Ongnam saw his mother, he burst into tears, rushed over to her, and cried out for her. Oksun had grown up weeping silent tears, alone in her room, for the last seven years. Her long-suppressed cries came bursting out, and she hugged Ongnam and wept loudly. Kim's wife and the nursemaid wondered why they had brought Ongnam. Kim's wife wept freely as she approached Madam Ch'oe.

"Excuse me, Madam Ch'oe. This is your son. Look here. Pull yourself together and look at this child. How did you get this way? Why are you stabbing that pillow? Stop that nonsense and hurry up and get better so you can instruct your daughter well and marry her off, so you can raise your son and bring in a daughter-in-law. You need to start living again. You cannot do anything about your deceased husband, but isn't it heartbreaking that your poor father-less son should be raised by someone else? Madam Ch'oe, hurry up and pull yourself together so you can raise Ongnam and enjoy life. Whatever happened to that kind, well-mannered Madam Ch'oe we all once knew?"

She became choked up and stopped there. Madam Ch'oe recognized Madam Kim somehow and sobbed.

"Look here, woman from Hoeo Valley. What bitter pill is this? Your husband came to our house and threatened to beat those officials to death, but I stepped forward to stop him. The officials knew nothing of my good deed and dragged Oksun's father away then killed him. I have gone to see the Great Jade Emperor. He heard my petition, and he has promised to fulfill all my wishes. He called forth the king of the underworld, who captured Governor Chŏng by trapping him beneath a thousand-*kŭn* iron tub[13] and threw him in hell. Then he cast a golden net over the officials who came to our house and turned them into serpents. The Great Jade Emperor told me, 'After you leave, I will examine and punish all of the people who have committed crimes against others.' Woman from Hoeo Valley, listen to me carefully. In a few years, the world will be overturned. The evildoers will be in a fix, and the people will be able to live and enjoy their wealth. Wait and see, whether I am right or wrong ... Everything Oksun's father said when he died on Taegwallyŏng will come to pass."

She said such crazy things for a while before later closing her eyes and lapsing out of speech entirely. She sat still and pointed

---

13. A *kŭn* is equal to 600 grams.

one finger like the hand of Buddha forming the center line of the water trigram to indicate silence. The only sound in the room was that of Oksun and her brother crying.

On the wide waters of the Pacific, an enormous steamship was making its way. All that could be seen beyond the mast was the blue sky, and all that could be seen beneath the water was the shadow of the blue sky. Where did the sun rise, and where did it set? Where had the boat come from, and where was it going? Even if one could see where it had come from, it would still seem to have come from the sky, and even if one could see where it was going, it would still seem headed for the sky. The wind was still, the waves were placid, and the setting sun was far away. Three people came out of a first-class berth and stepped onto the deck. The one in front was Ongnam, and the one behind was Oksun. Behind them was Kim.

Ongnam skipped about on the deck, saying, "Sister, sister, can you believe you almost missed this sight because you said you did not want to come when we left home? Would you have gotten to see this if you'd stayed at home?" He looked about, excited, while Oksun stood at the bow of the ship disinterestedly and looked only at where they had come. Oksun's grief was deep beyond measure and indescribable to anyone.

"What has become of Mother? It made my insides crumble to see how those grannies who attended to her would browbeat her and nag her, even when I was there. Those grannies try hard. I thank them. That's not empty praise. It is no easy task to look after our mother, who has become that way, day and night. But what will become of her now that I am not there either ..."

With that thought, beadlike tears rolled in pairs down her face. When she bowed her head, the tears had vanished into the boundless expanse of water. Worry followed upon worry, and her thoughts were without end.

"Where is Kalmo Peak? Where has Taegwallyŏng gone? When Father died, we were crossing Taegwallyŏng, and all the world below was mountains. I thought if I stood on that mountain, I would see the whole world. *Aigu*, that mountain, that mountain ..."

As she stood deep in thought, Taegwallyŏng seemed to appear before her eyes. A mountain has no feelings, so what drove Oksun to such feelings of attachment to that mountain?

At the summit of Taegwallyŏng Pass, her dead father lay in silence. In Kyŏnggŭm Village at the foot of Taegwallyŏng, her living mother was no better off than her father. She would not forget the sight of her mother. She saw her in her dreams when she slept, and before her eyes when she woke. When she saw a person, even a beggar, walking around, sound of mind, she thought about her mother's condition. And when she saw a person, even a cripple, who was sane, she thought it would have been better if her mother had gone blind or deaf or lost the use of her arms or legs. Then she would recognize Ongnam as her son and return to the world. Such thoughts made Oksun grieve for her mother. Everyone she saw reminded Oksun of how her mother had changed. Even the sight of a winged beast or a crawling insect conjured up wretched thoughts.

"Though they are mere animals, they must also feel happiness and anger and sorrow and joy and love and hate and greed and all those things. So how is it that our mother has lost those feelings? Father left this world, and Mother is oblivious to it. So now that my brother and I have no one to turn to, the ones who take pity on us and care for us like their own are Kim and his wife. If we were at least remotely related by blood, it would not matter, but we are from different clans and not even bound by the affection of being related by marriage. How will we ever repay their kindness after we've grown up ... They treat us with the kindness of parents, yet I call him Uncle since I cannot call him Father. Nevertheless, in our hearts, we think of him as a father and follow him as such. But no matter how careful we are to be on our best behavior and mind them, they can never be like our true parents. It is my duty to hide my worries and put on a good face."

With those thoughts, Oksun wiped away her tears, as if she would not cry again, raised her head, and looked once more at where they had come. All she saw was the steam from the ship above the boundless sea.

Though Oksun had come out onto the deck to take in the view for a moment, her thoughts and worries were still there. Her worries made themselves felt all the more when she was alone in a lonely place, lying on her pillow in the quiet dark.

Kim Chŏngsu was the one known as Ch'iil and Ch'oe Pyŏng-do's dear friend. He was a man who put the fate of the country before his own. He was not born that way, but after learning about the state of the world from Ch'oe, he had abandoned his obstinate ways, as if waking from a giddy dream, and examined the world carefully. Ch'oe had returned to his hometown, after hearing the lofty words of Kim Okkyun, having realized that he was just an ordinary man from Kangnŭng who had best dare not dream of saving the people and taking back the country. He was a man of Chosŏn, where you were not even respected as a human being if you were lacking in status, so as there was nothing he could do, no matter how talented a statesman he might have been, he had no choice but to return home and save up money. The purpose of saving that wealth was not to eat and dress well and live in luxury, but so he could take everyone who had some ambition, however many there were, and go study abroad. Like Kim Okkyun, Ch'oe was bent on reforming the country's politics.

After Ch'oe died, Kim had lost all hope. He was like Boya, the famous zither player, who cut the strings of his zither and vowed never to play again after his closest friend and greatest fan Zhong Ziqi died.[14] But when Madam Ch'oe told him what her husband's last words had been, Kim's eyes filled with tears of righteous indignation, and he did not have the heart to ignore Ch'oe's request.

---

14. Boya (伯牙 n.d.) was a famous zither player of either the Spring and Autumn period or the Warring States period. His surname may have been Yu (俞),

Ch'oe had made three final statements before he died. One was words of resentment toward the world. Another was a message for his friend Kim. And the last was a request for his wife.

His resentful words were delivered in the rash, uninhibited manner of a man not long for this world. Much of what he had said were words that should not be spread, but anyone listening would envy and praise the friendship between Kim and Ch'oe. Much of what he had to say to Kim was also related to events happening in the world, so those who heard it whispered it amongst themselves, keeping his words secret, so his message stayed in Kyŏnggŭm Village and did not spread out into the world. The only message of his that was delivered was his final request to his wife.

Ch'oe's final words to his wife were, "I am a man with a bountiful harvest. Ch'iil has nothing to eat. After I am dead, I want you to use my wealth and continue to make a living from it with Ch'iil. Do as he says, even if it means buying or selling off the household goods. Also, the baby is due soon, so ask Ch'iil to help raise the child, whether it is a boy or a girl." With that, he shed his last tears and died.

Long before Madam Ch'oe went mad, Kim was putting ten, no, a hundred times more work into Ch'oe's home than his own. When she lost her mind, Oksun was only eight years old. As Ch'oe's home had been dealt more blows and had no clear future, Kim had Ch'oe's household transferred to his, including the title deed to his paddy fields. Kim even provided the food, firewood, and all the ceremonial goods used in Ch'oe's home. Ch'oe's fortune swelled until, just seven years after his death, his wealth had grown by three or four times what it used to be.

With Ch'oe dead and his wife ill, it would have been easy for a household so overcome with such a succession of disaster and ca-

---

but he is commonly referred to simply by his given name. After Zhong, who always listened to Boya, died, the musician cut the strings of his instrument and vowed to never play again.

lamity to squander its wealth. So it was strange that their fortune grew. However, considering that Kim had added his wealth to Ch'oe's household, as well as his own household goods, it only made sense. For example, if they harvested a thousand bushels, then a hundred bushels went to feed both households, leaving grain leftover. Kim sold nine hundred bushels to buy more fields and began to increase the annual harvest, which made Ch'oe's fortune grow like wildfire. After Ongnam met his mother, the year he turned seven, he and Oksun cried day and night and refused to be apart. So Kim set aside the wealth that Ch'oe had amassed in his lifetime, sold the fields he had bought himself, and used the money to take the two of them to study in America. After they went to Washington and looked at the bustling sights, he saw to their education. Since Ongnam was young, he lost himself in the sights and did not think of home, but Oksun was indifferent to every place they went, museums and zoos alike, and thought only of their homeland. If she saw a flower, she saw it with tear-filled eyes. If she saw the moon, she looked at it through tears.

Kim gave no thought to the difficulties or what might come up during a long stay abroad, as he was determined to educate Oksun and her brother, and he was still young and strong. He put all of his energy into increasing their knowledge. Five years passed, during which the cost of an education in an expensive place like Washington was no small matter. He also spent too much money in other ways in order to keep Oksun and her brother from having to suffer, so the money he had budgeted for ten years or more was spent in just five years, and the funds for their education were set to run out in only a few months. When Kim left Kyŏnggŭm Village, he had instructed his son to increase the harvest from Kim's house each year so they could sell it for cash. His son was twenty-one years old when he left. Since five years had passed, he would be twenty-six. Kim thought, "Even if the harvest is not doing as well as before I left, the grain prices have been steadily rising back home. So if he did as I instructed him to do, there should be a lot of money. It will take me half a year to return home in order to retrieve the funds for their education. Even if the journey is slow, it will not be more than eight or nine months." So he bid farewell to Oksun and her brother. As soon as he returned home, he found that some things were the same and some things were different with Ch'oe's family.

Madam Ch'oe was still alive and insane as usual. Their wealth had been reduced and was not as much as before. Kim took a closer look at his own household. To his surprise, there were two things that were different. One was that his son had increased his debauchery, and the other was that his son's lies had increased exponentially.

Kim had never imagined that his son, whom he and his wife had trusted immensely, who was praised by kith and kin alike, and who was looked up to by everyone in their village, could fall to such a level. Had he done so of his own will, or had he been lured into it by others? It was not because his intentions were wrong. He had been led astray. Then, how had it happened? At that time, the Kabo Reform had just taken place.[15] The government was reorganized, and the magistrate of each town was renamed provincial governor. The eight provinces were divided into thirteen. Some Buddha-like governor had been sent down from the capital to Kangnŭng. But his connections were not strong, so he had to quietly extort money from the people instead of doing so broadly. He heard a rumor that the son of Kim Chŏngsu of Kyŏnggŭm Village had a tidy sum of money, even if it did belong to someone else, so he decided to investigate. He summoned Kim's son and showered him with praise and flattery, treating him well, while asking to borrow just a few thousand coins. Kim's son feared that if he did not comply, he might be struck down by lightning, so he quietly gave the money to the magistrate of Kangnŭng. As he suffered in silence, an elderly provincial governor with more influence than the

---

15. The Kabo Reforms (甲午更張) took place in 1894.

Kangnŭng magistrate summoned him and brazenly took even more money from him. Kim's son squandered all of the cash earned from Ch'oe's harvest as if it were his own, then worried and fretted over what to do. Finally, his greed got the best of him, and he took out the deed to Ch'oe's fields, which were being managed by his mother, mortgaged it for cash, went to Uljin to do business, and returned empty-handed after his first try.

When Kim's son first went to try his hand at business, he had done so thinking that he would easily recoup the money he had given to the county magistrate and the provincial governor. He went to Ulchin to make money off of fishing weirs, but the closest he got to the fish was their smell, his money all but cast into the water like so much bait. His attempt at business left him shuddering with failure. He did not tell his father what happened. He filled all of his letters with lies.

Once a person starts lying, even an honest man will find himself spinning wild tales. Kim's son not only lied to his father, he lied to everyone and racked up a pillar of debt. He exhausted Ch'oe's fortune and seemed maniacally intent on pulling the wool over everyone's eyes.

Kim Chŏngsu was so appalled, he could not speak. The fact that his son had fallen into debauchery was second to the fact that Ongnam and his sister were going to starve to death ten thousands of miles away. The thought of it kept him up at night. He tried to come up with traveling money to bring the children back. After being put in charge of Ch'oe's wealth, Kim, who had had no money of his own, had gained credibility with others. But once his son had become known for his wild ways, they were much criticized in the village. The rumor quickly spread that Kim Ch'iil and his son were bent on ruining Ch'oe's household, so he was unable to borrow even a single coin from anyone. If he so much as brought up the subject of a loan, he was met with only curses.

Kim could not sleep for several nights on end, and his attempts at devising a plan came to nothing. Blind with anger, he refused to eat and drank all day instead. He would sober up only to be greeted by countless worries, so he would drink again until everything turned hazy. Then, fortunately, he could pass the days in peace without a care in the world.

During the months after Kim's return home, the time that he spent sober only amounted to a few hours within the thirty days of each month. In the end, even during his sober moments, his mental faculties left him, and he was oblivious to the world.

It was not the alcohol that made him so, nor was it due to illness. He was oblivious to the world because he had entered a long, long sleep.

As with the days preceding, he gulped down booze like a whale. His body was healthy, unmarred by disease or illness. When he passed away, it was not due to any ailments; death itself was the ailment. The day before Kim died, he called his wife and son before him and told them he had a plan to bring back Oksun and her brother. There was no logic to his words, only insistence.

As if the value of their house, which only amounted to a few coins, would be enough to bring them back, he told his wife and son that he was going to sell the house then sell all of its occupants to others as slaves, and he would use the money to bring back Oksun and Ongnam. He had been drinking like a horse, gulping down *soju* so strong it stung your nose. It was the dog days of summer then, and after drinking *soju* all day, he fell asleep at dusk with all the doors flung wide, whereupon a fever came over him like fire rising inside his body. He looked for cold water. Leaving no time for a response, he urgently demanded that cold water be brought to him. He swallowed a bowl in one gulp and died on the spot, as blue fire shot out of his nostrils.

Though Kim had died, Oksun and Ongnam were still alive and waiting day and night. Had Kim's family sent them a telegram immediately to inform them of Kim's passing, they would have given up and stopped waiting. But Kim's son was a country boy, and the thought of sending a telegram did not occur to him. So

Kim had been dead for five or six months, while Oksun and her brother were completely in the dark. Oksun and Ongnam's money for school had run out, and they were on the verge of starving to death in a foreign land where they had not a soul to turn to. They sent several letters but received no replies. Then, one day, Ongnam came skipping in with a letter that had arrived in the mail. "Oksun, we got a letter from home! Hurry and open it!"

He set the letter in front of his older sister. She was so excited that she did not look closely at the envelope and tore it open straightaway to find that the letter had been written by Kim's son, and that the content of the letter was the news of Kim's death.

At that time, Oksun was nineteen years old, and Ongnam was twelve. Upon hearing that Kim, who had been like a father to them, had died, the two were as grief-stricken as if they had become a filial son and daughter mourning the death of a parent. And not only were they sad about losing him, they were sad about their own pennilessness.

They had thought they would see their mother, who had gone insane and knew nothing of their whereabouts, once more while she was still alive. But it seemed that Oksun and Ongnam were going to beat their mother to the grave. Oksun clung to Ongnam and cried.

"Ongnam! How could anyone be more ill-fated than us? Just think of our dead father, our living mother. Our whole lives have been filled with grief, and now we are to die here without visiting our father's grave or seeing our mother's face once more? The worst thing a child can do is die before their mother. But how are we to live when we are in a foreign country with nothing to eat?"

As they wept, Oksun and her brother decided it would be better to commit suicide. They were both bright children. Kim had guided them well. Though they were still young, they studied harder than others and poured in their whole hearts and devoted all their energy to studying so that they could return to their homeland and be of benefit to the nation. Oksun was seven years older than Ongnam, but as was usually the case with girls, she had not been sent to school in their homeland. In the United States, they both entered primary school together, and they advanced and graduated together. By then, they were in their first year of secondary school. They had studied the same amount, but there was a clear difference in their perceptiveness and in their manners. Oksun thought more often about their father, and she also thought more about their mother's condition. Furthermore, Oksun was at heart a woman. When she took her young brother to die, the sorrow she felt could not be put into words, not even if she were ordered to speak.

They had once been close with everyone at the hotel where they had stayed for the past five years. When Kim was with Oksun and Ongnam, spending money freely, he and the hotel owner had become like brothers, and the bellboys were happy to be at his beck and call, like they were an extension of him. After their school funds ran out and they had no money to pay for their meals, that brotherly owner and those helpful bellboys changed in a heartbeat, and did they ever change! Without money, they were not allowed to stay even a single day longer. But the fact that they had been staying at the hotel for that long on credit was because the owner thought Oksun's family was sure to send the money within a couple of months. They were allowed to stay at the hotel for exactly that long. But now those two months were up. Even if they only wanted to go ten miles, they had no money for train fare. All they did have was a single gold watch and a gold ring that Oksun wore. They quietly left without even telling the owner where they were going. They were on their way to die.

The setting sun hung in the western sky, and the bustling crowds were all heading home after work. Oksun and Ongnam waited for the sun to set then headed toward the train tracks. They looked for a place where there were no signs of other people. It was growing dark, and hardly anyone was around after the last train had left. Oksun and Ongnam watched from a hill next to the tracks and waited for the next train to come. Oksun clasped Ongnam's hands in hers and wept.

"Ongnam, you're a man. You shouldn't die this way. You should stay alive. Find work as a bellboy if you have to, and study hard for a few hours every day. Then later, you can return to our country, find our sick mother, and take good care of her. I'm a woman, so even if I survive, I am of no use to our family. Whether I live or die, I am of no value. But you should do whatever it takes to stay alive. Don't let our ancestors' graves go neglected."

"Sister, how can you give no thought to the fate of our nation and the ten million lives of our countrymen that hang in the balance, and worry only about our own family? If there were a way for me to stay alive and help our country, I would work like a dog if I had to, let alone work as a bellboy. And I would never dream of neglecting our ancestors' graves."

"Aye, those are commendable words. The more you feel that way, the more you should stay alive and do what it takes to help our country."

"Stop saying that. Think about how frustrated someone must feel to decide that they want to kill themselves. Kim Okkyun was an Eastern hero who tried to reform the government only to die branded a traitor. What kind of high-minded ambition do I have that I could help the country? Now that we are in America and suffering with nothing to eat, dying is easy. You're the one who should endure, find work as a maid in someone's house and keep yourself fed."

Before he could finish his words, the next train came rushing in like a storm. Ongnam, who had been waiting at the top of the hill, closed his eyes and ran down toward the tracks with Oksun close behind. But just then, a man at the bottom of the hill shouted and ran toward them. As the man rushed uphill, the train, swift as an arrow, was already passing by. Two days later, a story appeared in a Washington newspaper.

Korean Students' Failed Suicide Attempt

Two foreign students from Korea were rescued from a suicide attempt two days ago at seven o'clock in the evening. Distressed that their school funds had run out, thirteen-year-old Ch'oe Ongnam and nineteen-year-old Ch'oe Oksun attempted to take their own lives by stepping in front of a train. A policeman by the name of Callaver had spotted the students at the top of the hill and became suspicious. Though unable to understand what they were saying, he waited at the bottom of the hill. As he watched them, the students saw the train coming and hurled themselves toward the tracks. The constable rushed to their aid. The hill was about ten lengths away from the twin tracks, with the northbound rails closest to the base of the hill and the southbound rails on the far side. When the students saw the southbound train approaching, they mistook the direction and fell onto the wrong tracks, where they were rescued by the constable.

As the news story made the rounds, one man read the story closely and took pity on their situation. That man's name was Shecky Anis. He was a devoted Christian who thought of God as his father and all the races of the world as his brothers. When he read the newspaper, his heart went out to Oksun and Ongnam, and he set out to find them. He offered to pay for their studies for as long as they needed. At that time, Oksun and Ongnam were more concerned with returning to their homeland than with returning to their studies. But since Shecky encouraged them to continue studying, they could not bring themselves to tell him they wanted to go home and instead resumed their studies in America.

When Kim was alive, Oksun and Ongnam had attended school and studied from textbooks, but Kim had educated their hearts.

Though their family names were different, Kim was like a father to them, and he had provided them with a family upbringing.

What was the nature of that heart's education?

Ch'oe Pyŏngdo and Kim Chŏngsu's minds were filled with pa-triotic sentiment. Had Ch'oe lived longer, he and Kim probably would have died for their country together. But now that Ch'oe was gone, Kim was as ineffective as one hand clapping, stuck without a penny to his name in that remote mountain village of Kangnŭng and too busy taking care of Ch'oe's household to es-cape the situation he was in, so unable was he to turn his back on Ch'oe's dying wish. As a result, the world remained un-touched by his ambitions. He complained of this all the time, but what he really meant was that he was concerned about the fate of the nation.

While Oksun and Ongnam were growing up, he spoke only of the nation, so Oksun and Ongnam had had those words drilled into their heads. Later, when they continued their education with the help of Shecky, their minds opened a little wider, and the scope of their goals grew a little larger. They came to see everything under heaven as one family and the whole world as brothers. Their bodies were infused with morality and their hearts with love for their fellow man. Weak thoughts were cast out and replaced with vigorous spirits. They began to enjoy their studies and abandoned thoughts of home.

However, that was really only true of Ongnam. Oksun, with her feminine bias, did not sway once she had set her mind to something. And to what was her mind set? Her mind was set to-ward worrying herself sick over their homeland.

She could picture like it was only yesterday her father being arrested and taken away to the governor's office. Her mother cling-ing to her and weeping. Her father dying at the top of Taegwal-lyŏng. Her mother giving birth to Ongnam and losing her mind. Her mother failing to recognize Ongnam when he came with

Madam Kim. Her mother stabbing the pillow with a kitchen knife, calling out the governor's name, and swearing her revenge.

Her worries would cease then start again, vanish then re-emerge. What she saw were the hills and streams of her homeland, and what she thought of was her mother. She wanted to quit studying immediately and rush back, but it was difficult for her to admit that to Shecky. The days and years passed in worry. In the meantime, Oksun and her brother completed secondary school and received their diplomas. Oksun sat face to face with Ongnam and unrolled her diploma.

"Look, Ongnam. Why do people bother to study? Are we in any position to be spending all this time in a foreign country, doing nothing but studying? Even if our mother were in her right mind, we would still miss her terribly after being away for so long. Since our mother is suffering an unusual illness, we ought to stop studying and return home to take care of her. You were taken away and raised by your nursemaid and never even saw our mother until the year you turned seven. Then, right after that, we left for America. So you don't know all there is to know about her, Ongnam."

She became choked up and couldn't go on, which made Ongnam cry as well, his tears pouring down like rain. Oksun tried to compose herself; she forced herself to hold back her sobs so she could finish what she had to say. Ongnam, as ever, was moved to tears.

"Listen to me carefully, Ongnam. There is a difference between the things you hear and the things you see. You heard about everything that happened to our family, but I saw it all with my own eyes. Our father died tragically, and our mother was stricken with that terrible illness because of that tragedy. Her fate is many times more tragic than his. Ongnam, listen. The year after Mother became ill, we had a little puppy. The puppy found a dried fish head somewhere and was holding it down with one paw while happily gnawing on it when this big shaggy dog came out of nowhere, eyed the puppy, snarled and flashed its white teeth, then growled and attacked the puppy. Anyone who saw it would have been repulsed by the way the big dog stole the fish head, but Mother's grief was especially keen, and her illness especially severe. She did not know what was what. When she saw the dog attacking the puppy, she had a sudden relapse and shouted, 'There's the governor! He attacks others, takes their food. Won't let someone as harmless as that get by. You evil wretch. As governor of Kangwŏn, you killed all the people, so now you must torment a puppy? You've made yourself my enemy, so today I'll have my revenge.' She screamed and chased after the dog. It was the dead of winter, and no one knew where she had gone. The entire household poured out and spent the whole night searching for her. We should never have left her side. So we have to thank Mr. Anis without another thought and return home. Ongnam, my body may be here, but all my eyes see is our ailing mother."

She wept again. Ongnam sat and cried for a while then struck the table with his fist as if he were trying to split it in two. Then he took a neatly folded white handkerchief from his jacket pocket and wiped his face. He rolled his eyes to clear them of tears and gritted his teeth. He brightened up and spoke firmly.

"Sister, we have come to a civilized country to learn civilized modern subjects, so we must undertake civilized work with civilized thoughts. Listen. Loving your parents does not just mean staying at home and taking care of them. It means using the body your parents blessed you with to carry out your duties and obligations as a national citizen. Back home, there are many corrupt officials and their lackeys who are killing the people in their drive to fulfill their own greed and fatten themselves up, even if it means destroying the nation by obstructing the divine king's wisdom and trifling with our national sovereignty. Our father died unfairly, and our mother became terribly ill as a result. If you consider the cause, you'll see that our country's politics are all wrong. We are not the only ones to have suffered unfairly. Thousands, tens of thousands, of people have suffered. They have died and withered away, faceless, casting a wretched light over the entire peninsula. Two million people are living in misery, and the country is as precarious as a pile of eggs. Our race is collapsing and disappearing like snow melting in a spring breeze. If we are to help the country and save the people, we must reform the government. We must study as much as we can and broaden our knowledge, so that we may one day become a force for reform and work to improve our country. That is what it means to be filial to one's parents. Going home and taking care of Mother will not cure her of her illness. Visiting Father's grave will not bring him back to life. No matter how bad things are for our family, we cannot look back. We must study more for the common good of our country's brethren. If our country fares well, then our father, who died an unhappy death, will at last be able to rest in peace. And if our mother, who lost her mind to a bottomless grief, is able to release her grudge, she might get better. Stop thinking about what you should be doing for Mother and think instead of what you should be doing for the country. But, if you don't want to consider it, if you would really rather rush back home and take care of Mother, get married and live comfortably, then leave now. Since we have no choice but to impose upon Mr. Anis for traveling money, I will ask him for you."

Oksun sat quietly for a moment and thought it over. She decided that he was right and made up her mind to suppress her concerns and rededicate herself to her studies. After several more years of difficulty, she graduated high school and entered a music school in order to forget her worries. Ongnam completed middle school and began studying economics while also intensively researching social philosophy. Since he spent all his time with his nose in books, his nights were always clear and quiet, whether his window was lit with fireflies or the ground was covered in snow. But the world was changing day by day. Meanwhile, back home, those who had been blithely committing strange and terrible acts were, in a flash, becoming aware of the air of transformation being felt in the world. After the start of the Russo-

Japanese War, Ongnam turned his attention to the newspapers.
Each day, when he read the paper, his blood boiled. What had happened to make him that way?

For Ongnam, his home country was like Nolbu paying the price
for splitting open gourds.[16] What does that mean? Long ago, there
was a man named Nolbu who only cared about hoarding riches for
himself, even if it meant stealing from others and reducing his own
brother to begging. All of that evil energy over the course of his life
knotted together to form a gourd seed inscribed with the character
for wind, which could be interpreted three different ways: *entrap-
ment*, *demise*, and *ruin*. For someone like Ongnam, who was versed
in modern subjects, the character could mean northern wind or
western wind, western wind or southern wind. He felt a great wind
was about to blow, whether that meant something terrible was coming or not. But until the wind was already blowing, there was no way
of knowing what it would bring. Until you split it open, you never
knew what might come out of the gourd.

On what wind was that gourd seed carried? The willow trees
were drooping in the spring wind. Sparrows flew in front of the
houses of Wang and Sa and perched high up on a ceiling beam.
Twittering noisily about the warm countries to the south, they
dropped a gourd seed.

Nolbu picked up that seed and planted it. The Creator must
have fertilized the field well, because each vine had many nodes,
and on each node a flower bloomed, and each flower bore fruit,
which ripened day by day. But there was an evil blight on those
gourds. In the Eighth Lunar Month, when it was time to harvest
them, Nolbu plucked a gourd from the vine and split it open. Even
as he was splitting it open, he was thinking about how to close it
back up again.

---

16. Nolbu is a character in the dramatic story-singing performance of *Hŭngbu-ga* (흥보가 Song of Hŭngbu). Nolbu is the elder, morally corrupted brother of
the protagonist Hŭngbu.

He cracked one open, and out popped a chief mourner. He cracked another one open, and out popped the fierce general Zhang Fei.[17] He cracked open another, and out popped a slave master. Afraid of what the remaining gourd might contain, Nolbu did not dare split it open. But since it was already fully ripened, it seemed that whatever was inside the gourd was bound to come out, even if Nolbu did not open it himself, even if it had to open on its own. In the end, Nolbu lost all his money and was ruined, but thanks to his moral and loving brother, he was able to keep his house. This is a meaningless story from the past. In this civilized age, scientifically speaking, there is no way that the cruel general Zhang Fei and a slave master could have come out of a gourd. So it is not that Ongnam truly believed it. But, for Ongnam, it seemed like a speculative, figurative version of five hundred years of history since the founding of the Chosŏn dynasty, as there had always been doctors of science there. Nevertheless, Ongnam thought you could never be too careful, and he took the story to heart just in case.

Ongnam believed that his homeland was full of Nolbu. The rulers were all Nolbu. The governor of each province was a Nolbu. Even the town magistrates were Nolbu. He thought that when reformist forces came forward to reform the government, all those flocks of Nolbu would meet their comeuppance at once and retire.

Every hour of every day, Ongnam waited for reform to come to Korea. But it was not because he hated those Nolbu. He was waiting for the country's future to begin in earnest, and looking forward to an end to the people's current misery. But even if the country were roused from its deep sleep, as if from a dizzying dream, it would not awaken. And even if it were struck with a club, it would not be roused. Ongnam believed that until the day light-

---

17. Zhang Fei (張飛 d. 221) was a general who served under the warlord Liu Bei (劉備 161–223 CE) in the late Eastern Han dynasty. He is also a major character in the fourteenth-century fictional work, *Romance of the Three Kingdoms* (三國演義).

ning struck and a change came that could overturn heaven, it would be difficult to wake the country from its dream.

1907 AD: 516 years had passed since the founding of the Chosŏn dynasty. Summer had come, and sunlight was pouring down from the sky. The light shone into the guest room of a hotel in Washington, D.C., United States of America. The room faced southeast. The window in the southeast wall let in the morning light. Inside the window hung white hemp curtains. Below the curtains was a bed, and on the bed was a female student. That student was Oksun. Her jadelike face glowed cherry red in the heat of the morning sun then turned to peach. Beads of sweat formed like dew on sweetbriar. She was the fairest of the fair, yet on closer inspection, her face was starting to show her age, which was closing on thirty. After waking up then dropping off to sleep again, she stretched, opened her eyes, looked at the alarm clock hanging at the top of the wall, and gently sat up.

"Already eight o'clock! I should not have slept so long, even if it is a Sunday." She got dressed, washed her face, and finished her usual morning preparations. Then she looked in the mirror and sighed.

"Time does fly. How can I already be this old? Mother was my age the year Father passed away. And I was barely eight years old. If this is how old I've grown, how old must Mother be now? Children should only come into the world when times are good. What fate was I cursed with that I should have been born at the wrong time? If this were a peaceful, joyous world, where the ordinary folk can plow fields and dig wells and know nothing of wealth and power, no one would have to die before their time, like my father. And no one would have to go crazy, bearing a grudge, like my mother. Alas …"

She broke off mid-thought and sat down without a word. Her face had turned pale. Someone tapped on the door and came in. It was Ongnam. Oksun tried to hide the worry in her face and look natural, but Ongnam knew at once from her complexion that she had something on her mind. He perched on the edge of the chair.

"Sister, have you read today's paper?"

"The paper, already? I just got up and barely finished washing my face."

"If you go to bed too late, you sleep more before breakfast. How late were you up studying?"

"You think I stayed up late because I was studying? Last night, I read a book until twelve then lay down at one o'clock. But I started thinking about Mother and could not get to sleep. I lay awake all night."

"But really, have you seen today's paper? It's quite funny ..."

"What could be so funny? What does it say?"

She started to look at the newspaper lying on the table, but Ongnam placed his hand over it.

"It'll take you too long to find the article yourself," he said, "so I'll tell you what it says. Listen carefully. The title of the article is 'Schoolgirl Sleeps In Late.' Ch'oe Oksun, a foreign student from Korea who has been lodging at the Sherman Hotel in Washington, sleeps when the sun rises in the east, believing that to be early evening, and sleeps some more when the sun is high overhead, believing that to be the middle of the night. I don't recall what the rest of the article says."

"You made that up. You're just making fun of me to try to convince me to stop worrying and sleep more easily at night. But Ongnam, do you think I'm doing it on purpose because I want to worry? Again last night, I read until twelve then went to bed, but thoughts of home started popping into my head. I tried all night, until Venus was rising in the east, to fall asleep, but I only managed to get some rest around daybreak. There's no difference between you making up your mind to forget your cares, and me being unable to forget them. I ..."

She broke off mid-sentence as tears dropped onto her collar.

"Sister, please don't say another word. Look at the paper."

Oksun hurriedly grabbed the paper and held it up to her eyes, as if suspicious that what he said might have really appeared there. Ongnam pulled his chair up close to Oksun, flipped through the newspaper, then pointed his finger to an article.

"Read this."

Oksun's eyes widened when she saw what he was pointing at. Originally, since Oksun spent too much time worrying about their homeland, Ongnam had tried to cheer her up each time he saw her. But the headline in the newspaper read: "Major Reform in Korea. The king had abdicated the throne and handed it over to his son." After Oksun read the entire article, she and Ongnam were once again deep in discussion.

"Ongnam, in every country in the world, there is no bigger or more difficult event than a revolution. Back home, people have been trying for dozens of years to carry out reforms, and they have been extremely loyal to the nation. But the people of our country have thought of reformist forces as traitors and opposed them, hating them like they were the enemy. Even loyalists like Kim Ok-kyun, who led the reformists, could not avoid assassination. After he died, many different reformists were called traitors and were unable to succeed. So now that this major reform has taken place, what do you think will happen in the future?"

Ongnam sat quietly for a while then sighed. "If the reform succeeds now, then after a few dozen years, the country will be restored. Up until now, I have only said things you wanted to hear and refrained from saying things that would worry you. But today, for the first time, I will tell you everything that's been on my mind. If our country had been reformed seventy years ago and progressed well, we could have stood among the most powerful countries in the world, and we would have taken Vladivostok before the Russians grabbed it as their base. If Korea had been reformed fifty years ago, Vladivostok would have been ceded to the Russians, but Qing China would have been under our influence. If reform had come forty years ago, the expansion of our army and navy would have been second only to Japan, but we would have been a strong, civilized nation. If reform had happened thirty years ago, we might have been a mid-level nation in terms of power. Japan would have been our ally to the south, and we would have blocked the spread of Russian influence in the north. Together, we would have reaped the benefits lost by the Qing and opened the path to future advancement into the continent. And we would have become one of the leading nations in a few years. If reform had come twenty years ago, even if we did not gain much strength during those twenty years, we would have opened more doors to education and opportunity for the people, and the state would have had the strength to stand on its own. Reform ten years ago would have been too late, because that was a tremendously difficult time for the country. Even if we had carried out political reform without outside help, it would have been an irreparable wreck. But even if only ten years had passed since reform, there would have at least been a foundation for preserving the nation. So when you look at it that way, those are the gains and losses to the timing of reform in Korea. But since there was no political reform, and the country has been steadily ruined instead, things are terrible. Judging from the state our country is in now, it is hard to say in detail how bad it is. For example, if we compare it to a house, all the provisions have run out and the children are running wild. Anyone who saw it would say that this house is on the verge of falling apart. It would be quite difficult for the family to set a new budget and manage the household well in order to pay off all of their debts, as well as to educate their children so that the ones who go about striking others, fighting with their brothers, and getting up to mischief day and night, would become a benefit to their families. That is the situation our country is in right now. Because he reformed the government while ascending the throne, our good and wise king will go down in history as a hero. We, too, must rush back to our homeland and do something beneficial with our education."

With that, Oksun and Ongnam set out for Shecky's house and explained their situation. By then, Shecky had grown very old and was not well. He had spent all of his money on donations to orphanages and charity hospitals. He instructed his own children to use their education to support themselves with their education, and he offered five thousand dollars to Oksun and Ongnam and told them to return home. The two of them firmly declined the money and refused to accept it. Instead, they took only five hundred for their traveling expenses and left the United States. Three months later, Shecky left this world behind and started along that long road to heaven.

Oksun and Ongnam reached Pusan where they took the Kyŏngbu Line to Seoul. Along the way, they gazed at the far-off mountains and wept in silence. At the sight of the bare mountains, stripped of all vegetation, they wondered, "Who would tear up all the trees like that?" They thought of the old days and wondered when the mountains would once again be lush and green. They also thought about the days to come. They saw tiny, flat-roofed houses by the road in the middle of fields at the base of the mountains, and they wondered if people really lived in those little shacks. Though they had seen such things when they were young, they felt taken aback, as if seeing them for the first time. But there was one thought that comforted them: that year was the first year of Emperor Sunjong's reign, the year His Highness had reformed the government. They cheered themselves up and headed to Seoul, then continued on to Kangnŭng without stopping to rest. In Kyŏnggŭm Village of Kangnŭng, a man and a woman dressed in Western clothing appeared, riding a palanquin. They stopped in the middle of the village, alighted from the palanquin, and asked about the home of Ch'oe Ponp'yŏng. It was the first time that village had seen a woman in Western clothing, so there were many onlookers gathered on all sides, and their voices could not be heard clearly over the barking of the dogs.

The woman in the Western dress was Oksun, and the man was Ongnam. The villagers heard that Oksun and her brother had returned, and they surrounded them and led the way to their family home. Along the way, more people kept joining the crowd.

The wife of Kim Chŏngsu heard the news and came running so fast that her straw shoes went flying, as if she had kicked them off mid-stride. She saw them fall into the rice paddy below the road, but she kept running in her socks without stopping to fish her shoes out. She clasped Oksun and Ongnam to her, crying, and took them to their family house.

It was autumn by then, and the only sound they heard was the rattling of the frostbitten pumpkin leaves hanging on the fence in the wind. The courtyard was overgrown on all sides with weeds, and there did not seem to be anyone living in their house.

There were many things Ongnam had forgotten about and many things he still remembered, but the more Oksun looked around at things, the more it seemed that she had just seen them yesterday, and the more she thought about the past, the more it really seemed like only yesterday.

Oksun and her brother went into their mother's room. Though she was still alive, she was just skin and bones. She had grown old in their absence; her hair was dotted with white, and the symptoms of insanity that had turned her into little more than a ghost were the same as ever. Oksun ran to their mother.

"Mother! Ongnam and I left you to study in a foreign country, and now we're back. Mother, what happened to you? Why are you still not better?" Shocked to tears, Oksun could not go on. Ongnam approached their mother and sat in front of her, crying.

"Mother, look at me. I am your son. After Father died, and you were stricken with grief, you gave birth to me and became sick. If only you had never had this unfilial son, you would not have become so ill …"

Before he could finish speaking, Madame Ch'oe suddenly shouted.

"What? Unfilial? You scoundrel! How dare you accuse someone of being unfilial just so you can steal their money? You villain!
Have you stayed alive all this time just so you could take money
from the people?" She was still not speaking rationally. Ongnam's
throat was choked with tears.

"Mother! I see now why you became so ill. But no one is stealing the people's money anymore, and no one is trying to kill innocent commoners."

Madam Ch'oe, who seemed to understand what he was saying,
asked, "Then what happened to that terrible governor and the others
like him?"

"Mother, you understand me now, don't you? The world has
changed. His Majesty the Emperor reformed the government.
Now, the people in power cannot abuse their posts. Neither the
provincial governors nor the county governors can rule over the
people with cruelty and violence. They have gotten rid of those old
evil practices and established laws so that they cannot take anything more than their own salaries. If things had been like this
before, Father would not have had to suffer so, no matter how
much money he had. If he could see how things are now, he could
rest in peace forever. Mother, you too can spend the rest of your
life in peace. Mother, I am your son, Ongnam."

Madam Ch'oe became alert and clasped Ongnam and Oksun
to her as she cried. Like a bright moon emerging from where it had
been buried in thick layers of clouds, her sanity returned. The
clouds lifted; the sky cleared. She hugged Ongnam and cried.

"Child, did you just fall from the sky? Did you spring out of
the earth? Are you telling me that I've been unaware all this time
of the child that came from me? Where have you been? Your father was young when he passed away. Now that I see your face,
how is it possible you resemble him so closely? Oksun, you were a
child when your father passed away. I don't know if you remember
everything that happened when you were young, but if you have
forgotten your father's face, just look upon your brother! You're all

grown up already? Now that I've seen you two in my right mind, I can let go of all of my grief and die happily. I only wish your father could have lived to see you like this. He spent his whole life worrying about the country and the fate of the people, so he must be happy now to look down on this world from the top of the mountain and see that all of the corrupt officials have been run off. Go with me to the temple so we can pray for your father's spirit to move on to the Lotus World. You two must read a written prayer to your father there to tell him that this world is now at peace."

Oksun and Ongnam were overjoyed to see their mother unexpectedly recover from her illness. The next day, they took her up to the temple to pray.

The Buddha was seated silently in the Hall of Paradise. The smoke from the incense floated gently in the clear air and billowed up into a great cloud. Madame Ch'oe prayed in a forlorn voice.

At the entrance to the village, a gunshot rang out. Suddenly, a band of rogues, hundreds in number, swarmed in and dragged Ongnam and Oksun out of the temple.

As they were both well-educated, intelligent people, Oksun and Ongnam did not look in the least bit afraid and went along peacefully. The leader of the rogues pointed a loaded gun at them.

"Who are you, and why have you cut off your hair? Did you come down here to spy on us? We are the righteous army of Kangwŏn.[18] It's our duty to execute suspicious-looking people like you."

The leader seemed sure of himself. Ongnam stepped forward calmly and began to speak at length.

"Listen to me, my brothers. I speak impartially for you, so please set down your weapons and hear me out. The righteous army is made up of your fellow countrymen. I, too, am one of your fellow countrymen. We both want the same thing for this country.

---

18. The so-called righteous armies (義兵) were guerilla groups that rose up to fight against the Japanese encroachments into Chosŏn. They are quite revered today in Korea as nationalist freedom fighters.

We have been educated differently, so it makes sense that we should approach things differently as well. You, my brothers, raised a righteous army and sneer in the face of death. Do you do that for the good of the country, or because you intend to do it harm? Please tell me. If I tell you what I think, you will likely kill me because we are not of the same mind. But if I do not speak my mind, not only will my fellow countrymen be in danger, a grave harm will be done to the nation. It is only right that I warn you against obstructing the progress of this nation and keep you out of danger, even if it means losing my own life. Before you kill me, hear me out.

"My brothers, your loyalties are misplaced and your ideas wrong. They have caused you to go against the imperial order of His Highness, Emperor Sunjong the Great, take up arms, and hide out in the countryside. While robbing the people of their wealth, you are met by forty or fifty border guards, who outmatch your numbers. So you accept your losses and run away, or else face countless deaths. What you are doing is taking the lives of your fellow countrymen and disrupting the national government. For what purpose are you doing this? You say you are angry about the loss of national sovereignty. But if you were truly angry, you would examine the root causes for that loss and do what it takes to recover national sovereignty in the future. When you think about how many decades of tyranny our country endured, it is surprising that so many have survived. Is it not fortunate that our country avoided complete collapse? We all experienced the same decades of tyranny, so you are well aware of what it was like. But let me share with you what happened to my family. Because he had money, my father was arrested by the governor of Kangwŏn, accused of lack of filial piety, and beaten to death. As a result, our family was completely ruined. There is nothing I fear in this world like tyranny. Listen, have you ever heard a more pitiful tale? Please hear me out. I went to the United States for many years. I met a man there from our country and spoke with him for a while. He said he had served as a governor, so I told him about how the governor of Kangwŏn had tyrannized our family. I asked whether that greedy governor should live or die, and the man said, 'Don't speak such nonsense. How many men get to be governor for free? Do you have any idea how much it costs, not only to get that post, but also after you start serving as governor? Do you know how much those royal birthday banquets, held several times a year, cost? Did you think those were the only expenses? That's right. How can they afford that on a monthly salary that only amounts to a few meager coins? If they don't take money from the people, how else are they to make up the difference? If they were to hold out and not spend a single coin as governor, who do you think would suffer for it?' When I heard that, I was so appalled, I could not speak. Those people steal money from the people and use it to their own benefit under the guise of working for the public. They take greed in stride. How will the country ever survive, and how can the people endure? That is why His Highness considered virtue and strength as he ascended the throne for this ruined country, and undertook a program of reform that could affect national power. He got rid of the evil practice of paying people off for positions in the central government, and he removed all of the government officials in the provinces who had been abusing the people. Now that Emperor Sunjong's reign has begun, has His Highness tyrannized the people? Listen, my brothers. If you wish to recover our national sovereignty, you must work hard underneath the reign of His Highness, teach your children well, and fulfill your duty to advance this nation's knowledge. There is no worthier cause than the nation's interests and the welfare of the people. Today, I will die cheering for His Highness, who has brought reform, and cheering for my fellow countrymen."

With that, Ongnam raised his hands high.

"Long live His Imperial Highness! Hurrah, hurrah! Long live my fellow countrymen! Hurrah, hurrah!"

As he cheered, the shaggy-haired men who called themselves

righteous soldiers began to shout: "This scoundrel must have been sent here by the king to admonish us! Let's get him!"

They stormed down on Ongnam and Oksun and dragged them away. In the Hall of Paradise, Madam Ch'oe lay prostrate before the Buddha. Her prayers for Ongnam and Oksun to be saved were the only sound.

∽

∽ 2

THE BATTLE OF DRAGON
WITH DRAGON

Introduction

Sin Ch'aeho (申采浩 1880–1936) is today praised as an ardent nationalist, historian, and literary man, by both those in South and North Korea. His project of defining Korea by its own people, known as *minjok* (民族), free of boundaries or influence from China was an attempt to counter the Japanese colonial ideology that sought to put Koreans together with the Manchurian people and debase the idea of Korea as a historically independent country and people. It is not an overstatement to write that he is better remembered as a historian than as a literary man due to his writings on the history of the Korean people.

As Sin came of age at the very time that Chosŏn was losing its independence, his early writings were aimed at stirring feelings of national pride among the people and perhaps inspiring them to heroic resistance. Thus he wrote historical-based biographies of past heroes such as the Koguryŏ (高句麗 37 BCE–668 CE) general Ŭlchi Mundŏk (乙支文德) who defeated an invasion by the Chinese Sui dynasty (隋 581–617) and Yi Sunsin (李舜臣 1545–1598) who was the leading force in defeating the Japanese in a number of naval battles. Both *Ulchi Mundŏk* and *Yi Sunsin-jŏn* (李舜臣傳 Life of Yi Sunsin, the greatest admiral) were published in 1908; the following year *Tongguk kŏgŏl Ch'oe tot'ong-jŏn* (東國巨傑崔都統傳 Life of commander Ch'oe, the great hero of the Eastern Country) was published and similarly focused on a great general of Korea's past. However, with the annexation of

Chosŏn by Japan these such works were quite naturally banned by the colonial government.

Sin received a traditional education from his grandfather and eventually attended the Sŏnggyun'gwan (成均館 Royal Confucian Academy) from which he received his doctorate in 1905. Subsequently he worked on the editorial board of two newspapers and became a key figure in the clandestine patriotic group, the Sinmin-hoe (新民會 New People's Association). Under the threat of sure arrest once Japan colonized Korea, Sin went into exile in first Vladivostok before travelling throughout China. He would never return to Korea. He joined the Eastern Anarchist Association (Tongbang mujŏngbuju ŭi yŏnmaeng) in 1926, and in 1928 he was arrested by the Japanese police in Taiwan for attempting to smuggle forged banknotes out of the country to help fund a bomb factory and other activities of this group. He was sent to Lüshun Prison where he died in solitary confinement in 1936.

Sin's literary style was enhanced by his traditional education and knowledge of premodern literary traditions. He did write in a colloquial style, but also added Chinese characters for clarity. The end result was that his works were read with relative ease by the people of the day.[1] He oftentimes used traditional forms in his writing such as the dream-record (*mongyu-rok*) common in Chosŏn period fiction. This allowed the story to be told omnisciently at times and also avoided the author having to voice his/her opinions, but simply acting as a transmitter of a tale-told. The present story is one such example of this method.

Yong kwa yong ŭi taegyŏk-chŏn (용과 용의 대격전 The battle of dragon with dragon), published in 1928, is an anarchist work featuring the clash of great powers from the East and West. Surely reflecting the times that Sin lived, the clash is inevitably horrific and results in pure anarchy and destruction of the worlds. The tale

---

1. Cho Tongil, *Han'guk munhak t'onsa* (The complete history of Korean literature) (Seoul: Chijik sanŏpsa, 1992), 4:317.

is allegoric and instructive as Sin demonstrates the evils of the past and present societies that have resulted in the deaths and hardships of the people. This reflects his ideology of the people (*minjok*) and how the governments have abused and oppressed them. Perhaps the work is a fantasy, but at the same time reflective of Sin's own activities with the Eastern Anarchist Association.

***

THE BATTLE OF DRAGON WITH DRAGON | *YONG KWA YONG ŬI TAEGYŎK-CHŎN* 용과 용의대격전

SIN CH'AE-HO 신채호

Translated by Brother Anthony of Taizé

1. The Descent of Miri-nim

It is descending. It descends. The dragon Miri-nim[1] is descending. Behold, the New Year has come, 1928,[2] the Year of the Dragon has begun. Miri-nim is descending over East Asia.

Waves rise in the Pacific Ocean. Gales blow in the deserts of Mongolia. Five-hued clouds gather at the peak of T'aebaek-san. Each and all of them declare that Miri-nim is descending.

At the report that Miri-nim is descending, all living creatures to the East of the Urals have raised their heads. The rich and powerful naturally prepare food in Chinese and Western fashion to please their tastes, make ready every kind of music—*kŏmungo*, *kayagŭm*, piano, etc.—to delight their ears. But the wretched, naked, starving poor who have to pay their devotions to Miri-nim own nothing. All they have are their crimson, naked bodies. They have no choice but to let some blood and brew wine from it, weep tears with which to make rice-cakes, place those miserable, unappealing offerings on the high altar and await the descent of Miri-nim.

---

1. The first Dragon is designated by the Korean word *miri-nim,* which is an honorific form of the native Korean word for dragon "Mirŭ / Miri."

2. The Korean text has *mujin* (戊辰), which is the combination of one each of the ten *kap* and the twelve *tti* symbols used to designate the years of the sixty-year cycle; 1928 was a *mujin* year and the story was published in 1929.

At two in the morning of the first day of the first month, at the first cock-crow, without any fanfare, borne on a plane of clouds, Miri-nim comes near. The high and mighty welcome the sacred Miri-nim with singing and dances, while all the poor with one accord fall prostrate on the ground weeping. As they weep, they pray to Miri-nim:

> "Your Lordship, Miri-nim! This year may taxes not be set too high. This year may we not have to give too high a share of the harvest. This year may we not see the inside of a prison. This year may none of us throw ourselves under a train for hardship. This year may none of us have to become a beggar wandering in other lands, other cities. This year may - - - prosper."[3]

As they pray, they hold hands and raised their arms high, ceaselessly rubbing their palms together in supplication.

But the sound of those prayers does not touch Miri-nim's ears, it only notices the miserable, unappealing offerings. On seeing them, Miri-nim grows furious. It opens its mouth and roars:

"Wretches! Death to those wretches who dare ask for blessings without showing devotion."

Alas! Is that mouth Nolbu's[4] gourd? Out of it come pouring an emperor wearing a dung tub on his head, a general wrapped in cowhide, a sleek-browed wealthy fellow, a landowner with the bowl of his pipe pointing backward, a stinking constable ... every kind of frivolous hireling. Once out, they gobble up every one of the poor folk.

---

3. Possible greeting: This year may So-and-So prosper.

4. Nolbu is the wicked brother of kind Hŭngbu in the popular Korean tale of *Hŭngbu-ga* (Song of Hŭngbu). Having sown magic gourd seeds, he expected to harvest gourds stuffed with treasure as his brother had, but instead out poured all kinds of monsters.

They gulp down the blood, gnaw the flesh, finally even crunch up the bones. If they don't want to be eaten they're destined to become bullet-fodder, or doomed to prison. Ah, hellish world ... wretched people ...

2. Victory Banquet in the Heavenly Palace, Fear of Treason

The sound of the pathetic pleas and angry shouts of the people who were being put to death shook the ninefold gates of highest Heaven, reaching the inmost chambers. The supreme Lord of Heaven,[5] startled, awoke from deep sleep. He ordered a heavenly angel to find out what that noise was.

The angel replied:

"That is Miri killing humans who demand the right to live."

The Lord of Heaven said:

"Ah, Miri is a wise and virtuous servant! If such aspirations increase they become insubordination, if insubordination increases it becomes revolution, so the people who aspire must indeed be killed! Ah, Miri is truly wise."

Then he calls Miri, gives it a medal for killing people, awards it a higher rank. Summoning all the immortals in heaven, the ghosts on earth, the generations of sovereigns, ministers and generals, he offers a banquet in heaven.

On Earth people's stomachs are empty, so they die, while in heaven stomachs are so full they're fit to burst. Lifting up then cradling his belly, the Lord of Heaven looks round at all the spirits.

"These things called humans are congenitally rebellious, they are all the time raising the flag of revolt, so what shall we do? Sup-

---

5. The Chinese word for "the Lord of Heaven" used in this text, 上帝 *Shangdi* ("the emperor above"), is the oldest Chinese name for the supreme deity, usually identified with Heaven. It has sometimes been used to translate the Christian "God."

pose we suspend a cannon in space as big as the Earth and shoot it, we could kill them all, but once the world is destroyed and the human race abolished, there will be no blood left for us to suck, so that won't do. Suppose we grant them their freedom and then they refuse to let us suck their blood, that won't do either. How can we completely dry up those wretches' rebellious nature, leaving them half-dead, so that we have no worries as we munch them up from head to toe, suck them dry from the outside in, devour their children and grandchildren and following generations? You must each propose a scheme."

The angel reported:

"We should equip them with nose-rings and halters like cows, whip them and crush them."

"Ha ha, you are too naive! Are not the administrative laws they have more cruel than nose-rings? Ethics and morality more brutal than bridles? Are not the guns of the military and the swords of the police many times more terrible weapons than whips? Yet still they plot rebellion."

"Then let's summon all the doctors, manufacture an anesthetic, and put them to sleep forever, so that we can devour them without their realizing we are catching and eating them."

"Humph! I already tried that. I sent that Confucius fellow to write about Honor and Duty, fooling them that 'the poor and lowly should accept poverty as their lot and obey the commands of the powerful, passing to future generations their reputation as faithful, loyal subjects,' while I sent poor Shakyamuni and Jesus, fooling them that 'even if people make you suffer, if you accept it without resisting, after you die your souls will go to heaven or the lotus flower podium.' Where will you find better anesthetics than those? For over two thousand years now I have been enjoying the effects of that medicine but today its virtue is exhausted and those wretches are waking up, starting rebellions or revolutions, causing trouble."

"Then since today is a period when science and literature enjoy high authority, I think we should seduce many scientists and writers and turn them into tools of the rich and powerful, the ruling class, ready to support by their theories the rights of the ruling class, glorify in poems and fiction the dignity of the ruling class."

"Oh! I tried that recently and have seen remarkable results. But there are scholars who disobey my orders and go plunging among the masses, encouraging rebellion."

3. The Repressive Measures Devised by Miri

In this manner the Lord of Heaven worried endlessly about human beings with their entrenched spirit of rebellion; finally he sighed:

"In the human world there cannot be a winning strategy that continues to work for one hundred years, so why should there be one that works for ten thousand years here in heaven? Let's just drink wine, eat meat, and let the years pass by; what use would it be if we kept worrying?"

Then he sang an ode without any refrain:

"Who cares if the gardens before and behind our palace collapse? What does it matter if the arrowroot vines on Mansu Mountain grow tangled?"

At that, Miri came forward and fell prostrate before speaking: "Your Majesty is so august and dignified, all the hosts of living beings venerate you. Why do you speak such ominous words? The humans on Earth have a rebellious nature but I can subjugate them and confine them forever in a living Hell."

The Lord of Heaven replied:

"Ah, you are a rare combination of wisdom and valor; if you have a strategy, tell me."

Miri continued:

"The populace of the world can generally be divided into two parts, one part being the populace of powerful lands, the other part being the populace of colonized lands. The populace of powerful lands have preserved a conventional form of patriotism that functions by force of habit and at the same time they have mistakenly come to think that the state belongs to the ruling class, taking patriotism to mean supporting an increase in the power of the ruling class, so that their patriotism has become a false patriotism. Therefore, if we grant the populace of the powerful lands things like the right to vote in general elections or increased wages, while promoting that false patriotism, which goads them to conquer the populace of small, weak lands and to oppress the populace of their colonies, allowing them to see themselves as the vanguard of the ruling class and capitalism, their hungry stomachs will be filled with these unprofitable vanities and they will not even notice the pain while we go on sucking their blood for decades more. The degree of pain suffered by the populace of the colonies may be thousands of times greater than theirs, but with their groundless faith in good fortune those starving always hope for the luck of a feast, those freezing always hope for the luck of warm clothing, those being dragged to the gallows always hope for the luck of life. As a result, when they resist, they are unable to do so wholeheartedly. No people are as easy to fool as those who have been colonized. Railways, mines, fisheries, forests, fertile land, rich paddy fields, businesses, industries … take every right and source of profit away from them, increase taxation and sharecrop rents, exploit them to an appalling extent, if you then declare, 'We are looking after your welfare,' they are fooled. Apply whipping, clubbing, stabbing, branding, electrical shocks, or even such punishments as the xxx[6] that are too dreadful to mention, mobilizing troops to tear women apart, bury children alive, slaughter whole villages, set fire to granaries … employ fearsome methods such as these, but then, if you simply allow the populace to have a couple of newspapers and proclaim, 'Accept the benefits of our cultural policies,' they are

---

6. "xxx" appears in the original text.

fooled. Restrict schools and abolish learning, forbid the use of national languages and literatures so that patriotism cannot arise,
transplant the citizens within their own countries so that the original citizens have nowhere to live, destroy whole clans by harsh
punishments and massacres, if you then make inflated statements
about 'friendship between peoples of the same race and culture,'
they are fooled. Tell them to forget words or terms like 'founding a
nation,' 'revolution,' 'independence,' 'freedom' and such, making it
impossible for them to be used in speech or writing, then say that
soon self-government and political rights will be granted to them,
and they are fooled. Just look. Those youths sucking at the sweet
lips of female students in the love-stories produced by amorous
literary circles that have performed memorial rites for the demise
of the nation, how proud they are of themselves. Men robbed of
their native land and exiled, who live as menial workers in remote
foreign lands, if they once have a place to lie down, don't they start
singing about the comforts of their second homeland? Independence fighters go running off in the wake of the communist party.
In their play-acted beggar's government even the president's
clothes are ragged. Since it is so easy to fool colonized peoples,
your Majesty, you can set your heart at ease. Even though you say
that all the peoples of the world are waking up, at least the colonized peoples are still far from it. Even if we only devour the people of colonized lands, we have nothing to worry about for several
decades."

The Lord of Heaven listened to his words, then said:

"Why, my child! I may be vicious, you are even more vicious
than I am. How could I keep my throne without you?"

And he patted Miri on the back.

4. Jesus Cruelly Murdered, No Hope of Resurrection

"Dragon[7] has come. Dragon has come. This is the last day of the Heavenly Kingdom."

Ah, what voice is this? Where is this voice coming from? What voice is this, coming as the Lord of Heaven is frolicking, his mind relieved after hearing Miri's reassurances. Now the Lord of Heaven comes tripping along, demanding to know where this voice is coming from, so all the subjects from Miri down, awestruck, go searching but there is nothing to be seen, only the voice crying:

"Dragon has come. Dragon has come. This is the last day of the Heavenly Kingdom," keeps booming from somewhere, shaking the heavenly palace's walls, roofs, gates, windows, pillars, floors, and foundations. They recite all kinds of spells and prayers summoning the Buddha Shakyamuni from Paradise, but the voice only increases in volume, the heavenly palace only quakes more violently. Greatly alarmed, the Lord of Heaven stops the feasting, then sends all the spirits out and spends the night with the court ladies, but he is so worried that his spittle dries up.

What next? At dawn the next day the myriads of spirits in the Heavenly City were awakened by cries of, "Special edition! Special! Buy this special edition!" An angel on his way by carriage to have an audience with the Lord of Heaven glimpsed a copy, a special edition of the three-hundred-thousand-year-old *Heavenly Times* newspaper.

The main headline in large capitals was: "Tragic Slaughter of Lord of Heaven's Only Son Jesus Christ" and in smaller capitals following it: "At Dragon's Instigation." The accompanying article read:

---

7. The second dragon is designated by the English word "Dragon" used as a name.

"The Lord of Heaven's only son, Jesus Christ, was lecturing on the Lord of Heaven's Way in a Christian chapel in a rural farming village when suddenly the village farmers, shouting, 'Bastard! Cashing in on your Father's name you've swindled yourself a living for nineteen hundred years and that's enough; why are you still running around barking like this?' and 'Where have you put all the blood you've sucked from us poor folk over the past nineteen hundred years?' and 'You've deceived the West so much already, why have you come out to swindle the East as well?' and 'Do you want another taste of the nails from that day's cross in Jerusalem?' They attacked him with kicks and punches, chopped at him with their hoes, turning the body of Jesus Christ into a pulp and killing him with no further possibility of resurrection. The murderers were poor folk but the chief culprit is said to have been Dragon. Dragon is a monster of obscure origin, but it has been frequenting this region for many days, cursing the Lord of Heaven, saying he is 'A villain who deserves to be butchered and eaten or worse,' and denigrating Jesus Christ as 'A more vicious rogue than his father,' circulating a manifesto enumerating the crimes of the Lord of Heaven and Christ in ninety clauses, finally taking advantage of Christ's visit that day to commit the outrage of murdering him, leading the populace on."

There followed, on the same page, an editorial under the title "Jesus Christ Incapable of Resurrection" that ran:

"Jesus Christ was the Son, wicked and vicious in character exactly like the Lord of Heaven his Father. After his birth, at first he taught his Father's Way but then, when he was just over thirty, he joined the Jewish outlaws. But the Jews of those times, being slow-witted, let Jesus go free after they had caught him; he escaped carrying the cross behind his back, claimed to be 'risen from the dead' and fooled the people of Europe so that he united them all under the banner of that religion. After the Crusades, he launched great wars, such as the eastward Crusade and the Thirty Years' War, teaching ordinary people the art of killing one another, all the time lying that 'blessed are those who suffer, blessed are the persecuted,' fooling the populaces of ruined lands and the proletariat with holy words, so that they make them forget reality and dream of a false kingdom of heaven to the advantage of the powerful and rulers, so that his sanctity and grace remain eternally and are inscribed in history.

"It is not just that this time he has been slaughtered so cruelly, today the masses who have become aware and the youths of the anti-Christ alliance have acted in concert, killing Christ again with brush and sword, so that henceforth Christ has been slaughtered once and for all, he cannot return to life again. Since Christ has been killed once and for all, the Lord of Heaven, sunk deep in old age, is in a pitiful state too, for in whose name will Christians offer him prayers now?"

The angel, on seeing that special issue, did not read through to the end but pasty-faced went rushing into the heavenly palace and showed the paper to the Lord of Heaven, his hands trembling.

5. Dragon and Dragon: Brothers but Different

The Lord of Heaven glanced at the paper, then stared dumbly, as if he was out of his mind, at the angel who was standing before him, before collapsing onto the desk. The angel rushed to raise him.

"Your Majesty, this is an incident in which the very existence of the Heavenly Kingdom is at stake; how can your Majesty let go of your mind in this crisis? Your Majesty!"

He appealed to the Lord of Heaven in a hoarse voice, choking with sorrow, while all the spirits, high and low, from Miri down, came pouring in to comfort the Lord of Heaven.

Seeing Miri, the Angel cried, his eyes blazing fire, brimming with fury, his face crimson:

"You wretch! Aren't you meant to be his Lardshit the dreaded Bastion of the East? What has happened to the influence you are supposed to exert over the population, that you have allowed such an atrocious incident to happen, that his Majesty's impossibly almighty only Son Jesus Christ should be killed without any possibility of resurrection? You wretch! You should be beheaded …"

He thumped on the palace walls with his fists as he rebuked Miri, who sat there silent like a deaf-mute sick at heart, grimacing.

"Dragon has come. Dragon has come. This is the last day of the Heavenly Kingdom."

Once again, the voice shakes the Heavenly Palace. The angel abruptly falls silent, Miri opens his eyes wide.

The Lord of Heaven, who has been in a swoon, jumps up from his couch.

"Dragon! Dragon! That Dragon that killed my son Jesus! Catch that Dragon and sacrifice it!"

In peremptory and desperate tones the Lord of Heaven gives his severe command. At once troops of the Heavenly City's police and secret agents are mobilized and make a great fuss, but although the cry, "It has come, it has come, Dragon has come …," rings in all directions, there is not the least trace of Dragon to be seen.

Despite all the exertions of the Heavenly City's police and secret agents, not a clue could be found until Dragon's photo and history were published the following day in the *People's Newspaper*, the only paper in all the world, East and West, for ordinary folk. But on the front page, under the heading "Dragon's Portrait," there was nothing but a large number of '0's with an explanation in small 5-point print to the left of them. The explanation ran:

"Until the Heavenly Kingdom has been completely destroyed, Dragon's form can only be expressed by '0.' But Dragon's '0' is unlike the '0' of mathematics. In mathematics, if you add '0' to '0', it is still '0', whereas Dragon's '0' can become every figure, whether 1, 2, 3, 4 or ten, a hundred, a thousand, ten thousand. The zero of mathematics occupies a space but corresponds to no reality, whereas the Dragon's '0' can become every kind of terror, whether gun, sword, fire, or thunderbolt. Today Dragon is expressed as '0' but tomorrow Dragon's enemies may be reduced to '0' so that empires become '0', the Heavenly Kingdom becomes '0', a capitalist becomes '0', every ruling power becomes '0.' When every ruling power has become '0', Dragon's original identity and form will be revealed to our eyes." Then under the title "Dragon's History" came the following:

"Who is Dragon? In the fifth year after the Lord of Heaven was enthroned as Supreme Being and began receiving superstitious worship from ancient humanity, in the midst of the void there arose a mysterious being, a monovular twin, one of them being Dragon and the other that renowned Miri-nim who is at present the Commander of the Guard of the Heavenly Palace and Governor of the East; Miri and Dragon are both written with the same Chinese character, 'long' 龍. Later, Miri grew up in lands such as Chosŏn, India, or China, becoming the dragon of the East, received passive education from Shakyamuni and Confucius, etc., becoming a loyal servant of the Lord of Heaven, then was venerated as a model divinity for humanity by every religious or ethical leader who had found his vocation in obedience and so become a tool of the ruling class, and therefore the dragon was highly praised and associated with the Lord of Heaven in the myths of Chosŏn, the Confucian classics of China and the Buddhist scriptures of India. So the Lord of Heaven chose Miri and appointed it to be Defender of the East. Meanwhile, Dragon stayed in places such as Greece or Rome, becoming the dragon of the West, always keeping company with rebels and revolutionaries, enjoyed wicked games such as 'revolution' or 'destruction' and suchlike, never accepting the bridle of religion or ethics, so that in Western history traitors and rebels were often given the nickname of 'Dragon.' In the modern world, Dragon has sympathized with Nihilism, practicing a more violent form of revolutionary action, finally becoming guilty of the murder of Jesus Christ."

Every one of the courtiers of the Heavenly Kingdom, high and low, was amazed to learn on receiving this newspaper that Miri and Dragon were originally brothers.

6. The Construction of the Terrestrial Nation and Consternation in the Heavenly Kingdom

Being the Lord of Heaven's favorite, Miri had for many millennia been Chief Governor of the East but now the rebel Dragon's act of murdering the Lord of Heaven's beloved Son had occurred in a region under his control and at the same time evidence that Miri was Dragon's brother had been published in the *People's Newspaper*, so that public opinion in the Heavenly City was widely inclined to suspect that Miri was a member of Dragon's party and, inevitably, the Lord of Heaven was furious.

Therefore he took away Miri's title of Governor of the East and instead dispatched the angel the same day with the order to arrest

Dragon and slaughter the rebels. The angel received his orders and after paying his respects before the steps of the throne he was about to set out when the Heavenly Kingdom's minister of Communications came puffing in and handed the Lord of Heaven a message from the world below. The Lord of Heaven read:

"After the common folk of the Terrestrial Nation had killed Jesus, they made short shrift of Confucius, Shakyamuni, Mahomet, etc., beating to death all the founders of religions and ethical systems, burned all the books concerning politics, law, education that supported the rights of rulers, destroyed the buildings housing churches, government offices, administrative offices, public buildings, banks, companies ... entirely rejected the past social system, and proclaimed the public ownership of everything in the world. All the members of the ruling classes mobilized troops in an attempt to subjugate the rebels, but the soldiers, who originally belonged to the common people, all deserted to the side of the people. They offered a large reward and tried to recruit new soldiers but noone applied. They had piled up mountains of cannon, field guns, rapid-fire weapons ... but were unable to fire a single bullet. Every member of the ruling classes had resolved to fight desperately, but not only were they far less numerous than the people, as owners of money, women, and all the other kinds of wealth they were unwilling to die in battle so they all fled into an impregnable fortress, where they were besieged by the people and starved to death, having nothing to eat. Among those who died of starvation, each one had a million *wŏn* on average clutched in their hands. Once the ruling class had been exterminated, the people renamed the world and called it the Terrestrial Nation, suspending all communication with the Heavenly Kingdom."

Never mind all the other events, what struck the Lord of Heaven most forcibly was the phrase "suspending all communication with the Heavenly Kingdom." Why? For tens of thousands of years past, the Lord of Heaven, his ministers and all the ghosts of the Heavenly Kingdom had not had to labor, being nourished and sustained by the tributes and sacrifices offered in the lower world.

Only now that the Terrestrial Nation had been established, and had proclaimed the suspension of all communication, tributes and sacrifices would no longer reach them. Which meant that all the ghosts would be forced to starve to death. The Lord of Heaven himself would be forced to starve to death.

The Lord of Heaven showed this message to all the ghosts, who were furious and demanded that the Lord of Heaven immediately issue a command ordering the slaughter of all the people. But the Lord of Heaven shook his head.

"While the people believed in us, we had power over them, but what power do we have now? Since we have no power, if we try to slaughter the people, we will simply be slaughtered ourselves. Slaughter the people? Those are vain words."

At those words, all their fiery rage evaporated.

"Then let's send an envoy to the Terrestrial Nation, imploring a resumption of communications and the continuation of tributes and sacrifices."

However, the Lord of Heaven had plenty of experience of the ways of humanity, he knew that any mention of tributes or sacrifices would do more harm than good, merely infuriating the people more, so he said it would not be possible.

"Then what are we to do? Shall we just sit here and starve?"

The Lord of Heaven sat in silence for a while, then spoke:

"There is only one solution. It means sending a messenger to the people, requesting that they give us as many gourd bowls as there are ghosts in the Heavenly Kingdom."

"What would we do with gourd bowls?"

The Lord of Heaven wept as he replied:

"We have no choice. We will have to stand outside people's doors every day, tapping on our bowls, begging for a spoonful of rice from 'our venerable people' ..."

His voice failed and he could not go on.

"But how could we ... we ghosts ... let alone your august Majesty ..."

All the ghosts raised their voices and wept aloud. The immortals' *paduk* games, the heavenly maidens' *kŏmun'go* tunes all ceased and lamentations shook the heavenly palace. Yet there was nothing to be gained, though they wept for a whole day, and the next day too, or for three hundred and sixty-five days. Finally the weeping stopped and the suggested request for gourd bowls was approved.

7. Miri's Departure for Battle and the Lord of Heaven's Anxieties

The Lord of Heaven asked the ghosts:

"Then who shall we send as the messenger to ask for bowls?"

The angel replied:

"Miri will be most suitable. As I heard from a dependable source yesterday, the common folk are not yet so strongly opposed to the Heavenly Kingdom, only our enemy, that wretch, Dragon, has gone inside their heads, and convinced them that since the power of your Majesty and those under you or the ruling classes among humanity only exists with the consent of the common folk, all our authority would turn into dead leaves in an autumn wind if ever the common people rejected it. It is only at his instigation that the people have started this kind of revolt. I believe that the people have more faith in today's Dragon than they had in your Majesty previously. If Dragon agrees, the people will probably give us bowls. Since Miri is Dragon's brother, I believe that it might be easier to gain Dragon's agreement if we send Miri."

The Lord of Heaven accepted this and, summoning Miri from prison, grasped him by the wrists and spoke, weeping:

"I have been so foolish, I nearly had you killed, my faithful subject."

He then explained in detail what had been decided concerning the gourd bowls.

"That's unacceptable. That's unacceptable. That's utterly unacceptable. Gourd bowls are used by beggars. Beggars holding bowls present themselves at the common folk's doors, saying, 'Please give me a spoonful,' and people give them rice out of pity. But if your Majesty comes along holding a bowl, they will point at you and mock you: 'Yah, beggar-emperor, what's become of all the dignity you used to have?' They will beat you with their fists, demanding: 'Give back all the blood you sucked from us in times past!' Far from putting anything into your bowl, they will smash your bowl. Forgive my frankness, your Majesty, but they may even set about your brow. … It's unacceptable. Asking for begging-bowls is absolutely unacceptable."

Miri wept as he protested. "Then what are we going to do? It would be better to commit suicide by throwing myself in front of a train, but where am I going to find a railway track in the Heavenly Kingdom? I could never kill myself with a knife …"

"If I once open my mouth, kings, consuls, capitalists … and suchlike emerge. I will go down to the Earth and open my mouth."

"Even if you vomit out kings, consuls, *et cetera*, today they don't have a shit's worth of power, the people won't be afraid of them. Your ideas are out of date."

"Then I will go down and inspire patriotism in the common folk of powerful nations, so that they gobble up the people of their colonies, and among the colonized people I will spread false reports they are being given self-government and political rights so they allow themselves to be gobbled up by the advanced nations' common folk, then while they are eating one another I will restore the authority of the Heavenly Kingdom."

"You think enlightened peoples will let themselves be taken in like that? Those are anachronistic ideas, too."

"Yet it is completely unacceptable that your Majesty should take up a begging-bowl. At least, I will go down to the Terrestrial Nation, spy out the real state of affairs, then return. If it's worth fighting, we can fight; otherwise, all the inhabitants of the Heavenly Kingdom will just have to join hands and starve, but begging-bowls are out of the question."

Miri then mounted a cloud-chariot and set off toward Earth while the Lord of Heaven and all the officials from the angel down, the immortals male and female, with all their kith and kin, all clutching their starving breasts, followed it down to the topmost layer of clouds, holding up their hands and shouting with hoarse voices: "Long live Miri-nim!" as they acclaimed Miri, who was bearing on his shoulders responsibility for the future survival or destruction of the Heavenly Kingdom.

"Miri-nim? Yesterday I was a villain in the Heavenly Kingdom and a hero down on Earth; today I'm a hero in heaven and a villain on Earth. Status in heaven and earth is so variable!" As he pondered inwardly, tears flowed down Miri's cheeks. He was not yet half-way down when the angel came panting after him and announced:

"You have to come back briefly. His Majesty has something more to say to you."

Miri turned back and arrived before the Lord of Heaven.

"You are not to use violence against the incensed populace. You must entreat them with kindness and reason, appealing to their tender hearts. This may be the last thing I ever ask you to do ..."

The Lord of Heaven squeezed Miri's hand hard.

"Yes, your Majesty, you must not worry. I will go down to Earth and do everything with the greatest care."

Miri quickly remounted his chariot.

8. Crisis in the Heavenly Palace, the Lord of Heaven's Flight

Once Miri has been dispatched, all the ghosts of the imperial court sit down together and begin to weep. They are not weeping over Miri's departure, they are weeping at the imminent destruction of the Heavenly Kingdom. Or rather, they are not weeping at the imminent destruction of the Heavenly Kingdom, each of them is weeping over his own individual misfortune.

The one weeping with the greatest anguish is the Lord of Heaven's favorite immortal maiden, Kokku.

The Lord of Heaven feels so sorry for her that he stops weeping for himself and starts listening carefully to the sound of her voice. He realizes that she is not weeping but repeating a curse:

"It's come. It's come. Dragon has come. This is the last day of the Heavenly Kingdom."

The Lord of Heaven is furious.

"Wretched girl! What's so good for you about Dragon coming?"

He draws his sword and cuts off Kokku's head; alas, poor Kokku, her head drops off and she dies. Once he has killed her, the Lord of Heaven listens to the weeping of all the others and they are all Kokku. Just like her, they are saying:

"It's come. It's come. Dragon has come. This is the last day of the Heavenly Kingdom."

"Ah! What is happening? Have all the members of the Heavenly Court turned into traitors and joined Dragon's gang?"

Now he listens to the sound of his own weeping, only his weeping no longer sounds like weeping but cursing:

"It's come. It's come. Dragon has come. This is the last day of the Heavenly Kingdom."

At this, the Lord of Heaven is obliged to stop weeping and issue a stern command:

"If anyone weeps inside the palace, they are to be executed."

After which:

"Why did I kill my lifelong sweetheart Kokku? Why is there no news of Miri? What will become of me if the Heavenly Kingdom is destroyed?"

Regret, depression, and distress keep rising in the Lord of Heaven's mind until he has a terrible headache. Holding his head in his hands, he enters the palace pharmacy to obtain medicine to relieve the pain but then, ah! how strange! There is nobody weeping in the pharmacy, yet it is ringing with the shrill cry:

"It's come. It's come. Dragon has come. This is the last day of the Heavenly Kingdom."

Full of suspicion, the Lord of Heaven cautiously searches until he finds the origin of the cry in a bottle of *aqua fortis*. Furious, the Lord of Heaven draws his sword and strikes the bottle; the liquid, as it spills and flows, transforms into a sword of fire, battering the beams, the pillars, the roofs, smashing the plinths, until with a *crack-bang*, *crash-bang*, flames whirring and roaring, the entire palace turns into an inferno.

The Lord of Heaven orders the Rain Spirit to be called and told to make some rain to put out the fire, but he does not come, instead the Wind Spirit comes roaring in, blowing a great gale so that the fire spreads from the palace to the entire Heavenly City. No wonder authority vanishes when the tide of power has been displaced. The Lord of Heaven is obliged to flee the fire but the moment he emerges from the palace gate he is swept up by the great gale and goes flying off.

The angel attempts to save the Lord of Heaven but the wind is too strong and he is helpless.

"This is indeed the last day of the Heavenly Kingdom," the angel cries.

But the angel is loyal to the Lord of Heaven, there can be no question of him changing course to follow the changing situation. He will follow the Lord of Heaven for better or for worse. He resolves to go seeking the Lord of Heaven wherever he may be, to the heights above the heights of heaven or the depths beneath the netherworld, so he dons canvas socks and straw shoes like the travelers of Chosŏn, working clothes like Chinese coolies, and goes seeking the Lord of Heaven high and low in all directions.

9. The Angel Goes Begging, the Sage's Divination

The angel thought: "If I want to find his Majesty, obviously I must go to the countries of Europe and America that have often turned to the Lord of Heaven as the only almighty God," so he passed through London, Paris, Rome, Berlin ... all the great cities.

But not only was there no sign of priests, ministers or suchlike, and when it came to emperors, kings, presidents, prime-ministers ... there was no hearing of such names, and as for banks, companies, trusts ... suchlike buildings were not to be seen, and there was nothing left from the old days, such as customs and traditions. But since the angel was incapable of thinking about anything except finding the Lord of Heaven, he just went rushing through at full speed and did not realize the situation. As he was passing Jerusalem, he met Paul and, thinking to himself, "Paul's a sincere believer in the Lord of Heaven, he'll know where he is," asked:

"Hey, Paul, where's the Lord of Heaven?"

"You idiot, you must be mad! You're looking for the Lord of Heaven nowadays? You're crazy!"

He punched the angel's cheeks until he took to his heels with a swollen face.

Reaching Beijing in China, he passes the Altar of Heaven located in a pine grove a couple of miles outside the southern gate, Zhengyangmen; there a crowd of spectators has gathered on hearing that the Emperor was going to offer the sacrifice to Heaven, wearing his crown and ceremonial robes.

"Ha ha, China is still a sacred nation! They have restored the monarchy and reinstated the sacrifices to Heaven!"

The angel hurries in and looks for the Lord of Heaven, but someone immediately holds up a restraining hand.

"You idiot, stop dreaming! This is a play commemorating People's Day. The Lord of Heaven? What goddam Lord of Heaven?" He too slaps the angel's cheeks. Alas, in faithfully serving the Lord of Heaven, the angel's swollen cheeks have no chance to recover.

Rubbing his aching cheeks, as he heads for the Tian-qiao Bridge he sees an elderly fortune-teller sitting at the roadside wearing his hair in a pigtail, wrapped in a Taoist towel. In front of him is a divination table to which is attached a paper bearing eight large characters: "Your questions all answered. Fee ten copper coins." He thinks:

"Ah, that old man's a rare bird. He has not cut off his pigtail and still believes in Fuxi's Eight Trigrams. The fee is only ten coins, all I need is ten coins before I ask him where the Lord of Heaven is."

He turns his pocket inside out but the pocket merely lets off a fart: "You don't have a clipped brass farthing, let alone ten copper coins." In such a situation, even an angel is reduced to tears.

"Before Dragon came, when I was in attendance at the Lord of Heaven's side, I only had to put my hand in my pocket and out would pour diamonds, rubies, platinum, gold, American dollars, French francs, silver coins from China bearing Yuan Shikai's head, but today my pocket refuses to give me so much as ten copper coins. …"

However, the angel is so eager to have his fortune told that he approaches the old Taoist smiling and makes a deep bow.

"Venerable fortune-teller, Sir, I beg you to tell me one thing. I am currently without money but, once this is over, money will be available and I will repay you then, not just ten coins but a thousand, ten-thousand coins, for sure."

"Indeed? Money is useless in today's world, of course, but I cannot forget the old tradition of being fond of money, so I just ask for it as a joke. What might your question be about? I will tell your fortune. Only tell me what the topic is."

Fearing he will be given another beating if he mentions the Lord of Heaven, the angel hesitates a little.

"Well, it's simply that I am looking for my master. I do not know where my master has gone …"

"Ha ha, you mean there are still people looking for their master in today's world? You are a loyal servant indeed!"

He shakes the case of fortune-telling spills and two divination signs emerge. He exclaims in astonishment:

"Ah! Oh! The first symbol is 'heaven,' which means 'the Lord of Heaven' and the second is 'flight,' which means 'run away,' so I reckon the master you are seeking is no human being, you must be an angel looking for the Lord of Heaven who has run away."

The angel could not help being surprised to hear those words. So he fell on his knees and humbly requested:

"Please, tell me where the Lord of Heaven is."

The fortune-teller replied:

"The first portion of the 'heaven' symbol, 'person,' changes into the first portion of the 'flight' symbol, 'Mercury,' and then the 'Mercury' turns back and overcomes 'person.' In divining, Mercury is a dragon, and the person is a rat, so the Lord of Heaven has fled Dragon's revolt and taken refuge in a rat-hole. In the old days, people used to say 'ever since heaven was established' but today they say 'ever since heaven was abolished.' Go and look for the Lord of Heaven in a rat-hole."

10. X X X[8]

Anxious to find the Lord of Heaven, the angel thanks the fortune-teller and sets off in quest of a rat-hole. Looking for a rat-hole he is startled to come across a shrine dedicated to the Dragon Spirit.

"Dragon is a nickname for Miri-nim and Miri must have come

---

8. As appeared in the original.

down here," he reflects, and on entering the shrine he finds Miri, only this is not the Miri of former times who could produce or destroy at will winds, rain, lightning and thunder, but just a clay image of Miri. Its ears have fallen off, its eyes are missing, its brow has been smashed. There is not a single bowl of offerings lying before it; clearly it has retired here after being defeated by Dragon.

"Miri, you wretch, how could you leave the Lord of Heaven somewhere and come here all alone? I cannot forget the Lord of Heaven and I'm looking for him ..." The angel scolded Miri, who smiled coldly.

"Angel, you idiot. What's the point of looking for the Lord of Heaven? The Lord of Heaven is Lord of Heaven when he's in the Heavenly Palace; now the palace has been smashed, how can he still be the Lord of Heaven? If the Lord of Heaven exists, he's a dead Lord of Heaven. A dead Lord of Heaven counts for less than a living rat. Let's assume it was right for the Lord of Heaven to be destroyed; then surely you and I and the Lord of Heaven are all nothing but fabrications of the fleeting superstitions of the ancient people? As fabrications of their superstition, just think how much harm we caused the common folk. It wasn't just the Lord of Heaven who pampered himself, surely everyone swindled the people of their money in the name of offerings and tributes to the Lord of Heaven? Surely there was no one who did not make use of the name of the Lord of Heaven to act wickedly as an earthly emperor? During the recent Great War that killed so many common folk, did not the emperors, rulers, and commanders of every country act in the Lord of Heaven's name? Did not the wretches who swallowed up other countries and melted down the bones of their populations claim to be doing 'the Lord of Heaven's will'? Now superstitions have been smashed, and the Lord of Heaven with them. How could you and I, who used to be affiliated with the Lord of Heaven, not be smashed too? Billions of common folk have turned into cats and all the powerful of days gone by have turned into rats. If you're looking for the Lord of Heaven, look in a rat-hole."

Hearing Miri's words, the angel thought it was a quite ungrateful wretch, but since its heart had already abandoned the Lord of Heaven, there was no point in saying anything more. Saying he would go on looking for the Lord of Heaven, he left the shrine and met people who had been mobilized to exterminate rats as pests. The angel suddenly remembered how the fortune-teller had said that the Lord of Heaven was in a rat-hole and wept as he begged:

"Please don't kill the rats. The rats are the Lord of Heaven who has run away from heaven."

He received no reply, but from all directions he heard ringing out a voice:

"It has come. It has come. Dragon has come. This is the last day for rats."

∼

～ 3

THE SHORE

Introduction

Ch'oe Chansik (崔瓚植 1881–1951) was a prolific writer of new novels during early years of the colonial period. His influence on the early years of modern Korean literature was substantial and helped establish the genre in the 1910s as something both marketable for magazines and newspapers, and as a popular one for the reading public. In all, he would write some ten novels over the period from 1912 to 1926. This is praised as his greatest contribution to the development of literature in this period.[1]

Ch'oe was born in Kwangju of Kyŏnggi Province and received a traditional education, including mastery of the Confucian Four Books and Three Classics. However, after the Kabo Reforms of 1894, the focus of his family changed and he began study of the modern sciences (新學問) in 1897. After returning from Shanghai he worked as a reporter for two different newspapers before making his literary debut with his first novel, *Ch'uwŏl saek* (추월색 Color of the autumn moon), in 1912. Like many writers of this period and genre, his writings were both didactic and entertaining. The focus on self-improvement through education is also a strong quality.

Ch'oe's subsequent writings include *An ŭi song* (안의 성 Cry of the wild goose) and *Kŭmgang mun* (金剛門 Gate to the Diamond Mountains) both in 1914, *Tohwawŏn* (桃花園 Garden of

---

1. Cho Tongil, *Han'guk munhak t'ongsa* (A complete history of Korean literature) (Seoul: Chisik sanŏpsa, 1992), 4:360–361.

peach blossoms) in 1916, and *Ch'un mong* (春夢 Spring dream) in 1924. In 1925 he published *Paengnyŏn hwa* (白蓮花 White lotus blossom). This novel centered on the life of a tenant farmer after a disastrous flooding of the Han River and is cited as a case of the new novels moving toward a realism, a hallmark of the works that appear after the decline of new novels.[2] His last work was written in 1926 and from that time forward he ceased his literary activities as the new novel had fallen out of favor among the reading public.

Haean (해안 The shore) is a new novella that was serialized in the magazine *Uri ŭi kajŏng* (Our household) over eleven issues from January 1914 through November 1914. The story has strong themes of critiquing past traditions such as early marriage, hereditary hierarchal relations, and blindly following superstitious practices. We can see Ch'oe's own disdain for the folk beliefs of Chosŏn—such as shamanic rituals—and also for the abusive relationships of in-laws with their daughters-in-law. Additionally the work shows the common theme of finding education and modernization abroad, in this case both Japan and America. Like many of the literary works of the early twentieth century, characters are driven to study abroad as a means to gain the knowledge necessary to help Korea find its path in the new age. However, and this is a different twist, the male protagonist seems to eagerly accept the banishment of his bride by his mother and proceeded to travel the world to gain his educational enlightenment. Upon reading the novella one wonders exactly what message Ch'oe wanted to send to his readers. Is it the need for education at all costs, or is it a more insidious message at the continuing disposability of women even in the face of modernization?

***

2. Ibid., 4:362.

∽ THE SHORE | *HAEAN* 해안

CH'OE CHANSIK 최찬식

Translated by Eugene Larsen-Hallock
Annotated by Michael J. Pettid

The seas around P'almi Island near Inch'ŏn are vast and of a single color with the sky. The evening sun streamed over the Wŏlmi lighthouse and threw a deep crimson steak across the Japanese Park. Its light fell across a young woman standing at the rail of the memorial pavilion there: there was a furrow across her brow and she sighed as she sat absent-mindedly watching a steamer surge in on the evening tide. Her hair was raised in a wispy *hisashigami* style, into which she had tied a fresh-looking light-pink ribbon, and she was neatly dressed in a lined purple and grey *ch'ŏgori* jacket over a jade-colored skirt.[1] She was eighteen or nineteen years old and, with her porcelain skin and clear features, easily one of the greatest beauties of her time, but she looked abstractedly out upon the ocean, her face was filled with concern, and a mountain of worry seemed to weigh upon her breast.

Looking out over the ocean and sky, she wiped away her tears with a handkerchief and said quietly, in a voice that would be barely audible to a person standing right next to her, "What honor is a life in this world if one has no hope for the future? Though my husband has not abandoned me, I don't believe he'll be able to keep his promise to return, and now I am sick and there seems to be no hope of recovery. It would be best for me to just end this wretched

---

1. A *ch'ŏgori* is a short jacket that was a part of a woman's costume in Chosŏn Korea.

existence quickly. This thing I am about to do is a sin against my mother—but who am I to even talk of a thing like loyalty to my parents, when I stand on the verge of throwing away the flesh and blood they have given me?"

After she said this, she took out a piece of paper from inside her jacket and, piercing the ring finger of her right hand, began to write out her story in a terrible letter of blood. She placed the letter in an envelope, which she sealed and upon which she wrote out an address in pencil. She walked slowly past the fountain and toward the exit of the park. There was no one else to be seen and all was silent, except for the unfeeling petals of the flowers and trees throwing off a dizzying fragrance as they were blown before the breeze.

Exiting the park, she deposited her letter into a mailbox, walked over Hwagae-dong hill, and then suddenly came to a stop at the shore on the bottom end of Shikishima, in a desolate place shrouded in a thick, inky fog.

It was seven-thirty. The brilliance of the setting sun had become a black cloud. Heaven and earth had grown dark, and it was impossible to see anyone that might have been nearby; all that could be seen was a faint shimmer on the waters of the channel stretching down to Ch'ungch'ŏng Province. Though it was unclear what had brought the woman to such a place, she stood silently staring at the southern sky. Then with a tremendous sigh, she began to silently speak.

"Am I not the same Kyŏngja that was raised by her mother like a precious gem, and who was loved by her husband like a special treasure? Kyŏngja, you've committed no crime since the day you were born, so how is it that you've ended up in this state? Oh, sadness! Poor Kyŏngja, who could know what bitterness lies inside your heart? When my husband had parted from me in front of the Japanese Park fountain he had said, 'Don't think of me, and instead focus on looking after my mother and father. In four or five years, I will return from Tokyo having learned many things, and then we will be able to ride in a car and take walks in parks like this.' How could he have known that I would now be working on a fishing boat? Ah, useless thoughts! I will be able to see him when the waves of the Pacific wash my body to the seas near Shinagawa."

Saying this, she turned around again, and bowed toward the north, "Despite the act of everlasting disloyalty I am about to commit; I, Kyŏngja, pray that my mother lives a long life."

Having finished her speech, she raised her hands to wipe away the bitter tears streaming from her eyes and plunged into the boundless waters of the sea. Who knows what despair she must have felt to end up in such a state, but a blameless mandarin duck was woken from its dreams by the startled waves and took to wing. The light of the Wŏlmi light house flashed, while the sonorous thrum of a *samisen* could be heard coming from the *Ilsallu* restaurant in Shikishima, and the moon threw resplendent beams light down before the *P'alp'allu* restaurant in the Japanese Park.

"What has happened to her? What has happened to her? Where has my Kyŏngja gone that she hasn't returned? She said she was going for a walk in the park, but she hasn't come home, so where has she gone? Oh, something must have happened!"

This was the worry of a flustered woman of about fifty years in front of the *P'alp'allu*. Looking in every corner of the Japanese Park, she called out, "Kyŏngja!" She even nonsensically asked a maid coming out of the *P'alp'allu*, "Are you Kyŏngja?"

She rushed about in that manner, and then when she had exhausted herself, she fell to the ground, looked up at the moon, and said to herself, "She has never been this late before, and it isn't like her to wander. What happened today? Something must have happened. How could someone unhealthy as her be out this late? I should go home to see if she came back while I was out."

Standing up, she walked out of the park, dragging her cane behind her. She went out to Yongdongt'ong Avenue and then headed for the Ch'ukhyŏn bus stop, she walked hurriedly past the stop and then entered a small thatched-roof house on the far side of Mansŏktong. This woman of course was none other than Kyŏngja's mother. But no matter how much she tried, how could she see Kyŏngja now, after her Kyŏngja had slipped without word into the briny palace of the dragon king? How tragic was this woman's plight! Kyŏngja's mother was the wife of a lowly farmer with the last name of Chŏng, and had lived with her husband in Oryu-dong, Pup'yŏng, where they had worked hard to eke out a livelihood farming. Faced with such poverty, they found no joy in the world, except for the comfort they found in the laughter and cooing of their beloved daughter, Kyŏngja. Spring of the year that Kyŏngja turned five, her father passed away; not only was there no place for Kyŏngja and her mother to depend on in their misery, they were left without any means to support themselves. Hearing that Inch'ŏn harbor was a good place to live, Kyŏngja's mother moved the two of them there and let a room in a house. At night, Kyŏngja's mother would sell needlework, while during the day she would go out to the gates of the harbor and gather stray grain that had been dropped there. She was neither young nor old, and she did whatever work she could lay her hands on, and worked hard so that she finally scraped together a little bit of money, which she then gave over to a trustworthy moneylender to be lent out on interest. As they say, hard work never goes unrewarded, so how could she fail to see some success after her frugality? Five or six years later, while it could not be said that they were well-off, they could put food on the table without having to gather stray grains at the harbor, and the money they had saved up little by little had become a thousand *wŏn*, which was enough for them to leave the room they had been renting and buy a small thatched-roof house at the base of Mansŏktong mountain. Life was a hundred times better than even when Kyŏngja's father had been alive and Kyŏngja's mother spent her days crying at the thought of him, and cared for her daughter as though she were a gem. At that time, society was moving toward enlightenment; even married women were able to go out into the street, and the number of girls in the schools was increasing year by year. Naturally, families with daughters thought to send those daughters to schools for girls, and society was gradually coming to think that it was unacceptable for even women to go without an education. When Kyŏngja was about ten years old and of age to attend school her mother began to think. *With the way that the times are changing, if I follow the old traditions and lock up my daughter inside the house, I'll ruin her life. Whatever it takes, I need to make sure Kyŏngja gets an education so that she can become a model for all the girls of Chosŏn.*

So, in the spring of her twelfth year, Kyŏngja was enrolled in a girl's school.

In addition to her refined character, since she was young Kyŏngja had possessed a good-natured disposition and an exceptional spirit. She was dutiful to her mother and diligently studied needlework. By the time she was ten, she had become quite skilled, and had even sold a ten-panel screen in a peony pattern for thirty *wŏn*, and she was praised by all who saw her. Even in a bustling place like Seoul, where people are keen judges of such things, a child like Kyŏngja would have been enough to make people wonder, so in a backwater place like Inch'ŏn, it was all people could do not to gape when confronted with a fresh-talent like her.

After enrolling in school with that sort of talent, her studies progressed by leaps and bounds, and she came out on top in every test that she took. Every semester she was promoted to a new grade, and talk of her was on the lips of everyone in the school community around Inch'ŏn and Seoul. At that time, however, there was one concern nagging Kyŏngja's mother. *Where will I ever be able to find a husband for a daughter with such an exquisite character and exceptional talent as my Kyŏngja? A husband with a character and talent like her own? The quality of a woman's entire life is determined by whether or not she meets the right husband, and to marry off a girl to the wrong man is to sin against your own child—so how will I ever find a husband for my Kyŏngja?*

This worry weighed like a great mountain upon Kyŏngja's mother, and filled her heart to the point that she could think of nothing else. But while she worried, time flowed by like water, and Kyŏngja was soon seventeen and close to graduating from high-school. Kyŏngja's mother worried all the more because of this and she believed that Kyŏngja was at a critical time in her life. Then, one day as Kyŏngja was returning home from school, she happened to encounter a group of students from Posŭng College who had come to Inch'ŏn on an outing. Kyŏngja lowered her head out of feminine modesty; but for better or worse, amongst the Posŭng students there was one who already knew Kyŏngja's face and watched her closely as she passed.

That student, whose name was Taesŏng, was the son of one Hwang Ch'amsŏ who lived in Kyedong, in Seoul. Taesŏng was of solid character and full of talent: he was eighteen years old, had already graduated from high school and enrolled in law school, and had promised himself that he would eventually become a re-nowned jurist. Since he had become an adult and was reaching a marriageable age, his parents were looking far and wide for a bride. His father, Hwang Ch'amsŏ, was not only stubborn, he was also stupid as could be. Even though he was incapable of under-standing how the times were changing and had no clue about how to manage his worldly affairs, he was stubborn and arrogant in everything concerned with finding his son a wife. He had no in-terest in whether a girl was educated or not, and was looking in-stead for a girl of the same class and not too poor to be unable to bring a very substantial dowry with her. All of the families he pro-posed marriage to, then, were families who were ignorant of the new ways of doing things and had clung to the old customs. But trying to match Taesŏng with a girl who had been brought up in that sort of household was like trying to pair a phoenix with a chicken, and there was no way it could have ended well. What Taesŏng wanted was exactly opposite his father's wishes. He was entirely indifferent to a girl's pedigree or social standing, and was only interested in whether she had been satisfactorily educated and had sufficient knowledge to become a role-model and teacher to all Chosŏn women, so that by marrying her he would be able to help bring about reform in the lives of ordinary women.

When Taesŏng saw that his parents were preparing to marry him off, he entreated his mother, "The pernicious custom of early marriage is certainly more fearful than any other. It is not yet time for me to marry; I want to wait on marriage until I have completed my studies, acquired sufficient knowledge, and am thereby prepared to take care of a family. Please tell what I have told you to Father and stop him from finding me a wife." He explained himself to his mother over and over, but his mother could hear nothing but the immature words of a child, and engaged the services of matchmakers to search far and wide for a bride for Taesŏng.

It's difficult to say that the customs related to marriage in Chosŏn are good. Marriage is not only an important matter and the greatest of the "three bonds" spoken of by Confucius, it is a single event that generally decides the fortune or misfortune of a person's entire life.[2] The single, small bow that a couple makes on the day of their marriage decides their lives, so how could that little bow not be an extraordinarily difficult thing for both bride and groom, requiring great restraint? In a lifetime, a person might meet thousands, if not tens of thousands, of other people, but the meeting of a bride and groom at a wedding is truly a difficult affair. When it comes time for that meeting, it is impossible for those involved to be anything other than cautious, careful, and especially restrained, so it cannot be said that marriage customs in Chosŏn

---

2. The Three Bonds (三綱 *samgang*) are loyalty between ruler and minister, filial piety between children and parents, and distinction between husband and wife. Thus the text is incorrect as marriage was not one of the Three Bonds.

are unrestrained or incautious. It is common practice, however, for parents who treasure their sons and daughters to marry them off at an early age before the blood of the womb has even dried on their heads or the smell of breast milk has left their mouths. Often, the groom has no idea of the appearance of his bride, nor the bride any idea of the appearance of her groom, and in a single morning they make the momentous promise to go through all of a hundred-year's joys and sorrows together. It is because of customs like these that mistreatment of wives by husbands and mistreatment of husbands by wives is so common these days, and nine out of ten lives are sadly squandered in that way.

If one were to ask Taesŏng what his opinion was, he would say that he intended to strike back against the custom of arranged marriage as it had been handed down through the generations; gradually reform that custom by becoming the first to advocate marriage arranged through the mutual agreement of the two people involved; and work to ensure that married life in the future would be free of evils like maltreatment and divorce. He detested the idea of marrying a woman who had received a traditional Chosŏn-style education, who was capable of no more than mending clothes and cooking food, and who would spend all of her time in the women's quarters of the house—no matter how pretty she might be. Indeed, if he was not able to marry the sort of girl he wanted—one who was capable of conversing with him on academic topics, could accompany him to banquets, and was comfortable leaving the women's rooms to receive visitors in the drawing room while he himself was out—then he would rather remain a lifelong bachelor. There was nothing, however, that he could do about his parents' wishes and this fact weighed upon him like a mountain. Then one day he came home from school to find an old woman sitting with his mother, saying, "I'll go over to the girl's house and ask them to make a decision quickly, then as soon we get word back we'll send over the details of his birthdate so that they can check his *saju* horoscope.[3] *Aigu*, you've certainly not made this easy for me!"

It was clear that the matter of his marriage had been settled. Instantly, his heart sank. He wanted to say something, but at that moment it was impossible for him to say anything, so he held his tongue, turned around, took his coat off and hung it up. The old woman greeted him warmly as though they had met somewhere before and then continued on without waiting for him to reply, "Did you just come back from school? It's because you're such a nice young man that I was able to find such a nice girl for you. I think she's about a forehead's length shorter than you. How are you going to thank me?"

The old woman seemed to be quite proud of herself, as though she had done something great. Even though Taesŏng didn't see it that way, there was no way for him to oppose his parents. Having these sorts of matchmakers frequenting the house was more detestable than he could bear, and what this one said had greatly displeased him.

"Thank you? Have you done anything that I should be thankful for? Why should I do anything for you?"

[The Old woman replied.] "What should you be thankful for? For my having found you such a beautiful bride, of course! Look here, young man, what even gives you the nerve to talk to an old woman like me in that way? Why should I have to take that from you? You should be bowing to me in thanks for the marriage I've arranged for you!"

When Taesŏng's mother heard this, she snapped at him, "Knock it off, Taesŏng, how can you be so insolent to such an old woman!"

Taesŏng pretended not to hear his mother and continued speaking out of an intense hatred for the old woman, "You're right,

---

3. The *saju* (四柱) are the four pillars on which one's destiny is made. These are the year, month, day, and hour of one's birth.

you're right. If you had arranged a good marriage for me, then I would have reason to bow down to you. But since you've made a mess of it, I'll talk to you however I please."

The old woman was stung by this, and said, "*Aigu*, what fickleness! What are you saying? What's wrong with the bride I've found you? For one thing, she comes from a good, *yangban* family with a substantial fortune, and she's pretty. Where could I find anyone better? I wore out three pairs of silk shoes just coming and going between your house and hers to arrange this marriage ..."

[Taesŏng said.] "Well, maybe she couldn't be any better by your standards, but what if I don't like her?"

[The old woman replied.] "You just say anything you want, don't you? You don't even know her and you're already spouting off. Why don't you meet her first and then decide whether you like her or not? Just stop badgering me and say thank you already. I thought I'd seen it all in my time as a matchmaker, but I've never once met a young man like you. What sort of wife do you want, anyway?"

"What's it to you?" [Taesŏng asked.]

"I'll set you up with whatever sort of girl you want." [Said the old woman.]

[Taesŏng said.] "First of all, no *yangban*."

"And?" [Said the old woman.]

[Taesŏng replied.] "I don't care if her family's rich."

"And?" [Prompted the old woman.]

"I don't care what she looks like." [Taesŏng replied.]

[Old woman, protesting.] "*Aigu*, you're impossible! I think I've heard it all now. What are you going to do when people make fun of you for marrying a girl from some unknown family living in a thatched-roof hut? If her thatched-roof hut family is too poor to be properly hospitable to you, where's the fun in that? What will you do if your wife is so ugly you hate to think of having to spend a life looking at her? What is it you're looking for?"

"You couldn't possibly understand what I want. No matter what she might look like, I won't marry a woman who doesn't have a few pearls of learning inside her heart and who's going to wear her hair up like some old-fashioned housewife. Just know that, and leave." [Taesŏng replied.]

[The old woman laughed.] "Ha ha ha, and what of it if she wears her hair up? As for pearls, the girl I found for you wears a jeweled *chokturi* in her hair that's encrusted with them, ha ha![4] How much could a girl even learn? A girl has no use for Chinese characters as long as she can read and write *han'gŭl*, and she doesn't need to know anything else except proper manners and how to cook and sew well.[5] If she's too educated she'll just look down on her husband, so what's the use in it? She's a good match, you just need to admit it to yourself. You say you want an educated wife— you probably want a girl who writes verse like Su Shi and whose calligraphy is like that of Wang Xizhi, ha ha ha![6] But, if you take that beautiful girl I found for you as your wife, you'll soon be thankful I brought you together."

"Well, yes, that may be true. I'm sure you have other things you need to get to though. Where do you live anyhow?" [Taesŏng asked.]

[The old woman replied.] "You were just playing with me, weren't you? If you're asking for my address, you must want to send me something good, but I really don't want anything. My house is at number 1, 1-tong, Chŏngja-dong, Saemunan, so send me five *sŏm* or so of rice, ha ha!"[7]

---

4. A *chokturi* is a black crownlike headpiece that women wore on formal occasions. ,

5. *Han'gŭl* is the Korean script. In Chosŏn era, this was generally reserved for women and the uneducated, as educated men wrote in Literary Chinese.

6. Su Shi (蘇軾 1037–1101) was a famous Song dynasty poet and Wang Xizhi (王羲之 303–361) is praised as one of the best calligraphers in Chinese history.

7. A *sŏm* is a unit of measure for bagged rice, equivalent to roughly 180 liters.

"Of course, if you find a girl I like I'll send you gold instead of rice." [Taesŏng joked.]

With those parting words, Taesŏng went out to the men's quarters. It was clear that the old woman would be brokering his marriage, and impossible to hope that his parents would give the matter up. It was such an unreasonably bothersome matter, but there was nothing to be done about it, so Taesŏng waited for the old woman to leave and then went back inside and eagerly asked his mother, "The wife that the old woman found for me, who is she?"

Smiling brightly, his mother said, "Why do you want to know? Would your parents be careless in choosing a bride for you?" This upset Taesŏng even further, and he was unable to say anything more. His mother continued,

"Don't worry about a thing. The girl we found will be perfect for you. *Everyone* knows the Pyŏktong Kim family. And everyone knows how rich they are. The girl is really without flaw. Her family must educate their girls well, so I'm sure she's good with a needle and knows how to comport herself. How much more could you expect from a wife? You shouldn't be so impertinent. I mean, what was that earlier with the matchmaker—how could you say such rude nonsense? I don't want to see you do that again."

"What does it matter how rich a woman's family is, or whether they're *yangban*? I, personally, have no idea. Good comportment is desirable in a woman, but the age of the *yangban* has passed and what meaning does being a *yangban* have now? As for the Kim family, they're also famous for their old-fashioned obstinacy. They're trapped in a *yangban* dream of a previous time and have no idea of the state of the world now—they didn't even send their son or nephew to school. Even if their daughter might adhere to the old ways and have some of that strict, old-fashioned uprightness, will she have gotten a proper education or know how to manage a household properly? Not at all. And how can you call me impertinent? These days, if a woman isn't educated, she isn't able to manage a household or assist her husband. How could you possibly think of marrying me to a woman who would cause me so much difficulty? Anyhow, I haven't even finished my studies yet and marriage is not what I need right now, so it would be best to wait on the whole thing."

Taesŏng expressed himself with angry intensity and clarity, but his mother didn't hear a word of what he said. With a cold smile, she replied, "Quiet down and do as your parents say. If your father heard what you just said, he'd give you a scolding."

Thinking about it for a moment, Taesŏng realized that acquiescing to his parents demands and marrying the girl they wanted him to would not only mean that everything he aimed to do would come to nothing, but also that he would have to spend his life joylessly. But, on the other hand, disobeying his parents orders would show a lack of filial piety and cause a discord in the family and a great deal of anxiety for everyone. He had no idea what to do and felt as though he were suffocating. Feeling anger rising suddenly within his breast he took the coat that he had hung up earlier and, putting it back on, went back outside into the early spring day. The willows had shaken off their frost, and their branches hung like golden streamers. The blossoms on the peach and plum were laughing gaily, the spring sun had drenched the land in beauty, strains of birdsong teased the season, and the plaintive sound of a flute blew with the course of the wind through the valleys and whistled in one's ears, making thoughts languid. With no place to go, Taesŏng went out to Kyodong Avenue and walked toward Pagoda Park.

The park was crowded with a sea of people, none of whom he knew, and it was boring walking about by himself, so he went to a shop and bought a newspaper. He read the newspaper intently, sitting under the shade of a tree, and tried to both forget his anger and his boredom. Whatever paper it was, on the third page in the miscellaneous articles section, there was an engraving of a young woman's picture, with the caption "Model Student" written large in No. 2 type. Next to that, in smaller No. 5 type, it said: "Chŏng

Kyŏngja, Inch'ŏn Girls' High School, Fourth Form." The article praised her in the highest terms for her educational accomplishments, womanly virtue, and outstanding studies in her major. Filled with adoration, Taesŏng tore out the picture, put it in his wallet, and thought, *If there is this sort of student amongst the girls in Chosŏn, then there is hope yet for the future of Chosŏn women.*

Thinking again about the business of his marriage, he sighed inwardly and left the park. Going around the side of the concert hall, however, he saw an old woman holding an umbrella looking with great interest at the pictures in a painting exhibition. As she passed, Taesŏng glanced several times at her face. It was someone he had seen several times. Looking more closely, he realized that it was one of the old matchmakers who had gone about trying to arrange his own marriage, but failed for some reason or other. The matchmakers of Chosŏn make their living as go-betweens for the parties involved in the marriage, and they are treated like queens in the homes of well-to-do families if it seems like they will be able to arrange a marriage. In such a situation, one can easily get ten *wŏn* or so by going back and forth between both sides making arrangements. If they're hungry, they might even occasionally badger the families involved for a bit of change or a bowl of rice, and generally think of the families as inexhaustible wells of money from which they may draw as they wish. When Taesŏng saw the old woman, a thought occurred to him, and he went over to her.

He called out a greeting, and the old woman turned around to see who was calling her.

She greeted him kindly, "But isn't this Hwang Ch'amsŏ's son? I can't see very well, so I didn't recognize you. Everyone gets this way when they're old. Don't be angry that I didn't recognize you. Did you also come to take a look at the paintings?"

"Isn't that the proper order for greetings? That whoever sees the other first should give the first greeting. Anyhow, why haven't you come around lately?" Taesŏng asked.

"After that business went bad, I was too ashamed to even show my face in your house. Is your mother well?" [The old woman replied.]

"She's fine. But what business are you talking about?" [Taesŏng asked.]

"What, you don't know about it? I'm talking about your marriage. When the match I tried to arrange didn't turn out the way I wanted, how could I even think of stopping by your house anymore?" [Asked the old woman.]

"Well, since you brought it up, I must say that in my opinion the match that you were trying to arrange was excellent, and I can't tell you how sad I was when it didn't work out. Anyhow, do you know if by any chance there's a matchmaker who lives in Chŏngjadong in Saemunan?" [Taesŏng asked.]

"There is, but why do you ask?" [The old woman responded.]

"That old woman has been coming by our house the last couple days, and from the way she's whispering with my mom, it looks like she's about to succeed in matching me with a girl from a terrible family." [Taesŏng said.]

"So what would you have me do? What family is the marriage being discussed with?" [Asked the old woman.]

[Taesŏng replied.] "Tsk, there's no reason for you to know. At any rate, I'd like to marry the girl you suggested, so would you come by our house sometime and then do as I instruct you to do?"

"If you'll marry the girl I was trying to set you up with before, of course. Even if I need to take all my meals on the run, I'll try my hardest!" [Promised the old woman.]

"Alright, then this is what I need you to do." Taesŏng then whispered a couple of words into the old woman's ear.

After saying farewell to the old woman, Taesŏng began to make his way home, stopping first to visit the wet-nurse who had raised him. Taesŏng's wet-nurse was a woman of about forty years of age, and she had taken care of Taesŏng from his second

year. She had fed him from her own breast and raised him like
her own child for more than ten years, so the two of them had
come to have great affection for each other. She came to love
Taesŏng as though he was her own son, and Taesŏng loved her as
much as he loved his own mother. If they hadn't seen each other
for four days, they would miss each other more than either could
bear. If Taesŏng didn't go to see his wet-nurse, then she would go
to see him, and if the wet-nurse didn't come to see Taesŏng then
he would go to see her, and the two of them had a very fond relationship. There was nothing that they could not say to each other,
and they would even go so far as to discuss family matters together. When Taesŏng went to see his wet-nurse this time, she
was exceedingly pleased to see him, and even though he was a
grown man she went to buy some cookies for him and doted on
him as though he were still a child. Taesŏng ate the cookies and
enjoyed being doted on just as though he were a spoiled child, and
after talking about this and that for a bit, he furrowed his brow
and said, "These days I've got a worry as great as a mountain."

He said this with a sigh while staring at the far-off mountains.
His wet-nurse was very surprised to see him like this and asked,
"Worry? What's bothering you?"

"It seems that the matter of my marriage has been decided recently." [Taesŏng replied.]

His wet-nurse heard that and said with a laugh, "When you
said you were worried about something, I thought that it must be
something terrible. If you're going to be married, that's great! What
is there to be worried about?"

The wet-nurse laughed again after she said this, as though
Taesŏng's worry had been a joke.

"I'm serious." [Taesŏng said.] "I'm really worried. Getting married is a happy occasion in a person's life, so of course it's a good
thing, but the girl I'm arranged to marry is from a very ill-omened
family. Not knowing that, my parents believed the matchmaker's
lies and agreed to the match. What should I do? I know of that

house's curse in detail, but I'm too embarrassed to tell my mother and father. The reason I can't help but be so concerned is because there is no one else who can understand this."

"I had guessed that your marriage was basically decided—but if there's a curse on that family, what sort of a curse is it?" [Asked the wet-nurse.]

"Would you really tell my parents for me?" [Asked Taesŏng.]

"If it's as bad a curse as you say it is, of course I will." [Said the wet-nurse.]

"You won't tell them that I told you to tell them, will you?" [Taesŏng insisted.]

"Of course not! I'll tell them about it as though I already knew of it myself." [The wet-nurse replied.]

"Make sure not to tell them that I told you to tell them. Pretend that you know all about the girl's family situation and tell my parents this ..." [Taesŏng again insisted.]

Then Taesŏng whispered a few words quietly into his wet-nurse's ear and went straight back home.

"*Aigu*, how long has it been since the last time I was here? How have you been?"

The old woman Taesŏng had met in the park greeted his mother as she burst into the front courtyard of his house. Having heard what Taesŏng told her and thinking she could profit from it, she had come to his house early the next morning.

Seeing the old woman come in, Taesŏng's mother said, "*Aigu*, it's really been a long time. Why didn't you come even once during all that time? I thought maybe something had happened to you."

"Oh, not at all, but thank you for asking. I was so busy running about and struggling to make a living along with my kids that I just couldn't find the time to come by." [The old woman said.]

The old woman came inside the house and sat down in the main room of the house with Taesŏng's mother. After rambling on for quite a while about all kinds of things, darting dizzily back and forth from this topic to that, she said, "Ah, I almost forgot. I didn't congratulate you on the deciding of Taesŏng's engagement. I heard he's to be married with the daughter of the Pyŏktong Kim family?"

"Yes, it's not final yet, but it looks likely." [Taesŏng's mother said.]

"Ah, that's wonderful. Even with that flaw they say she has, it's not easy to find a girl as good as that. *Aigu*, at any rate, that's one less thing for you to worry about." [The old woman replied.]

Taesŏng's mother had no idea what flaw the old woman might be talking about.

Curiosity took hold of her, and she urgently pressed the old woman for more details, "A flaw? What sort of flaw?"

"What use is there in knowing? It's best not to know. It's so unlucky you'd rather not hear it." [The old woman responded.]

[Taesŏng's mother persisted.] "What are you saying? If there's something wrong, don't you think that the kind thing to do would be to tell me about it? I'm not sure what you could be talking about, but if you don't tell me, I'll feel as though you're keeping me in the dark."

Then, as though she was reluctant to speak, the old woman said, "*Aigu!* It was rash of me to even bring it up. My tongue seems to be growing looser as I get older." Then she continued with a sigh, "The girl is very nice and comes from a good family, but there's a small problem. It's something that might put off a more capricious or fickle family, but I'm sure it's nothing that would bother you." The old woman said only this and did not give any specifics.

[Taesŏng's mother was adamant.] "*Aigu!* I can't stand it anymore! Just spit it out already."

"It was pointless even bringing it up. It would be wrong for someone in my position not to tell you, but it's really better if you don't know." Then moving right up next to Taesŏng's mother, the old woman quietly whispered, "They say that the girl is being haunted by a *Son-kaksi*."[8]

Taesŏng's mother's tongue began to wag as soon as she heard this, and she said, "Is it true? I had no idea!"

These were all just the things that Taesŏng had told the old woman in the park, but now she made these insinuations so naturally that anyone would have believed that what she was saying was true.

"Of course it's true! Have I ever lied to you? When the girl's older sister got married, that ghost followed her and stirred up trouble for her there. In the end, she was left a widow after only three years."

As it happened, the girl's sister had been widowed, and hearing this, Taesŏng's mother shuddered and said, "*Aigu!* That's awful! So that's how her sister became a widow. If you hadn't told me, there's no way I would have known. *Aigu!* Thank you."

Generally speaking, the foolishness of Chosŏn women knows no bounds. Their brains are awash with superstitious customs, which they believe in no matter how ridiculous the superstition might be—even things like "Don't comb your hair on a rainy day"; "One's parents always die on rainy days"; "Don't trim your fingernails on a moonless night"; or "It's impossible to avoid poverty your whole life." As trifling as these things are, Chosŏn women believe and follow them—so how could one of those women not get upset when told that her son's bride was being followed by a *Son-kaksi* that might come and ruin her home? The so-called *Son-kaksi*—or ghost bride—is the ghost of a fully-grown girl who died before she could marry. They say that girls who die without having married in life become extremely vicious spirits of vengeance who interfere with marriages and the other joyful occasions of life.

---

8. Son-kaksi was a young woman who was shunned by those in her village for being unattractive; she died, and came back to seek revenge on the young unmarried women in her village, causing their deaths. There are various renditions of the tale, but all involve a vengeful ghost seeking revenge for past mistreatment.

Son-kaksi are recognized as the most fearsome of spirits, and these ghosts are amongst the spirits that are most detested and feared by the foolish, ugly women of Chosŏn—to the point that anytime a family is looking to decide the matter of a son or daughter's marriage, one of their first questions is always whether or not there is a *Son-kaksi* haunting the other house. How could Taesŏng's mother not have been shocked when she heard that her prospective daughter-in-law was cursed by just such a spirit? However, there was a reason why she only half-believed what the old woman had told her and couldn't decide with certainty whether or not what she had heard was actually true. That reason was that the matchmakers of Chosŏn are infamous for being inveterate liars who will shamelessly slander marriages that have been arranged by others. Furthermore, insofar as the old woman had failed in arranging a marriage for Taesŏng herself, it was only natural that she would disparage to no end the match that had been made for him by another. Because of this, after Taesŏng's mother heard what the old woman had to say, she was—to put it vulgarly—as uncomfortable as if she had shat and not been able to wipe herself afterward, and she was unable to make up her mind on the matter. The old woman went on about these things until she was blue in the face, and then as she was leaving, "Everyone knows that there is a curse upon that house, I can't believe that you didn't know yourself. If you asked Taesŏng or his old wet-nurse, I bet both of them would know something about it, too. Need I say more? It's a deplorable thing that anyone would arrange a marriage for you with that house."

The old woman tossed out those parting words and left. Taesŏng's mother always fretted terribly, and after hearing what the old woman had said, she was suspicious of what she had heard but also concerned. It was certain that she would want to find out whether what the old woman said was true or not before she could decide on Taesŏng's marriage to the girl in question, and that she would ask around and investigate. Taesŏng's wet-nurse was kind and trustworthy, and Taesŏng's mother thought that asking her would be the most expedient and trustworthy way to find out the truth, so she sent for the wet-nurse that very day.

When the wet-nurse came, Taesŏng's mother asked her about the matter, "You've heard that our Taesŏng is arranged to be married to the daughter of the Pyŏktong Kim, haven't you?"

"I did. I heard about it and was actually just thinking about coming to see you." [The wet-nurse replied.]

"Have you heard the rumors about the Kim family?" [Taesŏng's mother asked.]

"Well, I know of them." [The wet-nurse said.]

[Taesŏng's mother continued.] "Is it true that something awful has befallen their family?"

Taesŏng's wet-nurse remembered what Taesŏng had requested she say and, without hesitating, replied, "Well, there was one thing—something truly terrible. Because of it, any man who marries one of their girls is bound to be unlucky. I heard about it the other day and wanted to come tell you, but I was waiting until I could look into it closely. Yesterday though, I heard it again from someone trustworthy, so it seems like it's true."

As soon as she heard that, the color drained from Taesŏng's mother's face. The wet-nurse was someone that Taesŏng's mother trusted, and the mother was a petty woman who put such faith in superstition that she would "not even move a floor cushion after she'd once put it in its place." So after having heard what the wet-nurse said, how could she continue with Taesŏng's marriage? The possibility of that marriage happening had grown so distant that the girl might as well have been in the middle of the Atlantic.

After Taesŏng's mother heard what the wet-nurse said, the impatience she had felt for the conclusion of Taesŏng's marriage was extinguished in the blink of an eye, and she told Taesŏng's father that it would be impossible to go through with the wedding. Taesŏng's father, Hwang Ch'amsŏ, was an exceptionally foolish man and would do whatever his wife told him to. Whether they had discussed the matter together or not, it was as good as decided. So when the go-between who had arranged the marriage came with the marriage agreement from the bride's family and pressed Taesŏng's family for the letter with the details of his birth date and time so they could verify his *saju* horoscope, Taesŏng's mother scrawled it out in language fit for a dog, and in that way succeeded in having the marriage called off.

Taesŏng was such an exceedingly upright young man that he would never think of deceiving a stranger, much less his own parents. The matter of one's marriage, however, has such a profound influence over the entirety of one's life that he was compelled to trick his parents into cancelling his marriage, so in the final reckoning his actions are excusable. After having done so, however, he was beset by the worry that there might not be a woman in all of Chosŏn who would be suitable to become his wife. He had cleverly broken off his first engagement, but deceiving his parents a second time was not something a good son would do, so it seemed like he would have no choice but to do as his parents told him the next time. Even though he would not be able to immediately find a bride that would be satisfactory to him, if only he could find a nice girl who was at least educated enough to be not totally ignorant and who he himself considered worthy, he planned to marry her straight away so that he would not have to see any more matchmakers coming through the gate. It did not seem that there would be any way for him to find that sort of a bride soon enough, so he spent every night tossing and turning, and he would occasionally gaze at the copperplate engraving of Kyŏngja that had been published in the paper. Since the day he got that picture in Pagoda Park, he had looked at it so often that it had imprinted its image inside his eye, so that had he actually seen Kyŏngja it would have been as though he were meeting an old acquaintance whom he had known for years. One day, there was a school excursion to Inch'ŏn so that the students could go on a fieldtrip and get a bit of exercise. Taesŏng also went on this excursion, and almost as though it had been preordained he happened to see Kyŏngja as he was passing through Ch'ukhyŏn. Taesŏng was immensely pleased to see this girl whose face was already so well known to him, and he wanted to run after her and introduce himself. But, it would be foolish for a student like him to even look twice at a passing girl, so he passed by her sadly without even being able to look at her properly. In his heart, however, an idea had begun to take shape.

Deep in his heart, Taesŏng thought to himself, "Is it possible that such a smart, charming, well-mannered girl might actually exist in Chosŏn? Even when I saw her picture in Pagoda Park, I couldn't imagine that it would be possible, but having seen her beauty and manners in person, I should say that she is more than I had expected. If you look at those so-called modern Chosŏn women that you can see these days, none of them have ever set foot in an enlightened country. Their 'modernity' is nothing more than a Japanese hairstyle festooned with jeweled pins, gold bands on their fingers, flashy clothes, and gold watch chains, while their idea of 'accomplishment' is making men's eyes glaze over. As for their behavior, it's deplorable—even if they've only graduated from high-school they act as though they've finished at a girl's college, and there is no limit to the heights their soaring conceit might reach. The only things they think about are going to the theater to see plays, prostituting their bodies, and (if they're especially bold) divorcing their husbands. These women are the so-called modern women of Chosŏn. The frivolous attitude they show as they saunter about is almost an x-ray image of their hearts, and it's enough to make properly serious people shake their heads and sigh. But Kyŏngja is not like them, and is truly the ideal of a Chosŏn bride. One's appearance is not something that can be chosen, but her own fine beauty might be said to be something like a modern version of Xi Shi, that renowned beauty of ancient China, while her personality makes her seem almost the reincarnation of Queen Tairen, who was so famed for her refinement and moral rectitude.[9] Oh, I just need to find out who her family is! Looking into the background of a woman from another family is a truly improper thing for a student to do, but I have a grand plan in mind, so whether doing it is right or wrong doesn't matter at all. I'll find out about Kyŏngja, and if she's already married then there's nothing that can be done about it, but if she is not yet betrothed ..."

While Taesŏng was in Inch'ŏn, he quietly asked around about Kyŏngja's background. He discovered that she was the daughter of a *yangban* family that had been in Pup'yŏng for generations, but was currently living with her mother in Mansŏktong. It was also said that she had worked hard taking care of her mother and studying, and within a few days would be receiving her diploma from a girl's high school, having finished classes in the spring. He even learned that she was not yet married and her mother was trying to find Kyŏngja a husband who was educated and had a character as good as hers. Having been able to learn all of this in detail, Taesŏng was gladdened to the bottom of his heart and felt as though he had discovered a great treasure on his school excursion. On the way home, he went to the home of that wet-nurse who understood him so well.

Taesŏng went to his old wet-nurse's house nearly every day, but today's was not just another visit—today he had something that he wanted to ask of her, and so he was especially warm to her from the moment he walked in the door.

"Auntie, are you home?" he called out as he entered.

"Oh, Taesŏng, is that you? I heard that you went to Inch'ŏn— did you see anything interesting?"

Smiling embarrassedly as though he had something happy to say, Taesŏng said, "Yes, I was able to see quite a bit. But I didn't just

---

9. Xi Shi (西施 506 BCE-?) was one of the four beauties of ancient China and lived during the end of the Spring and Autumn period (春秋時代 770–476 BCE). Queen Tairen (太任) was the mother of King Wen (文王 1152 BCE–1056 BCE) of the Zhou dynasty (周 1111 BCE–256 BCE).

go sightseeing, I also …" But then he stopped in the middle of his sentence and just smiled.

[The wet-nurse was curious.] "*Aigu*, why are you acting so silly? Just standing there smiling without even finishing what you were saying. You didn't just go sightseeing—you also went to Inch'ŏn and smiled like an idiot, is that what you're trying to say?"

[Taesŏng laughed.] "Ha ha ha, if I can't help but smile when I see my Auntie, what of it? But, anyhow … Well, Auntie, would you arrange a marriage for me?"

"*Aigu*, why are you asking me that? Wouldn't your parents arrange a marriage for you? Anyway, a few days ago you made quite a fuss trying to get out of an engagement with a really remarkable girl, and now you want me to arrange another marriage for you? I did what you asked me to because you asked me so earnestly, without having any idea whether that girl was really haunted by a *Son-kaksi* or whatever, but I still have no idea what you're thinking. How could someone like you, who's been to a so-called school and supposedly possesses 'new ideas,' call off a wedding just because of some superstition? I don't know if that's really what's going on, but I think you made a big mistake in getting that wedding called off." [The wet-nurse said.]

"Auntie, don't you start saying things like that, too. What was so bad about it? It was because I've been to school and have civilized ideas that I got the wedding canceled—don't you know me better than that? No matter how foolish I might be, do you think I'm the sort of person who would believe in a *Son-kaksi*? What I was really afraid of wasn't any ghost bride—it was the living bride who would have come to my home!" [Replied Taesŏng.]

"So what kind of a bride do you want then?" [Asked the wet-nurse.]

[Taesŏng answered.] "Don't ask me—think about it for yourself. What sort of a girl do you think would be right for someone as well-educated and progressive as myself?"

[The wet-nurse asked again.] "So, you want a girl who graduated from school like you and wanders around outside of the house
showing her face like a dog?"

"Well, I can understand that you might think that way, but if
amongst those girls there was one decent girl, then you could say
she was like a phoenix in the midst of a brood of hens. In my eyes,
too, those girls going around outside with their faces bared for all
to see are like a brood of hens, but in Inch'ŏn I saw a real phoenix.
Auntie, if you helped me, I think that I could make her mine!"
[Said Taesŏng.]

[The wet-nurse replied.] "Are you saying that when you went
to Inch'ŏn you actually saw a girl that would be suitable for you?
Just what sort of a girl did you find tucked away in some corner of
Inch'ŏn? What sort of a girl might you have seen that she has you
going on like this? There are quite a few whores in Hwagae-dong—
this girl of yours isn't one of them, is she? Ha ha ha."

"Auntie, do you really think I'm such a fool that I can't tell the
difference between a whore and a student?" [Asked Taesŏng.]

"The girl is a student, eh?"

"Yes, and her name is Chŏng Kyŏngja. She graduated from
high school this year, and she was the most exquisitely beautiful
girl I've ever seen, and also the most mild-mannered." [Taesŏng
replied.]

"Ah, Chŏng Kyŏngja. I actually know her. And not only do I
know her, she's actually my older sister's daughter." [Said the wet-
nurse.]

Taesŏng was stunned for a moment when he heard this, then
he slapped his knees and said, "So Kyŏngja is your niece? You were
certainly tight-lipped about it. And why didn't you ever mention
before that your sister lived in Inch'ŏn? Anyhow, there's no reason
for me to go on and on like this. Please go to Inch'ŏn right away—
I'll pay for your ticket."

[The wet-nurse responded.] "You're not being very polite,
Taesŏng. Do you think the reason I've never mentioned I had a

sister in Inch'ŏn is because I didn't care about her? My family wasn't poor when I was a girl, but after we were reduced to poverty I had no choice but to go to work as a wet-nurse—your wet-nurse. As for my sister, she scraped a living off the floor of the harbor customs house, picking up kernels of grain that had fallen there. So what reason could I possibly have had to tell anyone else about these things? As for my niece, she seems to be an exceptionally nice girl, but your mother is very opposed to girls who have gone to school, and Kyŏngja is not even from a first-rate family, so I doubt your mother would agree to your marrying her. It wouldn't be any problem for me to introduce her to your family, but if I did that and it didn't lead to marriage it would just cause grief, so why would I even bring it up?"

"That's why I'm asking you, Auntie. Are you telling me that you couldn't manage something as trifling as this? We should at least give it a try, and if we fail, we fail. If you won't do this for me, then I'll never speak to you again." [Taesŏng said.]

When Taesŏng's wet-nurse heard this, she furrowed her brow and worked her lips, then said, "You really like Kyŏngja that much?"

"Absolutely." [Taesŏng replied.]

"Well, for better or worse, I'll give it a try. Don't you worry about a thing." [The wet-nurse assured him.]

After she said this, Taesŏng's wet-nurse got dressed to go out, and stepping outside, bustled straight over to Taesŏng's house. When she got to the house, she saw Taesŏng's mother and after talking about all sorts of things finally got to the real purpose of her visit. She told Taesŏng's mother as clearly and lucidly as possible that the modern world was gradually changing and becoming more civilized; that even girls would need to be decently educated if they hoped to manage their families skillfully; that, because Taesŏng was so against it, it would be difficult trying to match him with the sort of old-fashioned, ignorant, poorly educated girl who would never leave the house; and that Taesŏng wished to marry a girl who he could rely on, who was at least moderately informed and educated, and who could contribute to the betterment of the human race in her own way. Not only was Taesŏng's wet-nurse a woman that Taesŏng's mother trusted, she also spoke fairly and reasonably, so that when she said these things, Taesŏng's mother immediately accepted them as true. After the wet-nurse had piqued Taesŏng's mother's interest in that way, she got on the train for Inch'ŏn and headed to her sister's home in Mansŏktong.

Taesŏng's wet-nurse and her older sister had been particularly close as children, but after they married and left home not only was one in Seoul and the other in Inch'ŏn, but they also suffered from such poverty that they could only see each other maybe once in every ten or twenty years. Even sisters who were not very close would burst into tears if they met after so long, so imagine what it must have been like for these two sisters to see each other after looking forward to meeting for so long! Kyŏngja's mother and Taesŏng's wet-nurse held each other and cried an inexhaustible river of tears, letting out all of their pent-up feeling without saying a word. Then, from beside them, Kyŏngja spoke up and very politely said, "How do you do, Ma'am?" It was obvious from her comportment then that she had been raised well.

After holding each other and crying for awhile, Kyŏngja's mother and Taesŏng's wet-nurse went inside and began to catch up on all that had happened since they last met. As they talked, Kyŏngja knelt down beside them and served them tea and snacks. She was dressed plainly, but her character and polite behavior made it clear that she was a heaven-made match for Taesŏng. Taesŏng's wet-nurse looked at Kyŏngja, and asked her, "Kyŏngja, how old are you this year?"

"I'm sixteen."

"*Aigu*, time flies. You probably don't remember, but I came once when you were six, and now you're about ready to get married."

Then, turning to her sister, Taesŏng's wet-nurse asked, "So have you decided the matter of Kyŏngja's marriage?" She had finally brought the conversation around to the purpose of her visit.

[Her sister replied.] "It hasn't been so easy to decide. I'm actually quite worried about it. I don't mean to brag about my daughter, but it would be tough for any family to find fault with her, so it's a formidable task to find a husband worthy of her. If you know of someone you could match her up with, please don't wait to introduce him."

"Well, I know a really nice young man—but what is Kyŏngja looking for in a husband?" [The wet-nurse asked.]

"Why should she have any different opinion about a man than we would? If you think the man is suitable, then Kyŏngja will find him suitable, too—what sort of a man is he?" [Her sister replied.]

[The wet-nurse continued.] "He and Kyŏngja were almost ordained by heaven to be together. He is the son of Hwang Ch'amsŏ in Kyedong, Seoul. The boy has a firm character and is well educated, and not only that, he also has land holdings that yield a thousand *sŏm* of rice. With that sort of fortune, you could even say he's rich. I nursed him from my own breast when he was a child, so I know well that he is kind-hearted and remarkable—really an amazing young man."

"So, you nursed him at your own breast … Then no two words about it, he sounds like a superb match. But unlike the past, these days if the prospective couple aren't interested in each other, there's no way they can marry. Kyŏngja, don't be embarrassed, speak up for yourself. What do you think of what your aunt has said?" [She asked her daughter.]

But Kyŏngja only kept her head down and did not say a word.

[The wet-nurse continued.] "Kyŏngja, you will become a model Chosŏn woman. You don't need to follow in the old customs by acting so embarrassed. As you know, the matter of your marriage will affect your entire life, and it won't work out if you don't like your husband. It also won't work out if it's not something that you've approved of yourself, so don't let a little bit of embarrassment make you indifferent to such an important matter. Do you think the boy I've mentioned would be suitable or not?"

Kyŏngja thought about this question for a long time before finally opening her cherry-red lips to say, "I'm not really sure. There's no reason for me not to trust in what you've told me, but ..." Her forehead was tinged with the red of a blush, and she said nothing more.

"Of course, that's only natural. There's no reason for you not to trust me, but how could the two people involved make a decision without having seen each other first? The two of you really are a match made in heaven. The boy is also against marrying a narrow-minded woman, and said that he wouldn't make any promise of marriage before he had seen his bride with his own eyes. He even called off the marriage that his parents had arranged for him. And then, after he somehow managed to see you a couple of times, he couldn't praise you enough whenever you were mentioned, even without really knowing you."

[The sister then asked.] "How did he know about Kyŏngja to be praising her like that? He must have seen her in the newspaper. There were a couple of articles about her."

"Probably ... Let's try introducing them ourselves. You've never seen Seoul, and you've never seen my house, so bring Kyŏngja and I'll show you around the city. The weather these days is bright and clear: perfect for sightseeing." [The wet-nurse replied.]

"Ok, let's do it." [Said the sister.]

After the two sisters had this conversation, they stayed for a few days in Inch'ŏn, going to the ocean and talking about all of the fond memories they shared. Then, taking Kyŏngja along with them, they set off for Seoul.

After seeing his wet-nurse off, Taesŏng had no idea how things were going and was beset by tremendous worry; he was unable to sleep at night and spent his days waiting impatiently for his wet-nurse to return. After several days passed and she had still not returned, his impatience grew and he started going over to the wet-nurse's house five or six times a day. Oh, there really is nothing so hard in this world as waiting for someone to return! After four or five days like that, Taesŏng felt as though he would go insane; whenever a train was about to arrive from Inch'ŏn he would go out to Namdaemun Station and carefully watch the women getting off in the hope that she would be amongst them. When the wet-nurse still did not come, he grew cross and his spirits fell, he stopped going to the wet-nurse's house and the train station, and instead spent his days lying about the house thinking about this and that. Then one day, he heard the wet-nurse's voice coming from the next room, and he was so delighted that she was back and impatient to find out what she would say that he leapt into the greeting room in a single step, dragging one of his shoes backward on his foot, and looked first of all to the wet-nurse's face.

The wet-nurse saw Taesŏng burst in that way and laughed, saying, "Was it that hard not being able to see me for a few days? You must have missed me just as much as I missed you. I missed you so much that I couldn't stand it and came back after only a couple of days, though I had planned to stay longer."

Taesŏng saw the wet-nurse's cheerful expression and thought to himself, "Yes! Things have turned out in my favor." He smiled gaily at the idea and was so pleased that he was unable to even reply to what she had said. Taesŏng's mother had no idea of what was on the minds of Taesŏng and his wet-nurse, and said, "If Taesŏng goes more than a few days without seeing you, he goes crazy. While you were in Inch'ŏn, he was going to your house a dozen times a day to see if you'd returned home. How do I know where you had gone? When I asked Taesŏng why he was going over to your house so often, he told me that you had gone to Inch'ŏn and that he was going to see if you'd returned. That boy is so fond of you that he almost forgets about his own mother."

All three of them burst out laughing at this; but Taesŏng was so impatient to hear Kyŏngja's reply that he gestured to the wet-nurse with his eyes that they should move into another room and then dashed out.

"So, how did that thing you went to do for me in Inch'ŏn turn out? I was so impatient I almost thought I would burst."

The wet-nurse smiled teasingly and said, "It didn't work out. She's already engaged to another man."

Taesŏng's heart dropped when he heard this, and said, "Already engaged? Has the engagement already been finalized? If so, then everything is ruined." His eyes were nearly brimming over with tears.

Taesŏng looked so ridiculous to the wet-nurse at that moment that she nearly split her sides laughing; seeing this, Taesŏng became suspicious and said with a hurt expression, "Auntie, you tricked me, didn't you! Stop playing with me, and tell me the truth. I was waiting so impatiently for you to return, and yet you tease me like that? Even if she was engaged, I'm sure you could find some way to make things work out anyway. How can you be so indifferent to someone suffering as much as I am?"

The wet-nurse kept laughing and said, "Do you really have your heart so set on that girl?"

"Oh, I do! If I can't marry her, then I won't marry at all!" [Taesŏng replied.]

[The wet-nurse said.] "As long as that's the case, then I'll help you as far as I can, but there are more than a few obstacles."

"What sort of obstacles?" [Asked Taesŏng.]

[The wet-nurse answered.] "The first is that your mother is not likely to let you get engaged to such a low-born girl; the second is that while you've had a chance to see the girl, she has not had a chance to see you and won't know how she feels about you until she does. Then, even if the girl is interested and consents, there's still the matter of whether your mother will approve or not. If either one of them is against it, it's over. Seems like it'll be hard to pull it off, doesn't it?"

"Ha ha ha, is it all really so difficult? [Taesŏng laughed.] If the girl has said she wants to meet me, then I'll leave for Inch'ŏn today, and since she's bound to like me as soon as she sets eyes on me, there's nothing to worry about there. As for my mother, I'm sure that you can convince her, so stop saying it's so difficult and just get everything arranged."

"My word! Well, how about a trip to the zoo tomorrow? I'll be going with a couple of guests from Inch'ŏn, so it would be nice if you came along and took your mind off things for a day." [The wet-nurse replied.]

"Guests came down from Inch'ŏn? Who are they?" [Asked Taesŏng.]

Laughing again, the wet-nurse said, "Why are my visitors any business of yours?"

"You'll find out soon." [He replied.]

Taesŏng had a feeling about what the wet-nurse might be implying and his mouth fell open as wide as a wide basket. He said, "Ah, I'd do anything you asked of me, Auntie. So if you say we should go to the zoo, how could I refuse?"

"Your mother should come along, too." [The wet-nurse suggested.]

"Then I'll ask Mother to come with us." [He replied.]

After talking, Taesŏng and his wet-nurse went back into the room his mother was in and they made arrangements to go together the next day to the zoo. The day after, the wet-nurse went with her sister and niece, and Taesŏng accompanied his mother.

When the weather is fair and the flowers are in bloom, all sorts of people come out to the zoo in great throngs so that even if two people were holding hands they might be at risk of losing each other. Even if you make an agreement to meet someone there, it can be difficult to find them if you are not paying attention; but Taesŏng's wet-nurse went there with the goal of meeting Taesŏng and his mother, and Taesŏng was taking pains to find his wet-nurse and her companions. The wet-nurse got there before Taesŏng and his mother did, and they made their way toward the botanical gardens while looking around the park, then they sat down next to the lotus pond and had a snack while they waited for Taesŏng and his mother to come. Taesŏng and his mother were making their way through the park and looking for his wet-nurse and her companions. Then when they came to the lotus pond the two parties finally met; and right as Taesŏng warmly greeted his wet-nurse, he was shocked to see that Kyŏngja was sitting there next to them. At that moment, Taesŏng's breast was filled with a mixture of happiness, relief, and gratitude toward his wet-nurse. Every time he saw Kyŏngja, he was intoxicated by her beauty and poise and too embarrassed to look her in the face, so he stood off a bit to the side while his mother sat beside his wet-nurse and lit a cigarette. Seeing how neat and proper the young girl next to her looked, Taesŏng's mother asked the wet-nurse, "Is that young woman there with you?"

"Yes, she is … Kyŏngja, say hello," the wet-nurse said, and introduced Kyŏngja and her mother.

"This girl is my niece, and this is my older sister." [She continued.]

Taesŏng's mother was surprised by this and said, "Is that so? Why hello, it's nice to meet you! I've been close with your sister for decades—in fact, she even nursed my son here at her own breast, so she's almost as dear to me as a sister. It's really a shame that you and I haven't had a chance to meet before now. I really must compliment you on your daughter though, how did you ever manage to raise such a comely, polite young woman? I don't think I've ever seen a girl like her before."

Taesŏng's mother then turned and looked at Kyŏngja, who opened her ruby-red lips and said, "How do you do, ma'am? Thank you for having been so kind to my Aunt."

Taesŏng's mother was completely won over by Kyŏngja's voice and the refined bearing she showed as she spoke and continued to lavish compliments upon her.

"My, how polite you are! What's your name, dear? And how old are you?"

"Kyŏngja, ma'am. And I'm nineteen.[10]"

Then Taesŏng's mother turned back toward Kyŏngja's mother and continued her praise, saying, "You've certainly raised your daughter well."

[Kyŏngja's mother explained.] "Oh, this girl doesn't know anything. She graduated from one of those so-called schools, but she's really as old-fashioned as can be."

Whether Kyŏngja was able to get a good look at Taesŏng or not, as they were talking the short hand of the clock hand made its way all the way around to four o'clock, and it was time for the zoo to close, so everyone said their farewells and went back home.

Taesŏng's wet-nurse had accompanied Kyŏngja to the zoo to introduce Taesŏng to her and also show her off to Taesŏng's mother, and after they returned home she asked Kyŏngja about her opinion of Taesŏng: "Kyŏngja, did you get a good look at him? That young man who we met at the zoo was Taesŏng. So now that you've seen him for yourself, what do you think?"

When she heard this, Kyŏngja didn't say a word, instead her cherry-red lips parted in a smile and a blush rose in her cheeks, then she lowered her head and turned away in embarrassment. Then, Kyŏngja's mother said to her younger sister, "It's no use asking her. As long as she's in front of her mom, there's no way you'll get a straight 'yes' or 'no' from her. Anyhow, the boy's a good match. There's no need to talk about it any further—see about arranging for Kyŏngja to marry him. But is there any way that a house like his would accept a family as lowly as ours for marriage?"

[The younger sister answered.] "I'm worried about that, too. Taesŏng was the one who wanted it in the first place, so we don't need to worry about him, but his parents still have a lot of the old biases, and we might end up disgraced if we suggest marriage."

---

10. Previously reported as sixteen. Likely error in original text.

As Taesŏng's wet-nurse was saying this, she felt concerned and began to turn the problem over in her mind: *If I fail to arrange this marriage, it would leave Taesŏng in a fix and I don't think I'd be able to face Kyŏngja ever again. Taesŏng's mother certainly had many nice things to say about Kyŏngja, but that woman is awfully set in her ways and she greatly dislikes girls who pull their hair back in the Western style and go to school, so how would she ever approve of a girl like Kyŏngja as her daughter-in-law? And on top of that, she's such a terrible snob, so how disgraceful would it be if I suggested marriage just to fail and be embarrassed? So what can I do to make this happen? Maybe there's just nothing to be done about it.*

The result of these deliberations was the conception of a remarkable scheme. Whatever her plan may have been, Taesŏng's wet-nurse spent the whole next day making arrangements and then went on another day to Taesŏng's house. Taesŏng's mother had been lying on the balcony, having been soothed soundly to sleep by the freshness of the breeze, but hearing the wet-nurse's voice, she sat up and the two began to talk. For whatever reason, if two women with nothing better to do meet they always seem to have a great deal to talk about, and they will continue talking until well after dark without any idea of the passing of the day. Taesŏng's mother had been napping because she was so bored, so when the wet-nurse came Taesŏng's mother was happy to be able to talk to her about this and that to kill the time. Then, while they were talking an unknown young woman, her head covered with the *changot* veil of a *mudang*,[11] came through the inner gate, stopped suddenly before the balcony on which the two women sat, and said, "I have come seeking offerings. I am a newly made sorceress who has only recently been inspired by divinity."

This young *mudang* had come by the wet-nurse's arrangement, but the wet-nurse feigned ignorance and pretended not to know

---

11. *Changot* was a garment that covered a woman from head-to-toe and worn in the Chosŏn dynasty. A *mudang* is a female shaman.

her. Before anyone else could say anything, the wet-nurse spoke up as though she were coldly turning the young woman away, "The people of this house have no interest in offerings or sorceresses, so I would suggest that you move on."

"*Aigu*, don't say such things. They say that those who speak in such a way toward a sorceress will be denied fortune. Sorceresses never use offerings for themselves. They offer up in prayer the things they have received for the realization of the wishes of those who have made the offering. It's not as though offerings need to be a whole *sŏm* of rice or hundreds of *wŏn*, so why do you say such unlucky things?" said the *mudang*, and then looked cautiously at Taesŏng's mother.

Without being asked, she continued, "You must be the mistress of the house? I know hardly anything of value, but I know that you will soon have occasion to celebrate a joyous event."

Superstitious women are greatly afraid of hearing things like this. So when Taesŏng's mother heard what the *mudang* said, her interest was piqued.

"Oh? Just what sort of a joyous event? I'll be sure to make a large offering, so tell me everything you know," she asked, and then moved to sit before the *mudang*.

"What could a wandering sorceress like myself possibly know? But I do know that before long there will be someone new coming to live in your home. If you have a grown son, then a daughter-in-law will be coming to your house."

"Ah, is that so? It just so happens that we are currently looking for a wife for our son. Will we find a good bride soon?" [Taesŏng's mother queried.]

"Yes, if this month you happen to come across a young woman from the south with the last name of 'Chŏng,' then know that she and your son are a match made in heaven: they will live together until old age, your grandchildren will flourish, and the couple will enjoy incredible good fortune. However, there is also a bit of an obstacle. If you come to my home and perform a *salp'uri* rite then the marriage will be realized without any difficulty."[12] [The *mudang* explained.]

[Taesŏng's mother was curious.] "Obstacle? What sort of obstacle?"

"In your son's *saju*, there is an unlucky sign that will interfere in his marriage. His marriage will not happen unless you do a *salp'uri*, and should you force the matter without performing an exorcism it is sure to end in misfortune. So don't be stingy about giving a bit of rice or money and holding a *salp'uri* right away." [The *mudang* said.]

With her superstitious nature, when Taesŏng's mother heard this she was completely taken in.

"*Aigu*, this sorceress is really something! The way that arrangements for Taesŏng to marry fell apart right when they were almost finalized—there really must be an unlucky sign in his fortune, just like she says. If that's the case, then what reason do we have not to hold a *salp'uri*? Sorceress, I'll have a *salp'uri* just like you've told me to, but who is the girl my son is meant to marry?"

"As I told you earlier, your son's preordained wife, the one who will bring him good fortune, is a bride from the south with the last name of 'Chŏng.' If you come to my house for a *salp'uri* I'll perform a divination and tell you about it all in detail." [The *mudang* explained.]

"Then we'll visit you tomorrow. Where's your house?" [Asked Taesŏng's mother.]

"It's outside of Saemunan, in Wŏram-dong. The house just below the village shrine." [The *mudang* answered.]

Taesŏng's mother was extremely pleased and said, "We'll go tomorrow, so make sure you're there waiting for us."

Then she called the old servant woman who worked in their home and asked her to bring out two *toe* of rice as an offering.[13]

---

12. *Salp'uri* is a shamanic rite to expel misfortune.
13. One *toe* is equal to 1.8 liters.

The *mudang* once again implored Taesŏng's mother to come to her house for a *salp'uri* and then left. After she went out, Taesŏng's mother and his wet-nurse talked about how amazed they were by the *mudang* and about the issue of Taesŏng's marriage, and then Taesŏng's mother began to tell the wet-nurse about her dreams.

"Listen here, earlier I dreamt a strange dream. It's true what they say: that you see in your dreams what you are feeling in your heart. Earlier, before you came, I was drowsing on the balcony, and I dreamt that Taesŏng had decided on his own to get married without my assistance, and then when I went to the wedding hall and took a good look at him and his bride, I discovered that he was marrying that young woman I met yesterday at the zoo. And I thought to myself, 'How in the world did he end up engaged to that girl?' But then I was awoken by your voice and I realized it was all a dream. When I saw that young girl yesterday, I thought that she was so lovely that if I had a daughter-in-law I would like to have a daughter-in-law like her, and that must be the reason I dreamt that dream. But what a peculiar dream!"

Generally dreams are formed of thoughts that one has already had. Despite being so stubbornly old-fashioned, how could Taesŏng's mother not have recognized the value of something so pleasing to the eyes as Kyŏngja? Even though she typically despised girls who went to school, when Taesŏng's mother saw Kyŏngja dressed so neatly in her school uniform, the beauty of the girl's demeanor made her eyes widen with surprise, and the thought that she would like to have just that sort of girl for a daughter-in-law was what led to her dream. Hearing what Taesŏng's mother said, the wet-nurse jumped on the rare opportunity she had been presented with to put in a word, "Not just that, though. Your dreaming a dream like that just before that *mudang* came and said what she did—it seems that the engagement will come about easily. However, your dream and what that *mudang* said are not just coincidences. Your dream of Taesŏng marrying Kyŏngja and what that *mudang* said about a bride from the south with the last name of 'Chŏng' being lucky almost exactly correspond. Kyŏngja's last name is 'Chŏng' and she's from Inch'ŏn, which is south of here. But would you really consider marrying Taesŏng to Kyŏngja? Kyŏngja is not of particularly low class, but she's certainly not on the same level as your family. Could you accept as your daughter-in-law a girl from a lower class?"

[Taesŏng's Mother thought it over.] "*Aigu*, it's all so strange. Is that girl's last name really 'Chŏng'?"

She said this and shook the ashes from her pipe, which she refilled and put back between her lips. She stared vacantly at Namsan a moment before saying, "Look here, come over early tomorrow morning and let's go visit that *mudang*. It'll be a good way to kill some time."

Before either had realized it, the sun had dropped behind the western mountains and the long spring day had drawn to a close, so the wet-nurse returned to her home.

The next day, Taesŏng's mother and his wet-nurse went together to the *mudang*'s house outside of Saemunan, as they had agreed to do. The *mudang* was, of course, a part in the wet-nurse's plan, and acting out the instructions the wet-nurse had given her, so how could her performance fail to be special? Taesŏng's mother, however, had no idea about what was afoot, and so after having the *mudang* tell her fortune, she gave the woman an ample fee of a full *wŏn* and said, "Now, give me a detailed reading of my son's fortune, and then we'll do a *salp'uri* or whatever is needed according to the results. I'm paying you especially well, so concentrate and do a good job of it."

The *mudang* cast some rice on a table and began her fortune telling. Mumbling something to herself, she scattered the grains about with her hands and then finally began to tell Taesŏng's mother about his fortune.

"You have but a single son, but there is no reason for you to envy even those who have many children. Thanks to your son, you will live in great luxury. Furthermore, this year the butterfly will come to a field of flowers. The bride who is meant for him is in that field, but he will not know which flower he should land on. Also, because there is a serious obstruction to his marriage in his *saju*, he will face obstacle after obstacle and be unable to marry. It is as though the butterfly is being swept along by a strong wind, so that, try as it will, it is unable to alight upon any of the blossoms it would land on. If, however, you perform a *salp'uri*, you will meet by chance a girl from the south. As I told you yesterday she will have 'Chŏng' as the last name and she will be the daughter of a fruit grower. Her first name will contain a character for something like 'gem,' '*kyŏng*' perhaps, and if you let her slip between your fingers then even if you manage to marry off your son later, that marriage will be unlucky. I don't know anything, but that is what fortune foretells, so give it some consideration."

Foolish women are always taken in by nonsense like this. Taesŏng's mother thought about the way arrangements for his marriage had fallen apart the month before, and not only had the *mudang* been so right that it seemed she must really be communing with a god, but that *mudang* had also predicted that the girl Taesŏng was destined to marry was a girl from the south with the last name of "Chŏng." So the thought occurred to Taesŏng's mother that maybe the girl from Inch'ŏn whom she had seen in her dreams really was the girl Taesŏng was fated to be with, especially when she thought, *Right, that girl's name was Kyŏngja— just like the* mudang *said!*

Taesŏng's mother thought that the *mudang* was the most miraculous sorceress in the world, and did just as the *mudang* asked by buying rice cake and fruit for the performance of a very passable *salp'uri*. Then she went home and asked the wet-nurse about Kyŏngja in detail, and how could she fail to be amazed by how well the wet-nurse's answers accorded with what the *mudang* had said? As a result, Taesŏng's wishes were realized, and his horoscope was sent to Kyŏngja's family as a precursor to marriage. Then a day for the wedding was chosen, and with that Kyŏngja's fate was decided as well.

They say that even iron and stones yield when one puts one's will to a thing, and truly whenever someone decides that they will do a thing, no matter what it takes, there is bound to be some result. Taesŏng had anguished day and night, and he had done everything he could think of to bring about the beautiful union that he had desired. So when the day of his marriage finally arrived he arranged a tremendous party to which he invited a great number of guests, held his wedding ceremony in a dazzling restaurant, and his marriage was consecrated in a bridal bed swathed in candlelight. You could say that he had gotten everything he had wished for, and Taesŏng was unable to contain his happiness as a smile continually brightened his face.

The affection that Taesŏng and his wife felt was so great that they were sad only that they could not have become husband and wife even sooner. Because Kyŏngja had a naturally submissive character and was also educated, their relationship was exceptionally friendly, but they still maintained a cordial respect for each other and were not so friendly as to forget their manners toward each other. They were devoted to their parents and always did their best to put their parents' hearts at ease. Taesŏng's mother was delighted with the way things had worked out and thought the close relationship the two of them shared to be a rare, joyous thing.

Just as time flows by, the heat of midsummer came and went along with the monsoon rains, and on the top of the hill behind Taesŏng's house were some rooms that were lit by the setting sun and filled with the pleasant hum of the cicadas. These rooms were where Taesŏng's wife, Kyŏngja, lived. With the clearing of the cursed summer rains, Taesŏng and his wife set aside the books they had spent every day studying and studying again, and reinvigorated by the freshness of the cicada calls, closed their books and leaned one day on the railing looking out over the mountains and fields. Won over by the quiet joy of the moment, Taesŏng sang while Kyŏngja accompanied him on the organ, and the two of them had a bit of pleasant fun together. Taesŏng's mother, napping in the house, heard the singing and the organ playing, thought again to herself just how priceless the two of them were and took some snacks and wine up to the top of the hill. Kyŏngja took the snacks and wine from her and said, "Mother, you really needn't have gone to the trouble of bringing these snacks!" While Taesŏng smiled brightly and said, "Mother, did you bring this wine for me?"

[His mother replied.] "Let's drink it together. I thought we could have some fun together as a family. Get back to your playing! I was feeling so lonesome all day, so when I heard the sound of the organ, I thought I'd come and have a listen."

Hearing this, Kyŏngja simply lowered her head and smiled sweetly, and Taesŏng said teasingly, "Let's eat first, and then we'll get around to playing after that." Then he poured his mother some wine.

"Mother, why don't you have the first glass?"

Taesŏng's mother took the glass from him and drank a bit, then said, "Kyŏngja, why don't you pour some wine for your husband? And why don't you eat a bit of the snacks I brought?"

Kyŏngja picked up the bottle and poured some wine for her husband and his mother. This was familial harmony, and the sound they made laughing and talking proclaimed the Hwang family's bliss. Then a young servant came running up the hill, and said, "The master requests that everyone come down to the house."

Hearing this, Taesŏng's mother said, "What could he possibly want? For the first time in a long time, I came out to listen to the organ, and he's calling me now just to be a bother. But if one's husband calls, then one needs to go and see what he wants to say." Then they all walked down to the house.

Not only was Taesŏng's father, Hwang Ch'amsŏ, old-fashioned and stuck in his ways, he was also the most foolish, stupidest man there ever was. Thanks to Taesŏng's grandparents he possessed a significant fortune, but he was clueless and had no idea how to manage a household, so his wife took care of all the finances. Taesŏng's schooling and all that he had accomplished was done under his mother's supervision, and all that his father had done was sit in the house, wear the clothes that were given him, and eat the food that was made for him. That he had an official position, even if it was in name only, and was able to wear the skullcap of a civil servant was also thanks only to his wife's mediation. For whatever reason this despicable old man called Taesŏng before him. Then he began to speak, "Look here, Taesŏng, the reason that I called you down is to tell you that I've decided it's time for you to go to Tokyo to continue your education. A man who grows up as isolated and ignorant as a fish in a well is of no use for anything. Everyone these days goes to study in Tokyo and then becomes a lawyer or a doctor when they come back, but what do you intend to make of yourself? Don't waste another idle day and leave at once."

Then, looking at Kyŏngja he added, "Isn't that so, dear? I'm right, aren't I?"

Then, turning to his wife, "Give Taesŏng plenty of money for his schooling and send him off within the next few days. A gentleman scholar like myself can do fine with just studying the classics in his own home, but since Taesŏng has already started down the path of a modern education, he'll need to at least graduate from university before he can even think of putting on the airs of a scholar. So without delaying another day, send him off at once."

Taesŏng's mother thought that it was strange such a stupid man should be saying such things, and she said to him, "It's certainly a surprise to hear something like that from you. You were always dithering on about how useless it was for Taesŏng to even go to school, and now you want to send him to Tokyo?"

[Taesŏng's father replied.] "If you're not going to see a thing through, then it's best not to even begin it, but after the thing's been started it needs to be done right. At any rate, playing and lazing around, and making a hash of it doesn't get one anything. Taesŏng has already graduated from a law program, but can he act as though he knows anything with just that education? There's nothing else to be said, send him off right away—even tomorrow would not be too soon."

Whatever Taesŏng may have thought of this, he said, "I'll leave right away as you've asked, father. I've always dearly wanted to study in Tokyo, but I never said anything because I didn't want to leave you and Mother. But now that I am married, I can trust that my wife will look after you both just as well as I would, and I can leave with my mind at ease that you will be well cared for. But schools do not take admissions this time of year, so I'll need to wait here for half-a-year at least. There's no way to avoid it, so I think it would be best for me to study here at home for a while and then leave for Japan next spring." As Taesŏng said this, however, it was apparent that he did not really want to go. It was true that one reason for his not wanting to go was the fact that it was not yet the season for admissions, but the larger reason was actually that it was difficult for him to think of leaving the hill behind his parent's home.

Hearing Taesŏng's reply, Hwang Ch'amsŏ said, "That's not true. Admissions might not be until the spring, but don't you think it would be good for you to go to Tokyo ahead of time to study the language and check out schools? Stop dithering about it and just get ready to go."

Taesŏng had no idea what it was that suddenly prompted his father to push for him to study abroad, but he had no desire to leave home, and he looked particularly flustered as he said, "Even if I leave later there will be plenty of time to do all that. I can learn Japanese perfectly well here, and it's no problem to research schools from here, so there's no reason for me to leave before next year."

This enraged Hwang Ch'amsŏ, and he pounded the desk with his fist and screamed, "Whether I'm right or not is beside the question—how dare you defy your father! Don't say another word about it and leave as soon as you can."

There was nothing that Taesŏng could say to this, so he said simply, "I'll leave right away."

Taesŏng's mother was sad to be sending her son so far away, but she knew that studying in a place as lively and flourishing as Japan was something that a person should do at least once in life. So she began preparing to send Taesŏng's off straight away, and it seemed as though there was nothing Taesŏng could do to avoid being separated from Kyŏngja. As Taesŏng sat on top of the railing staring out over the far-off mountains, overcome by resignation, it seemed as though the furrows in his brow almost formed the character for worry. Looking at Taesŏng, Kyŏngja was filled with misery, but she put on a smile as she asked him, "You've seemed distracted for a while, is there anything the matter?"

"No." [Taesŏng replied.]

[Kyŏngja asked again.] "Then is there something worrying you?"

"No." [Taesŏng insisted.]

[Kyŏngja pressed on.] "Then why do you sit there not saying a word and looking so worried? Are you worried about going to Tokyo and leaving your parents behind?"

[Again, Taesŏng replied.] "No, it's nothing like that."

[Kyŏngja continued.] "Then what is it? What could it be that you can't tell me?"

"I'm not worried about anything. I'm just sad about having to leave you." [Taesŏng said.]

Hearing this, Kyŏngja said in a sudden flash of anger, "Here now, what sort of nonsense is that? And you call yourself a grown man? Your parents have ordered you to go study, a thing you love to do more than anything else in the world. I'd say that sitting around moping over some girl shows a lack of mettle in a man. And if you're still thinking miserable things like that when you go to Tokyo, it will distract you more than a little from your studies— just imagine how embarrassed you'd be if you did poorly in your studies because of a reason like that. Stop being so ridiculous and instead devote all of that feeling to your studies. I'll congratulate you a thousand times over if you come back to me with a doctorate in your hand, but what you just said is nothing that I've ever wanted to hear from you."

Kyŏngja's words carried such force and were spoken so fervently that Taesŏng was overcome with embarrassment, and try as he might he could not say anything in response, and so he just went back to his room.

No matter how Taesŏng hated the thought of leaving home, how could he avoid it when his parents had given him such a stern order and his wife had entreated so earnestly that he go? Finally he was packed for his journey and it was time to set out for Tokyo; despite what Kyŏngja had said, what love must she have felt as the time came for her beloved husband to leave for afar? On the day her husband was to leave she followed him down to Inch'ŏn, both to see him off and to pay a visit to her mother. They ate lunch together at *P'alp'allu* and then went to sit together in front of the fountain in the Japanese Park: it was finally time for that warm-hearted and loving couple to say their farewells to each other. They talked together, looking out upon the boundlessness of the sea beyond P'almi Island.

[Taesŏng began.] "The color of the water is wonderful isn't it? Our love for each other is as limitless as those waters and that sea. Even if that sea were to be changed into a mulberry patch, there would be nothing changed about our love. I am too overwhelmed by my love for you to remain stoic about our parting."

[Kyŏngja replied.] "That may be, but your leaving me is actually a good thing in a way. If you study hard in Tokyo, then I will be the wife of a Ph.D. And more than that, it will not be long before we meet again, so I think it's unfathomable that a grown man should get so upset about something so trifling."

"Fine, fine, you're right. If I think about the future there's nothing to be sad about … nothing at all. When I get to Tokyo, I'll apply myself to my studies, I'll learn a lot, and then we'll be able to enjoy touring parks like this one from the inside of a car." [Taesŏng was convinced.]

Then, looking at his watch, he said, "*Aigu*, it's already time for the boat to leave. Why don't you hurry back on home. I'm going to leave now, so let's keep in touch by letter. Also, even though it's not the sort of matter a man should ask of a wife, I'd like to ask you to take good care of my parents for a little while."

Taesŏng then left in the direction of the shore, and Kyŏngja was left alone in the park. As she watched her husband go, it seemed as though the shadows of the pines standing tall about her and even the swallows flying carefree through the air seemed to share in the sorrow she felt.

After saying farewell to her husband, Kyŏngja went to her mother's house. Kyŏngja had been her mother's dearest treasure when she was growing up, and her mother missed her terribly now that she was married, but a girl who has left the home to marry is as good as a stranger to her family so it was impossible for Kyŏng-ja's mother to see her often and all Kyŏngja's mother could do was think of her daughter night and day. How happy they must have been to be able to see each other again then! The two of them sat across from each other and were talking about all sorts of things when Kyŏngja said, "Mother, you must have felt so lonely, how did you bear it? I wanted to see you, but you know I can't just do whatever I want. Because of things like that, it really seems like parents can't even think of their daughters as being their own children."

This was Kyŏngja's expression of all that she had felt since the last time she saw her mother, and her mother said, "If you felt like that, can you imagine how I must have felt? It seemed as though I missed you so much I wouldn't be able to bear it for a single moment, but what can you or I do about the misfortune of having been born a woman? Be that as it may, however, it's more important for you to be a good daughter-in-law for your new family than it is for you to be a good daughter to me. I trust that your mother- and father-in-law aren't too hard on you and that life in their family is going well for you? Your husband is really quite an extraordinary person, so I trust him and that helps me worry a little less."

Kyŏngja had always been kind-hearted and genial, so even if her in-laws were hard on her, she was not the sort who would forget her manners and slander them before others or cry about it and complain about her mother-in-law. Not only that, her husband was exceptionally kind and her mother-in-law exceedingly loving, so why would she tell her mother anything but the truth? She even exaggerated all of this in answering her mother so that her mother's heart would be at ease. Kyŏngja told her mother about her husband's leaving to study in Tokyo, and then spent the next ten days or so doing this and that: she made rice cake, she cooked taffy, and she sewed new clothes for her parents-in-law, as is tradition. When she returned to her in-laws' house, they were as happy as could be to see her, especially that degenerate father-in-law of hers who seemed happier than usual and said, "Why did you wait so long to come back? I know that you were visiting your mother, but we missed you so much it was as though our eyes would fall out for wanting to see you."

Kyŏngja was incomparably happy to be loved so well by her parents-in-law, and she told them that she had seen Taesŏng off and that her mother was keeping well. They spoke without noticing the fading day, and it was dark before Kyŏngja went back up to her rooms at the top of the hill. The books were stacked staidly upon the bookshelf, and the shadows of the tree branches crisscrossed the garden. Feeling lonesome, Kyŏngja sat down and it seemed the image of her husband floated before her eyes as vividly as a photograph, and the sound of her mother's voice could be heard in her ears as clearly as a phonograph. Unable to overcome her sadness, Kyŏngja leaned upon the railing and looked up at the moon. But then, from the flower garden, she heard the tapping of a cane. The silhouette of a man's hat could be seen faintly making its way through the garden, and she knew that it was her father-in-law who was coming up. He stopped at the bottom of the garden, bowed his head in greeting, and said, "Look here, a letter came from your husband. It appears that it's for you."

Then he pulled out a letter, and guffawing loudly, continued, "I was so pleased to see a letter from him that I wanted to show it to you right away and so I brought it up myself. There's nothing wrong with me bringing you a letter, right? I guess he says that he's arrived safely in Tokyo and that he's taken a room in some house somewhere in Gojimachi-ku, wherever that is. He says that if he enrolls next spring it will take him four or five years to complete his studies and return, but I'd like to see him keep studying as long as he's doing well and return after he's finished his bachelor's or Ph.D., or whatever. Since he's already gone so far away to study, he might as well stay until he's made a respectable job of it. These days, a lot of the students who go abroad saying they're going to study look decent enough, but they're full of bullshit and good for nothing when they come back."

He blathered on complaining about this and that before finally saying, "You must feel pretty lonely having to sleep alone from now on. These days the police are really sharp, so you don't need to worry about thieves or anything like that, but you're still a woman and weaker of heart than a man would be, so you might be feeling a bit afraid? I always make the rounds of the house two or three times before I sleep, but I can't stay up the whole night like an old night watchman. Ha ha ha."

So Kyŏngja said politely, "Don't worry about me. There's nothing for you to worry about."

And her father-in-law falteringly said, "You're just saying that to be polite, how could I not think of you and how could I possibly say that I'm not concerned? I'm really worried about you."

While prattling on in this way, Hwang Ch'amsŏ had been carefully judging Kyŏngja's reaction and in the end finally worked up the courage to sit down, so that it was late in the night by the time he finally returned to his own room. After that, Kyŏngja's father-in-law would come up and wander around the outside of Kyŏngja's rooms several times a night, dragging his cane behind him, and sometimes he even sat down on the porch and talked to Kyŏngja before going. Late one night, Kyŏngja was having trouble sleeping, while the crystal-clear moonlight was streaming down through the branches of a paulownia and a strong westerly wind was shaking the trees in the woods. There was a chill in the air, and the sound of the insects lamenting fall in its passing pricked the ache which Kyŏngja felt within her breast, and her longing for her husband became especially intense, and she thought to herself, Aigu, *autumn has nearly passed and the weather is growing cold, how must my husband be suffering in that foreign land? The thought of it's enough to overwhelm me with worry here, so far from where he is!*

Kyŏngja wanted to calm herself with some music, so she went over to the organ, opened it, and played a rousing song. Then her father-in-law came and sat on the end of the porch and said, "Dear, the sound of that organ is far nicer than any Chosŏn music."

When he spoke up, Kyŏngja stopped her playing and greeted him, and then he continued with a laugh, "Keep playing, I'll just sit here and listen for a bit and then go."

With no choice but to continue, Kyŏngja resumed playing, but as she did so, her father-in-law slowly crept up beside her at the organ. Then, as though he was enjoying the music, he said, "Dear, why don't you teach me how to play a bit. I'm bored of singing, and have nothing else to occupy my time. I think it would be fun to learn the organ."

[Kyŏngja said.] "I'll teach you as much as I know, but it's not something that you can learn right away."

"Well now, you can't get full after drinking a single glass of wine now, can you? Just teach me a little every day." [Her father-in-law replied.]

Then he brought up a stool, sat down beside Kyŏngja, and said, "So what do I need to learn first? Why don't you come a little closer and show me?"

When he said this, it was finally more than Kyŏngja could stand, so she stood up and backed away from him. Without missing a beat, he laughed and said, "There's no reason for you to be uncomfortable, so just come back over here by me and show what I need to do. Why won't you come and sit next to your father?"

Kyŏngja was so flustered that she just stood where she was without saying a word. Then, even though he knew it was wrong, her father-in-law came over to her and grabbed her wrist, saying, "Come sit with me, I said. Why are you just standing there like a stranger when your father is calling you? Ha ha ha."

This was of course a very naughty thing of him to do, so Kyŏngja shook her wrist free, and said politely, "That's not right." But her father-in-law began acting even more strangely.

"Not right? What's not right? What's so wrong about your father asking you to come sit next to him and teach him how to play the organ? Come over here. Come over!"

Then, even though his daughter-in-law was trying to avoid him, he grabbed her wrist again and pulled roughly.

Often, when family harmony breaks down, all sorts of strange things begin to happen. Hwang Ch'amsŏ was a foolish man, with no sense of boundaries and no discretion, so when he saw his daughter-in-law's beauty, he was immediately smitten. He sent his son off to Tokyo so that he would be far away, and from the day his son left he entertained all sorts of brutish thoughts in that dark heart of his, and looked up to the top of the hill and plotted. His actions now were part of that same scheme, and Kyŏngja recognized this. Kyŏngja straightened her face and said firmly, but politely, "Please, watch your manners. It's fine if you ask me to come sit next to you, but how could you lay a hand on your daughter-in-law? Even if I were your real daughter, it would be unthinkable of you to touch me."

Saying that, she shook her hand free, and moved away from him, but that scurrilous Hwang Ch'amsŏ chased after her as she fled. With one running away and the other chasing after her, anyone who saw the two of them would have thought that they were playing around and flirting.

Kyŏngja was embarrassed as could be and tried to keep away from her father-in-law, but right at that moment the sound of someone clearing her throat was heard coming from the garden. As soon as he heard this, Hwang Ch'amsŏ knew he had been caught being naughty and was so afraid that he made his escape, running straight out the front gate without even bothering to put on his shoes. And who should come up onto the porch then but Kyŏngja's mother-in-law. Discomfort was written across Kyŏngja's brows, and her mother-in-law said, looking at her, "What were you doing just now? Your hair is all undone."

Kyŏngja stood silently where she was, unable to say a word.

"I asked you, what were you doing just now with your father-in-law? Why can't you say anything? I've already seen what you were doing with my own eyes, so why can't you tell me?"

Kyŏngja could make no defense for herself, and she could find no excuses, all she could do was stand quietly and cry.

"When a home goes to ruin, who knows what sort of mischief there will be? I hadn't wanted to bring an educated girl into home as my daughter-in-law, but it seems that my family was already on the point of ruin for me to have taken a liking to a girl like you and allowed you to marry my son … Your husband's away, so you chase after your father-in-law? It's disgraceful. Does it even matter why it happened? That man's behavior is wrong, both as a father and as a husband." Then Kyŏngja's mother-in-law let out a great sigh and turned around, stepped down off the porch, and mused to herself, "Could it be that that dog knew how shamefully he was acting? He ran off without his shoes."

Then picking up the shoes, Kyŏngja's mother-in-law went back down to the main house.

As she had lain in bed, Hwang Ch'amsŏ's wife had heard the sound of Kyŏngja playing the organ, and was so pleased by it that she was going up to have a listen when she heard the sound of

Kyŏngja and Hwang Ch'amsŏ roughing around and laughing, and was certain that something fishy was going on. Kyŏngja was so upset and mortified by everything that it felt as though even if she were to pierce her breast and wash her heart clean with cool water it would never be clean again. She felt as though her heart were being torn to pieces, and no matter how she thought about it, there seemed to be no way to exculpate herself, and she spent that entire night so filled with worry that it seemed her insides were burning.

After witnessing that scene, Taesŏng's mother went back to her room and thought about the best way to deal with the situation, but was unable to think of any solution. She turned over several ideas in her mind and was unable to sleep a wink. In the morning she arose early, called Kyŏngja before her, and said, "Kyŏngja, dear, you've studied in a school, so you know a bit more than the average woman, don't you? And because of that, you should rightly be a role model for all women—so just how is it that you could do such a crude thing as you've done? That sort of thing won't just ruin you, it'll ruin my entire family. How could I possibly forgive you? It's wrong of me to chide you this way, but how could you wreck my home like this? But I don't want to be long winded. So what I want to say is, first, I made a mistake by bringing the wrong girl into my home. And second, because your father-in-law is such a flawed person, there's no need to discuss who is to blame. I'd like you to go back to your own home this very day, and never come into my sight again."

When Kyŏngja heard this, she was unable to even explain that she was innocent and that her father-in-law had been in the wrong. The heavens and earth seemed to be reeling, her sight darkened, and she had no idea what to do. But there was no way that she could just sit by while suffering such a vague, baseless accusation, so she politely told her mother-in-law of the events as they had occurred.

"Mother, how could you say such things? I may be immature and foolish, but how could I possibly have done the things you say

I've done? As for what happened last night, Father asked me to teach him the organ and sat down close to me. I thought of my honor and I told him as much as that it wouldn't be right of me to do so—and I certainly did none of the things you've accused me of. Mother, please don't suspect me, and please don't say such things anymore."

Taesŏng's mother knew that her husband, Hwang Ch'amsŏ, had no sense of honor and that he always acted ridiculous in everything he did, so she suspected that he did not know how awkward his daughter-in-law would feel about his asking her to teach him the organ, and also that Kyŏngja had likely rebuked him.

"You know, you could very well be telling the truth. There's no way that you could have actually done those things, is there? Your father-in-law is rather lacking in sense, so be aware of that in the future. I spoke too strongly earlier without really knowing what happened. *Aigu*, there are really all sorts of scoundrels in the world. You can go back to your room now, and put your mind at ease," Taesŏng's mother said, as she comforted her daughter-in-law and sent the girl back to her rooms at the top of the hill. Taesŏng's mother then called in her husband and confronted him with what he had done.

"What in the world were you thinking? No matter how much of a rascal a person is, there have got to be limits. Did you really not know how uncomfortable you would make your daughter-in-law feel? You're over fifty now and an old man, and it's time for you to develop some sense, so what were you trying to do? You need to think about what awful things people would say if rumors about what happened last night were to get out. A mistake like that could ruin our family. Were you really so desperate for an organ teacher that you had to ask your daughter-in-law to teach you? You need to start acting more respectfully toward your children."

Hwang Ch'amsŏ became hopping mad as soon as he heard that and scolded his wife, "What was so wrong about what I did? In the civilized world of today, why should there be any worry if

I ask my daughter-in-law to teach me the organ? And what's all this about my ruining our family? You're the one who keeps making up this nonsense about the ruination of our family—so who are you to tell me that if other people start speaking ill of our family we'll be ruined? When the hen starts to crow, that's when the family is ruined! So stop your blathering and just keep your mouth shut."

Hwang Ch'amsŏ's wife was so stunned that she was unable to say anything, and instead just gave up and tried to placate her husband by saying what he wanted to hear. If there hadn't been any other incidents after that, they could have continued along and become a stable family, but when discord comes to a family, all sorts of strange things happen. After acting as though he was in the right and becoming incensed, Hwang Ch'amsŏ spent the entire day lying in his room and turning away visitors, and seemed to be extremely angry for some reason. Then, that night, he summoned his lackey, the servant Kyŏngch'ŏn, and said to him, "Kyŏngch'ŏn, tell the young mistress that I would like to see her."

Kyŏngch'ŏn was just a servant and was only doing what his master had told him to do when he went up to the top of the hill and said, "The master has asked that the young mistress come down for a moment to the master's room."

Kyŏngja was trying to be very cautious, and she was also a bit suspicious of what her father-in-law might have called her for. She thought to herself, *What could my father-in-law possibly want of me at this hour? Even if he has something to say, he should have sent a female servant and called me to the main room, not sent a male servant to bring me to his own room. This is quite peculiar, so what should I do?*

She did not have time to think about it carefully, so she pretended to be sick as an excuse, "Ah, I've suddenly got an excruciatingly painful stomachache. Tell him that I'll see him as soon as my stomach settles down a little."

Hwang Ch'amsŏ was so angry that he sent his servant a second and a third time, yelling at his servant in a terrifying voice, "How can she refuse to come when her father calls her? She's not on her deathbed, so how dare she disobey my orders? I have something urgent to say to her, so tell her to come at once!"

Kyŏngja knew that even if she were suffering from some illness she would be expected to come if her parents called, and she thought to herself, *Well, as long as I keep my wits about me, what could possibly happen?*

And, *Even if something does happen, I can always call Mother and ask her to intermediate.*

Having steeled her nerves, Kyŏngja went down to her father-in-law's room, but did not go inside and instead stood off to a corner of the porch. As soon as he saw her, Hwang Ch'amsŏ just laughed, and said to his servant, "Alright, Kyŏngch'ŏn, you may go now."

After sending the servant away, he continued, "Why didn't you come when your father called you? Ha ha ha. Why are you being like this? Anyhow, the reason that I called you down here is because your mother was going on about some nonsense this morning, and I wanted to ask you about it. Why in the world won't you just come inside? Come inside and let's have a little talk."

And then, without another word, he grabbed Kyŏngja's wrist to pull her inside.

Kyŏngja was shocked by this and said sternly, "That's not right. Let me go and then we can talk. Let me go!"

But Hwang Ch'amsŏ ignored her pleas and pulled her into the room with absolutely no regard for decency. He said, "Your father told you to come in, so how dare you talk back? Dear, your mother suspects you. It's only natural that since she suspects you, she'll accuse you. It doesn't matter if you're innocent and falsely blamed, or whether you're guilty and rightly accused; either way, it's the same for you!"

From his words and his actions, it was apparent that he was not in his right mind.

Kyŏngja pleaded with him, "Father, what are you doing? Are you going senile, what is all this? Please listen to me for just a moment. The thing which makes man special amongst all the animals is his moral clarity, so if you transgress morally, then how can you be properly called a man? How are your thoughts so muddled that you keep trying to do these sorts of things?"

But having reached the state he was in, there was no chance of Hwang Ch'amsŏ hearing a word she said.

"Hmph. What sort of nonsense is that? Do you think I don't know what I'm doing is wrong? I know, but since I'm going to be blamed whether I've actually wronged you or not ..."

In the midst of Kyŏngja and Hwang Ch'amsŏ's struggle, a voice boomed out like a clap of thunder.

"You scoundrel! What is this? Are all *yangban* as degenerate as this? Even though I'm nothing more than a low-born son-of-a-bitch working in your home as a servant, I would never do a thing such as this. You act like some important official and wear that horsehair cap on your head, but then you force yourself on your virtuous daughter-in-law? Take this, you bastard! I quit!"

It was the servant, Kyŏngch'ŏn. He thought it was extremely peculiar for his master to summon the young mistress out of the blue, and so he peeked in to see what was happening. When he saw how despicable Hwang Ch'amsŏ's behavior was, he was so filled with moral indignation that he could not stand it anymore, and he ran into the room. As he dashed into the room, a six-sided cudgel flashed in his hand, and with it he gave Hwang Ch'amsŏ two good strikes to the head. Fire flashed in Hwang Ch'amsŏ's eyes, and he yelled out, "*Aigu, aigu,* what treachery is this? There's a thief in the house! A thief! ..."

Then he dropped to the floor unconscious, bleeding profusely from where he was struck. Kyŏngja was in a panic, and scolded Kyŏngch'ŏn, "What have you done! It was only a quarrel!"

He replied, "If a person isn't careful, this is liable to happen to them. I wish you a long life. And with this, I quit."

And then he made a hasty getaway. That night, Hwang Ch'amsŏ's wife had been unable to sleep because she was so concerned about her husband's indiscretions. So when she heard the sounds of a scuffle and yells of "*Aigu! Aigu!*" coming from the next room, she was terribly surprised and came dashing in to discover her husband covered in blood, lying unconscious on the floor, with her daughter-in-law Kyŏngja standing next to him. Hwang Ch'amsŏ's wife had no idea what had just happened and asked Kyŏngja, "What is this? Speak up. Tell me what happened to your father-in-law and what you are doing here. What is the reason for all of this?"

Kyŏngja was unable to reply at first, and it was only after a great deal of hesitation that she said, "I don't really know myself. I heard a sudden, strange noise and came down to look, and this is what I found. But I saw Kyŏngch'ŏn running out the courtyard gate."

Taesŏng's mother thought about this for a moment, and then said, "Even if you don't say another word, I think I know what happened here. From the fact of you being here, and your having said that Kyŏngch'ŏn was the one who did this, I think I can guess. Kyŏngch'ŏn may be just a servant, but he has never been one to stand for injustice, so when he saw what your father-in-law was doing he wouldn't have just stood idly by. It would be no great loss if your father-in-law died, but I can't stand to see him die this way. First, help me send him to the hospital, then try to get some sleep as you won't be able to serve as a witness to what happened here." Taesŏng's mother then hurriedly called a rickshaw and took her husband to the hospital.

Kyŏngja went back to her rooms and thought to herself. *Whoever is to blame, there's no way I'll be able to show myself before another person again. How can I possibly face my husband when he returns?*

She wanted nothing more than to forget about the world, and with no hope that she would have any chance to exonerate herself, she decided to end her own life. She tied a towel about her neck, but she could not die without seeing her mother one more time and explaining the injustice of her situation. After she did that then she would do what she would, but for the time being she undid the towel from about her neck. How must she have been feeling then!

Taesŏng's mother wrote her son a long letter that very night and sent it off before summoning Kyŏngja the next day. She said, "Kyŏngja, listen carefully to what I have to say. From this moment, you are no longer a part of my family. I don't want to talk anymore about who is right and who is wrong; all I want is for the connection between you and my family to end, so I'll keep this short. I have already written your husband a letter, and whether you see the reply or not, from this day forth, you are no longer married. So, leave quickly and go back to your old home."

How must Kyŏngja have felt when she heard that? It was as though the sky were tumbling down upon her, and she cried until she was blind with tears. It was hopeless to try to explain at that point, for even if she tried to resist it would be no use! Filled with more than enough bitterness to last a lifetime, she went crying back to her mother's house in Inch'ŏn.

Hwang Ch'amsŏ had his banged-up head treated in the emergency room, and was well again within a week, but it turned out that more than his skull had cracked. He had gone completely out of his mind. He was behaving very oddly, jabbering on nonsensically and laughing erratically, so that upon examining him the doctor declared him insane and committed him to a mental hospital. Hwang Ch'amsŏ's mental disorder did not begin with his hit to the head: it had actually begun before he sent Taesŏng to Tokyo, but because he had always been so foolish, no one in his home had even dreamt that he was becoming mentally deranged. Even his sending Taesŏng to Tokyo had been a symptom of his disease—how could someone who hated the idea of a modern education so much even conceive of sending his son abroad to study? He was not in his right mind then, and it was his disease that led him to send Taesŏng to Tokyo. And could there possibly be any father who would behave so beastly toward his daughter-in-law? His actions toward her had also been the product of his mental disorder, but his wife had no idea about any of this and sent away her innocent daughter-in-law.

But how could Taesong's mother have known that her husband's mental disorder had begun so long before? She had no idea that the storms and waves that had borne down on her family were all the result of that disease, and had thought that he had gone crazy as a result of damage to his brain from being struck twice on the head by Kyŏngch'ŏn. She had even reported Kyŏngch'ŏn to the police, but by the time she had done so he was already far away and there was no way they could catch him. This enraged her beyond measure, and if she had only been able to catch him, she would have taken his life with her own hands.

After saying farewell to Kyŏngja, Taesŏng had gone to Tokyo, where he found a room at the Boenkan in Iida-chō, Kojimachi-ku, and prepared to enter university by enrolling in the preparatory program at Meiji University. Taesŏng was enjoying his studies, but there was not a moment when he did not think of Kyŏngja: if he had but a quiet moment to himself it was as though she were beside him, and all that he heard was her voice, and all that he saw was her face, and his brain was filled with nothing but thoughts of her. He would spend the day accompanied by her memory, and his nights were lit by dreams of her. One day, he returned home from school and was so overcome by thoughts of her that he was unable to study. He leaned on the railing staring vacantly at the blue, cloudless sky and thought to himself, *Ah, I can't keep going on like this! I came here to study, but if useless things like these distract me so much that I'm unable to study, how will I ever be able to go home and face my parents and Kyŏngja? I won't be able to devote my energy to my studies as long as I'm so preoccupied.*

Then he went back into his room, opened a book, and began to study, but just then one of the girl servants came in with a letter and said, "A letter has come to you from home."

Taesŏng thought that it was a letter from Kyŏngja and was excited to get it, but it was not from Kyŏngja, it was from his mother. He said to himself, "How is it that Kyŏngja has not sent me a single letter? If she thinks of me even half as much as I think of her, I'm certain that she would write! *Aigu*, she's being so distant. No, that can't be it—she wouldn't act like that. She must be ill, or something else must have happened so that she can't write me. I'm sure she would have written if she were well. I'm sure I'll find out what's happened if I just read Mother's letter."

He opened the letter, and this is what it said,

> After we sent you off on your journey, I was very worried about whether or not you had arrived safely, so I was as pleased as could be when we received your letter. In the time you've been gone, however, terrible misfortune has come to our home, so shameful that I cannot tell you all of it. I'm sure that what I have to tell you will come as a great shock, but there is no way for me to keep it from you, so I'll tell you in brief. I beg you to not be surprised and to try to be understanding so that you can focus on your studies. There is no way of estimating the quality of a person's heart, but who would have ever known that Kyŏngja would be so deceitful?

When Taesŏng reached this point in the letter, the color drained from his face, and he thought. *Aigu, what is this? What could Kyŏngja have done that Mother would call her deceitful?*

He was unable to look at the letter and sat numbly for a moment before he resumed reading,

> You thought that Kyŏngja was a woman of impeccable virtue, but isn't it even worse to be taken in by a person that seemed so trustworthy! I also thought that a girl of such grace would make for a kind and virtuous daughter-

in-law, and it is a shame that that is not what she turned out to be. But she has already passed on to the other world, and …

When Taesŏng got to this point, he grew faint, and the characters of the letter swirled before his eyes like so many sesame seeds, and his chest grew so tight that he felt he was on the verge of passing out. He threw the letter down, and laying his head on the desk tried to calm his heart, *How could Kyŏngja be dead? Am I dreaming? How in the world did she die? I need to read the rest of the letter.*
Then he continued to read.

There's no reason for me to tell you of her sins at length, but I'll tell you generally what happened. Please try not to be too dispirited by what I tell you so that you can focus on your studies. When I was deciding the matter of your marriage, I was very opposed to your marrying an educated girl, but somehow you ended up marrying an educated girl despite that. Anyhow, only a few days after you left, I discovered that Kyŏngja was carrying on a foul liaison with Kyŏngch'ŏn. Kyŏngch'ŏn ran off, and Kyŏngja was so ashamed that she took her own life. Can you believe such a horrid thing could happen in this world? Who could have dreamt that Kyŏngja would do such a thing? I suppose that this is the sort of thing that happens when one's family goes to ruin. But what could we do at that point? Without any rumors about what happened getting out, we quietly held a funeral for Kyŏngja, but then your father's rage about the whole thing festered into illness. Even after reading this, however, don't worry about a single thing except for your studies: you can comfort your aging parents after you return. A man may experience these sorts of things and more during his time in this world. If you just study hard and return with a Ph.D. or a bachelor's, I'm sure you'll have no trouble finding a woman to marry. Anyhow, don't waste another thought on that filthy woman—just do well in your studies. Know that if you read this and try to return home, I'll disown you, so think about it carefully and study or do whatever else you might want to do. I'll stop now, and write the rest to you in my next letter.

> Day / Month / Year
> Your mother.

Taesŏng's mother tricked him with this lie because there was no way that she could avoid telling him what had happened in their home or go without breaking off the family's ties to Kyŏngja, but if she had given him a truthful account of the beastly things his father and Kyŏngja had done, he would have been overcome with shame, and so she told him instead that Kyŏngja had been unfaithful to him with Kyŏngch'ŏn. She told him that Kyŏngja had died out of fear that Taesŏng would write to Kyŏngja and discover her lie, which would lead to a break in the trust between mother and son. Also, to make sure that he would not return home after reading the letter, she told him that if he returned home not only would he be unable to study, there would be other consequences as well—which is why she had sternly cautioned him: "Know that if you read this and return home, I'll disown you."

Taesŏng was overcome and sat dazed, lamenting his fate, "Is there no one in this world who can be trusted? I had believed in Kyŏngja to the point that I even thought of her as almost a reincarnation of Queen Tairen, but how could anyone have known this calamity would happen! What is to become of me? Sometimes shocking things occur in this world, but how furious my parents must have been when they discovered what had happened! I want to run home and comfort them right away, but my mother told me in her letter not to come. How, though, am I supposed to be able to face anyone again with this shame? How is a man in my position supposed to be able to do anything, much less study? My mother told me over and over not to be dispirited and to focus on my studies, but you can only study if your heart is in it, how am I supposed to study when the characters are swirling before my eyes and I am unable to read? I will leave here, tour the countries of the world, and then die."

Taesŏng's lament had become a resolve to tour the world; and, without a moment to lose, he set off right then and there. He called the servant boy to settle the bill for his rooms, packed his bags, and then left immediately for the train station. On the way, he sent off a letter to his mother, telling her that he would be going to America to study, and then he boarded the train to Yokohama. It seemed as though Taesŏng was to become a world traveler.

Kyŏngja returned to her mother's home, bemoaning the misfortune of being a beautiful woman. Her mother, having no idea what had happened, thought it strange that her daughter had returned home so suddenly and said, "What are you doing here again? A woman needs to find pleasure in life with her in-laws, so it's no good if she visits her parents' home too often. You were here less than a month ago, so what are you doing back again so soon?"

Kyŏngja was unable to say a word and simply wrapped her arms around one of the pillars of the house, unable to control her tears. Her mother thought it even more peculiar for her to be crying like that and said, "Why are you crying? You did something wrong and got kicked out by your parents-in-law, didn't you? What did you do? They say that if a girl wants to get along with her in-laws she needs to stay mute for the first three years, but you were so used to having your way with your mother that you forgot to watch your manners with your in-laws, didn't you? Why did you come back? Just tell me and get it off your chest."

Kyŏngja just barely managed to say, "If I had done something wrong, would I be crying this way? I seem to be fated to suffer!" Then she continued sobbing.

"So you really were kicked out? Tell me straight. Did they tell you to leave?"

"..."

"Why don't you say something? Did your mother-in-law tell you to leave?"

Kyŏngja reluctantly responded with a single word: "Yes."

"You really must have done something awful, then. You would have had to do something exceptionally bad to get kicked out. Something shameful. After a girl has been kicked out by her in-laws, she's ruined, and there's nothing she can do with her life. But what did you do to get kicked out? Say something!"

There was no way that Kyŏngja could say what really happened, even to her own mother, so after hesitating for a moment, she said, "Whether I actually did something wrong or not, the result either way is that I end up like this, so what point is there in talking about it? If I had done something to deserve getting kicked out, I wouldn't be this bitter about it!"

"What is that supposed to mean? What sort of hateful in-laws would reduce a girl who's done nothing wrong to this state? What in the world happened? What could it possibly be that you can't even tell your own mother?"

"You'll find out eventually. Is it really so urgent that you know?"

"What? How could a mother see her daughter in this sort of state and not want to know what happened? Tell me."

Then Kyŏngja, speaking with difficulty through her tears, said, "It's all because of my father-in-law."

"So if it's all because of your father-in-law, then you must have done something to upset him? Are you saying that he ran you out without any reason?"

"You'll find out eventually. I just can't bear to say it."

"Strange. What could be so bad that you can't even tell your own mother?"

"It's not like that. My mother-in-law suspected my father-in-law, so she kicked me out. Can you believe that?"

When Kyŏngja's mother heard this, her face flushed red with anger and her body shook with rage as she said, "How is that possible! That family has some serious problems. How could parents entertain vulgar thoughts about their daughter, and then kick her out because they suspected her? How could a disaster like this happen? We should go to the court and have them tried. But it's no use in talking about it. This all happened because your husband isn't here. If he had been here, how could something like this have possibly occurred? There's nothing to be done about it now, though. There's no use in arguing over right and wrong with such ignorant people, and unless your husband comes back and sets things right, there'll be no fixing it. Come inside now, dear."

Kyŏngja was filled with such shame and rage that she wanted to end her life right then and there, but she thought to herself. *If I die, then I will never be able to prove my innocence. But if my husband comes home, then he will know that I've been wrongly accused, so no matter the state I'm in, I must wait for him to return.*

With that, Kyŏngja stopped crying, followed her mother into the house, and took out the ink stone to write her husband a letter explaining to him the awful truth of the matter.

Kyŏngja mailed her letter to her husband, and waited day and night for his reply, but there was no response or even news from him, and time passed cruelly like the spinning of an automobile wheel, and before she knew it one icy morning she heard goose calls overhead. She was unable to wait any longer, she was curious why her husband hadn't replied, and she was growing suspicious— and all of these things were nagging at her heart. Later the thought of Taesŏng's promise to her welled up like a spring after the monsoon rains, but after that hope had run its course, she was filled with the misery of her condition, and she would at times look out upon the blackness of the sea and sky and pass the time with sighs. Who was there who could understand the depths of Kyŏngja's sorrow? None but Kyŏngja herself and her mother. If Kyŏngja had acted on the feelings pent up in her breast, she would not have endured another day of life, but the thought of her aged mother prevented her from doing the deed, so she kept the great, surging tide of her grief locked inside her mind, and lived her life day by day. What a state she must have been in! But Kyŏngja had always been a woman of refinement, so she never showed her worry on the outside, and spent many long years devotedly caring for her mother. One day, the letter she had sent to her husband returned to her, and on the envelope was written: "Unable to locate recipient. Return to sender." Seeing her letter come back to her after so long, she again grew curious and thought to herself. *Aigu, what could be the reason for this? If it was returned because the recipient couldn't be located, does that mean that my husband moved to a different inn since I last heard from him, or maybe that has he come home? If his address was known, there's no way that my letter would have come back like this. What could have possibly happened? Am I so cursed by fortune that everything I do is to turn out this way? Aigu, the things a person must endure!*

She then wrote to her aunt in Seoul to find out the whereabouts of her husband, and her aunt reported back to her, "Since the fiasco that took place in the Hwang household I haven't dared to go back there—but it seems that not even Taesŏng's family know what's become of him."

After hearing that, Kyŏngja's worry deepened, a burning wrath sprang up inside her breast and she was struck with a gradually worsening illness. Because it was a malady born of rage, the symptoms were not particularly severe, but as the days and months passed, it penetrated deep into her bones. She neither ate nor drank anything besides cold water, and her appearance was completely changed from her earlier beauty as she wasted away to skin and bone. As a year passed, then two, then three, then four, her illness worsened and there was no hope for a cure, and she was unable to see even a glimpse of Taesŏng, who she had wanted to see at least one more time in this life. Reduced to that condition, she knew that there was no hope for her, and that another day spent in the world would only mean another day of suffering, while another two days in the world would mean just another two days of suffering, and so on until her last day on this earth. Even if quitting the world before her aged mother was a terrible violation of a daughter's duty, her mind was overwhelmed with worry and despair, and she could think of nothing other than departing this world as quickly as possible. One day, unable to bear the feelings that filled her mind, she decided to take her own life. She told her mother that she was going for a walk in the Japanese Park, and then headed toward the coast. The feeling that filled Kyŏngja's heart as she did this was beyond description. After the first step, she turned and looked back at her mother, and it was as though she would cry tears of blood, but she held back, and put the other foot forward, but she felt as though she would faint, so she stood clinging forlornly to the post of the front gate. Kyŏngja's mother had no idea of the thought that was lurking in her daughter's breast, but the sight of Kyŏngja's skeletal frame was so pitiable she choked up with tears as she called out, "Kyŏngja, Kyŏngja, how can someone as weak as you are possibly go to the park? The doctor did say that fresh air would be good for you, but how will you make it to the park if you don't even have the strength to make it out the front gate? Knock it off and come back inside. The walk and the air would be too much for you. So just stop it."

These words pierced Kyŏngja's breast and she no longer wished to go, but she knew that no matter when she died that her dying before her mother and the extinguishing of the flame within her breast would be the same—and so there was no need for her to stop what now she had resolved to do, so she turned around to face her mother and said, "Not at all. Don't worry about me. I'll be back in a little bit."

And with that, she continued moving in the direction of the park but wavered with every step between going back to her home and going toward the sea. Why was it that this invalid found her walk to the beach so difficult, having already made her choice for death? Not only do people feel tremendous sadness over the thought of leaving the world, there is also no way for them to deny or forget the love they feel for those around them. In the bleak state she was in, and having decided to die, Kyŏngja put no great value upon her own life, but there was something about the sight of her mother that prevented her from moving forward, so that finally she was left vacillating between her home and the sea. After travelling for several hours down that difficult and conflicted path, she finally came to the Japanese Park. Sitting down in front of the fountain, she thought of the conversation she had had with her husband there and her breast was again filled sorrow, so that she was lost in her grief and finally overcome by the cruel feeling within her breast. She bit down on her finger and wrote out a letter in blood that she sent to her in-laws, said a prayer for her mother's long life, and then threw herself from the *Shikishima* coast into the endless expanse of the waves. How pitiable you are, poor sufferer! If there had been no one to save her as she left her poor mother and plunged into the water without having again seen the husband that she loved so much, she certainly would have been dragged down forever into the dragon king's palace beneath the waves, and her wretched spirit so distressed it would be unable to ascend to heaven. But a human life is one of the most precious things in the world, and even in that cursed moment, there was a glimmer of hope. As soon as the ripples from Kyŏngja's splash had beat against the shore, everything was again calm and it seemed as though there was no one around—but then Kyŏngja's final hope arrived in the form of a boat that came darting in from nowhere.

The boat came rushing over, and one of the men aboard it heard Kyŏngja gasping for air and called out, "*Aigu!* Someone has jumped in!"

They hurriedly grabbed her, pulled her into the boat, laid her in the prow and then began talking coarsely amongst themselves, saying, "Well isn't this a fancy one! What could have upset such a fancy girl so much that she'd throw herself into the sea? I was the one who fished her out, so I'll be taking her with me."

One of the people on the boat, however, did not say a word, and looked carefully at Kyŏngja's face before saying, "*Aigu*, what happened to you?"

And then, "Boys, stop that jabbering. This girl is the daughter-in-law of a *yangban* family in Seoul. You lot wouldn't know, but this is a girl who is truly worthy of our pity. How awful things must have become for her to do a thing like this? Our coming here, however, is a bit of great good fortune."

Then shaking the body of the sick girl, "Ma'am. Ma'am, wake up. What in the world happened to you?"

The two men who had been chattering on earlier carried on with their joking, and one of them said, "That's a vile one, he is. Hey, do you really think you'll fool me with that? Whatever happens, know that I'm going to be taking her home with me!"

Then Kyŏngja came to her senses and looking up at the man who had called her "Ma'am," said, "*Aigu*, could it be? Is it really Kyŏngch'ŏn?"

She was unable to say another word, and tears began to well up in her eyes. It really was the same Kyŏngch'ŏn who had struck down Hwang Ch'amsŏ and then disappeared without a trace. Kyŏngch'ŏn had no idea that Ch'amsŏ's mistreatment of his daughter-in-law was due to mental derangement, and seeing that mistreatment had caused moral indignation to rise up within him up to the very tip of his topknot, and it was because of that righteous anger that he had struck Hwang Ch'amsŏ and then run off. After that, he had wandered around here and there, working as a laborer and doing all sorts of odd jobs, before finally finding a place with an Inch'ŏn shipping company, on a steamer called the *Taebung-hwan*. He had been living the life of a sailor for several years, and that night he and a couple of his mates just happened to be heading to *Shikishima* for a drink together when they rescued Kyŏngja.

When he saw Kyŏngja coming to, he cried sorrowfully and said in a voice choked up with tears, "Ma'am, how could you do this? How could you do a thing like this? Though I'm sure you haven't heard anything of me, I occasionally heard the news with you, and even though you might be suffering now, if only your husband returns it will be as though spring has come again and everything will be set right. How could you have even thought of doing something so rash? Did you really commit some sin? Someday you're sure to be exonerated—so how could you do something like this?"

Kyŏngja was completely bewildered by everything and just lay there like a dead woman. Kyŏngch'ŏn wrung the water out of her clothes, hefted her onto his back, and carried her to her mother's house in Mansŏktong. Kyŏngja's mother had looked for her everywhere in the Japanese Park, but was unable to find any trace and returned home, where she sat crying as Kyŏngch'ŏn came up to the house. She figured that Kyŏngja had killed herself, and she was beside herself with grief. When she saw Kyŏngja, drenching wet and being carried on the back of an unknown man, she was so happy and so startled that she leapt up to her daughter and, throwing her arms around her, said, "*Aigu*, so you've finally come to this! Just as I thought. Stupid, foolish girl! How could you leave your old mother and do a stupid thing like this?"

Kyŏngch'ŏn set Kyŏngja down off his back and said, "Ma'am, my name in Kyŏngch'ŏn. You don't know me, but I was a servant in Kyŏngja's home—though I did something wrong there, and had to run away. My crime was that I discovered the master of the house behaving crudely to the young lady here and became so angry that I gave him a beating right there on the spot. After that, I wandered around every which place, and by the grace of heaven I just happened to come across the young lady tonight, and I've never been so pleased in my life as that I was able to save her in time. At any rate, I hope she gets well soon."

As soon as Kyŏngja's mother heard that, she knew that although Kyŏngch'ŏn was a person of the lowest class, he was truly a man of honor, and she was deeply impressed and showered him with praise. After asking him his address, she gave him a drink and sent him off. Kyŏngja was already deathly ill when she did what she did, and it was only natural that her illness worsened afterward. Not only was she delirious the night she was carried back from the coast by Kyŏngch'ŏn, her symptoms worsened the next day so that it seemed she wouldn't be able to cling to life any longer. Finally, after agonizing a great deal over what to do, Kyŏngja's mother decided to check her into Inch'ŏn Hospital.

Despite her condition, Kyŏngja never stopped thinking of her husband, and she would carry her love for him within her breast all her life. As for Taesŏng, after he got his mother's letter, he ran away from everything and set off to see the countries of the world. He had gone immediately down to Yokohama where he boarded a steamer bound for America. This was why he was unable to receive Kyŏngja's letter, and why his family had heard no news from him. He left in anger, but when he saw the grand sights of a civilized nation, he was filled with sadness over the realization of how foolish the people of Chosŏn were, and he thought to himself, *How can the people of Chosŏn become like the people here?*

Since he was already in America, he decided that he would take some of that civilized knowledge with him when he returned, so that he might help in some small way the progress of civilization in his country. He enrolled in the medical college at Washington University, and in his heart he planned his future. *I will become a modern Bian Que or Hua Tuo, and return to my home country where I will aid my compatriots and pass down medical knowledge of great sagacity to future generations!*[14]

Then without wasting a single moment, he diligently began his studies. ~

---

14. Bian Que (扁鵲 d. 310 BCE) is acclaimed as the first Chinese physician; Hua Tuo (華佗 d. 208 CE) was a renowned physician of the Eastern Han dynasty (東漢 25–220 CE).

⁓ 4

IM KKŎKCHŎNG

Introduction

Hong Myŏng-hŭi (洪命憙 1888–1968), pen name Pyokch'o, is a controversial figure in studies of twentieth-century literature and politics in South Korea. He was born into a prestigious family that had held powerful positions in the Chosŏn dynasty. Hong received a traditional education as a child in a *yangban* home and is said to have been able to compose poetry in Literary Chinese by the age of eight. In 1901 he moved to Seoul where he started his studies in the modern sciences (新學問). By 1906 he had moved to Japan where he enrolled at Taesei Middle School. However, his experience in Japan was not good as he suffered greatly from discrimination.

Seeing how his country was falling under Japan's control he returned home in early 1910. After the annexation later that year his father, Hong Pŏmsik (洪範植 ?–1910), who was Magistrate (郡守) of Kŭmsan county at the time, took his own life as protest. With this, Hong's path as an anti-Japanese nationalist was set in stone. In the following years, Hong would actively resist Japan's rule and thus be incarcerated a number of times. When not under arrest, he managed newspapers, directed schools, and worked in clandestine, anti-Japan organizations.

After liberation in 1945, Hong worked to avoid the right-left split and find a neutral ground for Korea to stand upon. He participated in several different political organizations, and most notably the North-South Joint Conference held in P'yŏngyang in 1948. He remained in the North from this time forward and held high positions in the North's government until his death in 1968.[1] As a result of this choice, Hong and his literary works were a taboo topic in South Korea until the mid-1980s.

In terms of his literary accomplishments, *Im Kkŏkchŏng*, a historical novel based on the life of the Chosŏn era brigand leader of the same name, is certainly Hong's finest work. Im Kkŏkchŏng (Im Kkŏkchŏng 林巪正, 1504–1562) was the most famous among a number of rebels who rose up against the Chosŏn government in the turbulent years of the mid-sixteenth century. A combination of corruption, increasing taxation and poor governmental administration led many of the peasantry to join brigands and make their livelihood through pillaging. Im's group was active from 1559–1562 in the northern Hwanghae Province before being put down by government forces. Such a tale of bravery and contesting a corrupt government certainly was something that appealed to Hong and his readers of the day.

Im Kkŏkchŏng is a lengthy work that was first serialized in the *Chosŏn ilbo* newspaper from November 21, 1928, through March 3, 1939, although there were gaps in the serialization due to Hong's circumstances such as incarceration; after the closure of the *Chosŏn ilbo* by the colonial government, a single installment was published in the literary magazine *Chogwang* 9 (朝光 Morning light) in October 1940. The novel was never concluded. It has since been published as a multivolume novel in both South and North Korea, most recently in the South by Sagyejŏl Publishers in 2008 as a ten-volume set. Other novels under the same title and featuring the same historic character have also been written by other writers.

Hong did use historic records for parts of his work; particularly, he utilized the so-called unofficial histories (野談) that contain much more colorful portrayals than do the official records.

---

1. The above is based, in part on Kang Young-Zu, "Hong Myŏng-hŭi: Korea's Finest Historical Novelist," *Korea Journal* 39:4 (Winter 1999), 37–41.

As his novel focused on a member of the lowest social group, the plight of the people is central to the work. But beyond simply the poor and oppressed, it is also a novel where the characters are aware of and concerned with the state of the country which is greatly reflective of the period in which it was written.[2] Following is an excerpt from the novel.

***

2. Cho Tongil, *Han'guk munhak t'onsa* (The complete history of Korean literature) (Seoul: Chijik sanŏpsa, 1992), 5: 312–313.

❧ *Im Kkŏkchŏng* 임꺽정

Hong Myŏng-hŭi 홍명희

Translated by H. Jamie Chang
Annotated by Michael J. Pettid

...

The old monk and the strapping lad set out together. They traveled past Hüich'ŏn and Kang'gye, through Huch'ang and up along the river via Kalp'a-jin and Hyesan-jin, and arrived at the vicinity of Mount Paektu about a month after they left Yŏngbyŏn. Although they had traveled through stretches of uninhabited areas many times before on this trip, they had before them two hundred uninterrupted *ri* of unpopulated area until they reached the summit of Mount Paektu, so the lad packed over a *mal* of potatoes in the knapsack he carried.[1] The lad was not one to be alarmed by a tiger charging at him, or a bear attacking him, or a brutish Chinese army descending on him, but he couldn't help being awe-inspired by the vast forest for he had never seen one so expansive in his life. The forest was so densely occupied by trees that had never heard the sound of an axe that it was difficult to see the sky. There were towering trees reaching for the sky, rotten trees fallen over and sprawled out like bridges, trees and only trees all around them no matter how far they traveled without resting. It was as though they were swimming through a sea of trees. Had they lost their way, they would not have been able to find their way out in ten, twenty years.

---

1. A *ri* (里) is historically an indeterminate amount, but roughly translates to 393 meters. A *mal* is equivalent to 18 liters.

"This damned forest goes on forever," said the lad, following the monk.

"This is truly a great forest," said the monk walking ahead.

"I can't tell which way is north and which is south."

"Don't worry, we won't lose our direction. Look, somebody went ahead of us and left a trail." The monk pointed out a footprint stamped onto a bed of moss as he turned to look at the lad. The monk and the lad walked on through the forest, losing track of time, before they reached a wide clearing. There was a village shrine in the middle of the clearing.

"Whew, finally. That looks like a village shrine over there." "That is a village shrine. Let's break our journey there."

They walked up to the village shrine to find a woman kneeling inside. She was murmuring to herself, her palms pressed together and her forehead resting on her hands. She seemed to be saying a prayer.

The woman, startled by the sound of the lad clearing his throat, found them behind her and yelped, "Goodness!"

"Do not be frightened," said the old monk in a gentle voice. The woman gave the monk a pensive look, got up, and came out of the shrine.

The woman had salt-and-pepper hair and looked over fifty, but there remained traces of her former beauty on her wrinkled, gaunt face. The woman took a good look at the monk once more and then looked at the lad's face. The old monk, leaning on two canes, was dressed in black monk garb and a bamboo hat. He had prayer beads around his neck.

His goodness shone through. The lad with a heavy club and knapsack big enough to fit a person in it seemed fierce but not malicious. Calmer now, the woman began to talk to the monk.

"What brings you here?"

"We are on our way up Paektu-san."

"Which temple are you from, *taesa*?[2] Chabok Temple of Mount Ch'ŏnbong?"

---

2. *Taesa* (大師) was a title given to great monks—here it is an honorific greeting.

"No. I'm from Mount Myohyang."

"Where is Mount Myohyang?"

"It's in Yŏngbyŏn, P'yŏngan Province."

"P'yŏngan Province? You've come from far down south." The woman seemed to contemplate on something and then said, "My home is nearby. Why don't you break your journey here?"

The lad who had been standing in the back until then stepped forward and asked, "Where on earth are we?"

The woman replied, "Hŏhangnyŏng. Did you climb forty *ri* of the Hŏhangnyŏng heights without knowing where you were? This is Ch'ŏnwang-dang, the Heavenly King Shrine."

The monk and the lad followed the woman five *ri* through the forest hill next to the Heavenly King Shrine and arrived at a three-room log house. They went inside at the woman's invitation and looked around. There were pelts of wild animal fur all over the walls that it nearly seemed the wooden wall had been wallpapered with fur. There were tiger skin, bear skin, deer skin, and skin from all species of animals. The stench from wild animal pelts prickled their noses. The guests followed the host into the room and settled in.

The lad pointed at the pelts and asked, "How did you kill these animals?"

"The children did. How could I have hunted them?"

"Children?"

"I have a daughter and a son."

"Where are they now?"

"The siblings went out to hunt. They'll be back around dusk."

"Why do you live in such an isolated place?" he asked.

"It's a long story," the woman sighed. "Want to hear the gist of it?" she asked as she looked over at the old monk.

The woman was a magistrate's slave from Kapsan where she had fallen madly in love with another slave. When the new governor of Kapsan lusted after the woman and tried to force her into lying with him, the lovers eloped in the dead of night to a mountain village in Unch'ong where they built a hut and settled down.

Someone gave away their location to the authorities, and they would have been caught had it not been for another who alerted them of the situation beforehand. They then fled to this uninhabited place. The couple lived together for thirty years before the man died four years earlier, and now the single mother lived with her two children. Ch'ŏnwangdong, the son she had after praying at the Heavenly King Shrine, was sixteen, and his older sister, Unch'ong, was twenty-three. At first, the woman was not only lonely and frightened but also weary from all the hardship that she bawled like a baby when the man left the house to go hunting, but thirty years of woe had hardened her so that she did not feel the need to take the trouble of venturing back into civilization. She would have had no choice but to leave the woods to marry off her children, but she felt reluctant to leave her husband's grave, so she had been torn. She was in no rush to find her son a wife, but her daughter, now in her twenties, was of immediate concern.

The woman concluded the story of her life and circumstance thus: "I've raised my daughter to be so boyish I don't know if anyone will take her even if we moved to a village." As she told the monk her story, she studied the lad's face quite eagerly.

"Why hasn't your apprentice shaved his head?"

"He is not my apprentice. He was my pupil when I was a layperson."

"So the lad isn't a monk," she said, relieved that the lad wasn't a monk. The lad, perhaps oblivious, smiled and nodded. The woman began to interrogate the lad.

"Where are you from?"

"Yangju in Kyŏnggi Province."

"What's your family name and what's your first name?"

"My family name is Im and my first name is Kkŏkchŏng."

"How old are you?"

"Just now twenty."

"You're three years younger than my Unch'ong."

Kkŏkchŏng pictured a girl past her prime who is as tall as the

Four Heavenly Kings, with face as black as coal and hands like an ox harness hook, racing about like a wolf.

Kkŏkchŏng grinned and asked half in jest, "Do you want me as your son-in-law?"

Unch'ong's mother answered sincerely, "I would be blessed to have a son-in-law like you."

This prompted Kkŏkchŏng to change the subject: "Do you live only on meat from wild animals?"

"We have a field in back where we grow potatoes and plant corn,[3] and we also exchange pelts for crops."

"What about fabrics for clothes?"

"We get fabrics by exchanging goods, too."

"Where do you exchange goods?"

"Hyesan-jin, Kapsan-ŭp—anywhere. My Ch'ŏnwangdong is as quick as a deer. He can get to Hoeryŏng and back in three or four days, so exchanging goods isn't as difficult as before."

She then added, laughing, "I'm sorry I got carried away. You must be hungry."

She got up to go to the kitchen and returned with steamed potatoes and corn on a small table for the guests.

"Teacher, let's have a bite and travel another few dozen *ri* before we stop for the night."

"Well ..."

"Travel? You should spend the night here. Besides, Ch'ŏn-wangdong knows his way up the mountain like the back of his hand, so wouldn't it be nice to get directions from him?"

"We may be imposing on our host, but getting directions would be good."

"As you wish," Kkŏkchŏng replied to his teacher, not completely uninterested in what the siblings looked like.

The host and the two guests were peeling the skin off the boiled

---

3. This is historically inaccurate as both of these new world crops did not appear in Korea till much later than this period.

potatoes and scraping the kernels off the cob when a voice called out, "Mom, we're back!"

"They're back early today," said the mother, peering out. "Oh my, you brought back a big one," she said.

Banging and clopping, two children came running inside.

"Where did these strangers come from," said one of the children, looking shyly at the guests.

"I'm hungry," said the other child, grabbing the potatoes and corn in front of the guests with both hands.

"Give me some," said the child who had remained standing until then, and tried to snatch the food away.

"There's more over there," said the child clutching onto his food, not willing to share.

"Sit down and be quiet. We have guests here," said the mother, all but grabbing them by the nape and sitting them down herself.

They were dressed in the same color and looked similar, so it was difficult for someone seeing them for the first time to determine which one was Unch'ong and which was Ch'ŏnwangdong. However, if one looked closely, one could see some girlish features around the mouth and eyes on one of them.

"This one's Unch'ong," thought Kkŏkchŏng. She was not at all the way Kkŏkchŏng pictured her—as tall as the Four Heavenly Kings, with skin like coal, or with hands like an ox harness hook.

Ch'ŏnwangdong was mature and looked like he was eighteen or nineteen, and Unch'ong, looking around twenty, was only a little taller than her brother. The siblings took after their mother and had round, flat, pretty faces, which were tan but not dark, and their hands were rough with thick knuckles but not ugly to look at. Their eyes, clear through and through, were full of vitality, and their thin lips made them look sober when firmly closed.

"Want some potatoes?" asked Kkŏkchŏng, tossing a few potatoes at Unch'ong.

"Who said I want potatoes from you?" she said, turning away without picking them up.

Ch'ŏnwangdong, who was plopped down next to them said, "More for me." He put the potatoes between his legs and wolfed them down, barely peeling them.

Unch'ong hungrily watched her brother eat and then whined like a child, "Mom, I'm hungry."

"Very well, I'll steam some potatoes for you," said the mother who turned to the monk as she rose to her feet and laughed, "Who would take a girl over twenty who acts like that?"

"The siblings look like brothers," said the monk.

Hearing this Ch'ŏnwangdong said, "He says we're like brothers. Aren't we brothers?"

"He doesn't know what he's talking about," said Unch'ong, and they snickered together.

Ch'ŏnwangdong, and Unch'ong, too, soon became friendly with Kkŏkchŏng and began to talk to him.

"What did you catch today?"

"We caught a big *kŏmdungi* [black]. My brother chased it and I stabbed it."

"What's a *kŏmdungi*?"

"Do you want to go outside and see?" said Ch'ŏnwangdong, pulling Kkŏkchŏng by the hand as he got up.

"Me too," said Unch'ong, and followed them outside. Kkŏkchŏng was led outside to see a dead black bear stabbed in the head. He pointed at the blood on its head and asked, "What did you stab it with?"

"With this," said Unch'ong, lifting the spear that was standing nearby. "Have you ever caught a beast?" asked Unch'ong.

"No, I have not," Kkŏkchŏng replied.

"What kind of a man hasn't caught a beast?"

"Not all men know how to catch a beast."

At the sister and brother's teasing, Kkŏkchŏng said, "Do you want to go hunting with me?"

"What for? You don't know how to catch a beast," said Unch'ong, still teasing.

"We should see if he can catch one," said Ch'ŏnwangdong. "Sleep here tonight and we'll go tomorrow," and laughed, slapping Kkŏkchŏng on the back.

"Unch'ong, your potatoes are ready," called Unch'ong's mother from the room.

Unch'ong dashed into the house, and Kkŏkchŏng and Ch'ŏnwangdong followed her inside.

"If you call a bear a '*kŏmdungi*,' what do you call a tiger or a deer?" asked Kkŏkchŏng.

"We call tigers '*ŏllugi*' [patches] or '*padugi*' [spot] and we call deer with antlers '*ppudagwi*' [antlers]. Our dead father named them," said Ch'ŏnwangdong. "We should catch an *ŏllugi* when we go hunting," he added, smiling.

"*Ŏllugi*? You mean a tiger," Kkŏkchŏng laughed, too. He sat down next to Ch'ŏnwangdong and asked, "Do you have a sword at home?"

Unch'ong, who was sitting on the floor eating potatoes, picked up a small dagger next to him as if to ask, "You mean this?" Kkŏkchŏng shook his head.

"What sword?" asked Ch'ŏnwangdong.

"A long sword. A *hwando*."

"There's a long sword that belonged to Father. Should I look for it?" said Ch'ŏnwangdong, getting up.

"Stop making a fuss," scolded his mother, sitting him back down.

Ch'ŏnwangdong egged him on to stay another day to go hunting and playing with him in exchange for taking them sightseeing all the way to the top of Paektu-san. So the monk stayed at home with Unch'ong's mother, and Kkŏkchŏng went out hunting with the siblings. The three headed out after a good breakfast, Ch'ŏnwangdong leading the way with a spear in his hand, followed by Kkŏkchŏng with the *hwando* strapped to his side, followed by Unch'ong with a spear slung across her back. They walked through the forest for a while, passed Ch'ilsŏng Swamp, and entered a valley. They were traveling up and down valleys along the mountain ridge in search of animal tracks when Ch'ŏnwangdong took a whiff of the wind blowing past him and said, "There's an *ŏllugi* nearby." He walked in the direction whence the wind came and before long stopped and turned to signal at the others who drew closer. Ch'ŏnwangdong pointed at the ridge on the other side of the valley.

"It's *padugi*," said Unch'ong, recognizing it right away.

Kkŏkchŏng couldn't see it at first. He looked closely at the general area Ch'ŏnwangdong's finger was pointing, and saw something patchy under a group of short oaks. It was a leopard.

While the three on one side of the valley plotted to hunt the animal, the leopard on the other side must have seen them, for it got up from its rest, fluffed its fur, stretched with its front and hind legs digging into the ground, its sides lean and long, and began to saunter down the valley. The siblings saw this and began dashing down the mountain like a whirlwind. Kkŏkchŏng was about to follow them when he thought otherwise and ran toward the top of the ridge where the leopard had been resting. In the meantime, the siblings blocked the leopard's way down, coming up from both sides. The leopard stopped and growled, and then hissed angrily at the people closing in on it. It raised its upper body as if about to pounce on them and then turned around to head up for the ridge, as if it realized nothing good could come of pouncing on shiny spearheads. Kkŏkchŏng, who had been looking down at it from higher ground with his sword drawn, stopped the leopard charging up like the wind and struck it in a flash. Its throat slashed, the leopard collapsed on the spot. The siblings who were running after the leopard stopped in their tracks. Ch'ŏnwangdong walked up to the slain leopard and poked its head, which was now barely attached to its body.

"Scary what you can do with one swing of the sword!" he said, clicking his tongue. "We won't get more than a *mal* of hulled millet for this pelt," said Unch'ong, referring to the ruined fur. Kkŏkchŏng smiled and put the sword back in its sheath.

They did not come across any beasts after the leopard. They shared the potatoes they had brought to eat when the sun was nearly at lunchtime and were slowly making their way down when they reached the Ch'ilsŏng Swamp and spotted a deer drinking by the swamp.

Unch'ong turned to Kkŏkchŏng and kindly informed him, "*Ppudagwi* are scary from the front. When the *ppudagwi* is cornered and attacking with the antlers, it's scarier than an *ŏllugi*. Don't take it lightly and don't charge from the front."

The siblings and Kkŏkchŏng spread out and blocked the deer's escape route from three sides and cried out as they closed in. The startled deer turned to run, but there were people on all sides. It tried to escape through the gap but was marred by a sharp spearhead, and so it ran back toward the swamp. People began to close in on the deer. Fearing for its life, the deer bleated "*meh*" as if to call for help. Once the siege had become reasonably small, Kkŏkchŏng, who'd been standing in the middle dashed toward the deer like a bird in flight, and the deer in turn spun around, raised its bottom, and kicked at the air with both hind legs. The swamp lay before the deer, so it turned around again. It bowed its head to charge at him with its antlers. Kkŏkchŏng darted toward the deer and kicked its jaw from below, which made the deer raise its head. Kkŏkchŏng quickly grabbed the deer by the base of its antlers with both hands. The deer tried to push forward using its hind legs and also tried to shake its head. It could not move at all. Muscles bulged in Kkŏkchŏng's arms. All the deer could do was dig up the sand around the swamp with its front legs. When Kkŏkchŏng ran toward the deer, Unch'ong, who was standing beside him, had been stunned. She thought that Kkŏkchŏng was foolishly charging at the deer despite her warning him about how fierce deer could be. She raced toward him with her spear.

Ch'ŏnwangdong, who was on the opposite side, came running as well. Kkŏkchŏng had already seized the deer by its antlers by then, so the siblings froze and watched in awe. After a while, Kkŏkchŏng began to drag the deer toward him, taking steps back. The deer's front legs seemed to be giving out as well. It blinked as it was dragged out. Kkŏkchŏng turned to Ch'ŏnwangdong and told him to bind the deer's legs, and tipped it over. Ch'ŏnwangdong tied the front legs and hind legs with the hemp rope he had brought with him. Kkŏkchŏng let go of the antlers when he saw that it could not move anymore.

Unch'ong wiped the sweat off Kkŏkchŏng's brow with her sleeve. The siblings put a pole through the roped legs of the leopard with a dangly head and each held one end, and Kkŏkchŏng grabbed the deer, still struggling from time to time, by the hind legs, threw it over his shoulders, and carried it home upside-down. They arrived around dinnertime.

Ever since the hunting excursion that day, Unch'ong did not leave Kkŏkchŏng's side for a single moment. Unch'ong's mother specially prepared the good millet for the guests that evening. Unch'ong picked out a large bowl and placed it in front of Kkŏkchŏng, and mixed precious sesame into Kkŏkchŏng's salt. Kkŏkchŏng did not dislike Unch'ong's affectionate ways, but it embarrassed him to see Unch'ong's mother smiling a meaningful smile and his teacher acting obliviously. He sat with his eyes on the floor as Unch'ong showered him with affection, unaware of his embarrassment. Ch'ŏnwangdong was not as affectionate toward him as Unch'ong was, but admired him just as much as she did.

After dinner, Ch'ŏnwangdong told his mother that he would go sleep with Kkŏkchŏng in the room on the other side of the kitchen.

Before the mother had the opportunity to answer him Unch'ong said, "I'm going to sleep with Kkŏkchŏng, too."

"It'll be too crowded if you both sleep in there," said the mother.

"All right, you stay and I'll go so it won't be crowded in there," said Ch'ŏnwangdong.

"You sleep with mom. I'll go," said Unch'ong, and the siblings began to argue over who would go.

"Men are supposed to sleep with men and women are supposed to sleep with women."

"Sleeping is sleeping. What does it matter if you're a man or a woman?"

"There's such a thing as sticking to your own kind."

"If we're going to divide according to man and woman, then men and women are supposed to sleep together. When mom and father were sleeping in this room, you and I slept in the other room."

"Stop chirping nonsense, you two," scolded the mother.

Ch'ŏnwangdong was quiet for a while and then said, "Here's what we'll do. We'll have the monk sleep with mom and then the two of us can go sleep in the other room."

"That sounds good," said Unch'ong, clapping.

"Stop your prattling. We should give the room to the guests," said the considerate mother. Besides, Kkŏkchŏng said he would not sleep with anyone besides his teacher, so the siblings gave up. As they did the previous night, the two guests slept in the room on the other side of the kitchen by themselves. Kkŏkchŏng lay down and chuckled as he recalled the comical exchange between the siblings.

"It is rare and precious that they've been raised to be so innocent," the monk praised them.

"Don't you think they'll produce an offspring between the two of them if they were left to their own devices?"

"Perhaps. In the beginning of time when people were first created, there was only man and woman, no mother and son or brother and sister."

The teacher and pupil soon fell asleep after conversing like so, but the chattering went on well into the night where the mother and two siblings lay. Unch'ong and Ch'ŏnwangdong took turns describing the hunting from that day and praising Kkŏkchŏng.

"I spoke with the old *taesa* all day, and he is truly a *tosŭng*. I saw many monks at the Chaboksa at Ch'ŏnbongsan, my village, when I was young, but I've never seen a *tosŭng* like the *taesa*, so I asked him to read the scripture for your father on his memorial day, and he consented. It is a great blessing for the dead to be led into the next world by a *tosŭng*. Kkŏkchŏng is a pupil of the *tosŭng*, so of course, he's extraordinary." The mother continued to praise the monk by calling him a *tosŭng*.

Unch'ong, who did not know what "*tosŭng*" meant, asked, "What's a *tosŭng*?"

"A *tosŭng* is a monk who will become a Buddha."

"What's a Buddha?"

"Buddha is as holy as the Chŏnwangsŏngje (Heavenly King and Wise Ruler) of the Heavenly King Shrine," she replied.

Ch'ŏnwangdong, who did not know his father's memorial day asked, "When is the memorial day?"

"Ten days from today. Only nine more nights."

"Including tonight?"

"No, not including tonight," she replied.

On the subject of Ch'ŏnwangdong's guiding their way around Paektu-san, Unch'ong said, "It'll take two nights if they bring the monk along."

"I'll just come back on my own if I get impatient," said Ch'ŏnwangdong.

"You'll do no such thing. You will attend them there and back," she bade him.

Early next morning, the monk and Kkŏkchŏng were about to leave for the mountains with Ch'ŏnwangdong as their guide when Unch'ong noticed Kkŏkchŏng's unlined summer pants and shirt, and informed him, "The summit is as cold as winter."

So they tied about six or seven pieces of pelt onto Kkŏkchŏng's food sack to share among the three.

Ch'ŏnwangdong was raised to be no different from a wild animal. Not only were his legs strong, but he was light-footed from birth and could walk about 400 *ri* during daylight even in the winter. Pyŏnghae *taesa*, in contrast, had the strength of a young man but was nevertheless an old man in his sixties and naturally walked slowly. The great difference in speed between the two made traveling together difficult.

Even Kkŏkchŏng, who had become accustomed to traveling with the monk, was occasionally bothered by the monk's pace, so it went without saying that a wild, untamed horse like Ch'ŏnwang-dong would have a difficult time keeping his restlessness in check. Ch'ŏnwangdong walked twice as far as they did. He walked ahead of them thinking that they would catch up, and when they did not, he came back to find them and then went ahead again. When they had reached Ch'ilsŏng Swamp, Ch'ŏnwangdong turned to the monk and Kkŏkchŏng and said, "Let's see the swamp and go home," unable to contain his impatience. The monk did not say anything and Kkŏkchŏng laughed.

"Tsk, don't walk ahead of us. Let's you and me follow the teacher slowly," he said.

They rested by the swamp, and the guide Ch'ŏnwangdong and Kkŏkchŏng followed the monk. Before long, Ch'ŏnwangdong began to complain and then a while later began to squirm as though he was having a fit. Kkŏkchŏng found this funny and unfortunate at the same time.

"Teacher, Ch'ŏnwangdong is going mad," said Kkŏkchŏng. The monk laughed and said, "You should return home."

"Will you come with me?"

"We'll return after we get to the summit."

"Then no. I'm coming with you."

Kkŏkchŏng, who was listening to the exchange between the monk and Ch'ŏnwangdong, commended him, "How good of you to not return by yourself." He added, "Hey, how would you like to carry the teacher on your back?"

"Shall I?" said Ch'ŏnwangdong, and came around in front of the monk and showed him his back. The monk got on his back without refusing. At first, Ch'ŏnwangdong ran as though he would get to the summit in no time, but began to whimper before long.

"Ugh, I can't go on," he said as he put the monk down.

Seeing this, Kkŏkchŏng smiled and said, "Why don't I carry the teacher? You take the knapsack."

So Ch'ŏnwangdong lead the way carrying the potato sack and the pelts, and Kkŏkchŏng followed with the monk on his back. Kkŏkchŏng lagged behind but not so far behind that Ch'ŏnwangdong had to return to find them. They were able to move much faster.

"If we had done this sooner, we would have gone much further," said Ch'ŏnwangdong happily. They were delayed a good deal for this reason or that, but were still able to walk over a hundred *ri* and spend the night at the rounded peak called Muturi Peak, wake up the next morning, and hike the stone path without trees to the Paektu-san summit. The wind blew and shook the earth as though there was an earthquake and the clouds and fog formed an ocean. The three cloaked themselves with animal pelts and sat huddled together. When the clouds and fog lifted, they walked all the way down to the iridescent Ch'ŏnwang (Heavenly King Pond) before turning to leave.

The party returned after sundown that day.

"How far did you get?" asked Unch'ong's mother.

"We were at the summit," said the monk.

"My Ch'ŏnwangdong often makes the trip in one day, but how did you return so soon in your elderly gait? I thought it would take at least two or three nights."

"Two or three nights? It would have taken the monk at least four nights," Ch'ŏnwangdong interjected.

"So you got around to Muturi Peak," she fancied and said, "Muturi Peak is not the summit," turning to the monk.

"I dipped my hand in the Ch'ŏnwang Pond," he said.

As though she doubted the monk, who wouldn't lie, Unch'ong asked, "Did you really get to the summit or not?"

"Of course we did, didn't we?" said Ch'ŏnwangdong. "He carried the monk on his back," he said, pointing at Kkŏkchŏng. And so Unch'ong and her mother knew how they managed to return so soon.

"How did you carry the elderly man through the perilous mountain path?" The mother looked at Kkŏkchŏng.

"That's because it's you," said Unch'ong beaming at Kkŏkchŏng.

Ever since the day she buried her husband, Unch'ong's mother visited his grave near the Heavenly King Shrine and stopped by the shrine on the way back to sweep the place inside and out. What first began as her way of preparing for her afterlife turned into a ritual for her children, too. She would clean the shrine and bow before the Heavenly King and Wise Ruler three times, one for each wish. Her first wish was to meet her husband again in the afterlife, her second wish was for Ch'ŏnwangdong to live a long life, and her third wish was to find herself a good son-in-law. For four years, she never missed a day, rain or shine, save a few days when she was ill. Unch'ong and Ch'ŏnwangdong knew that their mother went to the Heavenly King Shrine often but did not know what she was praying for, so Unch'ong's mother was surprised to find out that her guest, the monk, knew. While the siblings were out hunting with Kkŏkchŏng, Unch'ong's mother divulged her concern about finding a son-in-law to the monk and esteemed Kkŏkchŏng's character, to which the monk replied, "Your devotion will not have been in vain."

She pretended not to understand and said, "Devotion?"

"What would praying at the Heavenly King Shrine be, if not devotion?" the monk said knowingly, and she could not hide it any longer.

Thus Unch'ong's mother recognized the monk as a *tosŭng* and inquired, "Will I have Kkŏkchŏng as my son-in-law?"

Smiling, the monk answered, "If it is the Heavenly King's will, you need not be worried."

Unch'ong's mother later went to the Heavenly King Shrine and prayed before the portrait of the Heavenly King, "I offer you my gratitude for a son-in-law like Kkŏkchŏng," giving thanks in advance.

As the monk had agreed to read the scripture on the memorial day of Unch'ong's father, he and Kkŏkchŏng stayed another seven or eight days. The siblings delighted in it, and Kkŏkchŏng likewise did not find it disagreeable. Kkŏkchŏng hoped to spend time alone with Unch'ong, but could not find the opportunity, for Ch'ŏnwangdong followed them around like a shadow until he went off to exchange the animal pelts for articles that would be used on memorial day. That day, after Ch'ŏnwangdong had left, Kkŏkchŏng followed Unch'ong's mother and Unch'ong to the Heavenly King Shrine.

When Unch'ong's mother had finished her affairs and was about to return, Unch'ong said, "Mom, go on ahead. We'll go off and play for a while."

"Very well, don't be gone for too long," and disappeared into the woods by herself.

Kkŏkchŏng and Unch'ong sat in the yard of the Heavenly King Shrine shoulder to shoulder. Kkŏkchŏng searched for words.

"Unch'ong," he said, and remained quiet for a while. Unch'ong looked at Kkŏkchŏng, as if to urge him to speak.

"Do you want to live with me?"

"What about mom and Ch'ŏnwangdong?"

"We'll all live together."

"Let's ask mom."

"Do you know about going *chang'ga* and going *sijip*?" he asked, and waited for Unch'ong's answer.[4] He laughed when she said nothing, and said, "You don't know, do you? When a man takes a woman, it's called going *chang'ga*. When a woman takes a man, it's called going *sijip*. Do you want to go *sijip* with me?"

---

4. *Chang'ga* indicates a man living with his bride's family and *sijip* refers to a woman living at her husband's home.

"What do I do when I go *sijip*?" she asked. It was as though he was talking to a wall.

Kkŏkchŏng laughed again. "You give birth to sons and daughters. Your mom went *sijip* with your father, so she had you and Ch'ŏnwangdong."

"I think I'd like to have a son like Ch'ŏnwangdong. Yes, I'll go *sijip* with you," and then begged him to hurry and have her "go *sijip*." Kkŏkchŏng lifted Unch'ong, sat her on his lap, and put his hand on her breast, and found that although she acted like a child, her age had given her breasts and proper nipples, too.

"Is this 'going *sijip*'?"

Kkŏkchŏng laughed once again.

"When mom had Ch'ŏnwangdong, mom and father came to the Heavenly King Shrine to pray. I saw them. It's true. Let's go inside the Heavenly King Shrine and pray, too." She begged and begged, and dragged Kkŏkchŏng into the shrine. Unch'ong kneeled down and made Kkŏkchŏng kneel, too.

Unch'ong prayed, "I went *sijip* with Kkŏkchŏng today. Send me a son like Ch'ŏnwangdong." She turned to Kkŏkchŏng who was mumbling a prayer to himself, and told him to say his prayer out loud. Kkŏkchŏng had walked into the shrine half in jest and had been mumbling whatever came to mind, but he suddenly felt solemn.

"Kkŏkchŏng takes Unch'ong as his wife," he said as he bowed his head. Unch'ong nudged him to ask for a son. "Please send us a son soon," Kkŏkchŏng prayed for a son, too, without cracking a smile.

When Kkŏkchŏng and Unch'ong walked out of Heavenly King Shrine, he took Unch'ong by the hand and studied her face. In the pretty pupils of her clear eyes, he could nearly see the Heavenly King. Kkŏkchŏng thought to himself that he would not find such lovely, divine eyes if he searched the entire world.

"What are you looking at?"

"Nothing."

"What do you mean, nothing? You are looking at something."

"It's only that my wife is pretty."

"Am I your wife? What are you?"

"You are my wife, and I am your husband."

"Husband? Then my husband is pretty, too," laughed Unch'ong.

"My sweet," Kkŏkchŏng smiled, lifted Unch'ong off her feet, and walked into the woods.

When Unch'ong and Kkŏkchŏng returned home, her mother and the monk were sitting across from each other and talking. Unch'ong sat by her mother, and Kkŏkchŏng sat near his teacher.

"I told you not to stay out so long. What were you doing?" said Unch'ong mother, turning toward Unch'ong.

Unch'ong replied without a moment's hesitation, "Mom, I went *sijip*."

"What do you mean, you went *sijip*?"

"With him," said Unch'ong, pointing at Kkŏkchŏng who shook his head, signaling her to stop. Unch'ong beamed as she continued, "We went inside the Heavenly King Shrine and prayed for a son."

Although Unch'ong's mother had been hoping for this, she was speechless. The monk looked on Unch'ong fondly, and Kkŏkchŏng turned red.

"Mom, and then we went into the woods ..." The instant Unch'ong said this, Kkŏkchŏng's face flushed as though it was on fire. He was about to get up and leave the room when Unch'ong's mother said, "I want to have a word with you. Sit down." Kkŏkchŏng sat down where he stood and hung his head.

Unch'ong continued to glow as she said, "We went to the woods and raced each other up trees. Kkŏkchŏng will get better at it." Kkŏkchŏng made a face at Unch'ong, finally relieved.

"I don't follow what she's saying," said Unch'ong's mother to Kkŏkchŏng. "Tell me what's going on."

Kkŏkchŏng silently stared at the floor for a while and then raised his head. "I have chosen Unch'ong to be my wife."

"Choose her, and that's it?"

"What do you mean?"

"You have to have the ceremony. What will you do about the ceremony?"

"We don't need to do the ceremony again. We made our vows before the Heavenly King."

"Even so," Unch'ong's mother was about to go on when the monk called her aside.

"Madam, it seems they have already had a magnificent ceremony. All you need to do is call Kkŏkchŏng 'son-in-law' from now on." The monk laughed and Unch'ong's mother followed suit in spite of herself.

"My new son-in-law must be hungry," said Unch'ong's mother, and brought some steamed potatoes from the kitchen."

"I want some, too," said Unch'ong.

"You ate with him just fine when you were strangers. You can go eat with your husband, can't you?" said Unch'ong's mother, laughing.

Kkŏkchŏng laughed, too, and beckoned Unch'ong to come closer.

"What are you going to do about Unch'ong? Will you bring her with you?"

"I can't take her with me this time," said Kkŏkchŏng, and looked at the monk. "She can't come this time," said the monk definitively.

"What will she do, then?"

"Send her later."

"How can I send her to such a faraway place?"

"It is far away, but there's nothing to worry about. Just tell her to find Im Kkŏkchŏng of Yangju. Besides, with Ch'ŏnwangdong around, sending word shouldn't be any trouble since he can travel a thousand *ri* in two days, isn't it so?"

"Well ..."

While Unch'ong's mother conversed with the monk, Unch'ong ate potatoes with Kkŏkchŏng and poked Kkŏkchŏng's side or pushed his chin up. Kkŏkchŏng made a face telling her to stop, and Unch'ong said to Kkŏkchŏng, "We agreed earlier that we'd bring mom and everyone, right?"

The day for the memorial rites came. After breakfast, Unch'ong's mother cleaned the room thoroughly, placed the ancestral tablet against a wall, put a small table with plates of fruit before the ancestral tablet, prepared a brass bowl containing coals and a wooden saucer full of incense instead of an incense bowl and an incense case, and made space for the monk to recite the scripture. The monk sat down, lit some incense, and began to chant. Unch'ong's mother and Ch'ŏnwangdong kneeled and bowed before the ancestral tablet, and Kkŏkchŏng and Unch'ong bowed behind them. The monk was not accustomed to the Buddhist scripture, so he read the Purification Mantra and Mantra of Avalokiteśvara first and then opened up the Diamond Sutra he had brought with him on the trip and read on. It was a strange scripture to read for a memorial day rite, but Unch'ong's mother, who did not know what scripture he was reading, felt as if the sedulous reading of the noble monk would reach the underworld and that Unch'ong's father would receive the Bodhisattva's guidance owing to the offering and soon reincarnate as a human again.

The sound of the monk's recitation brought tears to Unch'ong's mother and made Ch'ŏnwangdong restless. The monk kept on reading when Ch'ŏnwangdong wanted him to stop, and he read slowly when Ch'ŏnwangdong wanted him to get through it quickly. This frustrated Ch'ŏnwangdong. In his mind, the monk's reading was even more frustrating than his slow gait. As the monk turned page after page of the Diamond Sutra in front of him, Ch'ŏnwangdong's frustration grew into anger. Kneeling behind him, Kkŏkchŏng and Unch'ong glanced at each other and snickered silently, and then began making faces at each other. Kkŏkchŏng would wink, Unch'ong would stick out her lower lip, Kkŏkchŏng would flare his nostrils comically, and Unch'ong would stick out her tongue. Kkŏkchŏng, who was better at containing his laughter than Unch'ong, nearly split his sides as they made faces at each other with their eyes, noses, and mouths. Unch'ong, of course, couldn't help herself. Already upset, Ch'ŏnwangdong was even more irritated by the giggles from behind and scolded sullenly, "Stop laughing! What's so funny?"

At this, the mother also turned around and looked daggers at her, "You're over twenty and Ch'ŏnwangdong still behaves better than you!"

Scolded by her younger brother and reprimanded by her mother, Unch'ong cried dolefully. Kkŏkchŏng drew two lines with his fingers going straight down from the eyes and over his cheeks, but Unch'ong bit her lips and ignored him. The monk stopped reading to rest for a moment, so those kneeling and bowing could sit up. Before the monk resumed his recitation of the scripture, he suggested to Unch'ong's mother, "Why don't you have them go outside and play?" So the siblings and Kkŏkchŏng were able to avoid kneeling and bowing for the rest of the scripture reading. The scripture reading went on all day. Kkŏkchŏng bowed with the siblings, and Unch'ong's mother had a fit of bitter weeping. Early morning after the memorial day, Unch'ong's father appeared in her mother's dream to speak highly of the chanting and tell her how happy he was that his new son-in-law was able to attend the memorial. Unch'ong's mother woke up early next morning and delightedly told them about her dream.

The monk and Kkŏkchŏng stayed a few more days after the memorial. Seeing that Kkŏkchŏng had little intention of leaving, the monk pressed him, "Let's move on now." So they decided to leave the next day, and Unch'ong barely spoke to Kkŏkchŏng for not letting her go with him. Kkŏkchŏng tried to appease her and then her mother tried to appease her, but Unch'ong would not budge.

"I won't come find you later," she glared at Kkŏkchŏng. "Do as you like. I don't care."

Early next morning, Unch'ong's mother and Ch'ŏnwangdong saw them off at the Heavenly King Shrine while Unch'ong stayed in her room and refused to see him. Kkŏkchŏng felt disappointed. The hosts and guests were exchanging goodbyes at the Heavenly King Shrine when Kkŏkchŏng saw a shadow lurking in the forest path and went after it. "It must be Unch'ong," he thought. Unch'ong saw Kkŏkchŏng running toward her and threw her arms around his neck.

"Take me with you," she wept.

"Come later and bring mom and Ch'ŏnwangdong with you. If I were going straight home, I would take you with me, but the teacher and I are going to travel here and there, so we can't all go together. We'll have our happy reunion later."

Unch'ong, who was listening to Kkŏkchŏng with her head pressed against his chest, said, "Goodbye."

She freed him from her arms, turned around, and began to run off, stumbling a few times.

...

～

～ 5

NAKTONG RIVER

Introduction

Cho Myŏng-hŭi (趙明熙 1894–1942) was a writer who was heavily influenced by the socialist literary movement prominent in 1920s Korea. Born in Ch'ungch'ŏng Province, as a child he attended both a traditional educational institute (書堂 village school) and a primary school before moving to Seoul where he attended middle school. He was imprisoned for taking part in the March 1, 1919, independence movement, and shortly thereafter traveled to Japan where he attended Tokyo University and majored in philosophy.

This was also the time when his literary activities began. In 1921 he published the play *Kim Yŏngil ŭi sa* (김영일의 사 Death of Kim Yŏngil) and followed that with a collection of poems entitled *Pom chandibat wie* (봄 잔디밭 위에 On spring grass) in 1924. However, much change was afoot within Korea's intellectual circles that was in some ways spurred on by the relaxation of censorship on Korean literary activities under the so-called cultural rule that followed the March First Movement. While there was still heavy censorship of newspapers and other writings by the colonial government, there was increased production of literature and other writings. Out of this more vibrant literary community, there developed an ideological split within Korean literary activities. On one hand, there was nationalist literature that sought to glorify and promote the Korean state and, on the other, class literature. The New Trend School (新傾向派 Sin'gyŏnghyang p'a) was born of this and focused on real life and the difficulties of the people. It was the hardships and sufferings of the protagonists in these such works that highlight the lives of the proletariat, and through this critique the colonial government and the abjection of the Korean subject.[1] The writings of Cho are very representative of this new trend.

When Cho returned to Korea in 1924 he soon joined the newly formed KAPF (Korea Artista Proleta Federation; Chosŏn p'ŭrol-let'aria yesul tongmaeng), which resulted in his writing shifting to fiction with the publication of the short story "Nongch'on sa-ramdŭl" (농촌사람들 People of the farming village, 1927) and *Naktong-gang* (洛東江 Naktong river, 1927) which is translated here. The former story tells the story of a person who dies at the hands of the Japanese imperialists who had destroyed his family; the latter tells of the brutality of the Japanese rule among farmers and others. *Naktong-gang* was published in the magazine *Chosŏn chi kwang* (朝鮮之光 Light of Chosŏn) in its seventh issue of 1927. Soon thereafter, Cho fled to the Soviet Union where he would continue to live until his death in 1942.

Naktong-gang is set in 1920s Chosŏn and shows the hardships of the people under the colonial exploitation of the Japanese colonial machine. It is the most representative work of Cho in that the focus is clearly on the oppression and exploitation of farmers and others of low social status. The protagonist is a broken fighter for freedom who realizes that the only hope for the Korean people is to unite in the face of the Japanese imperialists. Cho's diatribe against factions in the socialist movement is rather interesting and perhaps also a statement against what he viewed to be the same problem experienced in the late Chosŏn period. Such a viewpoint would be influenced by the Japanese view of Korean

---

1. Kimberly Chung, "Proletarian Sensibilities: The Body Politics of New Tendency Literature (1924–1927)," *The Journal of Korean Studies* 19 (Spring 2014), 39–40.

history and the stagnation brought about by conflicts stemming from personal interest rather than the good of the country and people.

We can also note in this work the Marxist rhetoric against the bourgeoisie and those who seek to oppress the weak. This, of course, was one of the main aims of the KAPF and the New Trend School. The sufferings of the people are a means to illustrate the inequities of the class system and the imperialist ideology that sought to strengthen the state at the expense of the people. Yet Cho did not write this story for the masses, but rather for the intellectuals of his day as a means to demonstrate the lives of the people and their hardships. This is another trait of the writings of the New Trend School: a hope to bring relief to the suffering people by raising consciousness of their plight among intellectuals. In this way, *Naktong-gang* is a masterpiece of the New Trend School and its aims.

***

〜 NAKTONG RIVER
| *NAKTONG-GANG* 낙동강
CHO MYŎNG-HŬI 조명희

Translated by Brother Anthony of Taizé
Annotated by Michael J. Pettid

Once the waters of the Naktong River reach this spot, after flowing on and on for seven hundred *ri,* all the river's diverging branches draw together into a single body before heading seaward. The checkerboard pattern of fields following the river lie open toward the far-off sea while tightly clustered villages snuggle nestling here and there in the breast of those broad fields.

This river and these fields and the people living here! While the river flowed on and on, the people lived on and on. So how could this river and these people ever be parted from one another?

> Every spring, every spring,
> the swollen waters of the Naktong River
> on reaching the plains at Kup'o
> overflowing, overflowing flow,
> flow on, *ehey-ya.*
>
> Lapping, lapping, the overflowing waters
> spread across fields and plains
> and so become the mother's milk
> of many lives, of many many lives,
> become the mother's milk, *ehey-ya.*

The plains lay open,
these waters flowed,
and from that time onward
we grew up sustained by that milk,
we grew up, *ehey-ya.*

Naktong River! Naktong River!
Where we lived a thousand years, ten thousand years!
Even though we journey to heaven's end
how could we forget you, even in our dreams?
How could you ever be forgotten? *Ehey-ya.*

In the early spring one year, as a group of people bade farewell to this land and crossed the river for one last time on their way to distant Manchuria, it is said that one youth in their midst beat the side of the boat as he sorrowfully sang that song, making all his equally sorrowful companions shed bitter tears.

They had long lived attached like a brood of pups to the teats of this motherland. But those teats had already begun not to belong to them a long time ago. Things had gone from bad to worse, then a pack of people came upon them like wolves out of nowhere and began to push and jostle them and rob them of their share. Now it had become difficult to obtain so much as a single sip of milk. They had found themselves obliged to leave home and set off. Let us consider briefly how that came to be.

Since the time their ancestors first caught fish in this river, gathered grain and fruits on these plains, long ages have passed, countless, when they were truly free. Singing in harmony, they worked together in harmony. The plains to the south and those to the north, all belonged to them. What lay to west and east was equally theirs.

However, the wheel of history turned. A class arose that ate without working, and a class arose that worked and fed the other class as well. A ruling class arose, and a ruled class. From that time onward, the ownerless plains had owners, the common people who had never known hunger began to starve. They no longer noticed that the sky's sunlight was lovely, no longer recognized that the clear waters of the Naktong River were clear. For a thousand years. For five thousand years. Through all that long age they lived on in this unequal peace without a word, in silent grievance. They reached a point where they did not think their inequalities were inequalities. Like considering cloudy weather to be truly clear weather. Only history was intent on turning her wheel further. Wind heralds a shower. The flag was raised. The 1894 Tonghak uprising.[1] The 1895 reforms.[2] Since then, a monster roamed this land, this entire peninsula. Like an eagle beating its wings. That monster is Socialism. It passes everywhere, like a female butterfly ejecting innumerable eggs behind it, ever laying more eggs as it goes. Youth movements, women's movements … the weather of the past five thousand years has now become a mass of black clouds. Torrential rains are sure to fall. It is easy to tell what weather will follow that rain.

A dark night in early winter; it is a moment when, at the mouth of the Naktong River communicating with the distant sea, the lights of fishing-boats drowse anxiously, while the sound of cold waves breaking on the river shore grows louder. A group of people just off a bus were standing grouped in the flickering lamplight at the top of the embankment waiting for a boat. It was mostly composed of members of the youth movement, the equality brigade, the women's alliance, the tenants' union, and other social movement groups. Poorly dressed villagers with old hats askew carrying

---

1. The Tonghak Uprising was a peasant revolt that erupted, in part, due to widespread dissatisfaction with the corruption of the Chosŏn government in the 1890s. The Uprising ultimately failed, but was significant in that as a result of the weakness of the Chosŏn government, both troops from Qing China and Japan entered the Korean peninsula and set off the Sino-Japan war of 1894–1895. The end result of this was Japan's hegemony in Chosŏn.

2. These are the Kabo Reforms discussed above.

bundles, people wearing black or white *turumagi* overcoats, scruffy suits or Russian *rubashka*, girls with bobbed hair so short it did not reach the collars of their coats, or "new women" with their hair twisted up, and an invalid sitting in a rickshaw. They have just welcomed this Pak Sŏngun off the bus, he having been released on bail from the prison where he was being detained on account of his critical condition; after loading him onto the rickshaw, they are on their way back to the village.

"Why, they must have been as merciless as they are said to be. To reduce a man with the constitution of a mighty tiger to such a state, how harsh their punishments must have been, those wicked bastards."

The speaker seemed to be seeing the invalid for the first time since he had been imprisoned, having come out to the bus-stop to welcome him. Someone replied:

"They treat him like that, then if he dies they'll say he died after falling ill."

"Then he ought to have gone straight to a hospital, why come all the way here?"

"I have no idea. It was the invalid himself who insisted he was coming here ..."

"Why is the boat taking so long?"

"Ah, now the boat's bow has turned. It'll be here soon."

One man is chattering, looking toward the river bank. Then, turning to the man in the rickshaw:

"Aren't you cold?"

"It's alright. I'm not cold."

"No, you must be cold. Shall I get you another coat?"

"No thanks, I'm alright."

The invalid replies in a sickly voice.

"Hey, get that boat over here quickly."

Someone shouts to the boatman on the far side of the river, who has managed to turn the boat's bow and is rowing hard.

"Okay."

The voice sounds indifferent. Having rowed part of the way, he has stopped again.

"What's he doing?"

"Looks as though he's stopped to smoke a cigarette. Hey, you leper there!"

Several people burst out laughing. The boat has arrived. The man in the rickshaw is first.

"Hey, can you get the rickshaw up onto the boat with him in it?"

One man eyes the rickshaw driver and asks, "How could I?"

"No, I'll get down."

People help the invalid down from the rickshaw and up into the boat. As soon as everyone is in, the boat heads out toward the far bank, to the squeak of the oar in its slot and the splashing sound of the oar in the water. Even in the lamplight, the face of the invalid seated at the prow can be seen to be dreadfully emaciated.

"Hey, boatman, let's have a boat-song!"

"What? Why on earth do you suddenly want a song?"

Someone sitting beside him asks.

"I want to hear it ... after all, this may be the last time in my life I cross this river. ..."

"Hey, why do you keep saying such stupid things?"

"No! I really want to hear a song. Hey, boatman, won't you sing?"

"No, I can't sing at all."

"Well then, is there anyone who can sing? ... Ah, Rosa, sing, won't you ... sing the song I made."

He pesters the girl with bobbed hair singing next to him.

"You want me to sing?"

"Yes, sing 'Every spring, every spring,' won't you?"

"Every spring, every spring,
the swollen waters of the Naktong River
on reaching the plains at Kup'o overflowing,

> overflowing flow,
> flow on, *ehey-ya*.
> … "

The melody has some of the characteristics of the traditional Kyŏngsang song "Nŭiliri" combined with a trace of a more modern style, it is resonant with the power of sorrowful indignation and firm determination. As a female voice, Rosa's tone is rather too strong for a woman and might even be considered too bold, but the sound of her pure voice covered the sound of the waves stirred up on the river by the wind and wafted sadly across the night sky. The stars in the sky seemed to be blinking as though in sympathy. The people in the boat might not be headed for Manchuria at that moment, but their hearts could not help but echo anew.

At the end of the third verse, Pak Sŏngun joins in, in a high-pitched voice, looking quite hysterical.

> Naktong River! Naktong River!
> Where we lived a thousand years, ten thousand years!
> Even though we journey to Heaven's end
> how could we forget you in our dreams?
> How could you be forgotten? *ehey-ya*.

The song comes to an end. Sŏngun, twitching like a maniac, rolls up his right sleeve and dips his arm in the water, wetting his arm, feeling the water with his hand, splashing it about. His neighbor seems to feel sorry for him:

"What a fellow! We have a real problem here. This invalid, in the state he's in, goes dipping his arm into cold water! What does he think he's doing?"

"If I die now, it's fine. Don't go worrying too much."

"You're crazy … quite mad …"

Becoming increasingly agitated, the invalid turned toward the woman beside him. "Rosa! Roll up your sleeve. Let's dip both our arms into the water together." Seizing the woman's hand, he dipped it in the water and stirred it around.

"Five years I spent roaming overseas, and in all that time, whenever I thought of a river, I never forgot the Naktong River. ... Whenever I thought of the Naktong River, I never forgot that I'm the grandson of a Naktong River fisherman, the son of a farmer ... and therefore from Chosŏn, too."

Their two hands were simply hanging feebly above the water at the prow of the boat. The invalid again gazed out at the expanse of water before him and murmured to himself:

"Once I was crossing the Songhua River in Manchuria when I remembered this Naktong River and started to cry. ... If a person leaves home with a willing heart, no matter how far he goes he never feels heartbroken like that. ..."

He had no sooner spoken than the atmosphere in the boat grew quiet, almost as though they had stopped breathing. Rosa's head, which she had been holding high, dropped and she raised her other hand to her face. Likewise, a large tear rolled down from Sŏngun's eye.

For a while only the sound of the water could be heard. Using the hand that had been hanging over the side of the boat, Rosa grasped the man's cold hand tightly.

"That's enough, eh?"

The flavor of the accent with which she ended her words was the sweetest sounding of the tones employed by Kyŏngsang Province women. She wiped the water from his hand with her handkerchief and rolled down his sleeve.

The boat arrived at the embankment on the far side. Once everyone had landed, they loaded the invalid back on the rickshaw and headed through the darkness toward the village opposite.

As he had said, Pak Sŏngun was the grandson of a Naktong River fisherman, and the son of a farmer. His grandfather spent his whole life as a fisherman, his father spent his entire life as a farmer.

Perhaps his father had decided to encourage his son to get ahead out of regret at his own ignorance, or perhaps he was just following what others were doing at the time; in any case, although he was barely scraping a living by farming land he rented from its owners, he made sure his son received an education, at the traditional Confucian academy, at the modern-style primary school, then at the provincial agricultural school. ...

Once he had completed agricultural school, he worked for a couple of years at the county office as an agricultural assistant. In those days, his family thought of their son as some kind of high official, and boasted of him to everyone they met. On that account, the neighbors became immensely envious and made up their minds to have their own sons educated too.

Then the Independence Movement exploded. He made a clear decision, gave up everything he had been doing and joined the Movement. When it came to the point, he was an ardent militant. Like everyone in those days, he too spent a year and a half in prison.

Once that was done, when he came back to his family, his mother had died, while his elderly father had lost his house and gone to live with his daughter, Sŏngun's older sister. That same year, life there having become impossible, the number of people leaving for Manchuria increased suddenly. Father and son were obliged to join those setting out on the long journey, turning their backs on their former home. It was at that moment that Sŏngun composed and recited the Naktong River song quoted earlier.

Once they reached Manchuria, they found that it too was not a place where they could live comfortably. Pressure from the local officials, the Manchurians' arrogance, extortions from bandits, all were extreme. Father and son moved from place to place like everybody else. In the course of their travels he finally lost his father forever, in that foreign land far from home.

After that, he journeyed throughout Manchuria, up into Siberia, went to Beijing, down to Shanghai, all the time working for the Independence Movement. Five years passed. The whole movement was stagnating and declining. He turned and headed for home. Just as he arrived back in Chosŏn, a great change occurred in his way of thinking. From being a passionate nationalist, he changed and became a socialist.

Reaching Seoul, he tried to find something to do but could not act as he wished. The reason was that the country's social action groups, instead of using their energies for some kind of task, did nothing but form useless factions, although their ideas and principles were all alike, then spent their time quarreling with one another. He joined forces with some people with aims similar to his and started a movement designed to bring about reconciliation among factions, but to no effect; he tried to stir up public opinion but found no audience among people deeply steeped in factionalism. Finally he stood up angrily, declared in a kind of prophecy, "A time will come when these factions will be destroyed," returned to his native Kyŏngsang Province, created a social movement group covering the whole southern part of the country, and devoted himself exclusively to just causes, he himself taking charge of part of the area along the Naktong River.

Seeing the state of the country, his rallying cry was, "Into the midst of the masses!"

The first thing he did was pay a visit to the village where he had formerly lived but the sight filled his heart with immense sorrow. When he had left five years earlier, it had been a large village of some hundred families but in the meantime its population had shrunk considerably. Instead, a large building with a galvanized iron roof, that had not been visible before, stretched ostentatiously, seeming to be scorning and coercing the crumbling thatched houses. Without asking he knew it must be the warehouse of the Oriental Development Company[3] that had been

---

3. The Oriental Development Company (東洋拓殖株式會社) was established in 1908 by the Empire of Japan. It was designed to exploit Japan's colonies, first toward Korea and then other countries.

established by the Japanese government to exploit the lands and resources of Korea. People who had once been medium landholders had fallen to being smallholders, those who had been smallholders had fallen to being tenant-farmers, those who had been tenant-farmers had almost all left and scattered to the four winds. There was not one of his cherished childhood companions to be seen. They had all been dispersed, some to the cities, some to Manchuria, or to Japan. Not a trace, not a single post stone remained on the site of the house in which his family had lived for generations; the site was now the front yard of the warehouse, only the ancient zelkova tree that in the old days had stood beside their brushwood gate now stood in solitary splendor in the middle of the wide yard. He went rushing toward it like a child, spun around holding onto its trunk, laid his cheek against it, overcome with joy and sorrow at the same time. As he hugged the tree he shut his eyes. Memories from the past began to unwind like a thread. Memories of how in his childhood he used to hug the tree and spin around it as he had just done, of climbing to the topmost branches in summer to catch cicadas and being scolded by his bald grandfather, of the time when village youths had fixed a swing to its branches and he had pestered them to let him swing too, of playing at housekeeping in the shade of the tree with little Suni, the girl from next door, pretending to get married with Suni as the bride and himself as the bridegroom, and later, in his youth, he and the same Suni falling in love, then after she had been sold and was about to leave for P'yŏngyang, or perhaps it was Seoul, the two of them embracing in tears hidden secretly behind the tree late one night. Once all these memories had gone drifting through his mind, he breathed out a prolonged kind of sob and opened his eyes. He muttered to himself:

"This is not the moment to recall all those kinds of things … really … tst …"

He turned and walked briskly away, as though intent on banishing and abolishing such thoughts. He had originally been a sensitive person with tender feelings. But he had recently been making every effort to repress such feelings by willpower.

"A revolutionary has to have a willpower of cast iron!"

Such was his life's motto. But there were many occasions when his emotions cast off the bridle of willpower and ran free.

He began by establishing a program to be followed—publicity, organization, struggle, those three steps. First he set up a farmers' evening school and devoted himself to educating the peasants. He set to work, stripping off all pretensions in order to be really one of them and share their emotions, doing rough farm work with them, going everywhere they were gathered, whether farming in the fields, gathered to chat in rooms, or in night classes, doing his utmost to awaken their consciousness of their rights as human beings, whenever and wherever opportunities arose.

Next he organized a tenant farmers' union and launched a resistance movement against tyranny and exploitation by landowners, especially the Oriental Development Company, which was a great landowner.

The first year of the tenant farmers' dispute was a success, though there were a number of victims. The following year was a complete failure. The tenant farmers' union received the order to dissolve. The evening school was banned too. The tyranny and repression by the Oriental Development Company and the government were indescribable. No matter their zeal, no matter their endurance, there was nothing that could be done in such a country. Everything just came to a standstill. So in the autumn of the previous year one of his friends stood up in a rage and declared: "I'm getting out of here. What can we do here? Terror's the thing. There's nothing left but terror."

"Not so. We have to be here. To do the tasks of our class, it would be the same for us to go and work in China, to go and work in India, or any other nation of the world. But in our case, staying here to work is most convenient. Besides, even if we die, our responsibility and commitment is to die with the people living here in this land."

Notwithstanding such exhortations, in the end he had to see one of his most trusted friends leave.

This sleeping land, or rather this cowering land, finally cost him dear. The cause of his deep trouble was nothing but this. In front of the village, on the edge of the Naktong River, there was a reedbed several dozen acres in size. Thanks to that reedbed, ever since the river flowed and the village arose, people had cut the reeds to make mats, used them to make hats, sold them to buy clothes and food.

"The geese have flown off, over the Naktong River
    autumn winds blow, the reeds are fluttering."

Now the occasions for singing this song had been lost. That reedbed was now private property. Because of the villagers' ignorance, ten years previously it had been designated as government-owned wasteland, before finally being transferred to a Japanese man named "Kadung" on the pretext of "disposing of government-owned wastelands." From that autumn on, they could not even cut reeds. Representations had been made to the authorities several times but to no avail. Village folk had resisted, cutting the tip of a finger and writing protests in their blood, even organizing protest-groups bound by oaths sealed in blood. In the end, all failed. The villagers, beside themselves with fury, blindly cut and beat down the reeds that they had previously considered to be as precious as their lives. The owners hired guards, quarrels arose. Some people got hurt. Finally, Sŏngun was detained on charges of being the ringleader, and since he was very unpopular with the police he was severely tortured before being handed over to the prosecution, then after a further two months he had been released when the state of his health became too serious.

One additional episode should be mentioned here. It happened one market day that summer. At the market a big fight broke out between some members of the equality brigade, which were mainly drawn from the lowest classes, and market vendors, especially some of the resident merchants. It all started when one resident merchant spat out an insult as he was passing in front of the equality brigade headquarters, words were exchanged that turned into a fight, which spread, until hearing a report that enraged them, merchants had taken up clubs and attacked the village of the equality brigade, Sŏngun took the lead and, having mobilized members of the youth league, the peasants' union, even the women's alliance, went rushing off to support the equality brigade. Once the fighting was over, the opposite side heaped scorn and opprobrium on him, complaining, "You louts, you're a new kind of butchers," to which he replied:

"Butchers or us, we're all human beings … only our jobs are different … besides, no matter what one's job, no job makes a person higher or lower than another. People from bygone feudal times talk like that … besides, we of the proletariat are obliged to make common cause with the equality brigade members. We need to recognize them as our brothers and companions …"

He shouted such things enthusiastically within the hearing of many people.

From that time on the local women's alliance gained an additional member, Rosa, the daughter of a member of the equality brigade. Once she was an alliance member, she naturally began to be increasingly often in Sŏngun's company. Thus they came increasingly close, until finally they were deeply in love.

Her parents, being members of the equality brigade, and perhaps wanting like Sŏngun's parents to see their child, even a daughter, improve her lot, sent her to Seoul where after finishing high school she went on to attend a teacher's training school, after which she went to teach in a primary school in the faraway Hamgyŏng region, and this happened while she was visiting her home during a vacation. Their daughter's appointment as a state-commissioned teacher was the first and foremost honor her parents had known since the foundation of the world. Therefore her father reflected,

"My daughter has the rank of state-commissioned teacher, so how can I keep on with my present job?" so he had given up his butcher's stall and even nourished thoughts of going to live in the place where his daughter was teaching and enjoy his new high-class status.[4] This was something they had discussed and agreed on since his daughter arrived. Yet lo and behold, that fight had erupted out of the blue, after which his daughter had become a member of some kind of women's young people's association alliance, busily running around, taking up with some kind of extremist fellow, saying she wasn't going back to the place where she had been working, that she was giving up the honorable position she had reached. Her family found itself facing the biggest worry it had ever experienced. Coaxing, wheedling, all kinds of reasoning, their daughter would not listen to anything. In the end her father turned to shouting:

"You stupid wretch of a girl! A butcher's daughter, rising to such a privileged position, what could be better?"

To which she replied:

"Father, we have endured the abuses of those wicked men for hundreds of years, ever since our remote ancestors, yet you still retain the rotten ideas of that wicked breed, but I hate such a filthy job and all the rest ... I want to live as a human being."

She was retorting to him with such arguments, when:

"Why, you little brat. So cheeky. ... What do you mean, eh, what do you mean?" Her mother intervened in support of her husband.

"Hey, just you stop and think how hard we worked in that despised job so that you could study. How can you talk like that if you care for your parents? Among our children you're the only one that we sent to school, a daughter too, so surely we did that expecting some kind of reward from you."

"So, Mother and Father, you mean that you did not send me to

---

4. Butchers were one of the eight lowborn classes of Chosŏn.

study and so become a human being, but saw me as something that can be raised to bring back benefits, just like a pig that's raised for profit."

"What the heck are you going on about? I can't understand a word you say. Why are you talking like this? Why?"

"Stop, I don't want to listen … I'll do as I like."

At that, her father flared up:

"What? You little brat … Stay out of my sight. I don't want to set eyes on you."

With that he stood up and stormed out.

After which Rosa remained collapsed on the floor sobbing bitter tears. It was not simply that she could not stand the shock of being scolded by her father. She knew that her parents acted like that because they were ignorant, and while hating that ignorance, she felt much stronger pity for their ignorance.

As always at such times, Rosa went rushing to find Sŏngun in search of sympathy. Understanding that, he encouraged her:

"You have to be like a bombshell fired from the very lowest level. You have to stand up to family, society, other women, and men, everything."

At that point, Rosa collapsed, burying her face in Sŏngun's lap, trembling with emotion, and began to weep. He continued:

"You will have to stand up to yourself, too. You must kick aside your tears, those everyday tears, the weak things that women tend to be proud of … We all together have to become strong people."

In this way Rosa, by the power of love and thought, quickly became a changed person. Her name was not originally Rosa. Once, when they happened to be talking of Rosa Luxembourg, Sŏngun had laughingly remarked:

"Your family name is Ro, so let's really call you Rosa, eh? You must become a real Rosa."

From that moment what had been a joke came true and she changed her name to Really Rosa.

It is early in the afternoon a few days after the group surrounding the ailing Sŏngun crossed the Naktong River and headed for the village opposite, piercing the darkness. A procession many times longer than when they arrived emerges from the village and moves toward the river embankment. A host of banners are flapping. A double file of people hold a long strip of hemp cloth in their hands. In front a flag edged in black bears the inscription "The funeral of the late Pak Sŏngun."

Behind that are multicolored pennants with the names of this or that alliance, association, union, or brigade. Then a host of banners with commemorative inscriptions:

"The warrior has left us. But his hot blood leaps in our hearts."

"You have left us! Before the day dawned, you left! We will not be able to join hands with you in the dance welcoming the dawning day."

There were too many to count. Among the rest was one containing what looked like long lines of poetry:

"You often told me to become a bombshell fired from the very lowest level. You are right! I will become that shell."

"As you were dying, you told me to truly become a bombshell. You are right! I will become that shell."

It was clear without asking that that was Rosa's inscription.

Late in the morning one day later that year, as the first snowflakes come fluttering down, it is time for the train to leave Kup'o station and head northward. Until the train has passed the last fields, a woman sits gazing steadily out of the compartment window. It is Rosa. She seems determined to follow the path previously taken by her dead lover. But soon she too will return to this land that she will never be able to forget.

~

~ 6

Commoners' Village

Introduction

Yi Kiyŏng (李箕永 1895–1984) was born in Asan of South Ch'ugnchŏng Province during the last years of the Chosŏn dynasty. He attended school in Tokyo, but did not complete his studies but instead returned to Korea. His writings are said to be representative of class literature that sought to bring about cognition of the oppression of those in lower social classes by those above them. After liberation from Japan in 1945, he stayed in North Korea until his death.

Yi was influenced by the New Trend school, which emphasized the realities of the lives of the people. He was also an active member of the KAPF (Korea Artista Proleta Federation), the major socialist movement of 1920s Korea. His writings are thus centered on the hardships of the people that were resultant from the inequities of the class system that privileged some people at the expense of others. Throughout his writing career, Yi's works resounded with the realism of the socialist movement and demonstrated both the evils of the feudal system from which the peasants struggled to break free, and the inevitability of the ultimate victory of the people in their revolution.[1]

Yi's writing career began in earnest with the publication of *Minch'on* (민촌), translated here, in 1925. His full-length novels. *Hongsu* (홍수 Flood, 1930) and *Sŏhwa* (서화 Rat fire, 1933), sim-

---

1. Kwŏn Yŏngmin, "Literature of North Korea" in *A History of Korean Literature,* ed. Peter H. Lee (Cambridge: Cambridge University Press, 2003), 502.

ilarly center on the lives of peasants and their struggles with poverty and hardship brought about by the class system and the difficulties that plagued their lives. His *Kohyang* (고향 Hometown,
1933–1934) is highly acclaimed for its descriptions of events in the
lives of poverty-stricken farmers and their gradual recognition of
a class consciousness that leads them to fight the landlord class in
an effort to control their own lives.[2]

Yi continued his literary career in North Korea after the divi-
sion of Korea. He rose to prominence in the North as a key member of the North Chosŏn Federation of Literature and Arts (북조
선 문학예술총동맹). This group was crucial in the ideological
education of the masses in helping to establish the political order.
Kwŏn Yŏngmin describes the regulations for literature and arts in
the North as being "premised on the belief that cultural and artis-
tic activities must serve the homeland and the people, [and] stipu-
lated that literature, under the absolute rule of the proletariat, must
aim at developing a socialist mindset among the masses."[3] His
most prominent work after liberation, *Tuman-gang* (두만강 Tuman
river, 1961), centers on the struggle of peasants to overthrow the
feudal yoke and even incorporates the revolutionary struggles of
Kim Il Sung (Kim Ilsŏng, 1912-1994) into the work.

Minch'on is a close examination of how poverty works to destroy the people. The story begins with what seems to be a normal
occurrence of womenfolk gossiping, yet soon devolves into a vivid
work of poverty literature (貧窮文學 *pin'gung munhak*). The hor-
rible plight and helplessness of the poor peasants in this village is
contrasted by the wealthy young landlord who uses this to wrest
whatever he desires from the poor. Yi's writing was quite naturally
not for the poor themselves but rather to bring this situation to the
attention of other intellectuals. Thus his writing is interspersed

---

2. Ibid., 398.
3. Ibid., 498–499.

with rather sophisticated oratorical interjections detailing the historic roots for the inequity, and the means to solve such a situation are given to the reader. Surely this was not lost on Yi's readers, as almost all of the colonial subjects could have seen in at least some way how their own lives were being dictated by this framework.

***

∾ COMMONERS' VILLAGE
| *MINCH'ON* 민촌

YI KIYŎNG 이기영

Translated by Jung Ha-yun
Annotated by Michael J. Pettid

1

Water from the valley at T'aejo Peak wrapped itself around Hyanggyo Village then made a turn, flowing through the willow forest by the village entrance, while the narrow and serpentine road that led to Tongmak Village crawled up toward the mountain ridge, twisting this way and that between the banks of the fields and paddies on the other side of the stream. By the roadside banks stood an old juniper tree, its shape reminiscent of an elderly man with a stooped back leaning on a cane, and next to the hill was a small spring enclosed by a stone wall, from which clear water always flowed over the dike, light and gentle.

Drought had once dried up the stream, with only a meager drizzle from the spring flowing down like barbel on a catfish, but a recent flood had brought a marked rise in the water.

On the sky as deep as a tube of blue from a Western-style watercolor set floated a cloud as white as cotton from Tang China, while a cool buzzing sound of cicadas was heard from the thick willow forest. One side of the field that opened up in front of the forest shone green with rice stalks, their last leaves sprouting, and Mount Sŏlhwa glimmered in the distance along the southern edge of the sky. It is evening under the blazing sun, around the second and the steamiest dog day of summer.

Mr.[1] Cho's daughter-in-law, Chŏmbaek's wife, Sŏngsam's wife, Chŏmsun, and Ippŭn all sit in a row along the stream, rinsing barley in one corner or washing greens in another, and it seems that Sŏngsam's wife, famous for her chatter, cannot keep her mouth closed even on such occasions. It was her habit, each time she smiled, to carve springs in her two cheeks, and whenever she spoke, to tilt her head sideways and throw furtive sideways glances with her eyes under those vivid eyelids. Whatever you may think, she was considered a striking woman in this village, with her clear face, smiling eyes, and her lithe, loose ways. For a long time now there had been rumors of her many flings, but her father-in-law and husband were clueless, which had earned them a reputation as a pair of dunces. Now Sŏngsam's wife threw a quick glance at Chŏmbaek's wife with that expression of hers and called out, her voice sharp and sleek.

"Missus!"

"What's going to spill out of her mouth this time?"

Mr. Cho's daughter-in-law kept her thought to herself, taciturn as usual, her ears on other people's talk. As a new bride who has yet to overcome her timid ways, it was hard for her to break into conversation at such times.

Sŏngsam's wife rubbed and pressed the barley, her arms milky and fleshy under the rolled-up sleeves of her summer blouse made from Andong hemp. Rub, rub, press, rub, rub, press—she was having fun, moving to the rhythm, then after splashing a gourd full of water to rinse the barley in a single swing, poured the water, white from the rinsing, into an earthenware bowl next to her. With this done, she threw a glance and a quick smile at Chŏmbaek's wife, whatever this meant.

"Missus! I hear Clerk Pak's son got himself another concubine?"

---

1. In the text 첨지 is a title for elderly men that gives them respect, which has a softening effect when calling them. Here, the term is used as "Mr."

"Indeed. These rich folks, I suppose, can get as many as they want, the way we switch cattle."

Chŏmbaek's wife gave a sullen answer, as if it were nothing unusual. She sounded gruff even when she was chatting about nothing in particular.

"As for the concubine that came before her, she was kicked out against her will! Didn't get a single coin … chased out as she wailed and bawled."

"Well why wouldn't she? A concubine she may have been, but he took her in to live with her but kicked her out without a penny in only a year!"

"That's right, but I would never stand for it, being kicked out like that!" Sŏngsam's wife suddenly went into a sulk, her eyes narrowing.

"What could she have done? First of all, the man rejects her, and on top of that, the whole family casts her out. How can she bear such hostility? That's why old folks used to say, being someone's wife is like being locked inside a gourd with only a tiny opening. And she was a concubine at that, without the legal bindings of a citizen register."

"Couldn't she have at least vented out her anger, grabbing him by the hand and flipping him over her shoulder, and thrown him to the ground?"

Before Sŏngsam's wife could even finish, Chŏmbaek's wife, who had been glancing up ahead, suddenly poked her in the side, saying, "Shh."

At this, Sŏngsam's wife quickly turned her head, startled. Indeed, there was Clerk Pak's son, who they had been talking about. So she feigned innocence, pretending to be focused on rinsing the barley.

Wearing a traditional summer coat of ramie and a straw hat, Clerk Pak's son walked with a dignified gait, his head held high, his cheeks so fleshy that they flapped as he moved. Upon seeing Mr. Cho, who had, without anyone noticing, stepped onto the bank along the stream, his hand clasped behind him, Clerk Pak's son offered, without thinking twice, a greeting in casual honorifics.

"Tell me, old man, are you in good strength?"

Mr. Cho gazed at him for a long time, as if he were wondering who this was, then put on a jovial expression of recognition.

"Ah! It's you, sir. This fool's eyesight is poor … and getting worse yearly, you see. Would be better-off dead, I say … Ah, so, where might you be headed?" As he said this, he joined Clerk Pak's son in his way, meandering along.

"Well! Just over by the fields down there …"

He gave an arrogant reply, looking around at the women sitting along the banks with eyes filled with pride, then walked on.

"You should live on a while longer, though," he said, turning his head, as if he had just thought of it. This allowed him another glance at the banks of the stream.

"What good would that do, sir? The longer life goes on, the more hardship one has to endure, hum!"

Mr. Cho let out a sigh as he stands watching Clerk Pak's son approach the village, then turned around again, his gaze extending to Mount Sŏlhwa in the distance. Without realizing, he exhaled another long sigh and made an effort to straighten his back.

"The fresh little prick, talking all informal to someone old enough to be his grandfather!" Sŏngsam's wife said, pouting her lips.

"Plenty old to be his great-grandfather, I'd say!" Chŏmbaek's wife added in support as she poured water from the gourd. She glanced at Mr. Cho's daughter-in-law.

"Your father-in-law, he turned how old this year?"

"Eighty … seven!"

Everyone's mouths fell agape.

"Both may be from the noble class, but Clerk Pak's son down at the village acts in no way like that man."

"That's because he is a well-mannered man to begin with. Even if they address us informally, their origins won't ever sink low and even if we never address them informally, our origins won't ever rise up. Nowadays, though, it seems that if you're exceptional, you no longer have to live the typical life of a commoner. For those who are exceptional in what they do, or for those with money, this world is a pretty cushy place!"

"*Aigu*! For you, that may be true, since you have an exceptional son. I hear he always gets top grades at his school?"

"Well ... who knows what his future holds. We're an old couple placing all our hopes on him alone, but what struggle we go through to put him through school. By the way, you too should bear a son soon, but what could be the matter? No news yet! ... Why don't you try asking at your favorite haunt?"

"I already did!"

"So what did she say?"

Chŏmbaek's wife suddenly lowered her voice, glancing furtively. "She said what I need is an exorcism to chase away bad spirits!"

"What bad spirits? She should stop sleeping around, that's what."

This was what Chŏmbaek's wife thought, but she asked a different question instead, sounding as if she were not quite convinced.

"Then you should! So bad spirits have taken over your house?"

"No, over us. We're not a good match."

"Well, that gives her a good excuse!"

With these thoughts occupying her mind, Chŏmbaek's wife nodded, as if in agreement. Then, as if she just remembered something she forgot to do while lost in conversation, she began washing the barley, her hands big as pot lids. Her wide face was covered all over with pockmarks, which made it look like a beehive.

Chŏmsun, who had been washing young radishes without making herself noticed, suddenly lifted her head and spoke.

"How can a man as young as he speak so informally to the elderly?"

She looks at Chŏmbaek's wife with a quizzical expression, as if she had been keeping quiet all this time thinking about this.

"That's because he's of the noble class!" Chŏmbaek's wife answered.

At this, Sŏngsam's wife chimed in again, as if she just remembered something.

"It scares me to think I might be reborn as a nobleman in the next world! What fun would there be in life, locked up indoors all the time? Heh, heh!"

"It's nothing compared to how things were before. It used to be far more dreadful, you see. A woman could not even look straight at her husband's face, or plop down comfortably in front of her parents-in-law. Always had to stand with hands clasped in front of her. These noble people, for whatever reason, nitpicked over every whole and half as if cutting measured cloth, acting so polished in everything they did!"

Sŏngsam's wife held her stare for a while then said, "How did such folks do it under the covers, I wonder?"

She broke into laughter, while Mr. Cho's daughter-in-law covered her mouth with her hand, smiling as she said, "My, my ..."

"That's how they used to be, but now they're turning more and more like common folks!" Chŏmbaek's wife said, wearing a grin. Ippŭn hung her head low.

"Seems like they felt their noble origins to be a binding, as you said, and now they act like common folks, the only sign of their noble life left in their talk. In everything else, they are like commoners, except for the way they talk down at commoners. If that was no longer as well, well then they'd be no different from common folks, I'd say. Now they may be noble only in their skin, but in the old days, nobles behaved in a way that was becoming of nobles!"

"A nobleman like Clerk Pak is not even worth as much as a dog!"

"In the old days, they said nobles should not be knowledgeable about money, but nowadays it seems they have to be. Look at Clerk Pak, he's considered a nobleman because of his money—if he weren't rich, who'd think of him as prominent? That means, the day he runs out of money, he'd fall out of his noble status. So no wonder he attends to his money more intently than he does to his grandfather's mortuary tablet. They strive to make more money, even if they have to skin us poor folks whole, so that they can have more power as nobles."

"Well, I don't know if it is money or man that is flawed, but now this world is all about money, it seems. No loyalty, no compassion ..."

"Man's flaws brought money into use. Animals have no use for money, making a living on their own!"

"That is true. Never heard of any animals using money, even in old tales!"

"But in their case, the strong ones eat up the weak, don't they?" Chŏmsun suddenly asked, as if in doubt. The question was blurted out without her realizing it.

"Well, nevertheless. And it's the same with people, too, isn't it? Dear, I don't care if I have only one day left to live if I could only live it any way I pleased!"

"Like a lark flying freely across the spring sky?"

"Yes, you said it," Chŏmbaek's wife said, with a little smile. It was all thanks to things that her son had told her that she had gotten to talking this way. "The *yangban* from Seoul" was what the villagers called a young nobleman who had returned after attending middle school in Seoul. Whenever he was home, Chŏmbaek's son went over, then would relay the things he heard from him to his parents. Whenever his father heard such talk from his son, he would nod, as if deep in thought.

"To think of it, there's a point ..."

As they chatted on like this, the women headed back one by one. Sŏngsam's wife carried on her head the earthenware bowl containing the barley, filled to the rim with water, and in one hand a smaller bowl containing the water she saved after rinsing the barley. As she walked, she had to keep puffing to spurt out the water that overflowed from the bowl on her head, down into her mouth. Smoke rose up here and there from homes around the village busy preparing dinner.

2

This village called Hyanggyo-mal had for a long time been known as a *minch'on*, a settlement for commoners. And indeed, the village of some forty, fifty houses was filled with them, without a single nobleman in sight, even if you needed them. Occasionally, a down-and-out nobleman moved to the village, but he would soon leave, harassed by the villagers.

In the old days, however, the villagers were able to make a good living thanks to the noblemen, working some lowly jobs at the local county school and farming the land on the school's properties, but nowadays, the noblemen thought about nothing but their own interests, some of them so viciously shameless as to lick the crumbs off a servant's chin. All ties were not cut, except for one villager farming a few patches of the school's rice-paddy as a caretaker. The rest of the land was controlled by a few powerful noblemen and in some cases, they allowed tenant farming on this property, as Clerk Pak's son sometimes had done for one of his servants, a commoner from a neighboring village.

This being the state of things, life had been getting harder and harder for the villagers when in the previous year the village suffered a bad harvest, making life quite unbearable. Those among them who were slightly better-off were tenant farmers cultivating a few patches of other people's land and there were several who tenant-farmed Clerk Pak's paddies. The rest went back and forth between eating and starving, selling firewood or straw shoes or growing what they could in the mountains, many suffered damage this year due to a flood. Chŏmsun's family lost all of the rice plants in the flood, which they had planted on the few patches of paddies they had access to, leaving them without a single grain of rice to be harvested in the fall. Things had come to this even when they were fortunate enough to continue farming Clerk Pak's land this year. Perhaps it had taken something more than persistent pleading on the part of Chŏmsun's mother to keep Clerk Pak's family from cutting them off from their land. As one can see, despite Clerk Pak's insistence that Sŏngnyong, who had long been begging for some land while offering up free service as a servant at the house, be allowed to farm there, Clerk Pak's son got his way and let Chŏmsun's family continue …

Clerk Pak's family had lived in the neighboring village for generations now, growing more and more prosperous each year and now considered one of the wealthiest in the area. All in the family were known to possess a keen sense of financial opportunity, even Clerk Pak's deaf mother, whose ears cleared up bright as lanterns when it came to money—anyhow, the family members were all of a kind, people said. Clerk Pak's son, a young man who had just turned twenty, was especially keen in such matters, so much so that his father, money-minded as any other, had handed over management of the household to him. The son was currently enjoying immense influence as a tenant-farm manager for the Oriental Development Company, as a member of the Township Council, and a trustee of the Finance Cooperative. There was even talk that he had the connections to be recommended as a member of the Primary Education Council, for whenever a sword-carrying police officer or a district official came out here on business, they stopped by the house first for a casual and friendly get-together, and even the primary school teachers paid occasional visits to share a drink or two with him.

There is no need to go on about this, however. For people like Clerk Pak or his son will never die out from rural villages anywhere around the country.

Now, back from the stream, Chŏmsun placed the basket of greens and the jar of water on the clay stove in the kitchen. Her mother had already gotten a pot of barley ready and started a fire. The barley straw flared up.

"Wasn't it too heavy for you, to carry so much water on your head? Sunyŏng came by to see you."

"She did! When?"

"Just now. Said she'll be back. Why don't you and Sunyŏng sew up your brother's shirt?"

"But you'll be too busy on your own."

"I'll be fine."

As soon as Chŏmsun's mother answered, Sunyŏng entered, saying, "Just returned?"

She glanced at Chŏmsun with a beaming smile. One could not say Sunyŏng was prettier than Chŏmsun, but she was an attractive girl, her face round, with soft, fleshy cheeks. She was sixteen, the same age as Chŏmsun, and her hips were now quite broad, her long locks streaming all the way down to her ankles. Chŏmsun, on the other hand, was tall and had an oval face, her figure not too fat or not too thin, her complexion white.

"I was about to go see if you were still at the stream. What took so long?"

"The young radishes were worm-eaten all over so I had to wash them thoroughly. Let's go inside."

"What for, it's so hot. Let's work out here!"

"But it's cool by the back door."

So they went into the room and sat down with the sewing kit. "Whose quilted socks are these?"

"They're Father's."

"Quilted socks on these dog days?" Chŏmsun asked, glancing at Sunyŏng with a curious look. The look suddenly shifted into a smile, a teasing one, it was clear.

"Ha, I get it! So that's why!"

"What do you mean? Can't one wear quilted socks during dog days?"

"Quilted socks for a meeting with a prospective groom? ..."

Before Chŏmsun could finish, Sunyŏng jumped to cover Chŏmsun's mouth with one hand, pinching her thigh with the other.

"Ou, ouch! I surrender! I won't do it again! Heh heh ... Then you're lying? Again!"

"Come on, stop that talk now and teach me how to sew this.

I need to hurry, I tell you," Sunyŏng said, her cheeks flushed as if in embarrassment.

"Why the hurry again?"

"Again, you say! Because Mother told me to hurry, that's why. My mother tells me that every time I come over to your house."

"Why is that?"

"Who knows? She says I shouldn't stay too long at a house with a lad that's all grown up. How could a grown-up girl be so ignorant, she says."

"Do you like my brother?"

Out of the blue, Chŏmsun popped this question. This seemed to have left Sunyŏng speechless.

"Well, don't *you* like your brother?"

"No, I don't. He's so mean."

"They say guys should be that way. Unabashed and bold."

"So you're saying you like him!"

"Says who? … It was just an observation."

Sunyŏng threw Chŏmsun a sideways glance, looking vexed, the whites of her eyes pushed to the corner while her lips spread into a grin.

"*Oppa* is quite taken with you."

"Oh, listen to you …" Sunyŏng looked at Chŏmsun, dumbfounded.

"I know everything … The two of you were whispering by the wall last night, there in the corner, right?"

At this, Sunyŏng pouted.

"Well, last night you were alone with the *yangban* from Seoul at the lookout hut in the orchard, weren't you? I could see clearly from the banks."

"Yes, I was. I never said I wasn't! So why didn't you walk over to us then?"

Sunyŏng was quite surprised that Chŏmsun would admit it without reserve. I shouldn't have accused her if I'd known how she would react, Sunyŏng thought.

"Why would I go interrupting other people having a good time? If I had gone over, you would've shot bullets out of your eyes ..."

"That's not true. It was my first time speaking to him. And ..."

"And what? But why were you out there alone? To greet him? Ha ha ..."

"Just listen to yourself. Hear me out now. I was waiting with lunch all prepared when Mother returned from the orchard and said to me, 'Eat up and head out to the lookout hut. Keep an eye on the orchard while I take lunch out to the field.' Father and Brother were plowing the field that belonged to a family on the other side of the mountain, you see."

"That's right, your family were working yesterday. I saw the smoke spewing out at lunch time!"

"So I had just sat down at the hut and was about to start my sewing when I suddenly heard someone's footsteps. I looked up, startled, and it was him! I didn't know what to do and just dipped my head."

"So what did he say?"

"You know already. Why are you acting like you don't! He said, 'Why are you so shy when it's just a person looking at another person.'"

"Huh! He sure is funny. So what did you say?"

"What could I say? I just smiled and looked at him. Then he said, 'Yes! You should have raised your head like that from the very start,' and stared at me as if he could see through me, I think. Then he took out a melon from the sack and kept offering me one, too!"

"What! What's gotten to him? So what happened next?"

Sunyŏng drew closer and looked at Chŏmsun with wide, curious eyes.

"Then he told me this. Chomping his melon, he said, 'I suppose you are all shunning me because I'm of the noble class, but nobles are people as well. If you think about it, the fact that we draw lines between men as nobles and commoners, between the rich and the poor, just shows that humans are flawed. So then, why shouldn't you and I enjoy each other's company? We're all of a kind. What I most long for is to hear you call out to me by name, 'Hey, Ch'angsun!'"

"Huh? What is that all about?"

"That's why I asked him, all startled, 'How come?' And this is what he said. 'Then you and I would be friends, wouldn't we?'"

"So he wants to be friends!"

"So I said, 'You're just like us commoners!' and guess what he said? 'I want to be a commoner.' How funny!"

"Why would he say such a thing? Could he be mad?"

"I don't know ... Then we talked about many different things. About Seoul, about girls, and he made a big fuss about the world being evil and this and that."

"Now what is that about? My, it must have been some chat! I should have been there!"

"Then he fumbled inside his pocket and pulling out whatever he found, he handed me the money without even counting and headed back with a swagger, not even looking back!"

"Huh! So how much was it?"

"There were coins and white brass coins, about four, five *nyang*[2] in all. For a while I sat there like a fool, then called out 'Come back for a moment!' but he wouldn't. He waved his hand, saying, 'Never mind,' and kept going."

"How many melons did he have?"

"He said he had three. Although he also took a bite each from two unripe ones. Counting only the ones he finished, even if I charged three *ton* for each, it'd come to just one *nyang* and a half, right?"

"Right!"

"And I wasn't even going to charge him for the melons in the

---

2. *Nyang* is a unit of measure for money. One *nyang* was equal to ten *ton*, and ten *p'un* were equal to one *ton*.

first place. So how could I take that money? When I counted it up later, it was four *nyang* seven *ton*!"

As soon as she finished speaking, Chŏmsun glanced ahead and jumped with a startle. "*Oppa*, why are you standing there pressed against the wall like an alley cat?"

At this, Sunyŏng gasped in fright, crouching.

"Let me join in! What's all this interesting talk about?" the fellow said, grinning. A towel was wrapped around his short hair and he had an affable face, with a certain noble quality. He still had the boyishness of an eighteen-, nineteen-year-old, but his taut, muscular thighs and solid arms gave him the appearance of a strong young man, full of energy. He looked like he had come from working in the fields, his hands powdery with soil.

"Sunyŏng here was speaking ill of you, that a grown fellow is chasing the rear of a maiden that's already taken."

"Says who! You're impossible! ..." Sunyŏng laughed anxiously, her face turning red.

"You said that, did you?" the fellow said, pouncing on Sunyŏng ... Chŏmsun, beaming with a smile, gave her brother a sideways glance and slipped outside.

"Hey! What are you doing? Go away! ..."

Hearing Sunyŏng whimper, Chŏmsun's mother called out from the kitchen. "Chŏmdong! What is the matter? The girl should be married off any day now ... now you leave her alone! You'll get her upset."

"Well, you're not married yet!"

The fellow grinned and glanced again at Sunyŏng, who threw him a sideways glare, looking vexed. Then she abruptly dropped her head, tears flowing from her eyes.

Seeing this, the fellow rushed to hold her tightly. And he pressed his heated lips against hers.

At that moment, Clerk Pak's son arrived outside the gate. "Is Mr. Kim home?"

"*Aigu*! It's you, sir. He's out working."

As soon as she heard his voice, Chŏmsun's mother rose to greet him, pulling herself away from the fire, the poker still in her hand.

"You come all the way out here and I don't even have a decent seat to offer ... Our home being the way it is ... Here, please have a seat on the wheat straw mat here!"

Her face appeared perplexed, as if she were overcome with anxiety, as if she had committed some crime. Indeed she believed that poverty in itself was a crime. Clerk Pak's son put on a faint arrogant smile as he kept glancing furtively toward the inner chamber of the house.

"That's quite alright. I shall be on my way soon!"

His expression seemed to carry the recognition of his own happiness, that he had become an even better person.

"But ..."

Chŏmsun's mother slurred her words, but after hesitating for a while, she started again, as if she had thought of something. She looked as if she were barely getting the words out, using up all her energy. As if she were finally speaking after much hesitation.

"Sir, I beg you, please allow us some more rice paddies to farm next year! Oh, such unexpected rain we had this year did so much damage not just to us, but to you as well, sir, I imagine."

"Rice paddies? No paddies to go around, it looks like. But let's look into it again when fall arrives."

At this, Chŏmsun's mother took a step closer, as if in delight. "We have faith in you, sir. We've nowhere else to ..."

"I understand, so let us wait and see ... Why don't you come over sometime! You're an old woman now, you should get out a bit! Let your daughter take care of the house and ..."

For some reason, he did not finish his sentence.

"Will I find the time, I wonder? Housekeeping is such trifling work but keeps you busy day and night. It would be too rash to think that far ahead ... But come to think of it, I should pay a visit to meet the new madam."

"Do that then! I shall be going now."

Clerk Pak's son, who had been perched on the large mortar in the yard, rose with pomp and walked out, puffing on a cigarette.

"Ah, are you off already, sir? Well, good-bye then."

Chŏmsun's mother saw him off, following him with her eyes for a long while. For some reason her eyes incomprehensibly filled up with tears.

3

From Mount Hŭksŏng in the east, dark rain clouds appeared out of nowhere, floating around, then bringing in a black spray of shower, accompanied by a rumble of thunder. Before long, a high wind whirled in and raindrops the size of fists began to fall, d*rip, drip,* then came down in a single, roaring pour, loud and disorienting.

Heaven and earth, completely quiet until now, were suddenly in an uproar, as if all hell had broken loose. Farmers ran inside from the field, gasping. Rainwater fell from the eaves, forming a stream, and creeks rushed down, swollen red and muddy. The leaves of the rice plants in the paddies out front, and on the poplar tree in the garden, swung and swayed as the raindrops fell, creating a roar as they moved. But before you realized it, the rain turned gentle, accompanied by flashes of lightning and a frightening rumble of thunder as dark rainclouds flocked north. A series of cracking noises were heard, signaling a bolt of thunder! In a matter of minutes, however, the sky cleared up, as if it had been washed clean. A crescent moon rose in the eastern sky, fine and vivid.

After a meager dinner of steamed barley or barley porridge, they began gathering at Chŏmbaek's yard as they always did. Chŏmsun's father also headed out this way after finishing his meal, carrying his pipe. Mr. Cho and his son, considered a pair of dimwits, were already there, as was Wŏndŭk, said to be the most knowledgeable among the adults in the village—the most knowledgeable member of the "intelligentsia" in this village, although he had barely mastered the Korean alphabet and all he could manage was to read storybooks, falteringly, during winter days. Sudol the village's head bachelor, Mr. Pak who snorted at anything that caught his eyes, and all the others sat back in a row, resting their tired bodies after a long day. The elderly used long pipes to smoke their cigarettes. Hardly anyone could afford the expensive Hoeyŏn brand, but Sun-ik, known for his guts and audacity, an avid gambler who was generous with his winnings, secretly grew his own tobacco and often gave away rolls that he had cut and dried himself.

The elderly spoke with an earthy charm in their voices, Mr. Cho being the oldest among them and also the most eloquent. Younger folks were smoking in another corner, sitting or lying on a separate mat, while some had come over to where the elders were seated to listen to their stories. Recently, their topic of conversation centered on the floods that had been occurring everywhere.

In the courtyard, women were milling barley in a mortar to prepare for the next day's field work, and Sŏngsam's wife, assigned as one of the beaters, was having fun pounding away to a three-beat rhythm, *thump, thump, thumpety-thump.* Even when she beat grains, Sŏngsam's wife did it with flair, adding a tap on the mortar's rim in between beats, which heightened the excitement.

Chŏmbaek's wife, Ippŭn's mother, Mr. Cho's wife, and others were winnowing in another corner, while Sun-i's mother, a charmer; Su-dol's wife, a talker; and Sŏngsam's wife, famous for many things, were beating the barley as a team. Anyhow, they made good teams.

Of course, even on such occasions, Sŏngsam's wife did not keep her mouth idle, whispering this and that even when it made her run out of breath and gasp for air, bursting into that famous glossy laughter of hers. Then Su-dol's wife would say something funny, everyone would break into a roar of laughter, their hands clasping onto their bellies, their wooden pestles clashing. This was when Sun-i's mother suddenly broke into song.

> *Thump, thump, thumpety-thump*
> Beat, beat, beat away the grains!
> When we're done beating them away
> Who shall I share them with?

With this they once again resumed milling, but out of the blue, Sun-ok's wife, who ran a pub and was known as the Mortar Whore, stepped in with a pestle in hand, dancing with her hips.

> A jarful and five bowls I'll use to brew wine
> A jar and two bowls to make cake
> Then invite all my friends
> To eat and prance and have fun
> Dance and prance, *thumpety-thump!*

She wrapped up her song, did a little spin with her pestle held high, then started beating the grain to the rhythm, while everyone else broke into laughter. Mr. Cho's wife broke into sweat as she clasped her belly, trying to suppress her laughter. But the grain beaters pounded down even harder, their shoulders swaggering, their spirits high.

> Some bitches have it easy
> Wrapped in silk robes, served white rice
> How did I end up like this
> My hands blistered from all the pounding
> Darn, darn, *thumpety-thump!*

This time Su-dol's wife took off with the song, then Sŏngsam's wife stepped in again.

> Sister-in-law, that slutty bitch!
> Why go around talking behind my back?
> Can't help it if I fell for my beau

While furrowing and weeding the fields
Dance and prance, *thumpety-thump!*

There they went again, making mayhem as they burst into laughter, banging their pestles, the barley scattering here and there. And Sŏngsam's wife, her laughter was quite something, creating as much clamor as she could muster, sounding like a hen pheasant.

Out in the front yard, the *yangban* from Seoul had just arrived and people were busy greeting him. They all liked him. This was not only because he did not make much of his noble standing but because they were drawn to his openness and sense of loyalty. He looks handsome as well, with large eyes and a sharp nose. And in fact, Sŏngsam's wife had been the first to fall for him. Whenever they saw him, the villagers would ask him about affairs of the world, as if they viewed him as a sack of information. And every time, he would talk to them about many different issues. He told them about things he had read in the newspaper, things he knew about, and the many problems in this world. The villagers would listen with interest. During the recent floods, he told them about a weathy man named Min from Seoul who had donated a thousand *wŏn* for hunger relief. This had left all the villagers so amazed they could not close their mouths.[3]

He would also add things like, "That's what they call rich folks' sugar coating. An attempt at squeezing out even more from people."

When the villagers first heard such talk, of course they were shocked and in doubt, but he was insistent in his views.

The things he told the villagers could be summarized as follows:

"First of all, money is not rice, nor can it ever turn into cloth. Furthermore, rice and cloth do not come from the hands of one

---

3. *Wŏn* is a unit of measure for currency and was used from the time of the Great Han Empire (1897–1910).

who sits there doing nothing, so how is it that even one who does not once lift a finger can become a rich man by possessing this piece of paper called money? That is wrong from the start. For instance, if one *mal*[4] of rice costs two *wŏn* these days, the expenses that went into producing one *mal* of rice, from spring to fall, especially for those who farmed the land on a fifty percent annual interest loan, would have been several times that amount, and it is unfair that the traders raise or cut market prices as they please, paying no regard to the cost of labor.

"All this is an attempt at turning even people into commodities in order to expand their own fortunes, taking only their own interests into consideration. Therefore, the righteous thing to do would be to allow money to be spent only by those whose work benefit people and not by those who are idle or commit evil deeds, so that everyone would work according to their skill and talent, with the exception of the handicapped, the elderly, and children."

These were his words. And so he condemned the rich, including Clerk Pak's son and Official Yi in the neighboring village, saying they were not noblemen, not even human, worse than dogs that don't know any better than to go around sniffing dung.

When the villagers first heard these words from him, they were astounded. It was because he was criticizing those that they had until now looked up to as honorable men. As they kept listening to him, however, they were soon able to be rid of their suspicions. And they came to understand that the wealthy Min's donation of one thousand *wŏn* was nothing to be amazed at.

Once he also said, "Money is all people care about in this world today. If there was a dog that possessed money, people would address him with respect, as Sir Bark!" This made them all burst into laughter.

Now, after speaking at length once again about these issues, he rose to leave.

---

4. A *mal* is a unit of measure equivalent to 18 liters.

"Ah, do stay for more fun."

From here and there came words attempting to keep him longer. But he set out immediately, saying he had some business to tend to. He was visiting his uncle's house in the next village and it had been only a few days since he arrived from Seoul. With looks that seemed no older than twenty-two or three, the young man had been raised in his uncle's household since young and had yet to marry.

Heading along his way, he made a stop at Chŏmsun's house. He opened the bush clover gate and stepped in but it seemed that no one was there. He was about to turn around and leave when someone suddenly rushed out after him from the inner chamber. He saw that it was Chŏmsun.

"Look here! Um … do take back your money from yesterday!" she said, in a fluster.

"What money? Ah! You mean take back what I paid for the melons."

"It was more than what the melons cost!"

"Is that all you think about, whether it's more or less than it should be? If it's more, why don't you use it for yourself!"

"What! People will speak ill of me."

"Speak ill? What for?"

"That I take money from a man for no reason."

"Why should they speak ill of it if the money had been given in pure spirit. You are one who adheres to principles, aren't you? In that case, why don't you give me more melons next time in exchange!"

"Come tomorrow, then. To the lookout hut."

"All right, then!"

After giving her this answer, he headed straight home. He could not quite understand why he had wanted to stop by Chŏmsun's house.

That night, Chŏmsun readjusted her pillow several times, thinking, "What a peculiar man he is …"

4

It was the following night. Chŏmsun went with her mother to the lookout hut. The *yangban* from Seoul was not there. Chŏmsun was looking forward to seeing him, secretly, but this was not why she had come out. She had suddenly gotten the urge to get out; perhaps it was the bright moon that had filled her with curiosity and she did not want to be stuck in her room.

Sunyŏng had come over earlier in the evening and upon hearing of Chŏmsun's plan, she had offered to come along, saying she would get permission from her mother. And indeed, as Chŏmsun was about to set out, Sunyŏng had come running, with a broad smile on her face. Chŏmsun's father had left right after dinner, saying he had some business to tend to over on the other side of the hills. This was why Chŏmsun's mother was heading to the hut to watch the orchard.

The hut was built on the long embankment along the stream that runs down the corner of the hill by the village. Here, the sound of the gushing stream could be heard and the cool breeze from the water blew gently toward the hut.

Moonlight glimmered on the stream and fine crystals of mica glittered on the white sand beach on the other side of the water, while on the hill across the stream, a green forest of poplars cast a dim shadow. Closer to the hut, Mount Sŏlhwa appears to be shimmering, as if in a haze, while from the dark blue sky myriad stars gaze down at the human world, smiling and blinking.

Chŏmsun and Sunyŏng were enjoying the evening, intoxicated by the night scenery, when they suddenly heard people approaching and looked around to find the *yangban* from Seoul with Chŏmdong.

"What are you doing here? I told you to watch the house … And who's that?"

Chŏmsun's mother had only now noticed there was another person behind Chŏmdong.

When she heard his voice, she greeted him heartily, as if she had just realized who it was.

"Ah! It's you, sir. Had no idea you went around for evening walks. Do come up!"

"I ran into Chŏmdong and came by for some melons," the *yangban* from Seoul replied from below the hut.

"Now, I don't think we have any here. Chŏmdong, why don't you go pick some. Well, stay for a while, then. I must go weed the field now!" The old woman said, picking up the hoe and climbing down the hut. "The moon's bright and the night's cool, perfect for weeding. Why don't you get to work, too, since you're here!"

"Come now! I'm going to talk a bit with him here. You go on first, Mother." Chŏmdong said, heading to the melon field with a sack on his shoulder.

"How about staying for a melon before you start weeding?" He asked.

"I don't feel like having one right now. I'll eat later when I feel like it," she replied as she walked up to the furthest furrow and started weeding the field. Her hoe made rustling noises as it brushed against lumps of soil.

"It's okay, we'll just eat down here," he said, declining Chŏmdong's invitation.

"No, let's get up there! Nowhere to sit here. Girls, it's okay if we climb up, right? My big girls!"

They could hear giggles from the elevated floor of the hut, followed by low whispers.

Soon Chŏmsun called out in a shrill voice, "Do as you like!"

The two men climbed up to the hut. But before they took their seats, Chŏmsun pushed a fistful of coins toward the *yangban* from Seoul with a thump.

"What's this?"

Chŏmdong's eyes opened wide, which made the maidens giggle again.

"Ah, the money for the melons!"

The *yangban* from Seoul explained what had happened and added that vendors in Seoul had a hard time collecting payment from customers who try to hold on to their money.

"Well, let's use the money to pay for these melons then. Who cares where the money came from as long as we're paying. That's just how girls are, small-minded. As if they could scoop out an entire gourd with a tobacco seed," Chŏmdong said, handing out a melon each to everyone.

"What am I to do, then, take someone's money for no reason?" Chŏmsun yelled, glaring at Chŏmdong with a prissy expression.

But Chŏmdong simply continued to slice the melons and chomped off a piece. "Yes, yes, good for you. Why don't you have some more melons as a reward? And how about a song from each of you!"

"Horrendous! What kind of a girl would sing in front of men!"

"Why shouldn't you sing in front of men? You sing all the time among yourselves."

"What do you mean sing? Us, sing?"

"Didn't you sing, like this?"

Chŏmdong tried to imitate the girls' singing, his voice forlorn and head tilted.

> Shall we go, shall we go!
> Go gather wild greens
> climb the hills
> to gather wild greens.
>
> Let's gather some greens
> play the flute
> we shall have fun
> get a peek at my darling one.

"We never sang anything like it!"

The maidens whined, their voices desperate, their faces flushed red as if the embarrassment was enough to kill them.

"Forget it then! Or was it Sŏngsam's wife who sang it? Tell me, you from Seoul, do maidens in Seoul sing like this as well? What about schoolgirls?" Chŏmdong asked, turning to the *yangban* from Seoul.

"Sure they do, they sing Western *changga*."[5]

"Ah, *changga*. You mean songs that go like this. Young men, young men, listen all young men! Like that, huh?"

The maidens again burst into giggles. Thanks to Chŏmdong's easygoing playfulness, their embarrassment had diminished somewhat. They continued to have a good time, soon everyone was focused on the words of the *yangban* from Seoul. Once again he was saying that this world was evil and that the rich were evil. That was why all the youth around the country were in this current state, when they should be thriving in a world as beautiful as a mountain covered with flowers, he claimed in agitation.

"Look around! This beautiful scenery. These tantalizing stars. The luminous moonlight! The sound of the stream, deep and gentle. Think about it, in this season when every tree branch in that quiet, humble forest is draped in green, let us suppose that we are living in a nice clean house that we've built in this scenic mountain, with no worry about food or clothing. The fathers and mothers work out in the field while we study and run and play at school, and when we return in the evening, we help out our parents in the field or sing and play out in the mountains—how beautiful would our lives be? If everyone worked together and earned together, living with no distinction between the rich and the poor, this will result in the neighbors being truly friendly and loving, everyone enjoying themselves and having fun, saying, Today let's all get together at your place; Tomorrow, I'm inviting everyone over. That will be the day when the birds in the sky sing of the happiness of

---

5. A *changga* (長歌) is a long song or ballad.

men and the flowers on land smile at the joy that people feel. That will be the day when all the creatures in this world will finally bestow their blessings on humans, and we will feel genuine joy gazing at that moon. But what about the current state of things? We cannot afford to study when we should be studying, and our aging parents work day and night only to suffer in poverty. Young maidens' delicate hands are gnarled at the joints from all that pounding, and men and women in the prime of their youth cannot even afford to fall in love. The reason we are struggling like this, without enough to feed or clothe ourselves, tediously trudging through each day in our straw-roof huts the size of a crab shell, bitten by fleas and bedbugs and mosquitoes, is all because a few evil bastards have hogged all the money, shoving the good hardworking folks into the dark pit of poverty. Ah! The moon may shine bright but what good is that to us now? This breeze may be refreshing but our hearts feel more congested than ever, is that not so?

"A world where tens of millions of people, who work under the sun by day and rest their tired bodies under the moon by night, can all work and making a living together—that will be a truly humane world."

As they listened to his passionate outcry, everyone became completely captivated. Chŏmsun and Sunyŏng were in tears, unable to hold them back. How they longed to soon greet such a world ... which was why they felt further indignant and rueful about their present lives. Even Chŏmdong, who had been gibbering away, sat still and quiet, lost in thought. There was only silence all around, save for the roar of the stream.

Chŏmdong signaled to Sunyŏng with his eyes and they sneaked away from the hut. When only two of them were left, out of the blue Chŏmsun collapsed onto the lap of the *yangban* from Seoul and began to sob. It was not so much that she longed to love him but this was more a fitful outburst of emotion in response to his words. Indeed, looking back on her life until now, she felt that it could be described as nothing other than unhappiness.

"Why did you have to tell me all this?"

As revealed in these words, she seemed to have gained aware-ness of a sadness that she had not known until now.

At that moment, the man held her in his arms and placed upon her hot lips his own.

Faint, choking sobs could also be heard from the woods over there. It was Chŏmdong and Sunyŏng, also crying. What was it that was making them cry, these young men and women who had yet to step into the gate of life? Dear Moon, perhaps you might know …

The sound of the stream, the sound of sobs! Or the sound of the mother's hoe, weeding the field. These sounds mingled to-gether and quietly flowed on, wrapping themselves around this night symphony.

5

A month had now passed. The year was entering the seventh lunar month, recognized as a month of destitution, when poor families run out of barley. In Hyanggo-mal, few households still had grains left and it had been a while since Chŏmsun's family had run out of barley.

They had been holding on somehow, with the father and the son providing labor for this or that, but now only a dead end awaited them and they were lost as to how they could make their living. It was a time when rice and all the other crops had been planted, the ridges along the rice fields carved, and all the workers were heading up to the logging zone. There were no jobs left at all. The rice-heads were already out, white and cloudy.

Chŏmdong and his father had no other way to make a living other than gathering wood. The melons were done now for the season, with none left to sell.

Since Chŏmsun's family owned no land on the mountains, gathering wood was not so easy to do, either, but if both men were able to work, they might be able to make some money by logging other people's trees, but as the saying goes, misfortunes never travel alone, and Mr. Kim became unexpectedly bedridden. For seven days now he had been lying in his room, unable to move around due to a bad boil on his toe, growing worse. It was swollen pale now. Chŏmsun's mother, after much deliberation, went to see Clerk Pak's son to borrow a sack of rice, her last straw.

She knew well enough that Clerk Pak's son was a brutal stinker, but judging from how he had answered as if he would when she asked him for some rice paddies to farm, and how he had told her to come over some time, one thing seemed certain, that he did possess some sort of goodwill. She would learn later that this goodwill came at a high price, leaving her pale with shock, but for now, she was as good as dead, with nowhere to turn to, and at times like this, humans are bound to want to believe even completely unfounded things. Isn't that why they say a drowning man will clutch at a straw? How could she not reach out for help to a gracious man who had invited her over, responding to her request as if he would offer her land to farm? At a time like this, it did not matter whether the man was a wicked bandit or the farm manager for the Oriental Development Company. All she remembered was his offer that she should come over some time and his answer that had sounded as if he would give her rice paddies to farm. People might call her foolish, in fact. And indeed, Clerk Pak's son laughed at her foolishness. But what kind of a person goes around toying with an innocent and foolish person like her? That's right! In today's world, this kind of person would be described as high and mighty. After all, aren't people who deceive others in order to claim ownership praised as smart these days? If so, Clerk Pak's son would also be praised as a smart man, but he was so smart he had turned into a real stinker. This had made even people of this region, who had found much to praise about in smart folks, come to speak ill of him.

However, this was not the time to squabble about such things.

Chŏmsun's mother was headed to see Clerk Pak's son, carrying with her much hope despite her anxiety.

And indeed, Clerk Pak's son said yes, without a moment of hesitation. Saying that if one sack was not enough, she should borrow two.

How happy this made Chŏmsun's mother feel! Without realizing it, her mouth went agape. So after offering him many thanks, she stepped outside, her heart uncontrollably light, like a general embarking on his return after sounding his victory.

Clerk Pak's son, however, followed her out the gate and led her to a quiet corner saying he had something to discuss in private.

What he wanted to discuss was his conditions for the deal. Saying, I will lend you the rice as I offered, so give me your daughter in return.

Back home, clueless about all this, the family awaited her, wondering if there was some way out of their troubles. Even Mr. Kim, famous for his ability to maintain composure—and who had roared at his wife, telling her not to go—awaited her in hopes that there might be a way out. But his wife came back with nothing gained but tears. When she heard what Clerk Pak's son had to say, she felt something sink inside her chest, everything turning black in front of her eyes. Without answering, she had turned around and returned home, her mind in a muddle as tears fell like rain. Now she sat with one hand under her chin, down and discouraged as she stared out blankly at the hill facing her house, her eyes puffy and swollen. Mr. Kim was suddenly furious.

"So! What did he say?" he asked, shifting from his reclining position.

"He said we can borrow not one but two sacks if we need to."

"That's good news, isn't it? So what is it?"

"In return, he wanted Chŏmsun …"

The wife choked on her words and was unable to finish, turning away her teary face.

At this, Mr. Kim leaped up to a seated position.

"What in the world did you just say?" he roared, like a tiger.

The entire house shook and rumbled. Chŏmsun's mother jerked back in shock while Chŏmsun, who had been working in the kitchen, ran into the room. Mr. Kim clenched his fists as he gritted his teeth with force, his lips flat and quivering under his beard. Balls of fire moved back and forth inside his wide eyes.

"I told you not to go! So why did you have to drag yourself over there and take such dirty crap from him! Why! Huh?"

"How could I have known?"

The wife crouched down, as if she were afraid he might punch her with his fist.

"You wait and see if I ever give him what he wants, even if I have to starve to death. Does he think I'm going to sell my own daughter to serve as his third, fourth concubine? So what did you tell him? Huh?"

"What could I tell him? I was dumbfounded and said nothing!"

"You mean to tell me you just stood there listening to him? You bitch! You should have spat right on his face! Dirty bastard! You call a scoundrel like him the son of a nobleman? Go tell him, go! I'd rather give my daughter away to a dog than to you. You bastard, no better than a dog! You dirty *yangban* bastard! Go tell him this is what he deserves and spit right on his face! Go on now, you hear! Go!"

He continued to scream and shout, chiding his wife. The wife simply kept sobbing, without saying a word. Chŏmsun cried along with her.

"Ah—"

At that moment, Mr. Kim let out a scream and fell hard on the floor. The mother and daughter yelled, "Oh my goodness!" Chŏmsun leapt up.

"Father!"

She put her arms around him while her mother, stricken with panic, could say nothing more than, "Water, cold water." So Chŏmsun rushed to fetch some cold water and sprayed it with her mouth on her father's forehead. Right then, Mr. Kim fainted.

The mother and daughter did not know what else to do but stand there, their arms and legs shaking.

Chŏmsun had been in the kitchen cooking thin gruel with the bowl of millet that Sunyŏng had brought earlier, so she had heard every word of their talk. This was why she knew well the reason why her father had fainted.

After the news spread, the villagers of Hyanggyo-mal denounced Clerk Pak's son and came to the aid of Chŏmsun's family. Sŏngsam's wife was no exception. Clerk Pak's son had gone through the villages in the area picking up every single commoner girl with a decent face, but for some reason he had not been able to get his hands on Sŏngsam's wife. Actually, he had long been attempting an intimate affair with her, but Sŏngsam's wife, famous as she may be for her many flings, would not give him a nod. Clerk Pak's son had a go-between serving him in every village and whenever his Hyanggyo-mal go-between tried to drop Sŏngsam's wife a suggestive hint about Clerk Pak's son, she would pout her lips.

"You telling me that scoundrel is actually human? He may be a *yangban*, but he's no human, that's for sure!" she said, leaving the go-between with nothing to say.

And now this famous woman had come by with five bowls of rice and ten coins. Chŏmsun's mother was taken aback. Chŏmbaek's wife had brought two sacks of barley. Sudol's wife had brought a sack of barley as well. Ippŭn's family had brought two bowls of flour, Manyŏp's family a bowl of millet. Everyone brought what they could, a bowl of steamed rice or porridge even, and praised Mr. Kim's dignified spirit.

However, not even the state can relieve poverty, as they say, and there was no way people could keep up this effort day after day. That evening when Chŏmdong returned home after work and heard about the proposal, he was just as furious as Mr. Kim. He insisted that he would support the entire family on his own, telling them not to worry. However, it was hard to do, as hard as flying up to the sky to pick stars, for him to provide a living for the whole family by himself.

Mr. Kim later regained consciousness, but his illness worsened as time passed.

There were more and more things that called for money, including medication. Mr. Kim, however, did not permit anyone to mention Clerk Pak's son's offer ever again.

One day, Chŏmsun knelt down in front of her father, and politely and without even a hint of change in her facial expression., volunteered that she would get married to Clerk Pak's son. Mr. Kim, however, would not have it, jumping up and down in fury.

"Then you will no longer be my child!"

In the days that followed, his condition turned critical and he was barely conscious. The family wanted to get him some medicine but they had no money in the house, not even a thing to cook a bowl of thin gruel with. The mother finally broke down, unable to do anything but cry, while Chŏmdong gathered firewood to sell, barely making it through each day.

Chŏmdong had made up his mind, his teeth clenched tight. He tried as hard as he could to hold out on his own until his body crumbled. He went gathering wood even at night, and on rainy days he made straw sandals to sell. He worked without a minute of rest. He was determined to go on as long as he could, and if that didn't work out, then he would take up whatever kind of work that he had to. He thought he would rather steal or rob and end up in prison than sell his own sister for dirty money in order to live.

Chŏmsun, on her part, had also firmly made up her mind as to what she should do with herself. She knew clearly that she would never be able to get permission from her parents or brother to get married to Clerk Pak's son. So she had decided that she would go ahead with it on her own, without anyone knowing. All she had to do was to give her answer to Clerk Pak's son's go-between in the village.

For Chŏmsun to finally make up her mind, however, she had to lie awake many sleepless nights as her heart burned and throbbed. Many nights she wept, her heart burdened with the sense of indecision. It was a bitter thing, perhaps more so than death, to offer her body to such a man. If someone were to say to her, "I will provide for your family and in return you must die!" she would have said yes right away. In these times, however, such a gracious or chivalrous man was hard to come by. So no matter how she struggled, kicking her feet and gazing into the void, to tell herself that she would be unafraid of anything, anything but this, in the end, there was no other way but this. When there was no other way, one could only lie flat and await death, as the saying went, but how could she turn a blind eye when others could be saved if only she would offer her body? The key to their survival lay singularly in her hands. Furthermore, her father was ill in bed, moaning, but they did not even have enough to cook him a bowl of thin gruel. Even if what was asked of her was an impossible deed—a sad, sad deed, more painful than death itself—she had no choice but to endure it. No, if she could not live through it, then she would quietly choose to die on her own. Under the current circumstances, I have no choice but to go to him, even if the man were a heinous thief, let alone Clerk Pak's son! she told herself, in all desperation.

It was not that there were no other affluent families in the area. There were quite a number of so-called influential and rich noblemen as well. But they all turned a blind eye. They knew of Chŏmsun family's situation, still they turned a blind eye. A sack or two of rice to loan, what was it worth to them? If only they had the heart to do away with it, to them the significance would not even compare to a fistful of rice or a single coin that belonged to a poor family—furthermore, Chŏmsun's father's righteous nature had never allowed a debt to go unpaid, and he had asked to borrow the rice, determined to pay it back somehow—but no one gave up a single grain of rice. The circumstances were already dire but now a member of the family was close to death and a sack or two of rice would save a dying man. But the rich folks all turned a blind eye. It was as if they were enjoying an outing on their fancy boat with a phoenix figurehead, yet a stone's throw away people were drowning, flailing their arms and calling out for help, screaming *Argh! Argh!* but these folks just looked on, pretending they did not see the drowning. All they had to do to save them was to throw them a piece of rope, but they simply looked on, pretending they did not see. No, they were not simply looking on but gazing with a grin. And as they did, they were further savoring their own happiness.

Yes! This is the way of the world today. This is the world of humans, whom, they say, are superior to beasts. Exploitation by the rich, this is fair and just, they say. This is praised by the church of the holy God. Ah! Send down brimstone and fire here on this world! Here on Sodom and Gomorrah. Amen! Amen! ...

If Chŏmsun were to think such thoughts, she would run into the kitchen right this minute and set out with a knife. If only vaguely, she got to thinking that the *yangban* from Seoul was right in what he had said. She intuitively realized that the world was an evil place. She now saw that the things people said—about poverty being a punishment for the sins committed in our previous lives and affluence being appointed by the heavens—were complete lies. And so she had come to view rich folks as heinous thieves, no better than mice, the way he saw them. But right now she had no choice but to offer up her body to a dirty, heinous, no-better-than-a-mouse thief. She had no choice but to offer him her pure virginity.

Chŏmsun finally decided that she would send word to Clerk Pak's son the following morning. She intended to maintain her virginity through this final night. Only minutes ago, her eyes had been bright and dry with desperate fury, but now her decision made her choke up with sorrow. Unable to hold back the endless stream of tears, she sneaked outside, to the other side of the fence. She wanted to be where no one would see her and cry her heart out without having to hold back.

It was early in the evening and it seemed that it would still be a long while until the moon was out! As a curtain of darkness wrapped itself around the hazy dusk, the desolate mountain village was as still as the land of the dead. This made one feel as if one's fate were as dark as this night, nothing visible on the road ahead. While myriad stars twinkled in the sky and the Milky Way hung high above, the Weaver Girl gazed at the Shepherd Boy.[6] A warm breeze was rising from somewhere, making the poplar leaves shake and tremble, and beyond the hill by the village, the mountain path to the neighboring village appeared blurry. Reeds rubbed and rustled, creating a strange, stifling sound, and some bird flew into the air, letting out a single sharp screech. The ground along the ditches was already wet with dew. To Chŏmsun, everything appeared to be signs of sadness. And so she wept as she looked up at the sky. She wept as she bent down toward the ground. She wept as she gazed at the mountain. She wept as she gazed at the somber forest. No other words of lament came out of her mouth as she wept, calling out Mother ... Father ... Brother ...

She had not noticed him approaching but found the *yangban* from Seoul standing by her side. She jumped with a startle, then hung her head low. She had never imagined he would come out here in the middle of the night.

"Ah! What are you doing here?" he asked in surprise.

"No, nothing! It's ... it's ..."

Chŏmsun swallowed her tears. Her expression shifted, as if everything was fine. But he had already heard the news. He had brought what few coins he had over to Chŏmdong as well.

"I know everything, I know!"

---

6. This is a reference to the legend of the Weaver Girl and Shepherd Boy (*Kyŏnu-Chingyŏ sŏlhwa*), which dates to the Chinese Zhou dynasty (1027 BCE–771 BCE). The daughter of the Jade Emperor and a shepherd who lived across the Milky Way met and fell in love, neglecting their duties. For this sin, they were forbidden to see one another save a single day each year (the seventh day of the seventh lunar month), when their tears would drop down to the human world.

Before he could finish, Chŏmsun fell into his arms, holding on to him as she buried her face in his chest. Her voice trembled with passion.

"Please forgive me! Please forgive me! For leaving to be the concubine of a rich man ... a man you despise ... the son of Clerk Pak ..."

As she cried faintly, the man held her but said nothing, gazing blankly at the sky. At that moment, a meteor streaked across the sky.

6

The following day Clerk Pak's family sent to Chŏmsun's home a horseload of barley and fifty coins. According to the message delivered by the servant, the money was sent with kind orders that it be spent on medicine to cure the patient's illness.

Chŏmsun, however, had turned into a different person overnight, a gloomy person who let entire days go by without saying a word. Her expression, once so friendly and lively, had all but disappeared to who knew where. Mr. Kim was bedridden and in such critical condition that he knew none of this, but strangely, this morning, he had started to babble and drivel. Whenever he opened his eyes, whenever anyone caught his eye, he wagged his finger.

"He's the one who sold his own daughter to a rich family as a concubine in exchange for a sack of rice!"

Life is tenacious, however. Chŏmsun's mother cooked the rice to eat. Chŏmdong resisted—bawling and clamoring, insisting that he would never eat it, even if he should starve to death—but eventually began to eat the rice. The fact was, it was Chŏmsun who pounded the rice and cooked it up, wholeheartedly urging her mother to eat, and her brother as well. That day, Chŏmdong had been felling trees in the mountain until evening and when he came home he was greeted by Chŏmsun serving him an unexpected bowl of steamed white rice. Wondering if things had worked out somehow, he was about to ask his mother as he scooped up a spoonful of rice when he realized what was happening and threw his spoon to the floor. He sobbed out loud. Just then, Chŏmsun ran inside and collapsed at his knee, weeping and begging.

"Brother, please forgive me!"

Chŏmdong took to the floor, his hands around his head.

Their mother was speechless, sitting there and staring blankly at the two of them, as if she had been hollowed out of her spirit. But she decided that she should not further distress her young daughter. Behaving the way Chŏmdong did would only distress her, dreadfully at that, she thought. For this aging couple, a son and a daughter being all they had, their only wish was to do a good job of raising them, to find a good wife for the son and marry off the daughter to a reliable family and spend their later years watching them make it through life. They had never imagined, not even in dreams, that they would yet be unable to get a wife for their son at almost twenty years of age, nor that they would have to send off their daughter like this. Her husband was not evil, nor was any other family member, but somehow, try as they did day and night to live as others do, they were left struggling in poverty as they had always been, which made her wonder if she were being punished for a wrong committed in a previous life. But like frost falling on snow, unexpected circumstances now falsely accused them of selling off their daughter. Ah, what kind of fate had befallen her? She believed that it all depended on one's Four Pillars and Eight Characters, determined at birth by the heavens.[7] What was one to do under these circumstances, then? It would not be a difficult thing to do, for her to simply fall to her immediate death on her own with a knife in her mouth. But how could she take her own life, leaving behind her ailing husband and children? Then her hus-

---

7. These are the *saju p'alja* (四柱八字). This uses the two sexagenary characters for one's birth year, month, day, and hour to determine one's fate.

band would surely die! The children as well. The entire family would perish. Ah! She could not possibly allow this to happen. This was why she began eating the steamed rice before anyone else. She kept persuading herself like this as she scooped up rice for herself and fed her husband as well. But each time she was struck by the thought that she had done something she should never have to her daughter, that she had driven a nail into her young heart, she felt her bones ache and her innards melt! She threw her spoon to the floor, choking on the rice. Chŏmsun leapt up, putting her arms around her mother and rubbing her back.

"Mother, Mother! Please don't do this. I shall die with you then! ..."

She wept as she said this. Mother and daughter held each other and wept with grief, holding each other tight. When Mr. Kim opened his eyes and saw this, again he wagged his finger and mumbled.

"They're the ones that sold their own daughter in exchange for a sack of rice!"

Ah! What in the world is happening? Chŏmsun's mother thought things over, but she could not possibly let her ailing husband starve to death. This ailing husband who would never be given another chance if he died ...

Chŏmdong, on his part, concluded that there was nothing else he could do now that things had come to this. He had tried to hold out on his own and had no idea that Chŏmsun would decide to do this. But he did not blame his sister. He believed that in the end it was all because of his own uselessness. His incompetence was to blame for letting things come to this, for failing to do the job he was given as a man: to keep this small family afloat. As an uneducated man, even if he chopped wood all day long and sold them in town after walking twenty *ri*, the most he would make was fifty or sixty *chŏn*.[8] Even if he sat crouched all day making straw sandals,

---

8. *Chŏn* is a monetary unit; one hundred *chŏn* equals one *wŏn*.

the most he would make was forty or fifty *chŏn*. Ah! How could one save an entire family with this money? They had been barely getting by on what he and his father made, and now that his father was ill—and with their farming work all gone, they could not even borrow rice to eat—they had no other choice but to starve to death. How bad things must have been, for Chŏmsun to make such a decision? Naïve as she might be, she must have realized there was no other way. That he was now being sustained on this rice was indeed shameful. But wasn't it inevitable, given the current circumstances?

A few days later Sunyŏng also left on a palanquin, headed for the family that had already sent her family two sacks of rice. On the morning of her departure, she had come over before breakfast to see Chŏmsun and wept, holding Chŏmsun's hands. She could not let herself grab Chŏmdong's hands and cry so instead she wept in Chŏmsun's presence. Chŏmsun also cried as she sat face to face with Sunyŏng, but ever since that day, Chŏmdong appeared as if he had lost his mind. It was also apparent that the *yangban* from Seoul was no longer the same, either. He seemed listless, as if he were deep in worry. However, because his calm appearance suggested a firm conviction, one thought he might be up to something. As if to support this, his face turned frighteningly distressed.

Chŏmsun's mother was of course half out of her mind as well, but she did not leave her husband's side for a minute, squeezing out useless tears and sighs as she nursed him with full devotion. Only Clerk Pak's son rejoiced over his success as he awaited the day when Mr. Kim would recover. This being so that as soon as her father was better, he could take away Chŏmsun.

7

Rumors spread, however, that Mr. Kim's illness was getting worse. This was why it suddenly occurred to Clerk Pak's son that Mr. Kim might die. Keen as he might be about nothing but his own interests, Clerk Pak's son wondered how he could possibly take her away immediately following the death of a parent. One should be thankful that he had the capacity for such thinking, unexpected as it might be, but indeed he was capable of at least this much dignity. Because he had learned ever since he was young that the most important deed in the world was to care for one's parents, on the surface of things at least, no matter what he felt inside, he did possess the thought that other people's parents should be respected as well. So if Mr. Kim were to die, then it would take months, or even half a year, and it would mean serious trouble if they kept coming up with excuses, saying she would be sent after the first-year memorial service, then the second. Thus, he was determined to bring Chŏmsun over as soon as possible.

Another reason he was in a hurry to bring over Chŏmsun was because his newly acquired concubine was already proving unsatisfactory, causing a gap between them. Of course it was too early to completely push her away, not before he tried some more licks of her loving, but the new concubine was too gruff, even making him feel belittled sometimes. So by taking in Chŏmsun as soon as he could, he would be telling the concubine, Look now, and hopefully curb her strong temper, but that was not all, because the last time he saw Chŏmsun, he noticed that she had matured significantly from the year before, looking much like a woman now. His first thought about her had been, That's not too bad, but now her beauty made him greedy. So what he planned to do was get a taste of a young love, tender as a budding blossom, while receiving the love of his older concubine, subtle yet persistent, as if she would pull him into the ground, then when he got tired, he would turn his back on them both. And this was why this morning, he had abruptly ordered a palanquin to be prepared and sent to Mr. Kim's house.

The seventh lunar month had passed and it was already the first week of the eighth month. Over at Chŏmsun's, the family had just finished breakfast, as the sky, which had been clear and bright until the night before, filled up with clouds, making the day dark and chilly. Mr. Kim, who had recently become further emaciated, no longer capable of his crazy chatter, lay groaning in the warm corner of the room after taking only a sip of thin gruel, while the three other members of his family busily finished up their meager breakfast. The mother was unable to focus on eating, preoccupied with worry, and the three of them could not do much else but cry, but Chŏmdong still planned to go gathering wood and was about to head out with his wooden carrier. And that was when Clerk Pak's servants stormed in through the bush clover gate, carrying the palanquin.

Chŏmdong stood gazing at them, frozen like the village guardian totem pole. The mother suddenly could not see in front of her. Chŏmsun simply felt dazed. Flustered for a moment, she shifted her eyes from her father to her mother.

"Mother …"

She was barely able to get this one word out of her mouth. Then, without saying a word, she hung her head low and quietly walked to the palanquin. At this moment, her mother called out in devastation.

"Chŏmsun! Chŏmsun! Chŏmsun! Chŏmsun …"

She leapt into the yard, then fell flat on her face at her daughter's feet.

"Ah!"

Chŏmdong jumped in as well and wrapped his arms around his sister. Then Mr. Kim, who had been lying there barely conscious, not even capable of his crazy chatter, sat up by the door like a miracle and looked out into the yard.

"They're the ones that sold their own daughter in exchange for a sack of rice!"

At this, Chŏmsun turned her eyes to him.

"Ah! Father …"

She let out a faint cry, covering her face with her two hands.

When Chŏmsun was about to step inside the palanquin after taking one last look at her family, her eyes were met by another pair, ablaze with a frightening glow. They belonged to the *yangban* from Seoul, who was about to walk in but stood frozen by the bush clover gate, staring helplessly. Chŏmsun collapsed, face first, into the palanquin.

None of them, however, could outdo the power of two sacks of rice! Not the father's madness, the mother's passing out, the brother's tears or the frightening eyes of the *yangban* from Seoul could outdo the power of two sacks of rice! Not even her parents' love, her brother's affection, or pure love from the *yangban* from Seoul could outdo the power of two sacks of rice! Two sacks of rice were more than enough to drive the father mad, to cause unbearable pain in the daughter's heart, to bring everlasting grief to the mother and the brother. The love of her parents, who had raised her with such affection, the warm camaraderie she had shared with her brother, the rosy hope this maiden had longingly awaited, wishing, come, come, human happiness—they all disappeared like bubbles, helpless in the face of two sacks of rice. Thus, Clerk Pak's son was able to take away, with just two sacks of rice, their only daughter that they had cherished and treasured for sixteen years. Ah! But what exactly were two sacks of rice worth? Chŏmsun was now being taken away to Clerk Pak's house in a palanquin, sold for two sacks of rice.

∾

∾ ABOUT THE EDITOR

Michael J. Pettid is Professor of Korean Studies at Binghamton University where he has taught since 2003. Prior to that, he received his doctorate from the University of Hawai'i at Mānoa and taught in Korea at the Academy of Korean Studies and Ewha Women's University. The focus of his research and teaching is premodern Korea's history, literature, religion, and culture. His most recent books are the coedited volumes of *Premodern Korean Literary Prose* (Columbia University Press, 2018) and *Death, Mourning, and the Afterlife in Korea: Critical Aspects of Death from Ancient to Contemporary Times* (University of Hawaii Press, 2014). Among numerous other publications, his monographs are *Unyŏng-on: A Love Affair at the Royal Palace of Chosŏn Korea* (Institute of East Asian Studies, UC Berkeley) and *Korean Cuisine: An Illustrated History* (Reaktion Books, 2008). He is currently completing an annotated translation of a nineteenth-century guidebook for women, the *Kyuhap ch'ongsŏ* (The encyclopedia of women's daily life).

CORNELL EAST ASIA SERIES
Related titles in Korean Studies

CORNELL
East Asia Series

eap.einaudi.cornell.edu/publications

CPSIA information can be obtained
at www.ICGtesting.com
Printed in the USA
LVHW111906111119
637016LV00007B/12/P